EUROPEJSKI

EUROPEJSKI

MARK QUINN

Library of Congress Control Number:		2020920127
ISBN:	Hardcover	978-1-6641-1301-5
	Softcover	978-1-6641-1300-8
	eBook	978-1-6641-1302-2

Print information available on the last page.

Rev. date: 10/19/2020

To order additional copies of this book, contact:
Xlibris
UK TFN: 0800 0148620 (Toll Free inside the UK)
UK Local: 02036 956328 (+44 20 3695 6328 from outside the UK)
www.Xlibrispublishing.co.uk
Orders@Xlibrispublishing.co.uk
820199

For my Mum

CONTENTS

Warsaw, June 1988, the Europejski Hotel 1

Wyborcza, 1999 8

Belfast-Warsaw 1987–88 16

Ewa 1999. 144

Warsaw, May 1988 161

London and Warsaw, 31 December 1999 220

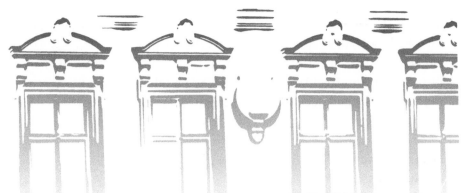

WARSAW, JUNE 1988, THE EUROPEJSKI HOTEL

A S THOMAS DAY NUDGED THE CURTAIN OF HIS HOTEL ROOM to one side, the nylon crackled cheaply against his finger. He cleared a circle from the smut on the glass. He wanted to see his girlfriend leave, recognise and memorise her walk, check for a backwards glance. The window was cold and made him feel cold despite the heat trapped in the room. He stroked his chest and stomach to smooth away the goosebumps, resting the tips of his fingers inside the band of his pants. She had left her scent in the room but nothing else that she might need to return for. A shapely dent on the edge of the bed. Words about love, about goodbye. Nothing she need come back for now. Gosia was in a hurry; he could see just then through the window. Because she was with the other man, Thomas didn't realise at first it was her. He knew the man too, of course. They walked together as far as the parade square before he peeled off to the left, and she strode on in the direction of the Tomb of the Unknown Soldier and the Saxon Gardens.

Spiro, from the embassy, had fixed it for him to stay at the Europejski Hotel on the edge of the Old Town. 'Just for two days, Tom. No more. We will get you a flight to London after that, but until then you had better lie low.' Spiro was being uncharacteristically diplomatic.

'I get it, Spiro. I am being deported and you would rather I didn't make any more fuss. Your job now is to keep this out of the papers at home. Sorry if I have messed up your day.' The two men were standing in Tom's student dormitory. The other three students, who until just that day had been Tom's roommates, had already cleared out. The tins

1

of meat, the Iron Maiden and Marillion posters, even the sheets from their beds, all had been removed. The cleaners had been in. They had left their caustic scent of dust agitated by bleach, the traces of their disinfectant still streaking on the walls and puddling in some corners of the floor. They had pulled back the curtains and opened the windows, letting in a summer light that was at odds with the smell in the room.

'I didn't realise we were allowed to open those,' said Tom, looking up at the windows. 'I wish I'd known earlier. I might have liked Warsaw in the summer.'

Spiro noticed Tom's bag and rucksack bulging at the end of his bed.

'You packed quickly,' he said. He wondered when he could have done it.

'It wasn't me.' Tom turned away from his bags, unable to look on them as his own. In the hours since the end of the strike, he had been confined in quarters assigned by the rector, unable to talk to his friends or even at first to call his embassy. With a speed that was disorienting for him and an efficiency he had not yet witnessed in his ten months in Poland, this episode had been brought to a conclusion and packed away. 'Someone else went through my things, folded them, sniffed them, whatever. They may have nicked stuff too, for all I know.' The diplomat reached for a pen and something to note down a record of goods stolen. Day was, after all, still a British citizen abroad. 'Don't bother.' Tom stayed him. 'It's not the worst thing to have happened to me.'

At that Spiro felt a moment of sympathy. His normal custom was to treat another's misfortune as a problem to either solve or disguise; if a solution did not readily present itself, Spiro would tidy it away or distract attention from it. Putting Day up at the Europejski was his tactful response to the student's eviction from his dorm; it put him out of sight until the first plane out. 'Is there something else I can do for you, Tom?' He didn't have to say the word for them both to understand he meant Gosia. 'Are you sure, Tom? I speak here as your friend. Are you sure you want to be messed up by the girl at this late stage? After everything I have already told you? When this is done, there will be no coming back—you are aware of that, aren't you? You won't see her, and you won't be hearing from her. Love, under the circumstances, is a non-starter. Oh, shit!' And so Spiro had agreed to do what he could. Tom thought it was the least he could do.

Tom did not know the name of her perfume. He breathed it in imagining even the pores of his exposed skin were joining the effort of taking in and holding this remnant of her. Warsaw's darkness grew deeper, so more of the hotel room interior appeared reflected in the glass just in front of him, separating him from the city. There was a soldier standing sentry at the military building opposite, four floors below. Tom had seen him there hours earlier and fancied that the soldier was guarding him and not the other place. It was not so ridiculous; however comfortable the hotel was, it was still his prison. His guard would not be looking up at him. There would be other lights on in other windows, people standing at them, some barely dressed. But Tom took a step back anyway, bringing his own reflection more into focus, making himself more a part of the room he was in. His foot hurt. The carpet pile where he stood was worn thin, and he could feel the reverberations coming from the disco somewhere else in the hotel. He had not noticed the music before. He tried to push it away; he resented it for entering his room and distracting him. The student demonstration aimed at the university authorities—and therefore the Communist government— had ended suddenly and violently. By missing a signal or saying too much, Thomas Day may have played a part in his comrades' defeat. He was being sent home. He had just seen the last of the woman he was sure he loved. Europop music was tingling the soles of his feet and making him want to dance.

It was like that other time.

Tom had been bundled into the back of a taxi across the laps of Agata, Wioletta, Norbert, and someone else, Aleks taking the seat at the front beside the driver. 'Where did you say we were going?' he asked, laughing, already halfway drunk from the vodka they had slammed in their dorm in Dom Studenta.

'Hades!' the girls replied in unison. To Tom they seemed sober despite having matched him and the boys shot for shot. The car swerved hard right, then right again and Tom quickly gave up any effort of working out their route. He had been in Warsaw for some weeks already but still only knew the roads he jogged along or walked to get to his classes. Every time he caught a tram or a taxi, one of his Polish friends took command and soon he was lost. Often he was drunk in any case. One of his roommates always seemed to have a half-litre of vodka, or if

3

they did not a visitor to their room would. *Irlandczyk*—Irishman—Tom was always expected to join in as if obligated by his country of origin. He had learned to drink *do dna*—to the bottom—by holding the fluid in his mouth until its fume and sting had subsided, then forcing it down his throat like a clean-and-jerk weightlifter resting mid-lift. Tom had still not managed to pay a taxi fare. He knew his friends were not well-off, and he guessed it could not be cheap to ride taxis every time, but every time so far they had refused his money.

They reached the *Hades* nightclub and showed their student identity cards to get in.

'Give me your jacket,' demanded Aleks. 'I'll check it in with mine and save some pennies.'

'Can't I keep my jacket with me?' Tom was unsure of the whiteness of his shirt under an ultraviolet disco light. In Belfast he was used to keeping his belongings on him.

'In Poland it is expected.' Aleks gave a shrug that suggested this was just one more way in which his country differed from the West. For him Poland often suffered by comparison. He could nearly always give an explanation that spared his personal shame, and it nearly always involved the communists. 'The man in the cloakroom has no skills, you see. Or the skills he once had he has lost due to old age or vodka. Under communism he must have a job even if he does no actual work. For that, taking the coats off people who would rather wear them is perfect. According to my own analysis, I ought to refuse to cooperate with this system, as it traps me as much as it does that man. My conscience tells me to resist, whereas my head tells me to wait and pick a better fight. And there, in the entrance to *Hades,* we have the Polish reality!'

Back home, the Prof had warned him of this technique. 'A Pole will happily abuse his government, and do it quite openly while at the same time staying comfortably within the law. This involves pretence on both sides. The people pretend to be loyal comrades, and the Party pretends to be communist.' The occasions when the pretences fell away provided the events for the course that Professor Carter taught Tom, the solitary Polish studies student at their university in Belfast.

The music was repellent but drew Tom and his friends into the mouth of the nightclub nonetheless. Wioletta and Agata needed no more alcohol to dance to it. Norbert sourced some beer and found a table to drink it at with Aleks, Tom, and the other guy. Then Norbert found some girls to talk to at the bar, Aleks and his mate disappeared and Tom was left guarding the table, happy to have a job which meant he could not dance. Instead he watched the dancers, moving—it seemed to him—regardless of the music, occupying the inexorably diminishing space between the dry ice around their feet and the cigarette smoke above their heads. Soon they would be faceless and footless, mere arms and bodies jolted by the electricity pulsing from the speakers. Norbert had found three girls and he brought them to Tom or to the table where Tom sat. They spoke Polish to each other and found other ways to ignore him. They had some make-up, which they seemed to be sharing:even in the hellish darkness of the nightclub Tom noticed the same shade of blue shadowing their eyes. They were all pretty. (His roommates had taught him a phrase to use with local girls that he was careful not to utter.) The smallest was dark-haired and wore a skirt that might have been leather. Beside her sat Kinga (he would learn her name later). Even sitting down, Kinga was impressively tall and quite possibly she was the most beautiful human being Tom had ever encountered. She noticed him looking and rewarded him with a mouth-open smile, introducing him—still in Polish—to her companions. The third girl was Małgorzata. Małgosia. Gosia. 'You choose,' she said in English. 'They all mean Margaret. Like Thatcher.'

You choose. After her name, they were the first words she spoke to him. If she had been flirting with him, she soon appeared to change her mind, squealing delight at the change of music and pulling her girlfriends to the dance floor without inviting him. Tom drew their chairs closer to his table. He couldn't see either Aleks or Norbert; Wioletta and Agata were dancing together in a way Tom remembered his parents doing. A blond boy, tall and in denims, was now chatting up Kinga, Gosia, and the other one. He was good-looking, certainly, Tom could see that. Someone tapped him on the shoulder, and Tom let two of his chairs go. He wanted a beer or he wanted to be doing something, so he shouldered his way to the bar. 'Piwo, proszę.' The barman reached him his bottle, popping the cap.

'We are thirsty too!' One of the girls—it was Gosia—was at his ear. 'You could buy sweet wine for us. It is expensive.' Tom shrugged his okay. He looked past Gosia for the blond in jeans: he had joined the

5

other two girls at Tom's table. Gosia took the bottle of Vermouth and four glasses, leaving Tom to pay.

'What's your name?' Gosia asked him while insisting he sit with them again. 'You didn't say.'

'Thomas. Tom. Some of my friends here call me Tomek.' *You choose.* But Gosia was taking charge of the Vermouth bottle, sharing it with the others. The blond boy placed his arm on Kinga's shoulder, and Tom wondered then whether he might be her brother—they were similarly handsome.

'Where is your glass?' Tom had not expected to split the bottle and preferred his beer anyway. Gosia splashed the wine into her own glass and slid it across the table to him. She waited for him to drink it with her chin in her hand. 'You like it?' He did not, but he did not want to say.

'I prefer the beer.'

Gosia seemed not to care, dragging her glass back to her side of the table to finish it off. She appeared to be finished with Tom too. She was more entertained by the blond and her girlfriends. Tom thought it was odd that they were not more curious about him. After all, there were not many foreigners to be found in student nightclubs in Warsaw. Something Carter had said to him in Belfast came to mind: 'It takes a lot for a Pole to call you their friend. In fact, I rather feel they disdain our habit in the West of calling people we have only just met our friend. But if you are lucky enough to make one there, you will find you have their friendship for life.' These girls had no reason for wanting to know him better, he reasoned with his bottle. Why, he asked his beer, should they find him more exotic for being from abroad? Why, more to the point, was the blond boy reaching for his arm to drag him to the dance floor? The Pole now had his arm over the Irishman's shoulder as much to prop him up as an expression of brotherhood, all the while pleading or conniving with his new acquaintance. Tom could not tell which, but he supposed the other could in fact be his friend and the two ended standing opposite the three girls on the dance floor and, after a fashion, Tom started to dance. The floor throbbed through the soles of his shoes as if to show him how to move. If Gosia took his hands, it was because she wanted to dance with him, not just to steady him. The music banged in his ears, rocked the floor, made him dance, and made Gosia dance with him.

The music was distant now and the bristle of the carpet agitated his feet only a little. He had an injury to be seen to back in London. The mood to dance was lost. His hotel room was large enough to hold a party in; the light he had left on in the bathroom brought to mind the bar shining bright in the gloom of *Hades*. The window was now a mirror, giving Tom a partner. It reflected his nakedness back to him. He was tall and lean; his muscle resulting from and suited for the running he did every day. But he did not want to dance. The air in the room was warm and tangy, barely perceptible eddies of air seeping through the ancient double-glazing from the city outside reached his skin and fingered it, caressing his chest and disturbing the minor hairs on his legs. Any firmer touch would have tipped him over an edge. He climbed back into the bed, curling up beside the hollow left there moments before by Gosia.

WYBORCZA, 1999

E WA KOWALSKA PAID FOR HER TAXI, SLOTTED HER PURSE back into her bag beside her mobile phone and pressed a pill to her tongue, confident it would target the hangover she had massaged to a point on her temple. No headache ever survived the second coffee of the day and Janusz—the new intern on her newspaper—made surprisingly good *caffè americano*. Ewa had refused to make the coffee for the staff when she had interned there, and she agreed with those who said then that she did not know her place. Not knowing her place meant that, just two years on, she was a full-time staffer with her photograph displayed in the lobby. As a matter of courtesy, she flashed her identity pass at pan Wojciech on the security desk and, to amuse himself, he pointed his finger at her photo in the gallery as if to say, 'You can come and go as you please, pani Ewa.'

She rode the lift alone, in its mirrored walls taking her first close look at herself of the morning. Her face was ruddy from the cold, her hair was all-weather short and highlighted blonde. She never bothered with make-up before lunch. 'There is no one I want to see before midday, and definitely no one I want to impress,' she told the mirror. The door opened and the old Gary Cooper poster greeting her on the landing told her it was high noon and she had arrived at the newsroom of *Wyborcza*. (It was an election poster dating from the time the editor himself was elected to the national parliament. With the right waistcoat, Stetson, and sheriff's badge, in Ewa's eyes her editor could be Gary Cooper.)

She thrust her shoulders back and strode—swaggered—into the office, expecting no one to be there. It was New Year's Eve.

Three colleagues were gathered around a computer screen as if it were a nativity scene and they were in Bethlehem—or rather as if they were *in* the nativity scene and the screen was the manger. 'Yeltsin is resigning,' one of them announced to the otherwise empty office.

Ewa spotted that one of the wise men was Janusz. But for what it would imply about her own news values, she would have demanded her coffee from him. Her head was still pounding. 'Jaś, what's he saying?' As punishment for his poor interning, she had addressed him with the diminutive she knew he hated.

He didn't attend to the slight. His mother often called him Jaś, and Ewa could occasionally act like his mother. 'He is apologising for letting down those who voted for him, blah, blah . . . for not fulfilling their hopes in his presidency, and so on.' Janusz was not the only person in the newsroom who could speak Russian, but somehow he had been nominated as the interpreter for this moment and he was seizing it. He took his hands out of his pockets. Then he straightened his back. He paused his breath. 'Dear God.' He exhaled. 'He's naming that FSB goon as his successor. Putin is in charge . . . until elections in March.' The intern appeared winded by the news.

'Is it really so bad?' asked Ewa almost in a whisper. She felt like the most ignorant person in the room.

'Ask the Chechens,' said Janusz crossly. 'There has been a massacre there right under everyone's noses. And do the Russians hate Putin for it? No, he's a bloody hero.'

Since she joined the paper, Ewa's interests had been mainly domestic; frankly she had barely punched her keyboard at anything beyond the capital city. She read the foreign news segment cursorily and then only as it touched on her country's relations with the EU. When Ewa strained her eyes to see into the future, she did not see Russia there. Russia it was that had denied her a grandfather by shooting him and burying him at Katyń. Russia was the frozen vastness that had swallowed her grandmother when she had travelled there, madly, to find her husband, leaving her infant son—Ewa's father—in the care of an aunt. Russia was the country *behind* her, the one she turned away from, the one that sent its icy winds across its barren plains to chill her city,

Warsaw. Being optimistic in Warsaw was an act of willed ignorance, like staying warm in December.

'He's KGB,' continued Janusz to the room. 'Or he was. Is, was, it's the same thing there. Mazur will be loving this! A communist in the Kremlin to go with the one in Belweder.' Ewa took a step back towards her own desk to take a better look at the intern. For all her refusal to make coffee, she was pretty sure she would not have been so trenchant in his position; interns are not columnists. Even now she held her tongue in the office while letting loose in the pages of the paper. She composed better sentences on the screen than she could with her lips. She might command the phrase to brand Vladimir Putin and Jacek Mazur as back-in-the-closet Commies, but the words would be unruly if she tried them out in the open.

'. . . coffee?'

'I beg your pardon?' Ewa had stopped listening to Janusz, the more to stare at him.

'I said, I suppose you would like a coffee?' the intern said, allowing a smirk. 'You look like you could do with one.'

'Thanks.' The word slipped out before Ewa could invest it with irony. Gratitude would have to do for now. She sat at her desk, lowering the chair so her feet touched the floor. She logged on to her computer and allowed the others in the office to deal with the Putin news. She had reserved her morning so she could re-read the notes she had made on candidate Michalski, on the meagre contents of his lustration file and the clippings archive she had called up regarding his anti-government activities in the '80s. Something about Dariusz Michalski did not quite add up. How did this one-time student protester, who with the same slogans and banners railed against Marxism and capitalism simultaneously, end up a sterling millionaire? Why did the informants, who reported on him so doggedly, report so little? And what (apart from making his import-export fortune) had he been doing in the ten years between his forced exile and his self-publicised return? Ewa wanted to memorise every word written about the would-be next president of Poland before approaching the one other man who might know even more. She was not going to look a fool in front of Cybulski.

Ewa knocked gently on Aleks Cybulski's open door and waited to be invited in. Legend held that one weekend, with no one around,

Cybulski himself arrived with timber and plasterboard and erected a wall across an alcove and created—out of nothing—an office suitable for the deputy political editor of the country's leading liberal newspaper. He invented the title too. Save for the one high window, with its view of the upper quarter of the Palace of Culture, the office would have been utterly dark. There was a chair with a disembodied hat and coat thrown over it, a two-seater cane sofa balancing an anonymous pile of boxes on its rickety knees, and a desk which once saw service in the Second World War. A paper mask of the pope, eyes popped out at an office party, hung by its elastic across the back of the computer monitor. Behind that was Aleks, crumpled and bald and twenty years younger than he looked. At the rap on his door, he lifted his face from his screen, and Ewa saw it as if in negative, shade substituting light. Ewa would name Aleksander Cybulski as the man most responsible for her own position on the paper; she was a watchful and articulate journalist, but she would not be able to pull together more than a hundred words to describe him. He lifted his glasses to his head. It was his salute and signal for her to enter.

'Ewka!' he called her in with more enthusiasm when he recognised it was her. Only he was allowed the use of her pet name; he assumed everyone did. 'How's our boy doing? What has Jacek Mazur been raking up?'

Three weeks before, Dariusz Michalski had announced his run for the presidency and passed his lustration declaration to the Public Interest Spokesperson. This was the deal for anyone seeking to hold public office; they made a clean breast of their past, and the civil servant did a trawl of Communist-era files to check they were telling the truth. In the three years since the parliament had passed the new lustration law, the Public Interest Spokesperson had developed a nose for *fałszywki*—the tiny but deadly falsities that the security forces used to place on a target's file, all the better for destroying their life should they somehow succeed in bringing down communism. However, although the spokesperson might pass them fit, the press could seize on any *fałszywka* and redefine it as the truth. *Oni*, the newspaper owned by the once-upon-a-time chief propagandist of the Polish United Workers Party, had the most fun with turning reality upside down. *Oni*, which was owned by the other man wanting to be state president.

'Mazur has been asking questions about Michalski's millions. *Oni* has a front-page cartoon of Michalski eating a metre high burger, with pound signs for eyeballs.'

'I saw it. Hardly original,' Aleks said dismissively. Jacek Mazur had been his bane since his student days when Cybulski had pulled every trick to distribute his underground paper and Mazur had done everything to stop him. 'Have you been lifting up those stones too, Ewka?'

'As per your suggestion, Aleks. Yes. Import-export—pretty much like any other wealthy Pole—seems to be the answer. Can I move those?' Cybulski nodded and waited impatiently while Ewa sat on the chair, dumping the hat and coat. The coat landed with an alarming metallic thud. 'Is that a . . . ?' Ewa began.

'It's a spanner. I will need it later. You were telling me about Darek's money?'

Kowalska noted but for now ignored her boss's use of the politician's forename. 'There is a lot of it, mainly in British pounds, amassed very rapidly over the past five years or so. Anything you pickle and put in a jar, he has been importing it to England from allotments in Ostrów Mazowiecka and farmers' markets in Iława and window boxes in Kutno—any damn place.'

'I get the picture, Ewka, thank you.' Being from Kutno, Aleks was sensitive to mockery. 'Michalski's fortune is in fact the good fortune of small farmers across Poland. People who grow food are definitively patriotic. We have the biggest gherkins, the sweetest carrots, the reddest beetroots, et cetera. And the smallest growers are the most patriotic of all.'

'He even puts their names on his jars,' Ewa added. She pulled a notebook from somewhere and prepared to read from it.

'Save those details for your piece, Ewka. So to get this straight, Michalski sells jars of home-pickled Polish vegetables to pound-earning Varsovians and Krakowiaks in London and Glasgow. He earns a mint and it's all legit?'

'He has even published his UK tax returns. Fully paid-up.' Ewa was consulting her notes. 'A handy opportunity to list the charities he contributes to, with the tax offset. Mainly, but not exclusively, Polish charities registered in London. He doles out the cash to RAF veterans, expat publishers, orphanages . . . any good cause that does him no harm politically.'

Cybulski reached out to take a look at Ewa's notebook for himself. He read down the list of good-doing organisations, satisfied himself that his colleague's call was correct and handed it back to her. 'Good work, Ewa. Any other lines to enquire into?'

Kowalska flipped her pad shut and made a jealous note to herself not to bring it into this office again. 'The Public Interest Spokesman was satisfied with Michalski's lustration declaration. Like other anti-Communists at the time he was spied upon, but he seems a fairly dull character then and his file is pretty thin.' With her foot, she nudged the coat (with its spanner) a little to one side. She looked the pope in its eyes. 'Would you say he was dull, Aleks, when you knew him?' Aleks had sat back in his chair away from the glow of his computer, so Ewa could not read his face. 'Was Darek not the charismatic figure he appears to be now?'

In the gloom of the office, the clicking of his pen could have been the tutting of his teeth. Ewa dared not speak next.

'I did not know him well, Ewa. None of us did. But he was not dull. No, I would not say that.'

'Some say, Aleks, that you were closer to him than most; that no one knew him better than you.'

'Some say? You are a better journalist than that, Ewa Kowalska.' Aleks considered leaving it at that. Ewa Kowalska *was* a better journalist than that, which was why he had given her the Michalski brief. If there were any holes in the candidate's lustration declaration, he wanted Ewa to find them first and then tell him about it. He could help her a little more with that. 'Dariusz Michalski did not get close to people. He allowed some of us into his orbit, certainly, but he did not betray personal confidences. We had the impression, or at least I had, that his mind was always occupied by matters outside of the room we were in. Whatever we were discussing—about the maltreatment of a student or the SGPiS strike—he was always placing it on a broader plane. He was an activist-philosopher, that bit older and smarter—and a whole lot more attractive—than the rest of us. Yes, he was certainly charismatic.'

With a sigh that was at once shallow and enormously effortful, Aleks turned fractionally towards Ewa, looking at her or into her, the glow from his computer lighting the younger features of his face. 'You know all of this, Ewa, you have read my reports. The NZS—the Independent Students' Association—was not strong at our university. SGPiS was mainly for the sons and daughters of loyal Party members, but there were some of us who saw things differently. All anti-government literature was *samizdat*. I relied only on people I trusted to circulate our little paper. Every publication was a coup against the Party, every reader who read it was a revolutionary. The thoughts in our heads, the presses we hid, the paper we stole, all were acts as punishable as any protest in the street.' Aleks idly tapped the spacebar on his keyboard and watched the cursor cross empty space on his monitor. He focused again on Ewa.

'People called our university the Red Fortress because of its imagined loyalty to Marxist orthodoxy. So when we went on strike— and when the usual threats failed to stop us—the authorities began to take note. We made Solidarity stand up too because we were the last place they expected to find support. You know about the confrontations with riot police, the ZOMO, where some passers-by got injured. Darek was always concerned about what he called "the balance of violence". He knew that, so long as the state was seen as the perpetrator, it would gain us more support, but he always saw it as a price, and someone had to keep an eye on how costly the price was becoming. Then the SB came.'

'The SB—the Security Service.' Even in the intimate gloom of the deputy political editor's office, it was Ewa's instinct to offer the explanatory parentheses. 'They broke up your sit-in in the vice-rector's office, dragged Michalski out and beat him up. You were there with your camera. You printed the pictures alongside your report. You were an underground paper, but everyone saw it.'

Aleks looked into Ewa again. He wondered had even she seen the report (back then—originally), not just from the archive. How old would she have been? Did ten-year-olds read *samizdat* newspapers? Maybe only ten-year-olds who went on to become staff reporters in the nation's leading daily. 'Darek decided—just at that moment, he decided that the strike had to end: the price of continuing—not to his life, but to the lives of the others he was leading was too high. He announced it right there in the stairwell where they assaulted him with the blood dripping from his mouth. *The SB were still standing there!* He announced it to me—and through me, to everyone—that the strike was off. I had my own feelings, of course. I was a protester too and I thought we were on the brink of a victory. But at that moment, I had to be a reporter. I would even say that that was the moment I *became* a reporter. My role was to relay what happened and let the comment follow later.' Aleks was tapping the space key again, seconds apart. 'He was selfless. It is an odd thought to have about a politician seeking the highest office in the land. To stand on a stage where the backdrop is your own hyper-projected image requires an uncommon sort of ego. He had ego then too and glamour. But I can tell you, at that moment—in the disused stairwell of that building with me, my camera and a squad of tooled-up gorillas— Dariusz was humble and selfless and . . . right.'

Ewa had only asked one question. She did not need to ask why her boss was backing Michalski for president now. She needed a coffee.

Cybulski leaned back into his computer screen and replaced his glasses on his nose. 'Ewka, this is for you.' He handed her an embossed card. 'Good work on the money thing. Now, go and write that up.' He watched her leave, rubbing the side of her head. He was satisfied with his morning's work.

Ewa Kowalska looked at the card in her hand. It was an invitation to a New Year's Eve party. The host was Dariusz Michalski.

BELFAST-WARSAW 1987–88

TOM WAS ACCUSTOMED TO ARRIVING DAMP TO HIS CLASSES. It drew amused comments from those fellow students fortunate to sit far enough away from him as inevitably they did. It was June, so it was not cold but it was still raining. Tom found mismatching shorts and T-shirt to wear, laced up his stinking trainers and strung his bag to his back. His jog always began the same way, with a ride down the Otis elevator from the ninth floor of his hall of residence. Alternatively, like this morning, the lift was out of service so he made a warm-up of the run down the stairs. He dodged other students sleepily exiting from their own halls and emerged on to the Malone Road. Although his parents were just streets away, Tom chose to pay extra to live in halls. He still kept a small bag at their place, but for the most part, he had managed to move his whole life out. His jog would be all downhill from here to the university, too easy and not worth the bother of getting wet. Before reaching the Eglantine and Botanic pubs, he turned a sharp right on to Chlorine Gardens, slowing down as he passed the Architecture Building where there were always female students making an early start. They never looked out at him. He had to stop for traffic before he could cross Stranmillis Road. As ever, he considered having breakfast in one of the bohemian cafés there, and as ever, he resisted. Instead he headed down a side street knowing it had a modest entrance to the Botanic Gardens. For his taste the park was too municipal—eked out by hand from the space between the university and the wickedly twisting, witchily smelling River Lagan. Still running downhill, he came to the Palm

16

House and an exit. Sometimes at this point, he allowed himself to walk through the university complex to get his puff back before reaching his class, but today he felt barely exercised so he continued his jog into the Quad, skirting the puddled shadow of the Admin Building and under the drippy bridge of the Main Library. He had arrived at University Square. He breathed deeply to recover the little he had lost on his run and to mask the awe he always felt standing before this multi-storey Victorian terrace. The departments here might have been classified by Dewey with Irish Studies and French and English and Law and History and Slavonics and Classics neatly shelved side by side. Two years before, Thomas Day had arrived to matriculate in the economics department, had been randomly assigned an admissions tutor from another, and decided with no stronger reason than that to take an option in Slavonics.

The table in Carter's room was large enough to accommodate eight students; as usual Tom had his pick of all eight chairs. He pulled from his bag the essay he had prepared on the events of 1956 and handed it to Carter, who read it in silence.

'So you think the international youth festival in June, in Poznań, was important?' the professor asked finally.

Tom pulled himself up in his chair. What would follow would be a few questions, disguised as debate prompts, which were in fact the warm-up act for Carter's own performance. 'It's hard to apportion relative causation,' began Tom (he had anticipated this question). 'The Communist authorities clearly wanted the kudos from hosting an international event, but they had no clue how to handle what might ensue. The fact that it followed Khrushchev's secret speech in February and coincided with the tentative reforms in Budapest, nudged the Poles into liberalising the press—at least for those months after Gomułka took over. Papers that had been underground, such as *po prostu*, could suddenly be read in the open. Workers and intellectuals with their own concerns used the Poznań festival as cover for their protests, and the newly free press reported it. Obviously, this was all a test for the new leader, who came under pressure from the Kremlin to clamp down on the liberals.'

Carter nodded so that the slack skin of his neck folded and stretched like a concertina. 'Good, Day.' He stopped himself short at the unintended pun on his student's name. 'Tom.' The professor looked over his shoulder at his bookshelves, scanning for a particular tome or skimming the accumulated wisdom of his personal library. From the specific to the general, from the general to the specific, that was Carter's explicit method. 'And what do you make of any comparisons with 1980–81? Was 1956 the progenitor to *Solidarność* and Martial Law?'

'Sorry, Professor, I have not read that far ahead yet.' Tom meant that Carter had not reached that point in the course. 'But . . .' Tom paused, expecting Carter to interrupt. When he didn't, Tom had to bluff. Not for the first time Tom wished that even one other student had taken this option. 'But . . . I think I would say that comparisons of that sort are more like games that historians play—like that game with the upturned cards, where you try to find matching pairs. The main action going on in a provincial city—Poznań then Gdańsk—away from the close attention of the central Party in Warsaw, under existential threat from Khrushchev or Brezhnev, Gomulka's clampdown in '56 gets matched with Jaruzelski imposing Martial Law in '81. They make neat enough pairs, but only when you stand clear enough from the events themselves.' Tom caught his teacher's eye and realised the wrong person was giving the lecture. 'I think a closer look would reveal them as more distinct than that.'

'*Do* read ahead, Tom.' Carter was looking at his shelves again, clearly for a particular item. 'And read back. Do as much reading as you can. You will spot comparisons, many of them illusory, but occasionally you will alight upon a genuine *match*, as you put it. The much more important point is that the people experiencing the events for themselves—not only the historians following in the ambulance—can say to themselves, "We have been here before, we know the dangers present." The people—in any case Poles, who seem more highly attuned to their past the more that it is deliberately concealed from them—they can be inspired by what they know about their ancestors. Don't scoff at that.'

'Sorry, Professor. I was just bluffing because I didn't have a proper answer to your question.'

Carter had moved on. He now pulled a box from under the bottom shelf of his bookcase and was standing at his full, proud, below-average height. 'Found it! Come over here, Tom, and feast your uneducated eyes on this!' Carter had removed from the box a broadsheet newspaper, which he folded out and spread smooth with a careful hand. 'It's the Catholic weekly, *Tygodnik Powszechny*, from just six years ago. A friend sent it to me.'

'Is it from the underground press? You say it's a Catholic paper.'

'Good question. No, it's not *samizdat*. Somehow, almost continually since the war, they have been allowed to publish in the open. For a while, after the events you wrote about in your essay, it was taken over by party publishers, but since then it has been in the hands of *Znak*, which is the closest thing the country has to an independent publishing house.'

'And they print what they like? That doesn't make sense.'

'No, Tom, it wouldn't. And you are right. They can't, not quite. But in a country like Poland, communism cannot coexist with Catholicism without at least some compromises. What I like about this edition is . . . well, where should I begin?' For a moment Tom could see his professor was lost in his own childish pleasure. Tom pointed to the date.

'*Marzec 1981*. That's March, right? So the Communists have already signed the agreement with Wałęsa and Solidarity the previous August— the Gdańsk Accords—agreeing to legalise the trade union and caving in to some of their demands.'

'I see you *have* been reading ahead, Tom.'

'And Martial Law . . . what did they call it?'

'*Stan wojenny*.'

'Stan wojenny is still some way off—December that year, right? So this was published within that period. Nice! What's it about?'

'Your language lessons with Professor Shaw aren't much help here, I suppose?' Carter had arranged for his student to take unofficial classes in Polish with his colleague in the chemistry department. Shaw was her married name; she called herself Janina Błońska. He knew that Tom often skipped other classes to sit with Janina in her lab, drinking hot chocolate laced secretly with cherry vodka. She had a supply she preferred not to discuss.

'The headline,' Carter continued, 'is *Prowokacja Bydgoska*. You can work that out for yourself. Bydgoszcz is a large town in central Poland. The Germans called it Bromberg.'

'What was the *provocation*?'

'It's what Solidarity activists called the attack on their members by ZOMO, the riot police. Jan Rulewski, who was a local organiser, was negotiating on behalf of farmers with Party officials in the regional assembly. They were expected to come up with some sort of joint communiqué, and a crowd of supporters had gathered in the town square. Out of sight of the supporters, Rulewski and other Solidarity people were attacked by the ZOMO around the back of the assembly building. Rulewski had his teeth knocked out, and his eye socket was fractured. He was smuggled to the hospital in a militia wagon and rumours spread that he had died. In the days that followed, Solidarity affiliates amongst farmers, schoolchildren, and factory workers planned a general strike throughout the region with support spreading across Poland. Wałęsa stepped in with the world's news media in tow. Reagan had his say. It's believed the pope had a line to Wałęsa, the General had just become prime minister and was no doubt leant on by the Kremlin. Then, having marched everyone to the top of the hill, Wałęsa called the whole thing off.'

'He was afraid of military law?'

'Yes, probably. The news bulletins carried none too subtle images of Soviet troops on exercises in Mazuria and Pomerania. He caved in. It was a terrible blow to the movement.'

'And all of this is reported in the newspaper?' Tom pulled the broadsheet closer to him with his finger.

'No. That's just it. That's what makes this interesting. Look here.' Carter pointed to blank spaces left within the text. 'They call these *białe plamy*. They are the censor's work. You can read in the text about Rulewski talking to Party officials and there is even a picture of him, but all mentions of the ZOMO and the attack have been whited out. You can see that *Tygodnik Powszechny* have pushed the boundaries of what is publishable in a non-Party paper.'

'It's full of blanks.'

'Indeed. And of course, your average Pole is quite capable of filling them in.'

'Reading between the lines.'

'Between the lines, outside the lines, within the words, they don't need to be underground when they can communicate this much. The censorship—the cover-up or the secret exchanges or the attack hidden from view—is part of the story, *is* the story. The *białe plamy* speak loudly for the words they replace.'

20

'Did Rulewski die?'

'No. But he was arrested under Martial Law. He became something of a celebrated political prisoner when he went on hunger strike. He was released in the amnesty of 1984. He's trying to live an unmolested life now. He drives taxis.'

'This friend of yours—the one who sent you the paper—it's Rulewski, isn't it?' Tom did not expect a reply, watching the care with which his professor refolded the newspaper and secreted it back in its box was answer enough. 'Professor, would you like me to get a message to him?'

'That won't be necessary, Tom. I can write to Jan myself any time I want to. He prefers it if I don't write letters because he is convinced that his post office steams his envelopes open. But postcards are fine. Every secret message in a postcard is hidden in plain sight. Those postal workers are not the brightest in the brotherhood.'

Carter sized up the boy in his office. He was intelligent enough although he carried it lightly. More importantly, he had the nerve to think for himself. Carter was sure he had chosen the right person to send to Warsaw. 'Tom, I shall miss our little chats in my office.'

'You mean our tutorials, don't you? Thank you, sir. I shall miss them too.' At that moment, Tom could not think of another person who would have talked to him in that way.

'I shall send you an occasional postcard, if I may, Tom?'

Carter blushed and that made Tom blush. 'I'm sure I will be craving words in English, Professor Carter. But I don't think I have an address yet.'

'Ah, yes, yes! I knew there was something else!' Carter rounded the large central table with such speed that Tom was sure he had dropped his shoulder like a biker to take the corners. He stopped at the narrow desk that sat below the three-quarter window and from one of its dainty drawers he pulled out an envelope. He began withdrawing papers before thinking better of it and handing the whole package to his student. 'These are yours, Tom.' The professor's squeezebox had developed a vibrato. 'Your temporary student visa is there, alongside references from me, the dean of the faculty and the vice-chancellor. There's a letter too. I have translated it from Wilk, a vice-rector at the Central School for Planning and Statistics, Warsaw. You'll be relieved to hear that they usually just call themselves SGPiS. It sounds like essgaypeece. They have already signed you up for some courses, including Polish lessons for their international students. You will be living in a dorm with them, most probably. UNESCO like to keep their children together.'

'What's this?' Tom had found some crumpled paper money in the envelope.

'I had some złoty leftover from my last trip. Not really meant to take it out with you. That was twenty years ago, so it won't get you far, I'm afraid.' Both men looked out of the window to avoid looking at each other. The concrete tower of the university library loomed opposite, full of learning, inscrutable.

'I will work hard,' Tom promised, wishing there was something else he could pay his teacher with.

'Actually, Tom, there is one more thing you can promise to do for me.' He handed his student a business card from the drawer below the window. 'He's called John Spiro. He works at the British embassy there. He knows you are coming, of course, but you should get in touch with him when you arrive. He would be a useful friend to have there, if you know what I mean.'

Tom pocketed the card, already feeling less intimidated about the adventure ahead.

The British Council granted Thomas Day a stipend to cover his living expenses and a travel allowance to get him to Warsaw in September. They advised him to take dollars or sterling in the form of travellers' cheques, which he could exchange at a bank or one of the city's international hotels. They warned him sternly against the temptation of selling his currency on the black market—a thought he would not have had had they not suggested it. 'The winters are cold, the summers are hot, and their glasses break easily. You should take a supply of toilet paper.' Even in the pages this was written on, Tom could sense a shrug of the shoulders. Tom squashed four rolls into his rucksack, hoping they would last him long enough before he could source a local supplier. With loafers on his feet and trainers in his bag, he had no room for other footwear. In the Oxfam shop on the Dublin Road, he found an old man's woollen coat and a tweed trilby. He stuffed socks inside his George Best mug and wrapped it for safety inside his good white shirt. He estimated he would be able to launder his clothes each week, so he packed seven pairs of pants. At the top of the pile, he placed a white T-shirt and a pair of white shorts, the only items he bought new for his ten-month holiday.

Tom waited with the chucked-out teenagers and stray elderlies brushed up against the hoarding for the 4 am Ulsterbus service to London from Great Victoria Street. The station behind the Europa Hotel had panels of hardboard rather than glass. The hotel was always recovering from its last bombing or preparing for its next. Posters on every panel apologised repeatedly for any inconvenience. The early shift cleaner picked up a tattered *Belfast Telegraph* in her dustpan. She changed her mind about putting it in the bin liner with the tins and crisp packets when she saw the headline; instead she neatened it and placed it on a seat next to Tom. The two plainclothes RUC men shot dead by the IRA in the Liverpool Bar, Donegall Quay, had been named. 'Hope it's better where you're going, dear,' the cleaner said to Tom, catching his eye. 'It'd be nice here without the people.'

The bus dumped its passengers outside the makeshift ferry terminal in Larne. It was not obviously raining, but Tom was mesmerised by the moisture particles hovering like flies around the orange balls of lamplight. The lampposts were so high they could light a football pitch or a prison. He and the others got in line to carry their bags onto the ferry. 'The country looks pretty through this window,' said one though Tom thought it must still be too dark to tell. He tried to sleep but the boat was as steady as a bucket.

Like experienced wild Westerners, coachmen from the National Express threaded their passengers and parcels through the shallow canyons of Galloway; they watered their horses at every service station on the M6 and switched riders. Tom slept for none of the twelve hours. To fill his time he had breakfast in Dumfries, lunch in Lancaster, and dinner in Banbury. His legs ached from non-use. He tried reading but he gave up easily. The oxygen in the bus—warm and sluggish—was something the travellers circulated and shared between them. By the time they reached the last post in Victoria, Tom felt securely sealed in, unsure he could efficiently breathe the London air. The coach door was sucked out and he and the rest disembarked, gasping and unsteady. Most smoked. Tom ducked low under the fumes trapped by the station roof, stooped by the weight of his rucksack and holdall and looked for a way to the Underground.

He spent a long night and morning in Heathrow, waiting for his 6 am flight out. Other tramps, cannier than he, marked out the benches for themselves to lie flat on or unfurled their carrymats below national flag-carrying help points. Tom squatted in France, brooded on his bags in Russia, and finally came to an uneasy compromise between sitting and lying in Switzerland. He wanted someone to switch the terminal lights off, but in there it was daytime all the time. He swallowed a bread roll and coffee that tasted of the airport, he brushed his teeth while men urinated behind him, and he got in line at the LOT departure gate.

On board the Tupolev, a stewardess in blue eyeshadow and matching uniform offered him a sweet for the take-off and a currency declaration form for the landing. Tom tried asking her, in Polish, for a bottle of water, but she gave him instead a miniature bottle of clear vodka. He gulped. The plane shuddered through a cloud. He had the middle seat. The man by the window sweated in a grey suit and was reading *Rzeczpospolita*; by the aisle was a *Trybuna Ludu* reader busting out of the same suit. The headlines in both Party-supporting newspapers were similar and concerned the imminent visit to Poland of Vice President Bush. The two negotiated across Tom, in defiance of him, animated to the point of hammering on his fold-down table to emphasise a point, reaching a settlement over a Marlboro and a shared bottle of beer. Tom caught a few of their words (potato, gas, Bush) and from those pieced together a likely trade deal between Poland and the US. The aisleman's cigarette burned with gratifying slowness as he nuzzled down onto Tom's shoulder. '*Dziękuję Panu.*' Through the window, as far as his vantage would allow him, Tom saw clear-blue borderless sky and below that only cloud. He could not know at what point he had crossed the Iron Curtain.

The plane held together as it landed. The people clapped. The stewardess refixed her hair with a pink plastic slide and nudged Tom's body man awake. 'Witamy w Polsce!' the captain announced. 'Welcome in Poland!' Music, which might have been the national anthem, was trumpeted through the vents; everyone stood up at once to reach down their duty-free bags, thus adding an arrhythmic clink to the martial beat. Tom's holdall held only his book, his papers and his money: not, he realised, an adequate survival kit for this country. In the immigration queue, he lost his grey-suit escorts. The line for international passport holders was a short one, peopled by Tom and a family of Poles from Hounslow who looked unhappy to be back. The soldier in the glass box inspected Tom's passport, checked his face, flicked to the visa.

'Pan jest studentem?'

'Student. Yes. Tak!' Tom pulled from his bag the letter from the vice-rector at SGPiS, the one explaining his study visit. The guard drew it under the glass. Then he stood up and departed out the back of his cubicle, leaving Tom where he was. Five minutes later, all passengers had passed through control into Poland proper and only Tom remained there standing on the wrong side, too warm in his hat and coat. A wall of frosted, reinforced glass supported by grey-green panels isolated him from the others. Vague, tinkling music drifted over the wall to him; he discerned through the glass a brighter block of something blue and white. He wondered had everyone gone home.

The border guard now appeared back in his box, this time with a troupe of other colleagues in uniform, who took turns at comparing the visitor's passport with the visitor while at the same time paying neither that much attention. Finally, the original guard sat down with a cigarette, opened an inkpad, took a stamp the shape of a hobby-horse, and rolled it over a blank page in Tom's passport. He squiggled something like a signature with a biro. He capped the pen, shut the inkpad, and closed the passport before sliding it, and the university invitations under the glass back to Tom.

He was through; his rucksack had gone. The baggage reclaim was a cart tagged *Heatrow,* wheeled in from the plane, and it was empty. He was tired. He tried to quantify how tired he was. *I haven't slept since the night before yesterday,* seemed the sort of thing Lewis Carroll might get Alice to say, and it seemed right. Tom inferred from a handwritten note at *i* that he might get some information when the desk opened at 9 am.

'Jeszcze zamknięte!' called a voice from behind. It was a woman in a café under the sign that Tom had seen through the glass. It read *społem* in a loopy blue script. She continued speaking in Polish, not reading the total incomprehension in the traveller's face. But that did not matter because she knew what he needed. She sat him down and brought him a glass filled with a hot brown liquid with a spoon balanced across the top and a glass saucer below. 'Kawa po turecku. Proszę.' And she left him alone with his coffee. The glass had no handle and was as thin as eggshell. Tom had to pick it up with his fingertips, but callipers would have been better. He took a mouthful and immediately spat the lot back into the cup. The waitress was alerted, so he turned his back to her to reach for a serviette from the fan on the table. He pulled one but got them all. Still he applied one napkin to scrape the roasting coffee grains from his tongue.

'Przepraszam,' he said to her, his scalded tongue still out as she gathered the remaining useable napkins, rubbed them back into a fan, and inserted them into an aluminium holder shaped like two triangles of toast. She restored the spoon atop the glass. He was to wait until the grains settled. He could take his time because it may already be 9 o'clock, but this was the People's Republic, and after all, there was no information to be had from Information. He had the time that's to be had in dreams, urgent but forever, sped up but not to be hurried. He had no bag but he had time. Time to read the spoon, also aluminium, also branded *społem*. Time for gravity to work on coffee grains.

The waitress, in white blouse and black skirt, was at his shoulder, her bumbag gaping. He had finished his coffee. He found one of the banknotes that Professor Carter had given him, and that was enough to make her go away. He called dziękuję to her ungratified back. For the first time Tom noticed two other employees there—one by the cooker, the other by the till.

He was relieved that the woman in Information spoke English.

'Hello, I hope you can help me,' Tom opened.

She said nothing but closed the Harlequin romance paperback she was reading.

'I have lost my rucksack,' Tom confessed.

She tapped her keyboard, either to spark her VDU to life or the opposite.

'Actually, you lost my bag,' Tom concluded. 'Sorry, you can speak English, can't you?'

'Yes, I speak,' she said at last, bored already despite this being her first job of the day. 'How I help you?'

'My rucksack.' Tom pointed to the still-there baggage trolley. 'It was not there when I came through passport control.' She did not ask for more information, so he added, 'I came from London.'

That raised an eyebrow. Tom saw that her eyebrows were painted rather than grown and appeared side by side like railway arches. 'You have documents?'

Tom handed her his entire envelope of papers. She tipped them out and efficiently brushed everything aside until she found his passport and inside it his immigration stamp. She spotted the date and compared it to the calendar laminated to the top of the information desk. 'You come today?'

'Yes, of course.'

She raised her other eyebrow. She tapped at her console again, the same key repeatedly. 'Your bag not here. Your bag in London,' she said the final word so the two syllables rhymed.

'How is that? How do you know that?' Tom did not believe her and was little more convinced when she swivelled the monitor towards him and showed him a screen of green cyphers. 'What is that?'

'That is your rucksack, Mr Day. It is blue and yellow, no?'

'Yes!' How did she know? 'Why is it not in Warsaw?'

Now she raised both shoulders together; that information was outside her scope. 'It will be on the next flight, we promise.' She was almost smiling.

'When is that?' But Tom feared he already knew the answer. She consulted the laminated calendar again, traced her finger one row down from today, and confirmed the worst—another week. The clothes he had already been wearing since the morning of the day before would have to last him another week. The Information lady filled out a form, made him sign it, signed it herself, stamped it, and dated that then did the whole thing again before keeping one for herself and giving the other to Tom. She also wrote out directions for him on a piece of buff-coloured scrap for how to get a bus from Okęcie airport to the Central Station, and a tram from there to the university. She told him how to get tickets for both. Finally, she showed him the exit, right below a sign saying *Welcome in Poland*.

The strap of his holdall tugged at the lapels of his coat so that Tom looked like a poorly dressed child. The sun was too high for shadows, and there were no trees for him to cool under. His legs were weak with sleeplessness. As quickly as they would allow, he ran for his bus when he saw it on the other side of the road. A cream-coloured taxi, stationary and battered, beeped at him to remind him that traffic drove on the other side here. The bus driver sold him a whole book of tickets and counted out the change in tiny copper coins. He watched an elderly man, who was carrying two tin pails of blueberries, insert his ticket in a red box and pull a lever. Tom did the same and saw that his ticket had been punched with dots a blind person could read. He sat, with relief, in one of the red bucket chairs. With a desperation he had not known before, he wanted to be in bed; he closed his eyes to conjure at least an image of comfort, but he found instead that his mind was assailed by another anxiety; he did not know where his bed was. The address he had was for the directorate of the university, where—he supposed—he would have to go to find out where he would be living for the next ten months. There was no picture in his head of what this might be like, no bed he could imagine, so instead he rested his head on the window of the bus and let his eyes roll over the road—long and straight, hemmed with dappling trees and low-rise blocks of flats. The bus stopped, someone told him to stand up, and he survived the rest of the journey, as on a fairground ride, on already unsteady legs. Tom followed everyone off the bus when it reached Warsaw Central train station.

He was searching for the correct tram stop, clutching his piece of scrap paper. It told him that he should have Aleje Jerozolimskie running lengthways in front of him and Marchlewskiego Street stretching away behind him. Tom dimly remembered one of Carter's seminars involving Rosa Luxemburg, Feliks Dzerzhinsky, and Julian Marchlewski. Communist internationalists, this was the company he was keeping now. As he oriented himself a car, small and noisy, buzzed past the station and bumped up a curb to Tom's left and stopped with a tiny screech. The driver, when he got out, stood taller and fatter than the car itself. He shut the door and walked away without locking it. As he was squinting into the sun, Tom had to readjust his focus from the driver to the building behind him in order to see it properly. He was surprised it had dodged his notice until then. No other edifice nearby (in fact, the tourist knew, no other in the country) came close to the height of the Palace of Culture. It was the colour of muddy river stones and against the near-white sky, looked like the discarded architectural drawings of a socialist Empire State Building. It was not a palace as a Bavarian prince would have conceived it, more the taste of the Kremlin. Its plain mass pulled Tom to it past the parked car and on to what could have been a parade ground. It was confusingly square and head-spinningly tall, and Tom realised that—although it certainly marked the land—it would be easy to become lost in its vicinity. It seemed to look in several directions simultaneously, and the buildings that faced up to it from the adjacent avenues were department stores, Party offices, and apartment blocks all of a similar hue and form. For a city, Tom thought, it was quiet—or quiet in a way that allowed you to hear things distinctly.

The clatter and clang of the tram he took were like that of an ancient lift cage. He franked his ticket as he had done before on the bus, and as he had there, he allowed an older person to take his seat. He was pleased with himself—despite having lost his bag, not having slept, and not knowing where and when he would sleep next. The woman at airport Information had advised him to alight from this tram after Stefan Batory Street, so he did his best to read the street signs through the scratched grime of the window. It would be a short walk after that, she told him, and the Central School for Planning and Statistics would be hard to miss. 'It's like if Aztec temple was built by socialists,' she had said. She had not meant it in a good way, he could see for himself now. It was about four or five storeys high, a plaster-and-glass block like many of the others but with jagged corner adornments. And it was red. Lowered on top by some ham-fisted god was a multi-layered skylight in the shape of a ziggurat.

'I'm a student here,' said Tom, not caring who might hear.

Inside the vast central hallway, Tom wondered whether Escher, rather than the Aztecs, had installed the staircases, so numerous they were and so pointless they seemed. He came to a hatch with a sliding window and a net curtain.

'Hello!' he called through the window. 'Dzień dobry!'

The person inside was a woman, sitting side-on to the window so she could watch her miniature black and white television uninterrupted. She slid back the glass but said nothing. Tom saw that the programme she was watching was for children, featuring puppets. He realised too that he was looking in on the woman's home; there was also a man in there—perhaps her husband—standing at a kitchenette and a small child in red T-shirt and blue tights reading a book on a rocking horse.

'*Hallo*,' she said finally, impatiently. The voice came to Tom as if through a tin on a string. Again he fetched the letter of invitation from his holdall.

'I'm meant to go here,' he said, pointing to the address at the top, knowing the porter would not understand him otherwise. She then began a conversation with her husband, which included the word *rektorat* and which ended with him emerging from a door behind a curtain and imploring Tom to follow him up some stairs. The baluster ironwork was like a circuit diagram of fuses and resistors as if it could be connected to a giant battery. Tom speculated that the landing they had arrived at was indeed the power source. A series of four or five doors lined the wall, installed so they overlapped their frames to minimise the seeping in or the leaking out of sound. Each door had a number, stencilled in white paint. The porter's husband knocked on 010 and without waiting for a reply (which he would not have heard anyway), pulled at the handle. The handle in its metal and curve reminded Tom of the spoon in the airport café.

Three women sat behind desks buttressing the three walls that did not contain a window. Each desk was identically appointed with a heavy green typewriter and a cream-coloured telephone. One secretary sprang up to dust the leaves of a giant cheese plant, which was potted in one corner but had ambitions on another. The second secretary began feeding armfuls of paper files into an overstuffed filing cabinet. The third picked up her phone—which was not ringing—and replaced it without speaking. None reckoned it was her job to deal with the two men in their office. The porter's husband began to talk in a way that suggested to Tom that he did not often get the opportunity. As he spoke, he himself filled the pauses that he had left for their replies. He warmed to his subject and stepped around the room with his hands in his pockets, hunching his shoulders forward, making him seem even skinnier than he was. He finished by extending his hand towards the foreign guest and giving the humblest of small bows. He'd have doffed his hat had he had one.

'Hello. Dzień dobry,' said Tom, again translating himself. 'Bardzo mi miło. Pleased to meet you.' He decided to focus on the one who was least occupied, which to him was the telephone lady. He extended to her the invitation from the vice-rector of the university. This was a woman with a reverence for official paper, and she looked upon this many-handled specimen with repulsion. Tom could see it in her eyes. 'I am Thomas Day.' He pointed to himself and to the name on the letter. He was aware that if these women had been expecting him, they would have been expecting him to look—and smell—like a Westerner. 'Yes, sorry about this—I know I must look a mess. I got no sleep on the coach or plane. I think I may have spilled coffee on my front. It's very warm in this coat. I lost ...'

'Chwileczka!' His nominated secretary interrupted him, picking up her still-mute phone. Again, she replaced it without saying anything, but now she got up and urged Tom to follow her. 'Come, Mr Day.' She led him through a door, which until that point had been obscured by the cheese plant. She left him there alone.

'Good afternoon, Mr Day. Or may I say, good day?' The voice was followed by its own laughter. Tom could not yet see its source. 'I am waiting to say that!'

The room was large but belittled by enormous furniture. A huge conference table, finished with the same high gloss veneer that covered a wall of cupboards, bullied the middle of the room. An oasis of glasses on the table called to the bottles on the drinks cabinet built into the cupboards. A long sofa, the colour of chicken stock and the texture of synthetic wool, was neighbour to an outsized television set. The curtains on the windows matched the sofa fabric and reached the ledge, whereas the nets behind them fell to the floor. Smoke was billowing from below a woollen tapestry so that Tom thought it must be on fire before the coughing made him take a closer look.

'Vice-Rector Wilk?' Tom guessed.

'I am!' the cough replied, standing up to become a man of below-average height and above-average girth. It was a long walk to his guest around first his desk then the conference table. A loose parquet tile rocked beneath his step. 'Sit, please!' He was already out of breath and Tom thought it best to allow him to recover.

'Your office is impressive,' said Tom, landing on an adjective that left some room for honesty. Wilk simply nodded, holding his next cough behind tight lips. 'It was not hard to find the university from the city centre,' he went on; he found himself making his own small talk. 'However, I did have some problems at the airport.'

'You must be hungry?' Wilk looked to the door that connected his to the secretaries' office. As if awaiting the cue from him, it opened, and the first secretary—the one who tended to the cheese plant—entered bearing a platter of open sandwiches and a plate of cake. She set them between her boss and the foreigner. 'Thank you, Elżbieta. Can you bring the tea in now too, please?' When she didn't move, he repeated the instruction in Polish.

'Actually, I am hungry. I am trying to think when I last ate. I somehow missed breakfast.' Tom bit into a sandwich with cheese and a disc of meat. The meat flipped on to his hand. The vice-rector seemed pleased.

'That is our famous *kabanosy* dry sausage. Very expensive. You must try it with vodka.' He registered his guest's alarm. 'It is also good with tea.' Again, the door opened and Elżbieta entered this time with tea. Wilk waited for her to leave, then he poured it himself. Into his own he dropped a slice of lemon, which he macerated with his spoon against the bottom of his glass.

Wilk waited until the student had finished his third sandwich. 'Elżbieta will give you a bag for the others if you like. Now you must have some cake! It's called by us *drożdżówka*. There is no word for this in your language.'

'It's like a Danish pastry,' Tom said, tasting one and not noticing the offence he had caused. He stirred the tea leaves to the bottom of his glass and sipped. There was no milk. Despite his lack of sleep the food had revived and emboldened him. 'You have another door, Vice-Rector Wilk.' Tom gestured to the corner nearest where the man's desk was situated. 'Is that where the secret recording equipment is kept?'

'That's a weak joke, I think, Mr Day. You enjoy spy novels perhaps. I have something better for you to read.'

'I should like that.'

Wilk had got up but became distracted. 'My toilet is out there. The door is . . . I have lost words . . . there is nothing after. Our building needs *remont* . . . renovation? There is corridor and more stairs, but they are dark and it rains there . . . not rain, but it is very wet. We need renovation but we need money for this. It's a hard situation.'

A silence fell between the men, allowing the noises from outside to come in. Tom went to the window to investigate the hammering and mechanical digging he could suddenly hear. He wondered how he hadn't noticed it before.

'We build the most modern metro in the entire world,' Wilk said with what might have been a rehearsed pride. 'The workers dig in the afternoon only,' he continued reasonably. 'The neighbours complain in the morning.'

Tom was still looking down on the street, the same he had travelled along by tram. He wondered at the psychology of the vice-rector, able to disconnect in his mind the excavation of a new underground and the leaking corridor in his own building, his vanity and his shame. And Tom supposed, it was not consideration for the neighbours that prevented the workers from digging until midday. 'What's the street called? It's very grand.'

'Aleja Niepodległości. Avenue of Independence. Is named from First World War.' The vice-rector had to climb over the Rs and Ws of the final words. 'We are independent almost seventy years. You know Polish history, Mr Day? But of course! Your professor Carter told us about you!'

Day was accustomed to professorial types questioning his reading habits. 'I have studied some of it, yes. But I want to learn as much as I can while I'm here. Sir . . . Vice-Rector Wilk . . . You would not say that Poland has been independent for all of that time?' The sound of the digging had again fallen into the background.

'No, indeed, the war with Germany. We were destroyed in Warsaw.'

'Not just the Germans, Vice-Rector. You had the Russians against you from the start too.'

'The Red Army liberated Poland, but you are correct, they were too late to save Warsaw.' Wilk had moved to the wall of cupboards. He opened a door to reveal a bookshelf. 'Here is the book I want you to read, Mr Day. Jerzy Topolski is a known Polish historian in these times.'

'*An Outline History of Poland.* It's in English.' Out of habit, Tom opened at the publication details at the front. 'Interpress. Warsaw, 1986. That's very generous, Vice-Rector.'

'I found it in the bookshop in the Palace of Culture. Is very fine shop.' He watched as his guest flicked through the pages. A booklet fell out of the back, which the vice-rector had not known was there.

Tom opened this booklet. They were historical maps. His curiosity drew him to one: *Nazi Occupation and Armed Resistance*. Wary of offending his host still further, he showed the map to the older man.

'You see these lines.' Wilk pointed to pink and green hatching and read from the key. 'They are areas of intense Polish and Soviet partisan activity. You see, Mr Day, the Soviets and the Poles fought the Hitlerites together.'

'Yes, I am sure that is true, Vice-Rector Wilk. But your historian Topolski has also included this line on the map.' Tom traced his finger down a boundary marked in green. 'He says this is the Soviet-German demarcation line of 28 September 1939. It shows the extent of pre-war Poland under Russian control after just one month. This is what the secret protocols of the Nazi-Soviet pact were about, Mr Wilk. You know this, I think.'

The vice-rector laughed. 'I see we have a lot to teach you, Mr Day.' His laugh became a cough and Tom guessed he was looking for words to evade the embarrassment. The man discovered a cigarette in his pocket, he lit it, and with his first drag, his breathing settled again. 'Do you know the expression *polska rzeczywistość*? Polish reality is called.' Tom shook his head. 'You have seen these maps, not only this one. You know it is our history, our geography. Sometimes even we have been invaders, but usually it is us invaded. It is our reality, our *raison d'état*. So now the Russians are our friends, they are our comrades. They made many sacrifice to protect our independence.'

'Who from? Who are they protecting you from now?'

'Aha, Mr Day! You are very funny. We are all friends today, no? Mr Bush is coming to visit us soon, you hear? And we would love if Mrs Thatcher was Polish. She is a clever, beautiful woman.' The vice-rector nodded in agreement with himself.

'Not everyone at home loves Thatcher quite so much.'

'No. That is your British democracy.'

'Is it yours, Vice-Rector Wilk?'

'You cannot ask one man his democracy. I think I should not give you lecture on that, as you have lectured me on my country's history. Democracy is what is the right path for the entire country. Democracy is when all the forces of society support each other. Our Party is the leading force now, but there are others—the Church, for example, intelligentsia, *Solidarność*—who must also help. The government wants a reform right now—our prices, bread, milk, meat. They are not at the right level—but the people don't want listen. They only listen to their priests, who say they can eat bread for nothing, that God will give them milk or vodka!' The coughing took hold of the vice-rector's body again, and Tom thought he might not go on. 'I am sorry, Mr Day. I am sick, you see. This is an important time in our country, I think. I am happy you are here with us. Please help us . . . Thomas. May I call you that? I think you can be very helpful to us. You will have friends here, and they will see that Poland is on a good path because you are here. You will tell that in a democracy people do not always get what they want. That's right? And your friends will see they must be patient. And we can also be friends, I think?'

'Yes, of course, Vice-Rector Wilk. I am sorry if I lectured you. You mentioned Professor Carter from my university in Belfast. He has taught me a great deal, and he also expects me to debate with him. It's a bad habit of mine. The truth matters, I believe.'

'I agree with you completely, Thomas. There is a historical dialectic and from this there are objective realities which society must accept. We may call this *truth*.

'And now, the truth is you must be tired. El . . .'

Elżbieta was already at the door. She leaned in to whisper in the vice-rector's ear as if it would be rude to utter Polish in front of the foreigner.

'Thank you, Elżbieta. That's a fine idea.' He watched her back out of the room with the remaining food. 'Thomas, my secretary has already obtained a friend for you. You will find him outside my office.' The vice-rector paused to allow Tom to stand and to gather his things. 'And pani Elżbieta will give you some sandwiches and . . . Danish pastries . . . for your bag. We will speak again soon, Thomas, I am certain.'

The friend that Tom had been assigned was a third-year Foreign Trade student named Aleksander Cybulski. 'Dude, no bag?' were the only words he spoke to Tom until they had exited the SGPiS building and turned left.

'No shit!' he empathised once they were amid the clamour of Independence Avenue. 'No worries, dude. I will arrange it all for you. But a goddamn week—what a country, man.' Aleks expressed all of this shame without appearing to burden himself with any of it. 'Didn't The

Wolf offer to help you? No, of course not.' Aleks saw the confusion in the visitor's face. 'Wilk, it means *wolf*. He's more of a sheep, actually, so we call him Wolf ironically.' The clang from the metro works stopped momentarily. One worker, buried waist-deep in a hole of his own digging, had called some of his colleagues over to look into it with him. With their hard hats and smudged faces, they could have been miners.

'Where did you pick up your American accent? Your English is so good.'

'The accent shows, huh?' Aleks gripped Tom's elbow and forced him to run with him across the tram tracks to the other side of the road. 'VOA, man. That's the *Voice of America*, but let's just keep that between you and me. Your new pal, Wilk, would not care to discover that his students were listening in to the enemy of socialism.'

'The vice-rector could convince himself otherwise, whatever the evidence.' Tom thought he might have to explain himself, but Aleks already seemed uninterested. 'Where are we going, by the way? Is this the way to the International House?'

'Dude, you aren't going there. Pani Elżbieta issued you papers for the International House as per instruction from Wilk, but you also have a dinner pass here for Dom Studenta. Which is where we are now.'

Tom looked up at the block, in colour and design the same as most other buildings he had seen that day. 'The Student House.'

'Yep. I aim to make you very much at home.' He walked Tom straight past the porter's window and up some stairs. Tom recognised the banister as being the same as in the university building, wired like an electric circuit. Shifting the strap of his holdall, he rubbed his shoulder on the wall. Chalky yellow paint came off on his coat. He tried to clean it.

'Tom, you must learn that, in our country, we only paint the bottom half of our walls with the good stuff. Rub your ass as hard as you like against this part, none of the gloss will come off. Give me your coat—I will fix it.' Tom was glad to be rid of it. Aleks also grabbed his bag.

They had arrived in a dormitory. Although a heavy curtain had been pulled across the window (obscuring most of the daylight), Tom could see in the gloom that there were four beds. Aleks dropped the bag and coat on one of them. 'That's yours now. The one under the window is mine. That mess over there is Norbert. Don't wake him—you'll see plenty of him later. This fourth one belongs to some guy we don't know yet. We think he has been suspended, but the old porter has his mouth zipped. In his absence, Norbert has christened him *Nikt.*'

'No one.'

'You understand Polish?'

'I learned some from an old Polish lady before I came, but it's embarrassing. I've been promised some language lessons, but I don't know how I will cope with my tutorials.'

'You'll skip most of those! Everyone here will want to practise their English on you, so you may not get the chance to learn much. Norbert, there, will teach you words you had better avoid repeating.

'Now, I have important work to do with the paper I stole from pani Elżbieta. And you, by the look of you, need to lie down. I will see you later.'

Tom shook hands with his departing friend. He had felt foreign all day. He could not drink a coffee, ride on a bus, or eat a sandwich without being alien. There was certainly something exotic about Aleks, but they were both students of a similar age and humour. Now Tom was glad to be alone. He stripped to his pants (he had no other clothes) and climbed into his bed. He was asleep in minutes.

It was because the sheet was a poor fit for the bed, or perhaps it was the coarseness of the blanket, for whatever reason, Tom did not sleep undisturbed in his new room. He was certainly tired enough to sleep soundly, but he could never surrender completely when his brain knew that it was light outside. Like the partially closed curtain of his dorm, he glimpsed his dream with partially closed eyelids. He could believe that the grey-suited passengers on the flight were placed to his left and his right to keep watch on him, provoking him into a political conversation with their newspaper headlines about Bush. He had been wise to them. They had disappeared in the terminal once their mission was foiled but had ushered Tom to the immigration queue. There the border guards had shilly-shallied over his passport just long enough for his rucksack to be isolated. What had they stamped in his passport, and was it an instruction for the lady at the Information desk? She could describe Tom's luggage with no help from him as if an edict had gone out to detain all blue and yellow rucksacks. She could not have shepherded the foreigner to the university more surely without escorting him there herself. 'Come, Mr Day,' had said the secretary who could not speak English. And her colleague, Elżbieta, must have been listening at the door, for how else would she know when to come with the sandwiches and cake? What sort of understanding did she have with Aleks, that he had delivered Tom to this dorm and not some other? If someone from his own embassy wanted to find him, they would go looking in the wrong place because here he was, lying semi-naked in the dorm of a man he had only just met. In fact a man he had not yet met, but who was asleep metres away from him, was somehow also at his side shaking him awake and demanding to know who he was.

Tom sat up in his bed, clutching the blanket to his waist, and waited for the blizzard of sibilants to subside. He guessed his assailant was Norbert. From the Polish, Tom plucked out the word for *bed* and assumed from their repetition that most of the rest were profanities: Norbert was without a doubt a master. Aleks appeared then, interrupting his roommate's flow, and Tom was almost sorry it had to stop. Satisfied, Norbert extended his hand to shake Tom's.

'Put it there, my friend.' He then translated this for Aleks' benefit. 'What's up?'

Aleks put his friend in a headlock and wrestled him away. 'That's about the limit of Norbert's English,' he explained. 'Wish I could say I was proud to claim I had taught him all he knows. He has a few more one-liners where those came from, but not many. But I suspect he will understand most of what you say. That is if you slow down a bit for him.'

'Do I speak too fast for you?'

'Yes, but don't worry. I'll ignore the parts I don't understand. Here, try these on.' Aleks presented the undressed man with some clothes, neatly folded. 'I commandeered them from the guys in the other dorms—but not Norbert. You would not want to catch what he's got. Mainly T-shirts, I think. No underwear, obviously. You can wash what you have on and dry them overnight downstairs in the . . . *suszarnia* . . . that's what we call it: drying room, I suppose. I will show you where. The same for socks.' He cleared his throat to shift the quality in his voice. 'Tomek, I am sorry that this has happened to you. There is a lot about life here that you will have to get used to, so I might need to apologise some more. But seriously, I can help you with most things, and I will be glad to. It's pretty amazing that you want to be in our country.'

Newly polonised, Tomek entered the next phase of his induction.

'Tomek!' hailed Norbert from his side of the room. 'What's up?'

That evening, Norbert convened a party in the dormitory in his Irish friend's honour. As the new semester had not formally begun, many had not yet arrived back in the capital from their hometowns. At one point, Norbert took a sort of register ('Is Olsztyn here? Have the girls from Kielce returned?') The official business of the evening was conducted in Polish—Tom was glad of that although he understood little besides what he could determine from the accompanying actions. So he soon learned the terms for *cheers* and *down the hatch* and *just a little more*. Piotr, a boy from the next room, had supplied and opened the first half-litre of vodka, having primed the bottle by smacking it on its bottom. Aleks had produced a full set of shot glasses from his cupboard. A slab of chocolate arrived with a girl called Wioletta; she divided it carefully into its squares and presented them on a plate. She later curled up in the bed belonging to *Nikt*, the suspended student, and stayed there until the morning. Aleks toasted a few rounds ('To absent friends and to friends we wish were absent!' he translated for Tom.) He then left the room and did not come back. Piotr attempted a conversation in English with Tom, relying on Norbert for reassurance.

'Piotr say you are a handsome bastard.' Norbert then checked back with his friend that this was what he intended to say.

'Why you in Poland, Tomek? Yes, yes. You are student, like us.' Norbert threw his considerable arms across both Piotr and Tom. 'But why you in our country?'

'*Do dna!*' Tom cried as if that were the only answer there could be. Drink up.

Later, Piotr sat on Norbert's bed and the two talked each other to sleep. Tom was so drunk he could barely keep both eyes open at once. He suddenly remembered his underwear; he would have none clean to wear tomorrow unless he washed the pair he had on now. He puzzled over how he could launder his pants without wearing any. Would he pull his trousers back on, or would he risk public nudity on his first night? 'It's how we do it in Belfast,' he could say. First, he had to find the washroom. He imagined it would be near the drying room, and he recalled Aleks saying that the *suszarnia* was downstairs. Shit, how hard could that be? Tom padded out to the landing; the cold of the linoleum told him he was barefoot. He could not recollect removing his shoes and socks. Christ, socks, yes! He dived back into his dorm to look for them, for he would surely want to wash all his smalls at once. Tom battled with himself to think logically. He could do drunk in charge of logic, so long as he drove it slowly. He was at the stairs again and reminded himself not to touch the walls on the way down. When he reached the porter's window, he held his socks up by way of a pass ('I'm doing these. These socks are my business. It's quite urgent.') but the hatch was shut. The porter may have gone home, but he had left every light on. *I will switch them off on my way back,* promised Tom to himself. He could hear a sound that was like the outside, like wind blowing at a high altitude or through caves. He was unexpectedly moved by the poetry of the moment, by thoughts of limestone and home. But he was approaching a washroom and the outside that he could hear were the taps running hard as if the water might run out tomorrow. A row of four sinks faced a row of four more. There was no plug and he had no soap so he rinsed his socks the best he could. He dropped his trousers and draped them over his shoulder then slipped his underpants off and washed them in the same way. He wrung them dry till they resembled a Polish sausage. *Kabanosy.* There was another door, and that door had a word stencilled on it, and (miraculously, triumphantly) that word was *suszarnia*. He entered. The room itself was dry. The air was hot and arid; the wooden rails were parched. He was stepping into a sauna with his trousers slung over his shoulder like a towel, and he instantly thought better of being unclothed from the waist down. He pulled up his zip with the care of a drunk man, tooth by tooth. He played quoits with his pants until they caught satisfactorily on a peg. He flattened a sock vertically on each side, displayed like rashers of bacon. He imagined them sizzling on the hot wood. They would dry quickly there; he could even wait for them. Or he might have to sleep amongst his new companions without even his pants, which they might find odd or they might not. The briefing by the British Council had not mentioned it. The other door—the one that was metal and with a studded plywood panel in place of a window—did not look like a toilet entrance, but the thought reminded Tom that he had better go before returning upstairs. The door opened before he could try the handle and out slipped Aleks.

Tom gestured proudly and wordlessly to his tiny array of laundry. Then, remembering his other requirements, said, 'Is that a loo in there?'

Aleks laughed and put his arm around his friend. 'No, Tomek, it is not the loo. I can show you to the restroom, or I can let you have a look inside. What's it to be?' Aleks was already opening the metal door and ushering the Irishman in and down some stairs. He pulled a cord and a light flickered on to show a room little larger than a prison cell. There was a broken chair, stacked upside down on another. Behind that, leaning against a wall, was a giant white sheet scrolled up around two wooden batons. Paint pots and brushes might have been the source of the chemical smell. Aleks had moved to a black box the size of a car battery.

'Ah! That's your radio, Aleks!'

'Longwave, shortwave, I've got the lot on this babe, dude. Of course, the reception is . . .' Aleks searched for the right word, but he was in too much of an elevated mood to think of a negative. 'But the cellar is basically soundproof, so it's quite safe. Be careful with that!' Tom was lifting the grey canvas cover off of something.

It looked like a sewing machine or a mangle, its black metal scratched but shiny, a crank at one end that appeared too big for it. A tray, that could once have belonged to a different device, was fixed to the front. With the cover off, Tom now knew where the odour was coming from.

'It's a . . . we call it a *powielacz* . . . for printing. I was putting oil on its moving parts, brushing off the dust, making sure that it will function when we need it.'

'Need it? What's it for? What do you need it for?' Tom was working hard to sober up his sentences, aware that Aleks was sharing with him something sacred.

'We have not needed it over the summer because there were no students around. We can't waste the little paper we have.'

'You got paper today!' Tom interrupted. 'You stole some from the rectorate.'

'Elżbieta helpfully looked away, yes. The *powielacz* is a very precious piece of kit. Tomek, I cannot say this strongly enough. You must not talk to anyone about it. You don't know who you can trust yet.'

Since he had arrived in the country, Tom had had no choice but to put his trust in people he did not know. Without relying on their direction, he would never have made it through the airport even or from there to SGPiS or from the rectorate to Dom Studenta. Making his way to the drying room was the only achievement he could call his own. 'Norbert?'

'Norbert and the others from Kutno all know, and they won't say anything. But they don't all feel the same way about the union, so it is best to say nothing to them either. Piotr, for example, was allowed to skip the *praktyka* due to his connection.'

'That's?'

'That's the month every student has to work in a factory before they can enrol as a student. This is a workers' paradise, remember Tomek. They can't just let the bourgeoisie get a higher education. I pushed trolleys in a hospital, which was all right. Everyone gets a certificate of *praktyka* and can then get their student identification. Pani Elźbieta said you can pick yours up from the rectorate tomorrow. They don't insist that you be a prole.'

'Union?' Tom had worked out that one-word questions were wiser in his condition, and they helped him focus on the answers. 'You said they don't all like the union?'

'The Independent Students' Association, NZS. It was banned in 1982 under *stan wojenny*. Now, even though martial law was ended, NZS is not legally registered, so the university authorities do not have to listen to us. The rector at Warsaw University is better. He sympathises with students. But here it is different. They call SGPiS the Red Fortress because the children of Party apparatchiks come here. They join ZSP— that's the official Polish Students' Association. Some on our corridor are ZSP partisans.'

'Wioletta?'

'Yes. How did you know?'

'She brought chocolate. Maybe the others can't get chocolate?'

'Her chocolate is from *Wedel*. That brand is made in Poland but for export only. Perhaps her mother got it because she is a Party functionary, or she could have bought it in a Pewex.'

'What's *Pewex*? There is a lot I don't know!'

'I'm your teacher, so you will learn a lot. I will let you take me to a Pewex some time—it's a store where you can buy great chocolate.

'This machine,' Aleks stroked the printer. 'It's my duty to keep it safe. Every photocopier every typewriter, even in Poland must have a licence, which lists the people permitted to use it. Not this one. This one is a monster—a beautiful monster. It is made from parts of older machines salvaged from earlier protests. My brother and I assembled it in our allotment. I must take you there! So this monster has no birth certificate, which is good because nothing it prints can be traced back to it. But equally, there would be no explanation for it if the wrong person happened to come across it. You understand, don't you, Tomek?' Aleks placed a hand on each shoulder and gave his friend a gentle shake.

'I do understand, Aleks. I get it that you have told me something that you probably shouldn't have and that you now need me to keep it a secret. I can keep a promise and a secret, so . . .' Tom put a hand out to shake. 'So . . . That's that. *Do dna!* Now, I want you to tell me more but really, I am totally knackered and quite pissed and I don't even know yet what I am going to wear in bed.'

'I can fix that!'

'No, this time I will manage. But thank you. *Dziękuję.*'

Over the next few days Tom got used to the rhythms of his new life in Dom Studenta. He honed his technique of washing his things and drying them overnight and putting on a long enough borrowed shirt to allow him to fetch them again in the morning. He picked up his student identity card from pani Elźbieta and enrolled in his classes. With Norbert's help he changed money in a nearby PKO Bank Polski and he spent some of his new złoty on bread and cheese and tea. He set aside coins for the phone in the hostel then found that it was permanently out of order. He purchased tram tickets from a kiosk, which also sold newspapers, cigarettes, and dressmaking patterns. He discovered that he could not buy *kiełbasa* or any meat without coupons, that he could not get coupons without a letter from the rectorate and that no one in the rectorate knew who could issue the letter. Tom was not sure he cared. His lunch pass allowed him to eat in the canteen in the Student House, and there he ate all the white sausage and offal he could genuinely want.

43

He discovered early on that the toilets did not come equipped with loo roll; the four rolls he had packed lay squashed still (he hoped) in a rucksack in Heathrow. He noticed a habit that Aleks and Norbert had of unwinding a length of paper from a roll they shared and taking with them only that amount. They let him share, but he could not shake the suspicion that they counted the segments that he tore off. In the toilet cubicles someone had thoughtfully hung strips of newspaper on a nail, so Tom augmented his ration with that. One long week after landing there, Aleks accompanied Tom back to the airport, and they reclaimed his bag. Someone had taken his George Best mug.

Tom stood tall in his white T-shirt and shorts while his roommates laughed.

'U nas, we don't run on the road,' said Norbert, pretending he was offering acculturation advice. 'Listen, Tomek. I beg you.'

Wioletta had entered the room. She sized up the Irishman and nodded her appreciation. This made him more anxious. 'Don't mind them, Tommy,' said Aleks, faking reassurance. 'But with those shorts, do keep an eye out for our Polish squirrels.' He laughed and—when he had translated it for Norbert—so did he.

'Laugh all you like,' replied Tom, tying the laces of his old trainers. 'I will outlive you all.' He stood up again to stretch and warm up, and this time even he laughed at his own ridiculous poses. He memorised the route he would take to the Łazienki Park, where he hoped to do most of his running. To leave the shade he opted to cross to the east side of Independence Avenue, to run past the university and into a large overgrown park, criss-crossed by a pattern of paths laid down by some optimistic post-war city planner. Perhaps the same planner had imagined that, on a hot day like this, children would paddle in the concrete pool he had designed for the centre—but now the pool was dry; the concrete was crumbling and the children were teenagers smoking in circles on the grass. As he left the park, Tom hoped that the busy road he emerged onto was Armia Ludowa. The street name, when he had spotted it on a map, had made Tom smile; the People's Army was a reminder of the type of country he now lived in. Professor Carter had taught him that the AL was a small fraction of the resistance during the

44

war, but because they were communists, they had inherited most of the credit in the years following. No doubt the book that Wilk had given him (and the history course he had signed up to that week) would tell a different story.

A rank of tiny cars was parked at an angle to the road, covered with the same grime that Tom could feel he was breathing. It was hot. The air was dry and acrid; man-high overground pipes ran down the central reservation and crossed overhead, leaking steam into the atmosphere. An open-backed truck lifted a tarpaulin and sold watermelons to a queue of people. Tom was thirsty. He was sure he was on Armia Ludowa only as he left it at the tangle of roads that Aleks would later tell him was called Plac Na Rozdrożu. ('It's the parting of the ways,' he would say.) A café, or bar, looked like it had been dropped in the middle of the circle. Its carved wood fascia and outdoor wooden benches gave it an incongruous, alpine appearance. He was thirsty, but he had not run far enough yet, so Tom pressed on southwards, confident that the park he could now see was Łazienki.

He had no guidebook, so he did not know the names of the grand buildings he passed—whose palaces they were, which ambassadors resided there—or the styles they mimicked. The trees and the water features, the promenades and statuary were all lined up according to a pleasant geometry. Tom breathed more clearly here, but he was not yet relaxed in his running. He dodged a family feeding sunflower seeds to squirrels. Peacocks, on full display, squealed at a father who came too close. Ducks hopped back into the artificial lake. Tom circuited the park twice before deciding he had run for long enough.

He sat on a bench already occupied by a man in a suit. The sun was still hot, but the man showed no discomfort. His dark hair was cut short and revealed no grey; his glasses were black-rimmed and were for looking at as much as looking through.

'That's Chopin you can hear,' he said in English, directing Tom's eyes towards a small crowd gathered around a bronze willow tree. 'Beautiful, isn't it? Every Sunday. What does it say about a people that they will make an appointment with themselves—the same time each week—to come and gather around their memorial to Chopin and listen to a classical piano recital?' He stopped to allow in more of the music.

'I don't know Chopin that well.'

'Well, you should, Tom.' A little Scots inflexion gave his admonishment more force. 'Buy a tape or something.'

The crowd clapped and a little man in tails stood up to receive the applause. He was little because he was some distance away, and although to Tom he looked young, that might also have been an optical trick. He sat down on the stool again, and tucking himself back under the piano, he resumed his performance. It may have been seconds before the music reached Tom; the pianist was in such command he could slow the speed of sound. Squirrels nibbled seeds and scampered away, ducks drifted across flat water, peacocks fanned their hens. They played a polonaise. Their notes marked out a walking pace, purposeful, aristocratic rather than martial, occasional dignified scurries balanced by genteel musical bows.

'I'll come here each week. That'd be better than a tape. Is it far for you to come?'

The man smiled inwardly. 'The embassy is on Aleja Róż, just a few minutes' walk away. I come here, but we are encouraged to be less predictable in our habits. You, on the other hand, should certainly come as often as you please.'

'What happens, Spiro, if I want to get in touch with you—after today?'

'You drop by Róż, like any normal citizen, if you like,' said the Scot. 'Or you could phone me from your Student House.' He slipped a card into Tom's hand. 'I don't know where you are going to keep that, in those ridiculous shorts, but I would ask you not to misplace it.'

'The Student House phone doesn't work.'

'It does bloody work! I thought that Aleks friend of yours was good with machinery and the like. Hasn't he shown you what a knife is for yet?' Clearly Aleks had not. 'Jam the knife into the coin slot—it connects the phone and gives you as long as you like. Just dial that number and leave me a message. Don't go abusing it, mind. I do have other business.'

'I'm going to Kutno next weekend, I have just remembered. I will have to give old Frédéric Chopin a miss.' Applause, carried by the smallest breeze, rippled again through the trees and disturbed the leaves above their heads. Tom leaned back on the bench as if sunbathing, eyes squinting.

46

'You will find the Cybulskis to be interesting people, Tom. Make sure you are polite and listen properly to them. Carter will be delighted, if a bit jealous at the same time.' Spiro sensed the quizzical look from the man on the bench beside him. 'Aleks' folks were well-known in the dissident movement at one time. They may not be now what they once were, but you should definitely give them the time of day. Their older son, now . . . I can't mind exactly what became of him.'

'Killed?'

'Christ, no! Tom, this is not Stalinist Russia you are in here, however bad it can get. No. Aleks' big brother is still around. You will probably see him, then you can jog my memory for me.'

The concert had finished and people were filing past their seat in greater numbers than before, causing the two men to be more self-conscious about speaking English to each other. Spiro moved to shake the younger man's hand then corrected himself—who'd give a jogger a handshake? He walked off in the direction of the ornamental lake. Tom retied his laces, gently stretched his calves, and started his run back to the hostel.

———— ⁓ ————

Pani Bańda was going to have a lovely time with her Polish class for international students; she always did. They came from such interesting places, and they always gave her such gorgeous presents at Christmas and on International Teachers' Day—chocolates and meats and cherry vodka and many more of her favourite things. This year she had her usual collection from the fraternal nations (they were always the dullest ones), a couple from Africa and one from Great Britain. Her plans from last year would serve her fine; her students always loved it when she invited the class to her flat to watch a film or discuss a writer. 'I don't teach you only Polish,' she would say. 'I teach you Poland.'

Pani Bańda taught Nelson to say, 'Hello, I am Nelson. I am a prince from Nigeria.'

Azil, who was from Libya and could therefore speak Arabic, Italian, and pretty good English, struggled to utter, 'I study cybernetics.'

Detlef, the East German, was certainly in the wrong class because he already spoke a lot of Polish on account of his Cracowian wife and his job at the Technical University. 'I want to become fluent so I can understand the sense of humour here.'

She was intrigued by the Brit, who turned out to be Irish. 'Hello, I am Thomas. I am studying the Production Economics course. I love vodka and Polish girls.' His roommates had taught him that phrase. She did not ask how he came to have roommates from the country.

That had made the two students from Czechoslovakia giggle. Jana and Hana would learn quickly because theirs was a Slavic tongue. But they might get lazy if they always sat together.

Bogomila from Bulgaria misunderstood. 'I also study economics,' she said, but no one laughed at her.

That was the whole group—three girls and four boys (or three boys, if she discounted Detlef—who was much older than the rest and therefore not really part of the group). There were no Russians this year, which always made the class more relaxed.

Pani Bańda wanted them to practise ordering a meal in a restaurant.

'Can I have chicken?' said Azil.

'We have no chicken,' replied Detlef in the role of waiter.

'I would like fish,' said Tom.

'We have cod, or trout by weight,' offered Detlef. Pani Bańda stepped in to explain the fish types and the custom of ordering food by weight to her less advanced speakers.

'Can I have beef?' tried Azil again.

'We have no beef. You can have kotlet schabowy,' recommended the German with a waiterly flourish. He then resorted to pig squeals and gestures indicating the tenderising of meat.

Azil stood up. 'Thank you. Good bye.' He then left the room altogether. No one was sure if the Muslim was actually offended or still in role. They gave him a round of applause when he came back. Pani Bańda finished the lesson with pronunciation practice of food-related vocabulary. Jana said that many of the words were the same—or nearly the same—in her language. Nelson wanted to know more about gherkin, beetroot, and cottage cheese. He declared, 'I am hungry in Poland.' Detlef proudly repeated some aphorism—taught him by his wife—about hungry Poles being angry. Bogomila responded crossly to that, but in Bulgarian so no one quite understood. Thomas revealed he had already learned the words for Turkish coffee, meat paste, and cheesecake. Pani Bańda set them a homework of trying a food they had never had before and dismissed them.

Outside, Azil walked with Tom. Like a wartime black marketeer, he opened the inside of his jacket for Tom to see. In English, he whispered, 'It's a banana. Do you like banana? Have you seen bananas in the shops? No. But I can get them for you.' He pulled the fruit out, peeled it, and gave it to Tom. 'For you, for free! Because your country and my country have . . .'

Azil did not need to complete his sentence. Tom knew he meant Northern Ireland, specifically the IRA, and the alleged purchase of Semtex by them from the Libyans. It seemed Azil was throwing in a banana to sweeten the deal. 'Thanks,' he said, cheerfully biting down. 'Where do you get them?'

'My secret,' said Azil, tapping his nose for emphasis. 'I can get dates too and figs. My embassy is very resourceful.'

They had reached a taxi rank, where Azil said he would wait. He had other places to go to that evening. Tom walked back to Dom Studenta, savouring his banana.

Tom was the first to wake the next day. Four giant pupae occupied the other three beds, their maturation looking in no way imminent. He was hung-over. He remembered the *Żytnia* vodka they had consumed the night before and the singing that Wioletta had led with her guitar. He had learned the word for scout but could not remember it now. In the semi-darkness he rummaged in his cupboard among his clothes and found a red plaid shirt that Aleks had scrounged for him. He had not been able to find its original owner to return it to him. He took the long walk to the bathroom to find that all the water had been turned off.

Back in the room, Piotr and Wioletta had made their way back to their rooms, and Aleks was up making tea with a heating element in a tin mug.

'You look like a Pole in that shirt,' he greeted his friend. He handed him the tea. 'No milk?'

'Thanks. I'm learning that tea is better black.' It also had a more salutary effect on his hangover. 'There is no water. How have you made tea?'

'In the desert, the owner of the oasis bar is a rich man. I filled these bottles last night,' Aleks said, pointing to the table beside his bed and the bottles with various vodka labels. 'Every year, they shut the central heating plant for maintenance. Those giant pipes you see along the side of some roads, those are from the plant. So they turn off the city's water for that and put a notice in the papers. Other times, the water stops because there is a leak. The plumbers try to fix it but they haven't got the right parts because someone has already used them to mend their father-in-law's or their boss's plumbing. So the guys patch the leak with whatever they can find until the next time. And so it goes on, keeping everyone in work while keeping the toilets out of order.'

'You have to be resourceful in this country,' said Tom. 'I'm thinking that's a good thing. You don't waste what you've got.'

'It will be better in Kutno,' Aleks said. He meant there would be water there, the toilets would flush. It did not sound like much to be proud of now.

'Kutno? Yes, I forgot. We are going there today? I had thought I might go into the Old Town today. I have been here for two weeks, and I have not really seen that part of the city yet.'

Aleks appeared to blush. 'You should,' he conceded. He knocked into the guitar that Wioletta had left behind, making a hollow, pained sound. Norbert groaned from beneath his pile of blankets.

'You say Kutno is better than Warsaw?' Tom challenged his friend.

('Fuck, yeah!' mumbled Norbert.)

'Then, let's go!' Tom started to pack his holdall for the short trip.

'You will have plenty of time to get to know Warsaw,' said Aleks, watching the Irishman. 'For some reason my folks can't wait to meet you. Don't forget your passport and your student card—you will need that for half-priced tickets. You should probably take a change of footwear with you too.'

Tom followed Aleks onto the correct tram then onto another then got off when he did, queued behind him in Warsaw West Station, and allowed him to pay for both train tickets. He paid him back when they found their compartment. The journey to Kutno was about an hour and a half through flat birch-wooded terrain. They did their best to sleep off their remaining headaches, not helped by the rocking of the carriage.

Aleks' brother Jakub met them at the station in one of the tiny cars Tom had seen everywhere. Jakub was shorter than his younger sibling but had a larger frame which he carried somewhat hunched over. When Tom greeted him in Polish, he responded in kind.

From the back seat Tom asked, 'What are these cars called? They are very popular here.' Although he had spoken in English, he had imagined Jakub might answer.

'Polski Fiat,' said Aleks. 'The government here got permission from the Italians to build them, sometime in the sixties, I think. We call them Baby Fiats.'

'Maluch,' Jakub added. Tom recognised the word; the car certainly was small, but he did not want to signal any criticism. Jakub drove the vehicle as hard as he dared, taking corners at a screeching angle, bumping over the tarmac softened to undulations in the heat, all the while maintaining an easy conversation with his brother. He parked, suddenly, outside a block of flats beside the concrete bay for bins.

'Top floor, I'm sorry to say,' announced Aleks. 'Five storeys up.' He added Tom's bag to his own and led the way up the stairs. Jakub drove away again without a word. 'Kuba has to fix something with the car,' Aleks explained.

Mr and Mrs Cybulski met them together at their door. With their similar height and black hair fading to white, they might have been brother and sister. Even their smiles were alike. They waited for Tom to take off his shoes, Mr Cybulski offering him leather slippers.

'Welcome, witamy, please do come in. You must be thirsty. Would you like tea or coffee? Magda has both ready.'

'Daddy, let him sit down,' protested Aleks affectionately.

'You mustn't speak English just because of me, Mr Cybulski,' Tom said, taking his place on a low corner sofa.

'Yes, but we must! You are a wonderful chance for us to practise our English. Please correct my mistakes, you won't offend. And please, call me Bogdan.' He pushed a coffee table laden with glasses and cake up against his guest's knees.

Tom ate two varieties of cake (thinking he was thereby doing his homework for pani Bańda), and when Magda Cybulska shovelled more onto his plate, he ate that too. Jakub returned but went straight to his room without joining the party.

51

Magda thought she had better explain. 'Jakub has been very busy lately,' she said softly, aware that her voice might carry to the next room. 'He is getting married in the new year, so he has been driving around the local farms and import suppliers trying to buy everything we will need. It is not easy in our country, Tomek, as I think you may know already. The normal shops do not have all that we need, and the black market has everything but at prices far above our wages. Still, we may combine.'

Tom nodded as if he understood before realising he hadn't. 'Combine—how do you mean?'

'It's a Polish word, Mom,' Aleks intervened deferentially. 'One of those *false friends* in the language. It means that Jakub can pull in some favours, fix things, make things happen. It's what we all have to do to cope. All who are not in the Party, at any rate.'

Tom, noticing how the volume of the conversation had quietened, himself spoke in little above a whisper. 'Earlier you said that Jakub had to "fix something with the car." Is that what you meant—he was doing a deal somewhere?' He noted the smiles around him. 'Slowly I am getting to grips with this language of yours. You must be really excited about the wedding.'

The smiles slipped. 'We are, of course,' said Magda.

In the corner of the room, Bogdan picked up a long-playing record and blew the dust off it before gently placing it on the record player and lowering the needle onto it. 'The Rolling Stones!' he announced triumphantly. 'They are the best.' He rejoined the group at the coffee table and spoke now in a voice just below the level of the music. 'Tom, you might know that Kuba is not entirely normal. I know that word sounds wrong to you—forgive me. I mean that he has had a difficult life—maybe he would have been ill in any case, but he has suffered traumas which are in some way our fault.' He held his wife's hand in both his own.

Tom recalled Spiro's instruction to be polite and to listen well to this family. 'I am sure—whatever it was—it could not have been your fault.'

'Of course it wasn't,' affirmed Aleks. His parents turned spontaneously to him as if he were the real authority in the home. 'He was arrested, or rather interned under Martial Law. The generals took him away and when they were done with him, he was never the same.'

'What did they do to him, if I may ask?'

All three Cybulskis shook their head. Bogdan spoke for them. 'We don't know. We can imagine—friends of ours produced reports of beatings, internees being told they had been denounced by their loved ones—we can imagine, but we do not know. He won't say. We took him to a psychiatrist, of course, but he would not tell her either.'

Magda was keen to change the subject. 'I see you have finished off the cake and I need to prepare dinner, so I must leave you boys alone.'

'Actually, Mom, I want to take Tom to the allotment. We can eat when we get back.'

The tiny shack on the edge of the Cybulski plot was sturdy even though it had been pieced together like a monster from a gothic novel. Aleks put his Irish friend to work digging up rows of potatoes and carrots while he plucked berries from their managed hedges. He watched the practised way the foreigner worked the vegetable rows. 'You have done this before,' he decided.

The Irishman straightened up, smiled, and wiped his nose with the back of a dirty hand and returned to the soil. The sinews at the back of his legs showed below the line of his shorts; his hands turned up potatoes in the ground like they were bingo balls. He strained but did not seem to tire or mind too much that his running shoes were getting very muddy. 'It must be an Irish thing,' he said. 'Both my parents grew up in the countryside. Perhaps I inherited something from them.'

'You don't tell me very much about yourself,' Aleks went on following no definite thought. Day did not lift his head. The sun, catching the ripples on the reservoir in the west, glinted like Morse code. Aleks shielded his eyes to look. He watched a single stork rise from the wetland—it would be young, fledged from its parents by now. It flew high then swooped down low—well-taught—to catch a field-vole or a frog from the earth before lifting up and settling in the nest it had in the barn near the road. This had been a dry summer. It was known that young storks were prone to abandonment by their mother when the weather was dry like this. Tom had limbs like a stork, Aleks thought.

'No,' Tom admitted finally, and long after Aleks imagined the subject had been lost. He stood squarely, his feet planted in the mud. 'I don't have a brother, Aleks. My parents are still around, but they aren't the sort to care too much about where I am or the trouble I get up to.'

Tom declined the crate his friend offered him as a seat. A breeze lifted at a strip of canvas sacking, revealing the dark vegetables beneath before dropping back in place.

'So that's it, Aleks, not much more to tell. Other people are a lot more interesting to watch and listen to.'

Aleks found two bottles of beer in the shack. He used the strike plate on the door frame to remove the caps. They tapped bottles. The beer was warm. They sat the next hour in silence.

'We should head back to the flat.'

Aromas of meat and gravy met them at the entrance. 'That smells amazing,' said Tom, removing his muddy trainers. 'But, Aleks, after all of that cake, I am not sure I can finish it. I don't want to offend your mother.'

'Telling the truth, Tom, you are more likely to offend her if you do finish your plate. In Poland, it means she did not feed you enough.'

'Pani Bańda did not tell us that. I didn't know. I am really sorry.'

'Don't be. It is just another lesson in socialism, to each according to his need . . . and not a thing more.'

Jakub joined them for dinner, making five around the low table near the corner sofa. He chose to speak in Polish, and so for a good part of the evening, Tom listened in hard, trying to follow the conversation. He understood when they were talking about work—Jakub's at the heating equipment factory, Bogdan's at the arms plant, Magda's at the hospital. There was discussion too about the wedding. Jakub's mother-in-law was making the dress from fabric someone in the family had brought back from Turkey. The Cybulskis were buying the couple a new bed and selling the one that Jakub had in his room. Tom gathered that the newlyweds would be moving into the same room. It would be their home.

'How long in Britain wait you for a phone?' Jakub suddenly asked Tom in English. ('Do you wait . . .' he corrected himself.)

'We don't wait. I would say everyone has a phone now.' He could recall a time when that was not so.

'So the state gives a telephone to every family in your country? That is very effective . . . efficient!' Everyone laughed at Jakub's apparent humour, except Tom who did not understand.

'Actually, it's no longer the state,' he said, killing the end of the joke. 'It was privatised two or three years ago.' Tom hoped he would not have to explain that aspect of Western capitalism, but it seemed his friends were either not interested or needed no explanation. Then, he realised he had missed his cue. 'So *your* phone. It looks new. Have you had it long?'

'Since the start of September.' They all tried to answer, but Bogdan got there first. 'We have waited nine years. Isn't it fine?' The mood slid from celebration to something more circumspect, so even Tom noticed. 'We have used it many, many times,' Bogdan reiterated. 'O, yes, we have!'

Tom was now sure of the change in atmosphere. He looked from face to face; each looked back at him in silence. The silence had to be held; it was too heavy to hover by itself.

'Everyone must have tea!' Magda announced, and in the flurry of noise which followed, Aleks whispered into his friend's ear, 'The phone is bugged, Tommy. We are sure of it. We have to be careful in this room what we say.'

Tom frantically rehearsed the entire conversation since they had returned to the flat, searching for anything he might have said that he should not have. And he recalled that most of it had been in Polish and therefore not of his making.

Later—after the tea and after the cake—Bogdan declared his intention to offer his foreign guest something else to drink. 'Come, Tomek, with me to the cellar. Aleks, you come too.' He led them down several flights of stairs to the bottom of the building where there was a double line of locked doors, a cellar for each flat.

Inside, the shelves were stocked with jars and bottles. There were fishing rods and nets, sets of skis, a suitcase stored on the highest rack. Aleks pulled out two stools, upended a crate, and invited his guest to sit. Bogdan selected a bottle and found some shot glasses.

'Do you keep those here for special occasions?' Tom asked.

'No, we often drink down here,' replied Mr Cybulski. 'Although, of course, this is a special occasion. This is a vodka I flavoured myself with lemons. It's not chilled, I'm afraid, but maybe you will like it anyway. To you!' He toasted the Irishman, and his son joined in. By now, Tom knew how to down a shot without gagging. He watched as the older man fetched down a jar, opened it and slid some of its blackish contents into a bowl. Aleks and his father used practised fingers to pick up one each—they were mushrooms, pickled in slime. Eating the mushroom and drinking the vodka were part of the same ritual. When it was Tom's turn it was like handling and then swallowing an eel; it was harder to stomach than even the spirit. The Poles watched as if monitoring his fitness.

'Good man, Tomek!' Bogdan smacked his back and for a moment, Tom was concerned the fungus might return. 'Now, tell me what made you come to Poland?'

Tom hesitated, remembering what he had been told about the listening device in the flat.

'It's safe down here, Tomek,' Aleks reassured him. 'This is where we come if we want to talk freely.'

Tom realised that his explanation was unclear even to him. 'My professor has links with Aleks' university. I chose courses in his department really by accident. Before that, I remember watching the news about Solidarity when I was young. I don't know why I remember, or why I wanted to watch. I don't have any family here or any connections.' Tom, sitting on the stool with the glass hard in his hand, knees touching his new friends', realised suddenly that he was very happy. He was smiling at Aleks and his dad, not really listening to them, letting their words slip by untranslated. He was picturing a man, a journalist, standing outside gates with crowds of men and women behind him clutching flowers and rosaries and banners with childish writing scrawled across them. The pictures were grainy, their colours faded either because of the quality of the film or because the people and places they depicted were drained of colour. The people were singing hymns; some were crying, many of the men wearing a moustache similar to the journalist's. The picture in Tom's head shifted as his memory flicked forward. The journalist was not on screen, but his voice spoke over pictures of stone-throwers being dispersed by water cannon, images of uniformed men gathered before armoured vehicles in threes and fours. The voice was urgent but no particular words survived the gap in time between then and now. The words he could hear now had a resonance and belonged to Bogdan. Tom realised that the older Pole was describing the events from his memory.

'Sebastian Thomson was my friend, I would say.' Bogdan was also reaching back. He refilled the three glasses. Mushrooms followed.

'I was the English professor. The regional branch of Solidarity here needed someone to communicate with the foreign press, so in that way I was put in touch with the BBC. Sebastian Thomson was the BBC man in Warsaw at that time. He had reported from Gdańsk in August 1980 during the sit-in strike at the shipyard that brought the union into existence. He got to know all the main men, Wałęsa, Kuroń, Rulewski, all the others. He wanted to know about the strength of the union in the regions, so he came here. Sebastian thought that we—not only Gdańsk—were the heart of the movement. When the presidium of national Solidarity convened here at the start of December, I contacted Sebastian to get him here. I wanted him to stay in our flat, but he would not do that—he knew that the SB would simply arrest me for espionage. The SB knew that the meeting was taking place. In fact, they even formally promised not to molest the top brass.' Bogdan interrupted himself to explain the idiom to his son. 'Solidarity was a legally registered organisation, remember. But they had to remain within the law. So they could organise but not plot, inform their followers of their demands, but not propagandise for the removal of the Party as the leading role in society. So we were open about our meeting at the Galeria club rooms. We knew the SB would attempt to bug the meeting room, but we had someone in the club who could tell us where the Service had placed the devices, in the three larger rooms. So we crammed everyone into a fourth room. We were very pleased with ourselves!'

More vodka and more mushroom crossed their lips. Tom made the toast to Solidarity. The two Poles were moved.

It had been a cheerful occasion. Jan and Krzysztof and Anna plus many more from earlier strike committees were there alongside Wojtek, Kamila, and Daniel Zając who were local Solidarity people, Guzy for the students, Kułaj for the farmers. Everyone there had been arrested at some point and had their wartime tales to tell. The little room filled with their cigarette smoke and laughter and occasionally a row would break out, and Lech would call for order. Each session began with a prayer led by one of the priests. There were reports from regional chairmen and from Solidarity affiliates. There were too many people for the room; chairs had been brought in from elsewhere in the club, but most were forced to sit on the floor. Magda had brought a pot of *bigos*, and it was like the whole movement subsisted on stewed cabbage. People came and went. The Gdańsk contingent wanted to finalise arrangements for the big convention being planned for that city later in the month. There was open talk of a general strike with pressure coming from Radom and Bydgoszcz. There were strike committees waiting to be activated in every factory and college in every town and region, but none would move until called upon to do so by the presidium. Lech could have called for a strike, and the country, very largely, would have followed. He had enormous power. He had all the power that the Party lacked. But he also lacked the power that he knew the Party had—firepower, military, the power to put uniforms on the streets. He could call a general strike and the army could be on the streets, and there would be more bloodshed and Wałęsa would blame himself.

'It should not have been up to him,' Aleks interjected. 'If the regime was to collapse, it was not the place of Solidarity to prop it up.'

'*Bydgoska prowokacja.* Have I got that right?' Tom was recalling the seminar with Carter back in Belfast when his professor had produced the newspaper from the box. 'Wałęsa was expected to call the country out on strike because of the treatment of Rulewski and the rest in Bydgoszcz. But he backed down. And you say Rulewski was back in the room with Wałęsa here in Kutno? Was Rulewski pushing for a strike again?'

Bogdan seemed to hesitate. He was suddenly sobered by the level of what the Irishman appeared to know already. 'I can't recall exactly. Rulewski was certainly one of the radicals among us, but others urged preparations at least for a strike.'

'Were you in the room with them?'

'Yes.'

'And you reported it all to Sebastian Thomson?'

'Of course, he didn't!' said Aleks, his voice heated by vodka.

Bogdan touched his son's hand. 'I would have told Sebastian everything, or nearly everything, it is true. But he understood what he should and should not include in his broadcast. For us, it was important that sympathetic journalists knew as much as possible so that if— when—the authorities clamped down on us, there would be someone who could tell the truth. Sebastian Thomson did not let us down. But someone, someone among us, did.' There was a tear in his eye. The light from the exposed bulb picked it out like it did the line of pickle jars. His son told the rest of his father's story.

'There was a traitor,' Aleks said. 'Someone had a mic on them. They recorded the meeting and handed the tapes over to the government. Jacek Mazur—the Party man in charge of propaganda—decided to broadcast the tapes over state radio. It was presented so it looked like Solidarity were plotting treason. "Disloyal elements in society" that type of thing. It was an almost complete fabrication. No one left that meeting thinking we were closer to a general strike, but Mazur re-edited the tape and broadcast the few killer words. They had their pretext. Within a week or two, *stan wojenny*.'

'Martial Law.'

'Yes. Hundreds were arrested.' Bogdan and Aleks both shook their heads at their memories.

'Including your son Jakub. Mr Cybulski, were you arrested?' It had been a question Tom had waited to ask for some hours already. It represented a curious gap in his knowledge of the family. Bogdan was a professor of English working in a weapons factory. He and his family had suffered humiliation and demotion due to their work within the anti-government opposition, which had at the same time earned him the trust of his friends.

'No. No, Tomek, I was not arrested. Then or any other time. Not with Magda in '68 or with my son and Solidarity activists in 1981.' He wanted to pour more of the lemon vodka, but they had drained the bottle. 'I cannot tell you why. I wish I had.'

'Why would you wish that?' Tom asked because that was the obvious question, but the answer too was obvious.

'Because now my friends can ask me the questions you have. Why was Bogdan not taken away after Galeria after the tapes? Why was he spared when almost none were? What does a man have to do to provoke the wrath of a hateful government, and why have I not succeeded where others have? Who—they ask this also, Tomek, although they will not ask me to my face—who is looking out for me in the Party?'

'Tom will know why, won't you, Tom?' Aleks had his hands planted firmly on his knees, his jaw jutted forward, in a pose designed by a slightly drunk man to suggest that this was the most important test of his friendship.

Tom was nodding long before the answer reached his lips. 'There does not have to be someone looking out for you in the Party. There might be, there probably isn't, you wouldn't have to know about it or to have done anything to win their protection. The person who recorded and passed on the tapes might not have been arrested, or they might have been. The Party is not rational. The ideology—Marxism-Leninism, I don't even know what they would call it—says that it is scientific, that it follows historical, unarguable logic. Maybe so, but the people in the Party, at the top of it and in the factory offices, in their grey suits and leather jackets, those people just aren't clever enough to be all that logical. I would say, Mr Cybulski, that there is a fair chance they didn't arrest you because someone overlooked it. The Party is stupid, am I right, Aleks?'

Aleks cheered. 'Can we toast that? To stupidity!' And the three men clinked their empty glasses. Mr Cybulski rounded up the glasses and the bottle and stood with his finger quivering on the light switch.

Upstairs in the flat, the glass door to the living room was shut and the lights turned off. The living room was also Bogdan and Magda's bedroom. Kuba had taken himself to bed hours earlier. In the final room, his mother had already pulled down the sofa that converted to Aleks' bed and made it for him to share with the guest. After the cool of the cellar, the flat seemed filled with the heat of the day. Aleks opened his bedroom window.

Tom listened. There was nothing, no traffic on the roads or helicopters overhead or people returning drunkenly with their beer tins and fast food. It did not sound like Belfast, for example. Even in his own room, with his head against the wall that he shared with his parents, he could hear the sounds of the city above the noise of their arguing. Foxes wailing like banshees, sirens blaring their way to—or from—trouble. The sounds through his window were as lullabies to Tom; he had slept with them all his life. They were his earliest memories. The silence through this window was foreign. He wondered what Aleks heard in it. Could he hear the cicadas, was there a dog wandering far from home, was there a woman crying herself to sleep beside a man living with lies? The net curtain breathed gently against the handle of the window. Aleks switched the light off to undress and was the first to climb into bed. Tom sat on the edge, with this back to his friend, and removed first his socks then his T-shirt then his trousers. He slid backwards into the bed so he would not have to wish his friend good night while looking into his eyes.

———

The Gdańsk train pulled in to Warsaw Central Station just a few minutes late with its cargo of soldiers on leave, traders on their way to Cracow and beyond, and students arriving in time for the start of term. Gosia found a taxi with ease and induced the driver to set her bags in his boot. Beyond telling him the address of the College of Tourism on Nowy Świat, she did not engage him in further conversation. She wanted the journey to end. To close the window would expose her to the smell of the man; to open it left her vulnerable to the stink of the city. She placed her nose next to the glass, the thin line between the one and the other.

She had an appointment with Dudek, the college director. He was a goat, who was shagging his secretary and would shag the students too if he could find one who would let him. It was generally not safe to be alone with him. Gosia wanted that journey over with too. But she was one of those students who owed her place in the college due to her father, who owed his place due to someone else, and Gosia was one of those who knew that sometimes a price had to be paid.

'Not yet!' the secretary barked at her as Gosia tried to walk straight into the director's office. 'Please sit and wait.'

Gosia plucked at the nylon balls on the armchair. She recalled how the secretary liked to own this space as well as the man on the other side of the door. She ostentatiously pulled a fashion magazine from her bag—one from a friend in Norway—and loudly flicked the pages over. A buzzer sounded and before the secretary could give her permission, Gosia was inside the director's office.

The first surprise was that he was not alone, she ought to be safe. The second was that the man who was with him was Stanisław Staniewicz.

'Hello, Gosia!' It was Staniewicz who greeted her; Dudek remained sitting on a couch, sunken and sullen. 'It is lovely to see you again. Do you know who I am?'

Although he was smiling, Gosia was not sure what the correct answer ought to be.

'Hardly,' he replied for her. 'It is six years since we last met. You could only have been twelve years old. You have, I see, developed into a pleasing young lady.'

'I was already sixteen. Perhaps I remember it better than you, panie Staniewicz.' She had recovered her courage. In all her dealings with the Party—even or especially where it involved her father—Gosia had found it best to retaliate early. She had not been invited to sit, so she perched as confidently as she could on the edge of the director's desk while gripping it behind her to steady herself. She resolved to smile as he had. 'Life has treated you well in the years since, pan Staniewicz. That's a nice watch you are wearing. A job in the Interior must reward you handsomely.'

Dudek sank morosely into the sofa. The insouciance of his students reflected badly upon him, even if—as undergraduates in tourism—they were renowned for it. He groaned.

'The timepiece is Ukrainian, Miss Kamińska. I wear it because it was what there was. Czech, I understand, would be better. It is not Romanian and for that, I can be thankful.' He took a moment to decide to respond to her second comment. 'A job in the Ministry of the Interior is indeed an honour to have, and one we are expected to be too humble to advertise. I am quite taken aback that you should know it.'

Her father had told her that all the goons in the Ministry of the Interior wore such watches, just as all secret SB wore zipped leather jackets. It did not have to be true for all for it to be true in general. He had also pointed Staniewicz out to her, watching the news on television not long ago.

'He is the man who came to our house, isn't he?' She had not forgotten his face. There had been snow outside, and there was a snow tread from his boots in their hallway. Gosia would have to clean that too because Mama was not fit to. The man had placed his hand on her head as if she were much younger than she was and as if he had a right to do so. He had then pushed her into the room where her mother lay while he spoke privately to Papa.

'He sent you out, didn't he? When Mama needed you home.'

'There was no choice, Gosia. Staniewicz had no choice either, I suppose. I was the doctor on call, so to speak. After the arrests, there was plenty of violence. I was terribly busy that night.'

'Because of you, Papa left me alone that night,' Gosia told Staniewicz calmly. 'I was extremely frightened. I could hear shots.'

'As you said yourself, dear, you were hardly a child.'

Where there are shots, that's where Papa will be, she had thought then. She had had terrible visions of herself in the orphanage or of being sent to unknown relatives in Lwów. She had located the blame for these nightmares in the person she later learned was called Stanisław Staniewicz.

'Sometimes one has to test one's love.' The ministry man was talking while lifting and inspecting the items in the office as if explaining his political philosophy was like taking an inventory. 'The good doctor abandoned his wife and child at a time of national emergency. Would not any true man do the same? Comrade Kamiński understands that his vocation is to the country. He must administer to its needs first.'

Despite the heat of the day and the stilled air of the office, Gosia felt a chill which forced her hands to cover her arms. She looked—but did not want to feel—defensive. She searched Dudek for a clue as to why he had called her to see him.

He remained seated, uncomfortably, on his office sofa. 'Miss Kamińska, this is your final year in the college?' His voice was reedy, inadequate.

'The start of it, yes, Dr Dudek. I passed all my courses last year.' As she said this, she spied a file open on the director's desk. Her grades from the young, persuadable PE instructor would be in there also.

'Well, let's agree that *passed* is one way of describing it,' the director continued, finding this still more excruciating than Gosia herself. The government man laughed heartily. 'You are nearing the end of your studies at the college, Miss Kamińska, without exactly fulfilling the hopes we all had when you were granted the privilege of a place. Only the most ardent of our young people can be admitted into the College of Tourism, thanks to our social and political realities. Excursions beyond the fraternal nations are inevitably reserved for the few who . . .'

'Oh, cut the bull, Dudek! What you are saying is that pretty Gosia here got her place on your crappy course because of Daddy's loyal Party work. She knows that already.' Gosia nodded. 'What she needs to know is, what's next?'

Gosia was uneasy being cast on the side of the man from the Interior. 'Please tell me what you want me to do.'

'Words to bring colour back to Lenin's cheeks! You are a smart girl—your father said so, and he was right. But this has nothing to do with him. Gosia, how good is your English?'

Szulman was closing up for the night. His was the glass-painting and engraving shop on one corner of the Old Town Square. Polish eagles with and without their crowns, Teutonic castles, or bespoke lettering: Szulman could trace and etch onto glass anything within reason. Amid the state-run craft and souvenir shops and cooperative cafés that occupied many of the other units on the square, he was a rare exception—a private trader. With this in mind, he stood by his window and looked out upon the square past the heavy curtains. The familiar vendors were there selling cordial drinks, ice cream, street art; many were gathering their wares already, enough business done for one day. Similarly, waiters were busy dismantling the large umbrellas covering the tables which spilled out from a few of the bars and restaurants. Szulman wondered what price their proprietors had had to pay for such licences: the Party did not hand out its permits for free.

The engraver was accustomed to the pattern of people passing through his square. They might linger for a portrait or refreshment or gaze in wonderment at the fidelity of the post-war reconstruction, perhaps even take a photograph. Lovers often met at the Syrena statue; secret police would sometimes malinger with an ice cream. Szulman rarely had anything to report, which was fine by him. One figure, however, had caught his eye. A tall, lean youth stood outside the Gessler restaurant, now peering into the thinning crowd on the square, now checking his watch. He was foreign, Szulman could see that, almost certainly Western—although there was nothing especially superior about his bearing or his clothing. It was the way he looked both assured and at the same time out of place. And there was another man now walking towards him.

Spiro had told Tom to meet him under the crocodile in the Old Town Square. He was to consider it an initiative test to find his way there without asking his friends. Was there any reason to tell his friends about Spiro at all?

It was early evening, still light but cooler now October had come. Tom knew that the square had been rebuilt since the war. He had seen black and white photographs of the devastation wrought by the Germans during the Uprising. But he was charmed by it nonetheless. It seemed old, it seemed authentic; perhaps it said something more about these people for having been reconstructed, for not strictly being true. Birds flew in and they flew out again anyway.

The crocodile was an iron sign hanging above the Gessler restaurant. Tom waited, intrigued by the arch over the portcullis-like door, which seemed to have grown an extra blind arch above it. A couple, obviously wealthy, left the restaurant cross with each other. A street artist was stacking multiple paintings of the same Old Town view, ready to cart home. A man in a suit and black-rimmed glasses emerged from among some tourists in the square.

'Were you watching me? I was looking out, but didn't see you.'

'That's me,' offered Spiro. 'I can melt into the crowd like ice cream on a sunny day. If you know what I mean.'

'How long have you been out of Scotland, Spiro?' Tom teased. 'You need to brush up on your idioms.'

They entered the restaurant and descended into the main dining area, a sooty cavern with candle-charred vaulting. They were shown to a reserved table, and Spiro ordered for both, ignoring the menu, speaking good Polish. 'I'm afraid I can't disguise my Scots,' said the diplomat. 'But since I get most of the words in the right order, they take me for a Bulgarian. Quite flattering, really.' He dropped his glasses to the right of his cutlery. He saw better close quarters that way.

Tom ate the beetroot soup and dumpling, the veal and potato, the pudding—whatever was put in front of him. To Spiro's amused glances he responded, 'The food in the Student House is good. Really, I have no complaints. But I think they struggle to put much on our plates. There is always plenty of bread, so every meal is bulked out with that. I can tell that my friends are embarrassed because they bring their own food around in the evenings—oranges, chocolate—and share it with me.'

They talked more about life in the hostel. Spiro was interested to know more about Tom's new friends, what they talked about in the evenings, his Polish lessons.

'Mrs Bańda made us all watch the news reports of Vice President Bush in Warsaw.'

'Oh, yes?'

'Obviously, I understood very little of what they said, but from the pictures, you could have assumed he had only seen the Party leadership.'

'Oh, yes?' Spiro waited for Tom. He was sure he would go on.

'But he didn't, did he? He also met Wałęsa . . . others from *Solidarność*.' Day tripped out other names. Spiro nodded. 'And he went to the church where . . .'

'The priest.'

'The church of the priest they murdered. Bush laid flowers on his grave. That's amazing, isn't it?'

'I agree.'

'I mean, that's a kick in the balls for the government. No wonder they kept it off the telly.'

'Indeed.'

'Come on, Spiro!' Tom admitted his frustration. 'Don't you want to know how I know?'

First he uttered something Scottish. 'The Bush pilgrimage to that church was no big deal really.' He looked for Tom's hurt reaction. It would be normal for the Irishman to feel that his information was privileged, coming as it had by clandestine means. 'There are secrets that the Party tries less hard to keep. A visit from a foreign dignitary is well worth the price they pay for it, a handshake with Wałęsa, a knee-bend at the grave of a murdered priest. Bush has to be seen in those places, which means there has to be a photograph, and the communists are simply not totalitarian enough to keep all the comrades' eyes averted. Do you know that there are paid-up apparatchiks who attend that church every Sunday? That priest was the biggest thorn in their backside, preaching his message of passive resistance until they intercepted his car and dumped his body by the roadside.'

'So why do members of the Party go there?'

Spiro had ordered two iced vodkas and downed his without a toast, twisting his mouth to control the bile. 'Bloody Catholics, aren't they? I mean, they may be atheists, but they are Catholic atheists! Anyway, why don't you tell me how you learned about Bush?'

Tom had crouched with Aleks in the cell down the stairs from the drying room with its printer and enormous radio and tuned into the Polish service of *Voice of America*. They had broadcast a fragmentary interview with Bush. He had declared his countrymen's support for democracy in Poland. It was not much more than that, quite bland really, aware obviously that the Party goons would be listening in, enough maybe to lift the spirits of the opposition. Aleks was quite excited.

'Will he be firing up the *powielacz*, do you think, getting a paper out?'

Tom's hand moved reflexively to his jacket pocket then hesitated. Spiro had uttered a secret word. He picked up a spoon instead. But he nodded. Spiro called the waiter over to order more coffee. 'He writes well,' he said. 'Or so I am told by our girls in the embassy.'

Tom was still wary. 'Why would you people know about that? Maybe a dozen students read Aleks' paper, hardly more. How could that interest the British embassy?'

'God, you're right!' Spiro joked. 'I didn't say it was interesting. You would not believe the crap some of these *samizdat* guys come up with. Believe me, your friend is a whole lot better than most.'

'He'd be pleased to hear that.'

Spiro chopped his hand in a lateral motion to say no. 'That would be to do neither him nor me a favour. It would not be good for him to think I was looking over his shoulder. I am not. Our approach is very light touch, believe me. Unlike Mazur, the government's propaganda man.'

'You think *he* reads Aleks' paper?'

'Not a chance. On the other hand, there is not a chance that someone in his department isn't aware the moment Aleks publishes. Jacek Mazur is a dangerous man, Tom. He controls information in this country—what people are allowed to know, what versions of events get to be heard about. Poles, being an unruly lot, make it hard for him of course. They have a way of sharing their messages in their underground comedy clubs, hiding their hatred of the system in their epic poems. But if they let their guard down for just a moment, Mazur is all over them.'

Tom had an image of Mazur's men raiding their cell beneath the drying room. It would not take them long to work out what the printer was for or the radio. 'You do monitor *Voice of America*, however.'

The Scot nodded. 'We certainly do. Actually, we have been keeping an eye on the Bush visit for some months, particularly his Sherpas. One of his advance men is Polish-born and therefore treated by Washington as someone of unusual insight. He has advised every president since Kennedy. Sports a grey pinstripe in all weathers. He believes in *peaceful engagement* with the Eastern Bloc, his theory being that there are dissident voices in Poland, Czechoslovakia, and elsewhere, strong enough to slip the leash of the Soviets. Some of those voices are within the Communist parties themselves. More often they are writers, theatre people, the churches. He engages with them, finds ways of channelling funds to them, helps them connect with groups elsewhere. He does it mainly under the radar because—strictly speaking—he is an agent of a foreign government plotting to bring down . . . blah, blah. So he was here four months ago, coming in through diplomatic channels. You won't find reports of his trip, not even on VOA. He met with all the usual suspects from Solidarity, sounding them out for what—short of the complete collapse of socialism in Poland—they would settle for. And he sat with about twenty independent journalists on the floor of a flat here in Warsaw. What do you think your friend Aleks would do with information like that?'

'What did they talk about?'

'That, indeed, would be good to know. But we, at least, have not resorted to planting bugs on our friends.' Spiro pushed the second vodka glass towards the other man. 'You should drink that. It's good. Then I can get more in.' He waited for Tom to empty his glass before sending the waiter off with another order. For all that the *Krokodyl* was a busy restaurant, it was also a place where two men could speak their minds. 'Tom, how did you find the elder Cybulski, Bogdan?'

'I think he took a shine to me.' Tom wrung the paper napkin from his lap into a thick twist and touched it to the lighted candle between him and the Scot. Spiro had mentioned secret recordings and Bogdan in the same breath. The candle guttered out without first catching to the napkin. The little darkening brought the walls closer in, so that the restaurant for an instant was like the cosy cellar in Kutno. A tear of wax dribbled down the candle. 'Mr Cybulski doesn't say much. Perhaps it's a language thing.'

Spiro lifted his spectacles back to his face and refocused away from his dinner companion. 'Yes. That will be it. Fewer from his generation had the opportunity to learn English. Unlike his son.' He hoisted his jacket from the back of his chair. 'I'm taking a cab from the Castle Square. Do you want it to drop you anywhere?'

The bar waiter was chatting to the cloakroom attendant. Had Spiro not ordered more drinks from him? 'No. Thanks. I think I will walk. Got all of this food and vodka to walk off.'

'Suit yourself.' Spiro picked a knife up from the table. 'Here, stick that in your pocket. They are always short of knives in that hostel of yours. And when you have done eating with it, you can always place a phone call to me with it. When you feel like talking.' Tom remembered: in this country, there always seemed to be a way of managing without money.

It was dark now. The tourists had stopped promenading and the locals had gone home. Tom walked without caring to notice street names or landmarks. He had a general, magnetic sense of where south was, where his room was in this city of straight lines.

From the inter-city train from Cracow and from the same inter-city service coming the other way from Gdańsk; out of trundling local services from Mazovian villages; from the muscle-bound Soviet carriages via Lublin and via Białystok; mixing with soldiers from Poznań and black marketeers from Olsztyn—from all across Poland, students of economics and tourism, languages, and mathematics, those entering their fourth year or dreading their first disembarked at Warsaw stations central, western and eastern and made their ways by bus, tram, or taxi to their dorms. They unloaded their sausage and cheese (wrapped by mums, sure that the capital was deficient in such things), snapped open their half-litres of vodka and toasted each other and the start of term.

Aleks, Norbert, Piotr, and Tom shared a bottle in the boys' room while Agata and Wioletta back-combed each other's hair and drank *ersatz* Vermouth in their own room. The Poles were teaching *Irlandczyk* some phrases they believed he would need in the nightclub.

'A beautiful girl is a ładna laska,' Norbert intoned. 'You speak. Say "ładna". Say "laska".'

'Don't say such words!' scolded Agata, entering the room with Wioletta, eyes shaded blue and hair held high. They sat in the ring with the boys and demanded their shot of spirit. They checked that Tom knew the difference in Polish between cigarette and ashtray.

'Polish laskas smoke.' Norbert dragged the last word as long as the thing itself while Wioletta and Agata puffed on imaginary cigarillos.

Piotr cut bread, chopped *kiełbasa,* and sliced tomato, and offered the supper around on a plate. 'Drink first,' he instructed the Irishman. 'Then . . .' and he mimed chomping down on the sandwich. Tom was already feeling the wooz of the alcohol. He bit down on the bread, jack-knifing the meat and flipping the juice of the tomato onto his shirt. He swore but not with sufficient vigour for his Polish friends, who dazzled him with more plosive, r-rolling options.

At a signal that Tom failed to notice, the Poles gathered themselves and their jackets together and followed Aleks down the stairs and out of Dom Studenta into a taxi with Aleks at the front, and the rest in the back—with Tom on everyone's knees. He could see the sky but not the road. 'Where are we going?' he asked helplessly. The car turned right and turned right again. The motion of his supine body mimicked the motion going on in his head.

'To *Hades*!' called the girls in unison. They danced as if they were not sitting down, as if an Irishman were not draped across them.

Tom could hear the Europop music from outside the nightclub. Someone paid the cab driver. They showed their student cards to get in. 'Give me your jacket,' demanded Aleks. 'I'll check it in with mine and save some pennies.'

'Can't I keep my jacket with me?' Tom—more vain when drunk than when sober—recalled the tomato stain on his white shirt. But Aleks insisted and lectured him on the role in society of the cloakroom attendant.

After the vodka, Tom was relieved to be drinking beer with the boys; the girls needed no more booze to carry them to the dance floor. It would have been hard for Tom to understand the Poles over the tinny bop, bop, bop, even if they had been speaking English, so he did not mind when they left him alone guarding the table: Norbert to speak to some girls attracting him from the bar, Piotr and Aleks simply disappearing behind smoke and dry ice. To Tom's ear, the music was bassless melody on short repeat, the lyric strained through equipment made entirely of metal. Still the couples danced, and they danced *as* couples. Was it swing? His mother would have known; his father would. He watched them once at a function in the King's Hall. They moved in and out, catching hands without needing to look (so not looking), fluid and old-time, Dad blowing the hair from his forehead, Mum the happiest he had seen her. Tom sat at their table, watching over their cigarettes, their smoke twining. He couldn't dance the way they had, and he saw them only once. Norbert brought over the girls he had found.

Norbert introduced them to the table rather than to Tom, whom he seemed not to recognise. In Polish, he asked the Irishman if the chairs were free; he looked at him as if at a stranger. The girls lost interest in their host once they sat down, so Norbert left. The table no longer felt like Tom's to guard, but he clung on. His only alternatives were to hit the bar or hit the dance floor. As his beer and his vanity were still intact, he allowed the noises to overwhelm him and concentrated on merely looking at the girls. One was shorter than the others and darker haired. Before she sat, Tom had noticed she was wearing a leather skirt. It may not have been leather, but the intention—and the effect—was the same. The middle of the three was very pretty but was made up more aggressively than he liked. The last girl was the tallest. The longer Tom looked at her, the harder he had to work at keeping his mouth from falling open. She was more photographic than female—a union of all the beautiful things he had ever seen. Perhaps she thought he was smiling for she smiled back, and when she did, her perfect teeth gleamed brilliantly in the UV light. Her name was Kinga—she told him—and even that sounded superior. Her short friend did not give her name; the other was called Margaret—she gave him a choice of Polish translations. Gosia seemed the easiest to say. Kinga was speaking to him excitedly, unintelligibly, and Tom was giving monosyllabic, unimprovably Polish replies. At one point she creased her pretty brow, displeased perhaps with one of his nods, but she continued undeterred, debating with herself until she agreed with his position. Really, he was not necessary to the conversation. The music changed (or there was a gap between it ending and restarting) and Kinga and her leather-skirted friend were press-ganged to the dance floor by the one called Margaret. Tom lost them in the murk. The ultraviolet could not pick out even Kinga's brilliance through the smoke. He busied himself with his beer, to be busy with something. He hoped Aleks and Norbert had not left already or that at least Wioletta and Agata would still be there to show him the way home. Even after a month Tom was easily lost in the city; its buildings were so uniform, its plan was so quadratic that he could not reliably distinguish features to guide him. And he was drunk. That thought led him back to the bar.

'*Piwo, proszę.*' The barman reached him his bottle, popping the cap. The beer was malty and strong, its glug making him hiccup. Someone pulled at his arm and he recognised it was one of the new girls, Margaret, who now had her head on his shoulder while stroking his hand. From an instinctive, more trustworthy place, he had an urge to push her away. Her scent was synthetic and corporeal. He hiccupped again.

'We are thirsty also,' she said in English. She pointed to their table. Sitting there now were the girl in the leather skirt, the impossible Kinga and a blond boy, tall and in denims. 'You can buy wine.' She had again spoken in English. Tom had not replied, and he wondered for how long he could pretend not to understand. Meanwhile she collected a bottle of Vermouth from the barman and bore it to their table, leaving Tom to pay and carry the glasses. There was no seat left for him, but Kinga made way by climbing onto the blond boy's lap, creating a tangle of limbs like a collapsed giraffe. The party proceeded in Polish as if English was a language only to be used at the bar, and Tom would have slipped into disinterested anthropology but for the moment he heard his name used by one of them: Thomas. It was Margaret, but she had not been addressing him nor even looking at him. He listened in vain for his name to be repeated.

The music switched, the girls went to dance, and Tom was left alone with the handsome Pole.

'What's your name?' Tom asked, not even attempting to say it in Polish.

'Dariusz Michalski,' he replied, and he reached over to shake the Irishman's hand. 'Or Darek. You choose.'

As a student of Production Economics, Tom took classes in social economics, production, planning, transport, shipping, and physical education. He was exempt from military studies; he was allowed to count his Polish lessons in place of the otherwise obligatory Russian. The theatre in which his social economics lecture took place reeked of chalk dust and perspiration. Both might have emanated from the teacher, Professor Paszyńska, who delivered her notes nervously from the dais. The English translation she spoke came from the same central source as the statistics she repeated, and she herself appeared convinced by neither.

'The economic system in Poland is based on three sectors, state, cooperative and private one. State sector have the large-scale industry, construction, transportation, and communications, the small-scale industry manages mostly through cooperative and private enterprisings, while agriculture is predominated by the private farm.' She paused there and seemed to bow as if anticipating applause for the country's progressive approach. It did not come and instead she picked up the pen that she had dropped beside the lectern. She continued, 'State and cooperative enterprisings constitute the socialised part of the national economy.' She turned a page. Tom was yet to make his first note. A student entered at the back of the lecture theatre and apologised to Professor Paszyńska with a stubby salute before starting an amusing conversation with a friend on the back row.

Paszyńska recorded a mark in the margin of her page. 'In 1987,' she said, hoping the currency of her next sentence might ease the boredom of her class, 'the proportions of the socialised economy in the production of national income amounted to . . .' She inflected the final words in order to make a question of them. No hands went up. 'It amounted to 81.2 per cent, while that of the non-socialised economy amounted to 18.8 per cent. Individual branches of the economy took proportions of the production of national income in this way.'

Tom took his cue from the more assiduous around him and wrote down: industry, 48.2 per cent; construction, 12.9 per cent; agricultural economy, 12.8 per cent; transportation, 5 per cent; trade, 17 per cent; other branches—Tom did a rapid calculation in his head and before his professor could speak, wrote down 4.1 per cent. 'Other branches, 10.6 per cent,' she said, not countenancing her error. No one else noticed, or if they did, they didn't care or, if they did, they didn't dare correct her. Tom wrote down the new figure beside the old one and circled it. That figure would be on the exam.

'Employment,' Paszyńska said, indicating the sub-heading her students should write down. 'Twenty-eight point five per cent of all the employees worked in industry in 1987. Twenty-eight point two per cent worked in the agriculture, 7.8 per cent in the construction.' Sounds of pneumatic drilling from the building of the metro could be heard at just that moment. The professor treated it as a distraction to be overcome rather than as a serendipitous illustration of her lecture. 'And 35.5 per cent in other branches of the economy. Seventy-one point five per cent of the total number of employees worked in state-dominated economy while 28.5 per cent were active in non-socialised economy.'

Paszyńska set aside the notes she had been using and reached in her bag for a separate folder. Tom looked around him at the other students. Several had faithfully filled every centimetre of space on their pages with the details their professor had dictated to them; others had sat back and had written nothing at all. Tom wondered whether there were two types of students or two entirely opposite ways of passing the course. He knew that they would all require zaliczenia—the teacher's mark, where anything below a three would be a fail. Clearly, some counted on ways of passing the exam without getting the answers correct.

'Economic power is the fundament of the prestige of state. In the middle of the Gierek decade, the '70s, the realisation of the ambitious programme for reform occasioned itself more difficult than expected, and the internal situation presented growing difficulties.' All note-taking had ceased; all young eyes were on the professor now. 'It became necessary to adjust the organs of state economic and governmental management so that they become more fully democratic functioning. Errors in implementation of indispensable policies led to inefficiencies in the social economy so that further reforms were essential in January 1982. Now,' she added as if to excuse the previous sentence, 'our foreign exports are more than double what was in 1970. Polish industry produced just less than two million telephone sets and six hundred and thirty-one thousand television sets last year.'

The final statistics provoked a muttering, which began on the back row, blended with the high-pitched rumbling from the metro, and spread to all but the least courageous rank in the front. The words for export, telephone, and television were prominent so that Tom—and plainly, the professor—understood that it was the view of the students there that too much of Polish production went abroad, and not enough of it arrived in Polish living rooms. Paszyńska miscalculated if she thought her lecture would end on a high. She left by a side door next to the dais which Tom had not noticed until that point. Somebody threw a scrunched-up paper ball after her.

Tom spotted Piotr as he left the lecture theatre, and they agreed to walk to the nearby milk bar. After the person-generated heat and sweat of the interior, the street-level cold ambushed them both so that they were glad of the sour warmth of the milk bar. They stood at a counter with their *pierogi* and tepid cherry juice.

'Paszyńska, huh?' asked Piotr in an eye-rolling sort of way. 'What you think?'

Not for the first time Tom thought his colleague shared the Italian habit of dropping words and raising their hands to show exasperation. He also recalled what Aleks had told him about Piotr, that he may be from Kutno, but he was not necessarily to be trusted. He had not had to prove his worker credentials by doing *praktyka* in a factory.

'Some of our lecturers in Belfast are not very good either,' Tom offered.

'Are your teachers in Northern Ireland dogmatic idiots? Paszyńska should not make us appear stupid. Especially there are foreigners there. There should not be talk of errors or necessary adjustments. It is capitalism we need! The facts prove that. This is a *statistics* university. The teachers should be kept to those. Do you agree?'

Tom had been chewing on his cabbage dumpling when the challenge came. It was clear that his colleague had been embarrassed by the lecturer's performance in part because it had played out in front of him, a Westerner. Tom had no wish to anger Piotr further. 'I like numbers,' he declared with a swallow. 'And I can make up my own mind when I have the facts.' He patted his jacket pocket. 'And I made plenty of notes!' He knocked back the cup of cherry juice as a kind of salute and stood up. Piotr reached a long arm around his shoulder and pulled him closer. Tom half-expected a kiss from the Pole, but he stopped short at an embrace.

'We agree with each other,' Piotr concluded happily. The two left the milk bar and departed for different classes. Tom had a history seminar to attend in the main SGPiS building. There a small crowd of students had gathered around as a fresh poster was pasted to a wall. It depicted a pretty girl in shorts and backpack, the letters ZSP chiselled above her head and some information to the right of her bottom. The gathering was talking excitedly and planning, it seemed, to follow whatever the instructions were on the poster.

'You should attend also, Mr Day.' Vice-Rector Wilk appeared at Tom's elbow. He was very pleased to see him. 'It's an excursion with the Polish Students' Association. They are very fine. They travel to the Lakes in Masuria. They do hiking and singing the songs, the . . . scouts, that's the word. They sing the old scouts songs by the fire. You don't have our scouts in your country—very fine.' Wilk would have been content enough to stand there all day, gazing upon the very fine young folk of his university.

'It was nice to bump into you again, Vice-Rector, but I have a class to attend.'

'Ah, yes, of course! I did not "bump into you", Thomas, I was looking for you. I have a proposition. You must come to my office.' And he marched off towards one of the flights of stairs, assuming Tom would follow.

'I have a class,' Tom called, but it was half-hearted because he knew that Wilk was used to getting his way. He took the stairs and entered the outer office, where Elżbieta and her two co-workers were engaged in activity identical to the first time he was there, answering a phone that didn't ring, wiping the dust from a cheese plant, filing duplicates. Wilk's door lay open so Tom went in. The vice-rector was not hidden behind his desk, where Tom had first found him but was instead sitting in front of the window where they had shared a feast in September.

'Have a beer, Thomas!' Wilk had already poured from a green bottle into a tall glass as fragile as a biscuit.

'But I have a class, starting now,' Tom protested. The liquid was golden, cool and fizzy. Wilk looked wounded. A rivulet of condensation ran down the glass from Tom's thumbprint.

'But you look thirsty, Thomas. And the beer is good. Even the Polish pope likes this beer!' Wilk howled at his own wit or maybe the irony of it.

Tom drank. 'It is good, sir. But my seminar is starting now.'

'Pepliński can wait! Look at that view—isn't it the finest city in Europe, perhaps after Paris? Venice is also attractive, I hear. And Athens too, perhaps. And among the socialist nations, Prague is indeed very beautiful. And Cracow has a claim as the prettiest in Poland. But Warsaw is—you will have to agree—a most fine capital.'

Since Tom had not been given a choice, he did not express one. He just drank the beer and wondered at Wilk's recollection of his timetable. How had he known that he was scheduled to have Pepliński next— unless their meeting downstairs in the atrium really had not been accidental.

'Thomas, you have spoken to your family?'

Tom froze. 'No, I have not. Has something happened to them?'

'No, no, not that. But there was a terrible bombing yesterday in your country. You did not hear? IRA, they say. It was a war ceremony, I think.'

'Remembrance Sunday.' Tom was picturing the scene. There would have been soldiers—serving and veteran—families, children. It was not hard for him to imagine it.

'Many killed there. Really, is not safe in your country?'

Tom wondered if this was the reason he had been shown into the office. 'Thank you for telling me. Was there something else?'

'Enjoy the beer! Would you like something more?' Tom expected Elźbieta at that moment to come through the door, he need only say Yes. Instead he fixed his gaze upon the uninspiring view. The workers on the metro were taking a break from their day's work.

'So, Thomas, you like the beer, yes? Excellent. I have found something you can do for me in exchange. Business is business!' And again Wilk succumbed to his own hilarity, his laughter finally dissolving into spasms of coughing. 'You will help the university to celebrate the anniversary of national independence.' Wilk looked out upon the avenue of that name, his chest visibly inflated as much through pride as through pleurisy.

'Sorry, Vice-Rector. What is it you want me to do?'

'Pani Bańda is most delighted by your progress in her class. I am sure that a few words from you—in Polish—would impress our guests.'

'Independence Day. That's . . .'

'Now, Mr Day, you study our history. You know it is 11 November.'

'Yes, but that's on Wednesday. I have no time.'

'Quite. So you had better drink up quickly and run to your history seminar. Professor Pepliński will be waiting.'

The class had begun by the time Tom arrived. One student was reading aloud her essay—something on the Second World War. There were eight other students present, plus Pepliński, whose face was the colour of his cigarette smoke. Tom, clumsy from the beer, tried to take a seat without disrupting the seminar, but its wooden feet sawed against the linoleum floor and his books dropped in a paper cascade. 'Przepraszam,' he said, sorry indeed.

'Nie szkodzi,' the girl replied, glad of the momentary interruption. Pepliński said something that Tom did not understand, and the girl continued with her essay.

The professor leaned towards Tom and whispered in his ear, 'You smell of beer!' His grey face was now suffused with red like the lit tip of his cigarette. Tom could only smile and nod in apology.

Pepliński held Tom back at the end of the lesson. 'This is a disaster.' He shook his hanging head as if devastated by his own loss. 'You know nothing, you have nothing to say, and you have not the words to say it in. And just two days! A disaster.'

'Wilk told you?'

'Oh, yes. He was very happy about it. He likes you, for some reason, although he must despise me to burden me with this. You understand, of course, that he will expect me to tell you what to say. The custom is every year that a student speaks for about two minutes on the subject of our national independence, our brave fighters, noble leaders, loyal friends, the end. This year, however, is the fortieth anniversary of the communists in power, and Wilk has been given the job of marking it with something special. You are his answer!'

'I am not a communist, Professor Pepliński.'

'No one here is a communist, Tom. Not even Wilk, most probably. But there are still plenty who pretend to be, and that is what is expected of everybody on Wednesday. So what are you going to say?'

Azil, the Libyan, gave Tom an orange after that evening's Polish lesson, and Tom brought it back to share with his friends in Dom Studenta. Gosia was there and Piotr, Wioletta, and Norbert. They recollected stories from their school days, of girls in pigtails carrying flower baskets of woven reeds, of school halls bedecked in red and white and dignitaries with matching lapel ribbons, of singing that Poland had not yet perished, the oath, the hussars' march. Wioletta had a grandfather who fought in the Ukrainian forest, as did Piotr, and for Norbert it was his grandfather's brother. Norbert spoke of family descending on Kutno from all corners of the country, of candles and special meals, and then Wioletta pointed out that he was probably confusing the national holiday with the religious feast of All Souls. Gosia sat with Tom at the head of his bed holding hands, their four legs stretched out before them. Piotr, sitting on the bed belonging to *Nikt*, had once given the vote of thanks at the factory where his father was director, had worn a one-piece suit his mother had made from a blue polyester fabric, had received a severely short haircut, had been photographed by the *Gazeta Kutnowska*, the clipping from which his mother kept in an old handbag. That same speech would serve for Tom if only he could recall any of the words. Everyone agreed that Pepliński should write the speech, that there was no danger of controversy there so long as Tom did not mess up his lines and that, just in case, Tom should give Pepliński a mention in his address. Then Wioletta said she had to leave, Piotr announced he had to get up early in the morning, Norbert yawned ostentatiously, and Gosia declared she did not want to miss the last tram.

Pepliński allowed Tom into his office the next morning. 'I thought I would be seeing you. Your friends did not help?'

'My friends told me to get your help. They said that you are the best at talking about history, without. . .'

Pepliński raised his hand. 'I don't want to hear the rest. Fine. As it happens, I was giving your address some thought overnight.'

Tom looked around his teacher's office. A pillow lay on top of some papers on his desk while a small blanket was draped across the back of his chair. Cigarette butts overpopulated the ashtray like gross maggots. 'You didn't sleep?'

'This is an important affair, Mr Day! The leadership of the university will be there, representatives of the Party, Warsaw city officials. They will be listening to you, but they will be *watching* me. Even if I had nothing to do with it, Wilk would make sure he avoided any blame, by pinning it all on me.'

'Blame? Blame for what? If there are any mistakes, they will just put it down to my clumsy Polish.' Tom took the seat opposite Pepliński's. 'Show me what you have come up with.' Pepliński lifted the pillow and pushed a crumpled sheet of paper towards him. There were fewer than two hundred words. 'It's in English.'

'I wanted you to know what you were saying. One of your roommates can translate it for you and practise it with you. Make sure it is someone you can trust.' Pepliński picked up the blanket and pillow and showed Tom the door. 'Now, Mr Day, I should like to sleep.'

Tom found Aleks alone in the dorm that evening, reading. 'Any good?'

'Of course.' Aleks indicated how far through the volume he had read. 'They're poems. Recommended by . . . You don't know him, yet. Różewicz is the poet, not in favour with the guys in charge, as you might expect.' Aleks set the poems aside. 'I hear you need my help? The Wolf has shafted you big time with this one.' He started to laugh.

'Everyone else is getting very nervous on their own behalf. I don't see the big deal.'

'You are lucky not to. The big deal is that these guys don't like saying anything in public that might get inspected for its political content. When they lecture, they stick to the official texts—sometimes the ones they have written themselves, the ones that have already passed the censor—and that way they feel safe. You will notice how different they are in their seminars, more ready to explore ideas, to entertain alternatives. There they have some academic freedom. It's the big spaces they fear. Wilk manages because he believes in nothing, so sounds no less convincing whatever he says.'

'Pepliński looks like he could die through lack of sunlight.'

'That's because he *does* believe in something. He cares enough to care. Did he write that?' Aleks pointed to the paper in his friend's hand.

Tom nodded. 'It's still in English. Can you help?'

Aleks read Pepliński's words aloud, "'I am very privileged to be asked to talk to you on the occasion of your Independence Day. The Poles are a proud people, independent of spirit and word and deed. Throughout their long history, as a state with its own borders or as a nation without, the Poles have conducted a dramatic relationship with their neighbours. Out of the disaster which was the First World War emerged a new Poland—confident of itself, determined to stand firm on the shifting sands of Europe. But those sands swallowed the young country in 1939, and six dark years were to follow. However, the idea of Poland was never lost and it rose once again. Because of the help of its friends in the east, it is again an optimistic country. It has rebuilt the social realm together, achieving a unity of social forces. Because of this unity, there is freedom, and because of this freedom, there is independence.'"

Aleks read these words again, this time to himself. 'Pepliński wrote this?' Tom nodded. 'And he definitely meant you to have it?'

'He handed it to me himself. He worked on it all night. I tell you, I don't think he slept.'

'And he told you to give it to me to translate? Why did he not write it in Polish himself?'

'He said he wanted to know that I understood it. He didn't name you. He just said to ask someone from my dorm, someone I could trust.' Tom stared at the book of poems, now lying closed on his bed. 'Of course, that means you. Does he know you?'

'I don't think so.' Aleks read the speech for a third time. 'But it is possible that he knows my parents. They must be of a similar age.'

'Is he trying to say something to you in there? Freedom, unity. That's the language of Solidarity, is it not?'

'It is. *Nie ma wolności bez Solidarności*: There is no freedom without Solidarity. And if he is not trying to communicate with me, he certainly is with someone.' Then, as if a switch had been flicked, Aleks was excited, bouncing off the bed and striding towards his own and the locker cupboard where he kept his dictionaries. Then, as suddenly, he paused. 'Is Gosia not coming this evening? Would you prefer her to help?'

Tom shrugged. 'I don't think so. I never quite know when she will call in. She has her own classes. Anyway, I think you would be better at this.'

'You flatter me, Irlandczyku. Okay, let's see.'

The translation did not take long. Several of the words were unfamiliar to Tom in Polish, and Aleks rearranged some constructions in order to render them easier to pronounce. The two practised long into the night, fuelled by tea, not tiring. Aleks ensured Tom knew precisely what he was saying and that he could say it as precisely as an Irishman could.

The morning was bright and mild for a Warsaw November. Tom jogged most of the length of Independence Avenue, going south then headed left through some scrubby allotments and into a vast area of green called Arkadia Park. For no reason he could identify, this made Tom think of the book of poems Aleks had been reading. Stone statues, depicting various animals and human figures in a socialist-realist style, surrounded the central lake on whose surface a modest Palladian palace was reflected. Winter had already entombed the park for too long for this to be a convincing paradise; the greens were too grey, but it was perfect for Tom to run hard in. He ran until he had achieved a sweat then exited the park for the short jog back to Dom Studenta. He felt the chill as he left the direct sunlight of the park for the shade of Independence Avenue. By the time he was dressing after his shower, he could feel the goosebumps on his arms that told him he had caught a virus. He should have slept more the night before or he should have taken breakfast before his run or he should have taken the jog more gently. Any of these precautions would have made him feel less responsible for his illness. Or perhaps it was not a virus but nerves which were attacking him and the responsibility for what he was about to do.

The grand auditorium was shaped like an enormous divot, the sides clad in sound-proofing pine, the front butting up to a vast stage. Patriotic swagging and sprays of flowers did what they could to pull in the dimensions, so the party on the stage could appear human. Wilk introduced Tom to some of them while the auditorium was still filling. The rector of SGPiS and the deans of each faculty; the Mayor, Bolesławski and his wife; Stanisław Staniewicz from the Interior, and Henryk Bednarski from the newly formed Ministry for National

Education. Some officials from the Office of Commemoration looked most nervous of all. Tom was sweating inside the suit he had borrowed from Piotr. He was among the first to take his seat behind the long table, covered like an altar with a stiff white cloth. He poured a glass of water from a bottle on the table, but he could taste only sulphur. Military music coughed out of a speaker mounted above his left ear, and he stood to attention with the rest of the party. The rector spoke and the audience laughed a little. Then a priest (to whom Tom had not been introduced) said a prayer and the mood became sombre again. Bednarski stood up next and gripped the lectern. His voice was too loud for the microphone setting, so he stopped abruptly and simply waited for someone to adjust it. The students in the audience—which included Aleks, Agata, and Wioletta—took the silence as a cue to talk. This seemed to irritate the minister, who perhaps saw himself as the nation's headmaster. He spoke again and the sound was just as distorted as before, which made several in the seats in front of him laugh inappropriately. He decided to press ahead, silencing everyone with a speech longer than even he planned. Tom—not even attempting to follow the minister's sermon—focused instead on not collapsing in his chair. He felt the heat on his back, his chest, his scalp, but all sweat had gone so that his mouth and even his eyes were dry. He slugged again from the glass, knowing it would disgust him. Polish glasses break easily, he once knew. He wrapped his George Best mug in a shirt to pack. You save water overnight in vodka bottles. Let the coffee grains settle to the bottom. Lemons. Bednarski sat down and music drowned out the response of the audience. Tom thought it might be Chopin, and he recalled his promise to Spiro to listen to more of the Polish genius. The piano on the recording rose and fell tidally, and Tom allowed it to soothe him. He was running again in a park like the one this morning or the one where he first met Spiro and heard Chopin. He should have brought his problem to Spiro—that's what he was for. No doubt he would have been told to give no speech at all or only one that the diplomat himself had written. Pepliński was a good man, Tom reckoned; he hoped he would come out on the other side of this day. He had made a promise to him (no, to Carter) that he would make the most of his time here and that he would listen to the Cybulskis. No, that was Spiro again. He did listen to the Cybulskis. The lights on the stage were hot, even the flowers were dry. The flowers were artificial, red and white buds in winter, strangled by green plastic vines, stretching from one corner to the other like a colonising cheese plant. Pani Elżbieta had plans to acquire the flowers for her office. She listened quietly at the door because the doors or the walls or the phones have ears. He listened quietly at the walls too, waiting for the silence. There was a sort of silence now or a noise without music. *Tomasz, Tomek,* Tom.

'Thomas, it is your turn,' Wilk told him gently. 'Will you be all right? You look unwell.'

Tom stood behind the lectern. It was angled so there was no place for his glass. Pepliński's address, and the translation, were in the pocket of the jacket borrowed from Piotr, but Tom began without them. He cited them from delirium, which felt safe, felt blameless, felt connected to last night but not to this moment. He said that he was very privileged, that the Poles were proud and independent, that their relationship with their neighbours had been traumatic, that the country had been swallowed in Europe's shifting sands. He said that Poland was not yet lost, but that freedom could be achieved through unity. He may have been standing through that, but it was over and he was in his chair again now, and there was a crashing sound, not music but clapping hands, boisterous applause coming from the people in the audience that he could not see past the lighting on the stage.

Wilk looked ill with a temperature like Tom himself. The education minister had left the platform. The man from the Interior was relaxed and chatting to the mayor's wife. The priest was speaking to himself or more likely praying. Wilk was in a huddle now with the rector and others from the university. No one spoke to Tom himself, but it felt to him like they were talking about him. Had he said *traumatic* when surely he had intended to say *dramatic*? These words were near homonyms in Polish as well as English. It was true that the sands of Europe had shifted, that Poland had suffered, that unity had brought freedom and independence to the country. That was what Tom had, in effect, said. That "freedom could be achieved through unity" was a lesson that Poland could teach others—a more competent speaker than Tom, perhaps only a Pole, could have articulated that additional message. They were fine words really. No doubt Pepliński was behind them. Wilk, be sure to see that Pepliński's contribution is recognised. The people from the Office of Commemoration, denying Elżbieta, untacked the flowers from the stage floor and rolled them into a box in a hurry to get to their next event. Tom was alone on the stage, then he wasn't.

'Hello, Mr Day. We were not introduced. My name is Stanisław Staniewicz.' Tom felt barely able to raise his hand to shake the other man's. 'That was not your speech, I am certain. Perhaps one day you will tell me more. In the meantime, it seems, we will have to keep a closer eye on you.'

'Closer?' Tom felt a chill which was not just his illness.

Staniewicz had left the stage. Aleks appeared and gripped firmly to Tom's elbow, raising him from the chair. 'I think you may have started something there, Tommy boy.'

***

'I like to run. Sometimes I run fast because I like to be tired. I can run for a long distance. I look at buildings and people and . . . all around me. I observe things. Running is not so popular in Poland.'

'Well done, Thomas. Try to lengthen your sentences, using words like but, however, despite. Poland has many successful athletes belonging to sporting clubs in every town. Nelson, your turn.'

Each student spoke for a few faltering minutes, trying out the new vocabulary pani Bańda had set them to learn. Bogomila talked about skiing. Jana discussed her favourite rock band, whom she was sure no one had heard of outside Czechoslovakia. Nelson was a keen cook but could not find Nigerian ingredients in Warsaw. Azil played football for his team in the Libyan army. Detlef liked travelling in other central European countries.

After the lesson, Azil had figs to give to Tom.

'It was Libyan Semtex, wasn't it, Azil? The IRA used your explosives at the memorial service in Enniskillen at the weekend?'

'Yes. It was terrible. But the British must have known after *Eksund* that there was Semtex in the country.'

Tom wondered at the devastation there could have been, had the French not stopped the ship, the *Eksund*, with its AK-47s, ground-to-air missiles, and tonnes of explosives bound for Ireland.

'You know that the Americans killed Colonel Gaddafi's daughter, when they bombed Tripoli last year. Those planes flew from airbases in

England. Gaddafi views the IRA as a way of striking at the British. He will make friends with any anti-imperialist country.'

'Is that why you are here, Azil?'

'Certainly! There are educational and cultural exchanges between Libya and all the socialist countries. I study cybernetics here, and I can earn good money at that back home. That is no secret. It is you who are the mystery, Thomas. Why are you here?'

Tom was bored with the question. He had never been able to answer it to anyone's satisfaction. And here he was, eating the figs of a Libyan soldier-student, and he must try again.

'I wanted to, Azil, and I had the opportunity.' Tom might have left it at that. After all, that was all there really was to it. But Azil still did not understand or believe him. 'In my country, I have the freedom to study what I like. My teachers are not controlled by the government. They teach according to their personal ideology or from no particular ideology. I have no practical reason for following a course in Polish studies. I mean there is nothing obvious for me to gain from it apart from the fact that I find it interesting. That's the best explanation I have for what I do. It is simply, of itself, interesting. Being here is interesting. I do not expect it will advance my career or ever earn me good money although it is fine that it should if that is your reason. I am here simply because I want to be, and I can be. And I love it. Do you understand?' At that moment, it was important to Tom that Azil should understand.

'Do you want bananas? I can get you bananas.' Somehow that was enough. The two laughed, unified in fruit.

Many classes were cancelled in the final week of term. Lectures were rearranged to suit the lecturers' holiday plans. The winter hike organised by the Polish Students' Association was sabotaged when it was discovered that someone had deliberately altered the date on all of their posters. Wioletta and Agata persuaded Tom to go with them to *Hades,* and he met Gosia and Kinga there too. There was no sign of the blond man Darek. The music was the same as before. Gosia had just learned that she would have to return to Gdańsk alone for the holiday; she had hoped to invite Tom to meet her father. Another friend, a boy from Norway, had unexpectedly shown up. She was leaving on the early morning train. She would go to Central Station directly from the nightclub. She was truly sorry, even heart-broken, not to be able to spend Christmas with Thomas.

It was 2 am. There were a few other sleepy bundles on the station platform, but otherwise Gosia and Tom were alone. The Moscow train groaned and sighed as if it were enduring a disturbed sleep; on another platform the train for Cracow let out a shrill whistle to shake itself awake. Out of the black and white three figures approached them. They were uniformed militia. They addressed themselves to Tom, but Gosia answered for him. He watched her make them smile and strip them of their official bearing—one even removed his cap and started kicking at an imaginary stone.

'Did you know them?' asked Tom as the three militia walked away.

'Of course not. They were just boys. Quite friendly.'

'Why did they want to speak to us?'

'They thought I was a prostitute. It is not normal for a young couple to be out at this time. They thought perhaps this was my area, and we would be going to a station hotel.' Gosia suddenly drew Tom close to her. She was cold and was shivering. 'Oh, Thomas! I don't want to go, but my father demand it. He does not understand that you are special to me, more special than this boy from Norway. He is only a pen pal, but he is in Gdańsk already and my father does not know what to speak with him.'

The train had pulled in and the few passengers waiting had already boarded, but Gosia remained on the platform clutching Tom, crying. 'You don't have to cry, Gosia. Be happy, you will see your father and your friend.'

'How can you say be happy? Perhaps you don't feel like I do. If you did, you could not say be happy. But I will try because you ask me to. I must go.' She separated herself from him at last and wiped her eyes. 'Promise me, Thomas, not to fall in love with Kinga or Wioletta. I know they are very beautiful, much more beautiful than me. I am quite plain beside them. Do promise me.'

'Of course, I won't fall in love with them, Gosia.' Tom was stunned by the way Gosia was speaking to him, and he did not feel adequate to it. He had not imagined, when he escorted her to the train station, that she would need anything more from him. Her feelings were deeper than his, or the words she used to express them were drawn from a deeper place. The same words would not sound the same if he uttered them. He wondered, had he not been drinking, would he have managed sincerity. It did not occur to him to doubt her sincerity or to assign her words to the Vermouth she had been drinking. He could feel the tear she had left on his cheek.

There were no trams back at this hour, so he walked. The city was asleep, cold enough for some of its living things to hibernate. Some distant, great engine hummed at a pitch so high only the night could hear it. Abandoned Baby Fiats studded the banks of snow along the roadside. Snow fell as polluted slush like frozen ash accumulating on the brim of his hat. The base of every building was dirtied by the splash and scatter of daytime traffic. Five floors up one block, the lights were on in a flat, friends and family gathered there perhaps for an early Christmas celebration. Tom tried to feel again the mass and warmth against his body left there by Gosia.

Tom did not watch his step. In his head he reworked the words Gosia had spoken by the train, tried to trace them back to other conversations that night at *Hades* or before, measure them against the weight of his own feelings. The imbalance made him experience actual dizziness, such that he thought he ought to feel something heavier on his side in order to put things right. The effort should begin now while he could still smell her scent and recall what she had done with her hair that night. The police thought she was a prostitute, or they thought he looked the type to be with a prostitute. Funny that Gosia had not met the suspicion as an insult as if to be considered a whore were an insignificant burden when compared to the rest of life. Tom—to shrug off such distractions—dredged up her voice again and what she had said to him not twenty minutes before. What was that? Something about her special Norwegian friend falling in love with Kinga. A train had exhaled a deeply held breath and that, to Tom, sounded like heartsore desire. He was distracted again. At a corner, beneath a pedestrian crossing sign, three men were standing, smoking, their car carelessly parked on the pavement beside them. The car (Tom recognised it as a local marque, a Polonez) was obstructing his path so he stepped onto the road, but one of the men peeled away to block him. Tom could smell alcohol on his breath and see white and ginger stubble on his chin. The man stood close. He spoke, but it was coarse and unintelligible to Tom. He repeated himself, supported by his two colleagues in similar fashion. With an effort, Tom did not move his hand to give away the pocket where he kept his wallet. He was not sure they wanted to mug him for though they had barred his way and talked loudly to his face, they had not touched him. Tom did not understand and said so, 'Nie rozumiem.' This was a mistake. It goaded the men, who took it as an offence. The lights were extinguished in the flat high above. The men raised their voices, beat their chests, and at last Tom discerned the word for papers and understood by the badge one flashed at him that he was being apprehended by plainclothes militia. He was not being mugged, but they could be arresting him. He had left his identity card in Dom Studenta. The doorman at *Hades* had asked for it, but let him in anyway. He had ridden the tram to the station without punching a ticket. Gosia—not he—had spoken to the uniforms on the platform. He knew he should have ID on him (he had been reminded many times), however much he might resent carrying it. 'Nie mam,' he explained to the three. 'I don't have it.' But the policemen had decided that if he spoke Polish, he must be Polish. Now it did not matter that he tried to talk to them in English. Again he could smell the alcohol, puffing out with their breath like an exhaust.

'My documents are in my room. I am a student—jestem studentem. I am from Northern Ireland, not here. Irlandczyk!' He pointed at his chest, now crazed as they were. Every Polish word he uttered confused them more. One took out a pad and a pencil and began to write out a ticket. 'I was at the train station,' Tom protested. 'My girlfriend is going to Gdańsk for Christmas, seeing a Norwegian apparently, leaving me here.' Tom was pathetic and the three companions sensed it finally. The one put his pad away; the others stood off the road to allow Tom passage around them. They uttered some further oaths. Tom was sure he did understand those but thought better of replying. He walked twenty metres more before glancing behind him. They were again standing by the sign for the pedestrian crossing, lighting each other's cigarettes.

Back in his room Tom found Norbert and Aleks already asleep. He wanted to wake them, to tell them about Gosia and the train station, about his near arrest. Instead he took his stories to bed with him and shut them in the dimness of sleep.

The next day Tom received a card from Professor Carter as if from an age and place long and far away. Yes, Tom had settled in, made friends, managed to pick up some things from his classes, improved his Polish. These seemed paltry ambitions to him now. He would try, over the holiday, to explain some of this to Carter, for if Carter could not appreciate his experience, no one else would be able to. One comment troubled him. 'Given recent events, you might consider coming home.'

'Carter sends his regards,' said Tom the next time he met Spiro. 'And by the way, the secret is out on your knife trick.' A long line of students had formed behind Tom on his call to Spiro, all waiting to speak to their families before Christmas. None of them was unduly surprised to see a dinner knife jammed into the telephone unit.

They were at a reception in the British embassy. Tom had again borrowed Piotr's suit.

'You look smart,' said Spiro, drinking an entire schooner of sherry. 'The only way to endure this shite.'

'Was that a compliment? Thanks.' Tom looked out onto the room of expats, recognising none of them. It surprised him to learn that others from Britain had made Poland their home. 'Will you be in Warsaw for Christmas?'

'Glasgow. Mrs Spiro did not accustom herself to the life here. She had hoped for a different posting, let's say.'

'I didn't know you were married.'

'Getting home for Christmas is an extra wedding vow now as far as she is concerned. It's a small cross to bear, I suppose, if you don't mind my mixing of Christian holiday metaphors.' Spiro brought the glass to his lips, realised it was empty, and let his drinking hand sag by his side. He seemed about to say something to Tom then changed his mind.

'Spiro. I hadn't given it any thought before. It's a Jewish name?'

Spiro nodded slowly. 'The wife too. In fact, we are both Polish-Jewish descendants. When I tell her that I am lucky to be here, I am making more than just the obvious point. My mother survived the war as a teenager harboured by a Catholic family in Lublin. She met my father in Israel before they came to Scotland to get married. My father—who could talk about the Shoah all day long—had no stories of his own as his entire family left Speyer near Karlsruhe just as Hitler took power in Berlin.'

'And your wife's family?' To Tom, Spiro looked tormented, with none of his usual composure.

'Her father came from Tykocin, way up in the northeast corner of Poland. There was once a bustling Jewish community there with a yeshiva and a beautiful synagogue. Right next to an impressive basilica. He used to tell her how the Jews and the Catholics got on so well before the war, before the Russians came, before the Germans came. But he was easily mixed up, and he also told her how the goys in his class would mock him for being circumcised. Anyway, the Jews of thereabouts—Tykocin, Jedwabne, Łomża—did not survive the end of Nazi-Soviet non-aggression. The book on that has not been written, but let's say my wife is disinclined to pay a visit back there. Can't say I blame her.'

'Carter told me how the Poles live in awareness of the history that surrounds them. That the more their history is concealed from them, the more devoted to it they are. Something like that.'

'Yes, he has written on the subject. I seem to recall. "The Poles are more highly attuned to their past the more that it is deliberately concealed from them" is the quote if I am right. I read that when I was doing my Russian Studies degree in Glasgow in the '70s. So I got in touch with him.'

'That would have pleased him.'

'Not exactly, not at first. You see, I told him he was wrong.' Spiro paused to enjoy the memory of his younger self. 'I told him that the Poles—like everyone else—were devoted to *an idea* of their history. That if it suited their self-concept, they would collude with the concealment of their past. If the truth hurts, you can focus on the censorship of it rather than the thing itself. What is there stopping a thorough examination of the wartime German occupation and localised collaboration? I don't know, but there isn't one. Instead, there is an almighty exercise in distraction going on, about whether the partisans and insurrectionists were communist or anti. That's not the issue, but it is the one that today's politicians and underground activists still ache over. A word of advice, Tom, from someone who got here before you did: if they are telling you a good story, ask yourself what story they aren't telling you.'

'Białe plamy,' Tom mused. 'Carter told me too about the blank spaces. So did you get to know Carter well?'

91

'Well enough for him to write me a reference for the diplomatic service. A recommendation from Martin Carter cut some ice then. He has got a lot to answer for.'

The ambassador was addressing the reception from a raised platform. A round man with a bald head, he held his whisky glass and microphone stand like a comedy stand-up.

'Brian Barder,' said Spiro. 'You would like him, Tom.' Spiro then looked hard at his guest as if really assessing the extent to which he and the ambassador from the Court of King James would rub along. 'He literally saved lives in Ethiopia. We got him here straight from Addis Ababa. He got the RAF in with supplies of food and medicine. That's a proper fucking diplomat.' Spiro had magicked another drink and consumed it.

'Is everything all right, Spiro?' Tom had not seen him like this; he seemed unsettled or frightened.

'Did Carter tell you anything in that card? Just platitudes or did he actually *tell you anything*? Like for example, did he tell you to keep your fucking head down and stay out of trouble? It's not good out there, Tom, in case you hadn't noticed. The government decided to have a referendum on the economy and predictably that has gone tits up. The betting is they will bring in their price increases anyway, sometime in the new year. And that never goes well for them. Every time in their whole bloody history they hike up the price of butter, they have a riot on their hands. Did Carter not teach you anything in Belfast?'

'He said something, that recent events might make me think about going back to Belfast.' Tom felt the disapproval building.

'Did he now? Too bloody polite, that man. That's a flaw when it comes to handling you, it turns out.'

'Look, Spiro. If you are talking about the little speech I gave, I am sorry. If I had been given enough notice, I would have asked for your advice. Wilk sprung it on me. Then on the morning, I came down with a temperature—I was delirious.'

'Not good enough, mate.' Spiro grasped two vol-au-vents from a passing tray. 'You are a guest here—I mean in this country—and you do not get to piss off the host without consequences. Do you get what I mean?'

'I think I do.'

'No, I don't think you do. Look, playing about with Aleks Cybulski is one thing. Giving an anti-Party speech in their fucking living room is another thing entirely. What were you thinking?' Spiro gripped Tom's shoulder to steer him into an adjoining room, where they could talk without interrupting Barder's speech. Tom noticed how gentle his hand was.

'Cybulski is for the high jump I suppose?' Spiro, recognising they were now in the catering bay, poured red wine into two glasses. 'Here. You look like you need this.'

Tom accepted the drink. 'What do you mean, is Aleks for the high jump? And what, while you're at it, do you mean by handling me?'

His diplomatic training had taught Spiro to ignore the second question. 'Not only did Cybulski feed you the speech, he wrote about it in his little secret publication, didn't he? He is playing a dangerous game, and he has dragged you into it with him.'

Tom explained Aleks' limited role in the affair. 'It was Pepliński really. It was really his speech that I gave. I think he wanted me to say it. Being foreign, I have a shield that he doesn't have.'

For the first time that evening, Spiro seemed interested rather than preoccupied. 'What is it with you and your teachers. First Carter sends you here—obviously totally unprepared. Then Pepliński makes you his ventriloquist dummy for his own political ends. Go on.'

'He's not the only one. It is obvious that at least some of the other teachers would prefer to speak their minds, but they are held back.'

'They are held back because SGPiS is the Red Fortress. The sons and daughters of the Party go there. If you are right, Pepliński was taking a huge gamble if what you said can be traced back to him. And Aleks, by publishing it, just made that a whole lot more likely.'

'He knew it would get back to him. Wilk as much as told him to help me with it. You don't think Wilk is playing a game too, do you?'

'I would not have said so before you said that. But who knows, that man has talents only for self-promotion and survival. As for Pepliński, I am not sure how courageous it is of an academic to fight for his intellectual freedom through the voice of his students, but perhaps for him right now that is his only option. You will have to keep an eye on him and Wilk for me.' Spiro realised he had overstepped a line. 'That's not what I mean, Tom.'

93

'You mean you do, or you do not want me to spy for you?'

'Not. Emphatically not. We have not got that sort of operation here, and I am not that sort of operator. I just mean that while you are here, I am responsible for your safety, and that means you need to take the right kind of precautions. Keeping an eye out for Wilk is just common sense, and if you hear stuff that can help me help you, then I want you to tell me. Deal?'

They saluted with their glasses. 'I thought you were going to Gdańsk for the holiday. A change of plan?'

'First of all, Spiro, how did you know that was the plan? And secondly how did you know it was off?'

Spiro laughed. 'That's handling you. You called me after you left your girlfriend at the station and after your brush with those secret policemen. Clearly you were more drunk or deranged than I thought at the time. You didn't tell me why she dumped you. What's her name?'

Tom was sure he had not called Spiro. 'First you pretend I have told you stuff that I haven't, then you pretend not to know stuff you plainly do. You know her name: Gosia. And she didn't dump me. She didn't want to go without me. She was a bit emotional actually.'

'You've got to watch those ones, Tom, those too eager to commit.'

'Is love advice now part of the consular service? We can rescue you from an emotional entanglement anywhere in the world. Just keep your passport handy.'

'Admittedly, it's not a service we like to advertise. But yes, Tom, do at all times keep your passport on your person. So you are off to Kutno instead? That was kind of Aleks. Will Jakub be there? Interesting character, he is too.'

Indecipherable fragments of Barder's speech drifted in from the next room followed by hearty laughter. The team of waiters and waitresses filed into the catering bay where Tom and Spiro had been talking. 'All right, Spiro, so you know that too. I'll let you know how I get on.'

Spiro sank another glass of wine.

⌣

Magda peered through the window up into the darkening sky, searching for the first star. Deciding she had spotted it, she excitedly started to clear away the cups and plates and crumbs of cake and to reset the dining table. She was helped in the latter by Mariola, Jakub's fiancée. The women brought in bowls of egg salad and pickled red cabbage, plates of potatoes and carrots and—on the largest platter of all—a whole carp, its head and skin waiting still to be removed. Bogdan, Jakub, and Aleks took their familiar places, and Tom was invited to take the seat of the unexpected guest. This was a place always set, but rarely taken, and therefore all the more honoured. Bogdan unwrapped the Christmas wafer from its paper foil, broke a piece for himself, and passed it around the table until everyone had their fragment. They consumed it quietly until, at some signal from Bogdan known only to the family, they began the feast. Mariola, speaking only in Polish and apparently still shy in the company of her soon-to-be in-laws, was happy to entertain Tom's faltering conversation, prompting him gently but never correcting him. Beside her, Jakub held her hand for encouragement, sometimes leaning in to whisper privately. Bogdan gave praise to his wife on the surpassing triumph of the meal, whose reaction suggested that this too was a family ritual no less sincere for being so. Bogdan then turned to Mariola to thank her also, apparently thereby establishing a new Cybulski tradition. It was then Tom's turn to be welcomed and thanked, and although he did not understand it well, he was nevertheless moved and spoke a few words in return. Aleks said something about promising that he had not prepared Tom's speech in advance, and everyone was amused at that.

The family exchanged gifts. Bogdan had found a French perfume for his wife who, just by receiving it, looked to Tom to be yet more beautiful. He had not thought it before, but it now seemed obvious to him. Jakub gave to his brother a counterfeit tape of a British rock band, recorded by someone at their concert in Katowice in the spring. Aleks and his father went immediately to the tape deck to play it. Jakub indicated to Tom to follow him to the hallway, where he opened a cupboard and eased out a cardboard box. This was for Tom. He opened the box. Inside was a pair of boots, deep tan in colour, laced at the front and buckled at the sides, not new but in good condition. Jakub told him he had noticed that his shoes were not suited to the Polish weather, that he needed Polish boots, that the best boots in Poland belonged to the army. These were his boots from his time doing military service, which he had not worn since. Tom again felt underqualified, not up to the job of expressing himself in any language. So he tried on the boots to show that they fit, that he liked them and that he would wear them with pride. Back in the living room, Magda and Mariola were removing every item from the table so they could dress it again with the linen table cloth that Tom had brought as his present to them.

Tom wanted to test his boots, so he persuaded Aleks to go for a walk with him. With all light of day disappeared, the chill was sharp, and Tom could feel it beneath his coat and under his hat. He was surprised that on Christmas Eve many shops remained open. A haberdashery, a butcher, a general grocery, a bookshop, a *Monopolowy* off licence. This was a Catholic country, but it was also a communist one, so Christmas was celebrated by everyone while not being formally recognised, Aleks explained with a shrug. Tom said that he wanted to buy the best vodka and the best chocolate. He was still speaking a kind of Polish to his friend, and through that he tried to say how grateful he was, how glad he was that events had turned so he could spend Christmas in Kutno. He gave his few words all the meaning he could give them, insisting that Aleks should understand him. 'Najlepsze,' he repeated. 'The best.' Aleks stopped outside an exclusive-looking shop with the word Pewex on its window. It was where goods could be bought only with hard currency, Polish produce made for export. Tom could get what he wanted in there if he had his sterling. Aleks waited outside as if minding the dog while Tom stepped into the shop. Inside he found that whatever language he spoke was all the same—the vodka and chocolate were to be distinguished only by the currencies they were purchased in. The woman behind the counter, wearing a flimsy off-white housecoat, wrapped his things in paper of the same colour. Through the window, he could see his friend, framed by the arcing letters of Pewex, impatient to be gone. He had a string bag waiting for Tom when he got out into which he carefully set the wrapped boxes and bottles.

Tom was concerned he might have offended his hosts. Aleks' demeanour hinted at it, but Bogdan and Magda, Jakub, and Mariola seemed very happy when they returned with the gifts and later, when they ate more cake and sang traditional carols, the vodka and chocolates helped make the evening more special still although Tom noticed that Mariola drank only tea. Later, when she and Jakub had retired to their own room, Aleks invited Tom into his bedroom. He had not yet given him his present, he explained. It was not a normal present, not one that he had paid for, although it had cost him a lot. It was a poem from the book of poems by Tadeusz Różewicz he had been reading, a poem he had liked and decided to translate so that Tom could understand it. He explained that Różewicz had written it only ten years after the war when it seemed absurd to be writing poetry in a world that had proven itself to be indifferent. To Aleks, it was about naming things again, making sense of the ordinary, doing the organic work. To him, it was about why poems still mattered even now. He had learned it by heart for Tom. 'It's called "Amidst Life". At least, that's how I translate the title.' Aleks continued, reciting the poem by heart. The lines were so simple, it was a while before Tom recognised it as a poem at all. 'This is a table,' Aleks said.

> this is a table
> on the table there is bread a knife
> the knife serves to cut bread
> people live on bread
>
> one must love a man
> I learned by night by day
> what must one love
> I replied man

There were several more lines—the father who picks the apple, the old woman with a goat on a rope, man talking to the water and the moon, the only reply being the voice of another man. They were quiet then because Aleks did not have to fill the silence, and Tom did not know how to. The poem was simple but Tom was certain he had not got it all; he would have to hear it or read it again. He did understand that Aleks had made himself vulnerable, by the mere fact of reciting a poem to him, that that was what he had meant by saying it had cost him a lot, much more than vodka and chocolate from a hard currency shop. Tom wanted to quote back the words—to say that the poem had value, was important—but he felt sure he would be missing the point. Their quiet persisted until Tom felt at last it had added its own comment, and it was appropriate again to talk. Music flowed in from the next room.

'Mom and Dad will be dancing,' said Aleks. 'They sleep late on Christmas Day.' Tom's eyes blinked and lingered in momentary sleep. 'You are tired. Help me with the bed.' The two men collapsed the settee they had been sitting on. They pulled a quilt from under it and flattened a sheet across it. 'Good night!' Aleks called out to the night.

'Dobranoc!' came the answering call.

History classes had been cancelled throughout December; a note on Pepliński's door simply said he was on leave. When he returned in January, he did not look rested. If anything, his skin bore the same frosted edges as the cold-painted window sills of his classroom, and his voice was as brittle. At least two of his students had transferred to another class. The girl, whose seminar Tom had interrupted on the day Wilk had forced him to drink beer, was again reading from an essay she had written. Her subject was the Holocaust, specifically the death camp at Auschwitz. Tom could not follow her argument easily, but she did provide statistics which he could note down. She emphasised the Polish sacrifice, the six million killed of whom perhaps only eleven per cent were military. She gave prisoner numbers in Auschwitz, one of what she said was more than two thousand extermination camps. The Supreme National Tribunal estimated 2.8 million were massacred there; the Soviet Extraordinary State Commission for investigating Hitlerite crimes put the figure at four million. Soviet forces had commandeered all remaining records when they liberated the camp, and this was the basis for the information supplied by the museum at Auschwitz. She did not give a breakdown of the murdered by nationality. Pepliński thanked her for her scholarship and invited comments from the other students. As there were none, he took in her essay and remained sitting in silence.

In English, Tom said, 'Sir, you must have other classes today?'

'I do, Tom. But I would like to finish this one first.'

The other students shuffled uncomfortably in their seats, but none of them left. The girl who had written the essay reddened and held her bag defensively to her chest.

'Really, Professor? I thought we heard quite an interesting seminar today.'

'We heard an essay only. There was no debate or deeper exploration. These students were too frightened to speak up. So were you.' Pepliński used a cloth (the one normally for wiping the board) to mop the puddle on the window sill.

'I have some questions,' Pepliński continued. 'Ones I did not put during the seminar in the hope that you, or one of your colleagues here, would. I don't mean to delay you for long. I can see that you are busy.'

Tom had never heard these students speak English; he did not know how much they understood the professor now.

'Do you trust the figures we heard—the ones for the numbers massacred in Auschwitz?'

'I have no reason to doubt them, Professor. She gave us her sources, and I don't know why the Soviets would exaggerate that particular figure.'

'You do not?'

'No, I do not. On what basis should we challenge them?'

'On the basis, Tom, that the Soviets allow no one else to inspect the original documents.'

'Sir, the history books in my own school gave the same number, four million killed in Auschwitz. This is accepted, it seems, the world over.'

'There you are then, Thomas, exactly my point. Who were the four million? The girl did not say. That surprised me. Were they French, or Polish, or Lithuanian, or Russian? What were they all?'

'They were all those nationalities, Professor.' This was the girl.

'Correct. And they were Gypsy, and homosexual, and political.'

'Yes, of course.' The girl was wishing she had chosen a different topic to write about.

'Your point, I imagine, is that they were Jewish. Am I right?' This was Tom. 'The inmates in that camp—and in all camps—were overwhelmingly Jewish. This was confirmed beyond all doubt in Nuremberg. She could have made that particular point clearer. Is that really the issue here? Is that why you have held us back?'

'No. Not only that. You did not question her numbers.'

'Because, as I said, I believe her numbers to be credible. The Holocaust devastated the European Jews, wiping out nearly six million according to recent international estimates. I hope you are not denying this fact?'

'Absolutely not. That fact—the six million—is key to this. How are we to arrive at that number if we are to accept that up to four million Jews died in Auschwitz? Were there no Einsatzgruppen, were there no ghettos, were Treblinka and Belzec and Sobibor not also responsible for the deaths of hundreds of thousands? Did no Jews die of disease, of hunger, on death marches? Tom—students—can you really imagine no reason why the Soviets would seek to claim such an enormous number of casualties for the camp that they liberated? And are you really saying to me that you have never considered these arguments yourselves?' Some colour had returned to his cheeks, whether through the struggle of debate or through exhilaration at the terrible risk he was taking. 'Thomas, you really are the most perplexing boy.'

'It is not so simple to count these numbers. Not every Jew who died was identified as a Jew, not every Pole was counted as a Pole. When the Russians arrived at Auschwitz, there were not the bodies for them to count, and many of the records—even the gas chambers themselves— had been destroyed. Auschwitz, and the memorial there, have become symbolic of the whole—they do, to an extent, stand for the Holocaust. In that way, the numbers there—though certainly enormous—may have been miscalculated. We do not know. We cannot know.'

'But we can, Thomas! We can.' The professor nearly jumped from his seat. 'You know that we can. Just not yet, not until Soviet historians allow others like me also to study the records they have.'

The rag, absorbing the wet on the window sill, was now dripping onto the floor. 'I think we can now agree that this seminar is over unless you have something to add, Mr Day?'

'Thank you, Professor Pepliński. Yes. I mean no.' Tom gathered his things. Before leaving, he turned again to his teacher. 'Professor Carter taught me this same way too. Then again, I suppose you knew that already.' Pepliński smiled to show he understood. 'Professor, do you really think we should have had this conversation in this way?'

'I can think of no better conversation to have, Tom, and no better time and place to have it.'

Tom nodded not because he was certain but because he wanted to be. 'Shall I write the next essay, sir?'

'That would be most interesting, Mr Day. I hope we will all be here to hear it.'

In the central atrium a small queue had formed at a table. Tom saw that Aleks, and another student he did not know, were sitting behind the table apparently taking signatures. Taped to the front edge of the desk was a small poster with NZS in boxy, zigzaggy letters. Tom recognised this as the Independent Students' Association. The banner for the rival ZSP had been taken down.

Outside, on Independence Avenue, the workmen had suspended their construction of the metro and were gathered around a smoking brazier for warmth. Beside them lay their shovels and pickaxes; the men had discarded their hard hats, piled together like a nest of hatched dinosaur eggs. A mechanical digger reared up behind them, inactive and ticking as it cooled. Nelson from the Polish class was waiting at a tram stop.

Tom removed a glove to shake Nelson's bare hand. 'Where are you going?'

Nelson indicated with his head. He was going to the city centre. Normally clean-shaven, he had allowed his beard to stipple his chin. He wore a raincoat over his sweater, but he had no hat or scarf on. He was shivering. His black skin had turned a shade of lead, the colour of Warsaw snow.

'Nelson! You must get inside. It is too cold for you out here.' Tom looked across the road and saw that the milk bar was not busy. 'Come with me.'

Nelson did not protest. He followed his colleague through the doorway, pushing back the heavy felt curtain that kept the harshest of the cold out. Inside, the windows and tabletops and even the stools were covered in a layer of condensation; steam rose from the tureens of soup and tin jugs of sweetened tea. Nelson devoured the plate of pale dumplings the Irishman brought him.

Tom waited until the Nigerian had finished his food and was no longer shivering. 'You must have warmer clothes, Nelson. Why don't you have a proper coat or a hat?'

'It is very expensive for my country to send me here. I am very fortunate. I have almost everything I need. But it is true. Warsaw is much colder than Lagos. In my home it is never below twenty-five degrees, many children wear no shoes—not because they are poor, but because they are too hot. Here, they would die. Even a prince might die here.'

Perched on a stool, Tom's feet swung with the weight of the army boots Jakub had given him. His neck was moist from the sweat of his scarf. He loosened it and gave it to his friend. 'Keep this,' he said. 'I will borrow one from a roommate.' He sized the Nigerian up, mentally measuring the width of his shoulders and the bulk of his chest. They were of similar build. Perhaps he could find a spare coat or buy one, he thought.

Nelson was standing, already happily wearing his new scarf. 'Thank you, my friend. Now I must go. I am much better!' He pushed through the felt curtain and was gone.

Aleks was the resourceful one; he was the man that Tom should see about a coat, but Tom remembered that he was busy in the university atrium. Dom Studenta was a short walk away. In his room, Norbert was still asleep in his bed, having missed all of his classes again. Piotr was sitting at the end of Norbert's bed, strumming his guitar, practising from a music book he had received as a Christmas present. When Tom had first met Piotr, it was as if the Pole spoke no English at all; later they had talked about the academic freedoms of the lecturers. Tom was never sure where or how to begin a conversation with him.

Piotr played a new melody from his book and looked to Tom as if to encourage him to sing 'Stairway to Heaven'.

'I don't know the words.'

'You must!'

'Sorry.'

Piotr continued playing. The mound beside him, Norbert, didn't stir.

'Have you no classes today?' Tom asked. Piotr smiled, shrugged, nodded and shook his head, and made it all seem like one carefree gesture. Tom recalled that Piotr had been excused from some courses, that he had certain undefined privileges. 'Piotr. I need to buy a new coat. A good one.'

Piotr wordlessly set his guitar aside. He stood and went to Norbert's locker, where he found a packet of cigarettes. He lit one. 'You have money?'

Tom blushed. He had not considered that money might be an issue. He lived off the monthly stipend given to him by the British Council in *złoty* and had rarely needed to exchange his British currency in the bank. Now he recognised he would require a larger sum.

'You have money?' Piotr repeated. 'You have dollars, Deutschmark, pounds?'

'I have pounds, yes. I will need to go to the bank.'

The Pole laughed. Norbert snored beneath his blanket. 'I will change money for you. See.' He lifted a pen from Norbert's cupboard, and on an inside blank page of his Led Zeppelin score, he jotted down some figures. 'See, I give you six times.' He was offering Tom six times the bank rate.

'I was told I should not exchange money on the black market,' Tom protested. 'It's a serious offence here.'

'Polish economy falls down without black market.' Piotr mimed the crash he had in mind, his fingers spraying like shrapnel. 'But listen, Irlandczyku. You say nothing. Even Piotr must go to the army if . . .'

'If you are caught.' The voices of other students skipping classes reached them from the corridor. 'It's OK. Forget it,' Tom decided.

Under his bedclothes, Norbert snored again. 'Fuck it! Do it!' he bellowed like a dragon from inside a cave. Somehow that obliged Tom to go to his own locker and extract his bundle of sterling notes. He unfolded three twenties.

'Will that be enough?'

'It may be,' Piotr replied, already reaching his wallet out of his back pocket and counting out several hundred *złoty*. He sucked on the cigarette to keep his hands free. 'Good business!' he declared, chuckling through his smoke.

Tom, with his bulge of cash, took the tram into the city, alighted near the Palace of Culture, and stepped into the Centrum department store. Pushing back the felt curtain, the orange glow of the interior barely lit the array of bicycles, kitchen utensils, and plastic goods. The floor was slick with the grey melt brought in on shoppers' boots. Heated bars hung haphazardly on the walls, doing little to dispel the cold inside. Tom progressed as through an abandoned bazaar with no hope that an assistant would accost him. Stairs led up through the ceiling to the first floor, where he found the women's and men's clothing. Mannequins dressed in trousers, socks, shirts and hats stood behind counters as if there to sell themselves. A small company of coat wearers stood to attention behind a counter in the far corner, and Tom headed there nervously. His Polish—as he explained the size, style, quality and colour he needed—would be stretched by his encounter with the shop assistant waiting for him there.

'I would like a coat.'

The assistant eyed him suspiciously. 'Sir is not Polish?'

Tom confirmed the fact, plain after only five words. 'I need a coat for the winter.'

'Sir is already wearing a coat. A little old perhaps, but . . .'

'For a friend.'

Somehow, for the assistant, this turned the transaction into a conspiracy, which he was determined to enjoy. 'Of course, a friend. What size is your friend, sir?'

'Like me.' Tom was glad, at least, for the simplicity of this. 'It must be warm.' The assistant disrobed a mannequin and walked around the counter to offer it to Tom, who tried it on. 'It is too small.'

'Yes. But it is warm.'

'Warm, but too small.'

Undeterred, the assistant hurried back behind the counter, pulled the coat off the next dummy, and bore it back to his customer. 'Sir is sure to like this one.'

'It is very nice,' Tom agreed. 'And warm.' He raised both arms above his head. 'But it is too large.'

'It is very nice on you, sir. Very nice and warm.'

'But too large.'

The assistant circled his customer in a professional manner. It really was very nice on him. But he helped the man out of the unwanted item, placed it back on the nude model, and returned with a third coat.

Tom put it on. There was no mirror so he had to swing his head one way and hips another to get a better look. It felt heavy on him, certainly warm. 'It fits,' he declared, thinking he would be pleasing the shop assistant.

The assistant looked doubtful. He tugged at the sleeves and boxed at the shoulders. He inspected the foreigner from every angle. Finally he said, 'It does not look right on you, sir. And the make is inferior.'

'It is not for me,' Tom reminded him. 'It will be fine. Good. I will pay!'

The assistant, defeated, reluctantly wrapped the coat in an enormous length of paper, quartering it with string. He keyed the price into the till (it came to the exact amount Tom had exchanged with Piotr) and presented his customer with the receipt on a tiny curl of paper.

He watched the foreigner walk off triumphantly with the bundle then stationed himself again amongst his mannequins.

The package was so large he wondered how he would ever be able to give it to Nelson without offending him. It was true, Nelson had accepted the scarf—and the dumplings—in the milk bar, but a scarf was only a scarf, literally a thing that can be shrugged off. A coat had tailoring, it was made to fit, it was *for* a person and could not therefore be so casually gifted. It was indeed expensive, in terms relative to local income possibly the most expensive single item Tom had ever purchased. The stitching was good, the material was thick if not elegant, the label said *sdelano v rossii*. It was not a language Tom knew, but he knew enough to realise that the coat must have been made in Russia. He could pretend that he had bought it at the Russian market, where all sorts of products, legitimate and otherwise, could be picked up for very little. Nelson might spot the lie but could at least hide his embarrassment behind it. Or so Tom hoped. He was back in his room, concocting this subterfuge alone when Aleks came in and dumped himself on his bed.

'What's that?' he asked, pointing at the package.

'I bought a coat at Centrum. I wanted to get your recommendation, but I saw you were busy.'

Aleks ignored this. 'You bought it there? You could have spent less dough just about anywhere else. Is it any good? Can I see it?'

'I think it is good. I don't want to open it—it's for a friend.'

'Really?' Aleks was suspicious. Still lying on his bed, he placed his wrist over his eyes, the better not to look into those of the Irishman. 'What rate did you get? Was it Piotr? What rate did he give you for your pounds?'

'That's not what happened.'

'You are lying. Do you think you could do something like that and I not hear about it? What do you think Norbert is for?'

'Six,' Tom said simply with neither pride nor shame. If he had broken a law, it was a silly law, and he had done so for a good reason.

'Okay. Six is okay. It was gonna happen sometime. Surprised it took you so long.' Aleks was still covering his eyes with the back of his hand. 'Piotr has plenty of cash.'

'He seems to have. Actually, it's a ton of money. What can he need it for?'

'My guess would be he needs it just for the reason you gave him, buying and selling hard currency, stereo equipment, cars.'

'Cars? Are you serious?'

Aleks pulled himself up easily to sit on the edge of his bed. He dragged his hand over his hair so that it spiked up. Tom regarded for the first time just how young his friend could appear. 'Especially cars. He travels to Frankfurt on the East German border, buys an old Mercedes, drives it back here or to his dad in Kutno, and sells it on. Polish cab drivers love them because they are roomy and don't break down as often as the Russian Ladas. I suppose he must make a lot of money that way.'

'Should I avoid selling my hard currency to him?'

'Of course, if you want not to be deported. But if you don't care about that, why would you not sell to Piotr? He is not a trustworthy character, but he is hardly going to admit his own crime by turning you in. You already do your shopping at Pewex. I can't see why PKO or the state should benefit any more from your exchange.'

This was the first time since Christmas Eve that Aleks had mentioned the hard currency shop Pewex. 'Look, Aleks, I am sorry about that. In fact, I am pretty sure you know I am. I went once, just once. If I go again—and I might—I won't drag you along. But I was grateful—grateful!—to you and your family for taking me in at Christmas, for being so bloody wonderful. And I couldn't tell them—at least I could not tell them the way I might want to, but I saw that shop and . . . It seemed like a fair enough idea. It *was* a fair enough idea.'

'Sure, go ahead. Any time you want to say anything you are too emotionally constipated to actually say out loud, sure, go ahead and spend some money instead. Nothing says thank you quite like overpriced export vodka or a coat from Centrum.' Although Aleks spoke angrily, his body language seated on his bed was still relaxed. 'I guess it is not your fault. You live your life in the West. It becomes the only ethic available to you. But, Tom, you might learn that there are other ways of valuing friendship.'

Now Tom was not sorry; now he was as sure of himself as ever he had been. 'He was cold, Aleks. He did not have a coat. I could perhaps have bought him a cheaper coat, but I did not need to, and anyway the more important thing was that the coat should fit and be warm. I took some trouble to make sure of that. When I give it to him, I will not emphasise how expensive it was, just how warm it is. When it comes to friendship, I am sorry that you have decided that I am not up to the job. It may be true. I have been hiding it—that's what you think—but I have been doing so in the hope that I might get better at it. I was hoping that, as a friend, you might realise that and give me some credit. And just in case you think I have not expressed it well enough or often enough yet, I *do* value our friendship, Aleks. But I am taking on a lot of stuff here.'

Despite himself, that last made Aleks laugh. "'A lot of stuff." Yes, you express yourself so well!' Aleks made sure Tom knew he was kidding. 'The coat, it was for a friend without one?'

'Nelson, the Nigerian prince. He was hypothermic at the tram stop.' It was Tom's turn to laugh. 'Two new hits off the Marillion album there, I think.'

'If they are not, they should be.' Aleks laughed still more, delighted that he had understood Tom's joke and delighted too that their argument had passed. He was glad to change the subject. 'You said earlier that you saw I was busy?'

'You were signing students up to the NZS. Do they let you do that at SGPiS?'

'Do they let us do it? That's a good question. No, would have to be the answer. They don't let us, but somehow we can do it anyway. I mean, today we could sit there in the atrium with a line of students. Tomorrow who knows? Officially the NZS is not a registered union, so if the rector turns against us, there is not a lot to stop him. We did just twenty minutes there today, long enough to let people know we exist, not so long as to annoy the rector or Wilk too much.'

'Will you need help with printing later on?'

'I'll meet you in the drying room!'

'You boys doing laundry?' Gosia was standing at their door. She invited herself in, turned away from Aleks sitting on his bed, and closed in on Tom standing by his locker cupboard. She enfolded him with her body and kissed him so he could not speak. Even when she broke off, it was for a second only to allow her to say how much she had missed him, that she had hated Christmas without him, that she would not go away without him again. When finally she let go, Tom, looking over her shoulder, could see that Aleks was still there.

'How long were you listening in on our conversation, Gosia?' Aleks was angry and he was speaking to her in Polish.

'A while, maybe, Aleks.' Gosia was looking past him rather than at him. 'I am sure you were being careful. I know how you like to keep secrets.'

'What are you two arguing about?' Tom interrupted in English. 'We had finished our conversation, hadn't we, Aleks?' Tom was keen to have some time alone with his girlfriend.

'Just about,' Aleks agreed. He found some dirty socks and held them aloft. 'Laundry,' he said and he left.

Tom and Gosia spent the rest of the afternoon alone. Her time in Gdańsk had been like hell. Tom even did not know how much she wanted him there. The boy from Norway was nice, handsome of course, and older than Tom, but he was boring to be with. Her father liked him, which was probably why he had come. She had had some nice days with her old girlfriends, just spending time together, going to only two parties; they understood her like her friends in Warsaw could not. She had written to Tom many times but had not posted the letters. She had been left so confused about his feelings at the train station, even she did not know what to say to him. It really was not fair that he should be so cool with her. But she forgave him because he was here now. There was one more thing that had upset her in Gdańsk. Her old boyfriend, Michał, had called around. He was very jealous of the Norwegian boy. Michał was a silly boy, he had problems with his stomach, but he was kind and loyal to Gosia and she had promised him she had no other boyfriends in Warsaw. She had to tell him that because he was going to hospital! Tom must try to understand. In Gdańsk, she might say she was even famous for having boyfriends. She did not have to try. Of course, usually they were too young or unintelligent, but despite this she liked to be with them because she wanted to enjoy herself while she was still young and beautiful. Michał was the only one of these boyfriends who still called on her, so you see, it was her duty to be kind to him. She would see Tom again tomorrow or the next day, soon. He would not have to wait long. She had a meeting with the director of her college. Dudek was such a fool, but she could not escape it.

Tom did not see Aleks at dinner so missed out on the extra portion of gherkin that he often set aside for him. Tom was still a little hungry after his meat and potatoes. From the bottom of his cupboard, he drew out some dirty socks and pants, which he took with him to the downstairs washing room. He rubbed soap in, using one sock to abrade the other, rinsed them, and carried his small laundry haul into the next-door drying room. He waited until he was alone then knocked on the metal door using the code he had agreed with Aleks.

Inside the underground cell, the *powielacz* was already grinding out the information leaflets that Aleks would use to attract students to the NZS. Tom picked one up from the pile and tried to read it. Even with his good eyesight, he struggled.

'We have to use the smallest setting,' Aleks explained. 'We never know when we might get our hands on more paper, and there is so much we need to tell people about. For example . . . here, let me show you.' Aleks switched off the machine. It gave a slowly descending whine, as if thankful for the rest.

There were chapters of the NZS seeking local registration in small colleges in Olsztyn, Elbląg, and even Suwałki near the Soviet border. SGPiS was not alone. Although certain rectors such as at Warsaw University had recognised branches, only national legal registration would ensure every student could be represented by an independent union. The ZSP was only allowed to organise its programmes because in their constitution they say they support the Party. For that, they get generous funding from the Ministry of National Education and seats on the University Senate. They run attractive events for freshers in their first weeks then bribe them to become members. Many students—especially at SGPiS—did not know that the ZSP was dependent on the communists, or they didn't care. It was Aleks' job to make sure they did know. There were NZS members around the country being arrested and beaten by riot police, just for publicly demonstrating their freedom of speech.

'Are you prepared to be arrested, to be beaten?' Tom asked.

Aleks had already considered this. 'There is what some call a balance of violence,' he said. 'Standing up to the authorities is never free. It has to be paid for. I would pay a high price, but the leaders of our organisation count not only the cost to themselves, but also to other students and to the society generally.'

'Let me understand this. You mean, there may be times when the NZS would stop a protest because of some other danger?'

'It's the Polish reality again, Tom. If our protests led to a Warsaw Pact invasion, that price would be too high. We would be counting the costs in the numbers lying dead on the street or locked up in prison. We have been there before. But sometimes the Party threatens us with such things when the truth is it will not happen. It's for our leaders to decide the balance. In any case, it will not be my decision to make. Michalski has that honour.'

'Who?' Tom thought he recalled the name.

'Dariusz Michalski. He is the leader of NZS here.'

'Why do I think I have met him?'

'I should not think you have. But that's his empty bed you lie beside every night in our room. He is the one we call *Nikt*. He has been suspended so many times by Wilk, but never quite permanently. So he still has a room. As he is regularly held back a year, and forbidden to graduate, he is much older than the rest of us. He is consequently also much better at organising an opposition, which is great for us. To many of our members, he is a legend. They rarely see him and they know little about him, but they have heard of his many confrontations with the authorities. When he said that the management of the university should be more open to students' opinions, he made his point by removing the door to Wilk's office. He was suspended for that. He never attended a single compulsory class in Russian, but turned up for the oral examination and scored a five. He dates the most beautiful girl in the university, and he reads philosophy in his spare time. Some assume he is from Warsaw. Others are sure he is from Białystok in the northeast of the country. In fact he grew up midway between the two, in Ostrów Mazowiecka, an insignificant, liminal place a hundred kilometres from any culture.'

Tom was glancing again at the leaflet in his hand. The print was too small and indistinct for him to read but, as he scanned, the word *Michalski* appeared then again, then again several times more. Was its repetition on the paper why he thought he knew the name? 'But you have met him, Aleks? I mean, you speak to him a lot?'

'A few times. I interviewed him for this. He wants to accelerate NZS demands. We need full academic freedom for our teachers. We need better books in our libraries and not just the ones from the official press. We need the SB, the security service, banned from campuses. He has plans, Tom, and he will need me to help agitate for them.' Aleks stretched his arm over the sides of the printer like he might the shoulder of an older brother.

'You could be suspended, or even expelled, from the university, Aleks. What would Magda say about that?' Tom had accidentally used his friend's mother's name. 'What would your mum and dad think?'

Aleks had known all his life what his parents would think of it, but still he hesitated. 'They would worry, of course. They do tell me to be careful. But they know that—by setting me the example they have— they have left me with no choice. My parents both lost their positions— and Kuba lost even the chance of one. It is not something they would want for me, but they know that a Cybulski always runs the risk. And they trust the people I put my trust in, like Darek Michalski.'

'How could I help, Aleks?' Tom thought at that moment of Spiro. Perhaps there were things that Spiro knew that the students did not. Or perhaps the balance was weighted the other way. Tom could channel information to the diplomat which could in some way help the opposition generally. Then he remembered what Spiro had said in the embassy about keeping an eye on Wilk for him before his emphatic denial that he wanted Tom to spy for him. Was being a spy such a dishonourable thing if the ends were worthwhile? 'I don't like being considered Wilk's pet.'

'Yes, he does like to point to you as if to say our system cannot be all bad if students come here from the West. On the other hand, it might be useful to us if you appear to remain close to him. Spend time with him, listen to him, if you can bear it. At the least, you might be able to pick up some more paper for me from behind pani Elżbieta's back.'

Aleks again turned the fat knob on the printer. Over the mounting din, he shouted, 'The revolution will be made of paper!'

Gosia's taxi dropped her at the College of Tourism administration building on Nowy Świat. It was early evening; the director's secretary had already left, so it was Dudek himself who let Gosia into his office. She scanned it quickly and saw she was alone.

'Comrade Staniewicz will be with us later,' explained Dudek, seeing the confusion on the student's face. He checked the sunburst clock on his wall. 'We have about an hour.'

Gosia calculated frantically. She would hardly be able to hold the man off for that long. 'In that case, I will leave and return later. I have an assignment to read for.'

Dudek cut off her exit. 'I am sure I will be able to explain to your teacher why you were too busy to complete your homework. See, I have chilled some vodka.' He pointed to two glasses and a frosted bottle of export spirit arranged on his desk where his family photographs ought to have been.

'I don't drink vodka,' replied Gosia, lamely. Playing the innocent would not work with this bully. 'I celebrate with Vermouth, if I can. What's the celebration? Is it your wedding anniversary?'

Dudek allowed himself to laugh at this. He was feeling supremely confident. Staniewicz had called ahead to give him permission to debrief the girl himself. The girl would be long gone before the minister arrived, and Dudek could give him his version of her report. The evening could only go well for him. He sat on his office sofa, leaving the student the option of sitting next to him or on one of the desk chairs. For now she remained standing.

'I am sure my secretary hides Vermouth somewhere if you want me to look. No? Suit yourself. We *do* have something to celebrate, Gosia, don't we?' He instinctively wanted to drink but realised he had stupidly sat down without pouring one for himself. He tried to dismiss his blunder. 'Tell me about our English friend.'

'I don't report to you, Dudek,' the girl said simply.

The director counted the multiple slights. She had called him by the informal *you*; she had used his name without his title; she had reminded him that he too had a superior. 'As we are dispensing with formalities, Gosia, I may as well tell you that Staniewicz has in fact requested I take your report. Now, pour me a drink. I am thirsty.'

Gosia was careful to place her body between the director and the bottle, so he would not see her hand shake as she poured it. She wished now she could also have one. Still with her back to him, she said, 'But

I don't have anything to report. I am afraid this celebration you have planned is premature.'

'Marx taught us patience, my dear. There may be many small milestones on our road to success. It is the Polish way to celebrate at each. You have the Englishman's confidence, that much you have secured.'

Now he had said it twice. Gosia decided to endure the director's error about Tom's nationality. 'I think he likes me.'

'How could he not!' Dudek licked the rim of his glass. 'I am sure you attend to him meticulously. Am I right?'

Gosia knew what he meant and that he was probably already aroused. 'Actually, he is a gentleman, and rather innocent.'

'Bah!' Dudek could not help his explosion. 'You are teasing him, just as I see you tease others. No doubt, it is why Staniewicz believed you qualified for the job. Tell me about his friends. Get on with it.'

Gosia listed the associates Dudek and Staniewicz already knew about. Tom had not yet made contact with other individuals of interest. He was attending his classes as would be expected. He especially liked history.

'Ah, that Pepliński fellow. Is he still around? I am surprised Wilk has allowed him to remain in post after that fiasco in November.'

'Pepliński appears straight. If anything, Tom is frustrated by how orthodox the professor is. They argue, apparently.'

'Is he—your boyfriend, the Englishman—is his propagandising, do you think? Is he trying to sway the others in his class? After he gave the commemoration address where he called into question our very raison d'état, it would not surprise me to learn that he was agitating still.'

'I don't think so. He hangs back after class. He doesn't speak at all during the lesson—he is still self-conscious about speaking Polish in front of others. From what I can work out, that was just him and Pepliński.'

Dudek ruminated. He was bored by Pepliński already, convinced there was nothing there apart perhaps from a frustrated academic. He had known many of those in his time. Wilk's problem, not his. 'What of Cybulski? You can't tell me that that young man, from that family, is not up to something.'

In truth, she did not know. Earlier she had walked in on Tom and Aleks talking, but she had missed the subject of their conversation. She had realised, too late, that she ought to have waited longer outside the door. 'I don't think he likes me,' she said at last. 'He leaves when I enter the room.' Then with sudden realisation, she said, 'He may be jealous of me.'

Dudek exploded again, this time wordlessly. The workings of the female mind were a constant mystery to him, focused apparently on the emotional rather than the political. 'Has it escaped your notice that arrests of dissidents have spiked again? Now that Bush is safely back in Washington and we will not be seeing the Holy Father again for a few years, the Interior Ministry has again decided to take some of its more talkative opponents in for questioning. So if you don't mind me putting it this way, I don't give a fuck for Cybulski's feelings, Miss Kamińska. I want to know what he is plotting.'

Now it was her turn to laugh. 'I think if they get through a day with their dinner eaten and their laundry done, they count that as an achievement. I think the state can survive any plot that Cybulski might be concocting.'

Dudek was dissatisfied with this. If his student had not seen or heard anything improper, it was because she had not been paying attention. At some point in the history of the People's Republic, legitimacy had given way to vigilance. Vigilance, attention, these were their mainstays now. If the daughters of loyal Party functionaries could not be trusted to look out, then what good were they? 'Gosia, may I remind you of your role here. It is to provide a regular flow of information. It is not for you to decide what is, or is not, significant. You have not the maturity or the social-political insight to make such decisions. You are the ears and the eyes, but you are not the brain. Staniewicz is the brain, General Kiszczak is . . . well, let's just say that these days Kiszczak does what Staniewicz tells him to. You see how important you are?'

'What are you, Dudek?' Gosia looked down at her director, sunk in the sofa nursing the wet but empty shot glass with both hands. 'What is your function?'

'I provide you, Gosia. I provide you, and others like you. I have learned that when eyes do not work, they can be ripped out, ears can be torn off. You would not want that to happen, believe me.'

Dudek remained on the sofa for some minutes longer, extending his metaphor to convince himself still more. His own vigilance was beyond question, that and his loyalty. He had initially taken a practical approach to Party membership, which had helped him to get where he was now. And now he was there, he appreciated all the more the need to watch out to defend with fervour its lead role in society. He did not notice the hands turn on his sunburst clock or the moment that the student left. He should not have said what he did about Comrade Kiszczak. Staniewicz would arrive soon. He would expect a report, something more substantial than Gosia had supplied. Dudek moved to his desk, picked up his pen, and poured himself another shot of vodka.

Sebastian Thomson was back in town. He had already done the rounds of the Lenin Shipyard in Gdańsk, the Nowa Huta Steelworks outside Cracow, and now he was back in Warsaw sniffing around his old haunts. The government had kept its promise of imposing one hundred per cent price increases then ballsed it up by also hiking wages by forty per cent. Thomson was no economist, but only a blind man could fail to see inflation on its way. The BBC turned to Sebastian Thomson for a Polish strike story, so here he was taking the betting. Barder at the embassy couldn't see him so had bumped him down to some guy called John Spiro. Funny glasses. Turned out quite useful in the end.

'Are you preparing your citizens for a strike here, John? Off the record, if you like.'

'Chatham House Rule for now, Seb. There will be a strike either this month or March. Guaranteed. We will issue the customary, about not engaging in local controversies. If it gets tasty on the streets, we will offer to repat, but I doubt it will come to that.'

'What makes you so complacent? You can't be hearing what I am. There is heat in this one.' Thomson poised his biro over his pad then dropped it, certain there would be no useable quotes from this one. Scots. They gave nothing away.

'You've been listening to the US guys getting all excited that the opposition is ready to make some coordinated move like a deal on prices in exchange for registration for Solidarity. Everyone knows the government can't reform the economy without Wałęsa, but the shit would really need to hit the fan for that to take place. No, there will be strikes. There will be a large demo or three, some arrests, then they will all go back to their boxes and a week later the manipulator-in-chief Jacek Mazur will announce at a press conference that the price rises have been reversed. As was. There's your story.'

'Thanks for the insight, and for the US angle. But no, you are missing something bigger.' Thomson picked up his pen again. Spiro shifted his position in his chair, unused to having his local intelligence trumped. 'Want to hear more?' Spiro nodded. 'This room safe to talk in?' Spiro nodded again. 'Kiszczak is not in charge of this one.'

'What does that mean? There is no one at the Ministry of the Interior who can rival Kiszczak, no one else in the government for that matter. That man practically *was* Martial Law. They have been making arrests all winter, ever since the fucked up referendum. They are worried about commemorations of the trouble in '68, so are lifting some likely lads on account of that. Low level still, but are you saying that that's not Kiszczak?'

'Not what I am saying, that's his guys for sure. It's the stuff still to come that I am interested in.'

'Is this journalists' gossip, Seb? Because if it is, I don't need to hear it. We have our own nags and soothsayers.'

'Tip-offs, whistle-blowing, humint . . . it's all gossip in the wrong hands, John. I have been at this a while, and my guess is you have seen your share of juicy information to be able to smell the shit from the roses. How's your Russian?'

'Fluent.'

'Of course, it is.' Thomson had heard enough diplomatic arrogance to know that some of it was justified. 'Your boss should really be the one to hear this, but you're his guy apparently.' Thomson had still not made up his mind.

'Go on.'

'Okay, so there's someone at the Interior who admires my work.'

'You have a source on Stefan Batory Street? Go on.'

'He was a bit nervous when I saw him yesterday evening. Not his usual, ruthless self. He had been in with Kiszczak earlier in the day, advisors' powwow or some such. He had papers. They all had papers. The country is fucking drowning in paper.'

'Go on.'

'So my guy picks up his papers that have been sitting on Kiszczak's desk, and he goes back to his own office, dumps his papers on his own desk, and leaves them there most of the day.'

'He's got General Kiszczak's personal documents.'

'For the General's eyes only. Only it's a defence-line telegram and it's in Russian, so he takes another look. He knows he shouldn't, but now he has done it he can't pretend he hasn't. He was trying to figure a way of slipping the telegram back on to his boss's desk when I showed up.'

'What, you just walked in?'

'By appointment, all above board.'

'You have an appointment with the Interior Ministry *before* you see your own ambassador. Should I be having you arrested?'

'Are you trying to avoid hearing this? What was on the telegram— that's the question you are meant to be asking me.'

'Wait. If you are about to leak foreign intelligence to me, you know what that makes you, don't you? Just so as you know, and you are comfortable with that.'

'I am not a spy, John. I saw the telegram, but my man would not translate it for me, let alone read it out loud. Not a man at ease in his own environment at that moment would be my assessment. He wasn't saying. But he was shitting himself. This was more than just the usual Kremlin interference in internal affairs.'

'How do you know?'

'Because the man was hyperventilating. He is usually super cool, you know, Paul Newman cool.'

'That's it? Your guy is having an off day and you call it a Soviet invasion?'

'You get me wrong, John. This was not an off day. This was the *best day of his life*. He could hardly contain himself. That's what is bothering me. You see, there's more. He let me copy down the sender's name—in Cyrillic, of course—and simply said, "Not Gorbachev". He meant, this was an order from someone else, behind the General Secretary's back. Here, here's the name.'

Thomson showed Spiro the page from his pad: Дми́трий Я́зов.

'Who is it? You can read it, can't you?'

'Yes. This is from Dmitry Yazov. He's the Minister of Defence, appointed by Gorbachev last May, but he's as old as the hills.' Spiro put his glasses back on to look into the mid-distance. He was trying to recall the ambassador's schedule. He heard a grunt coming from the journalist. 'Yes. Thank you, Sebastian. That is interesting. I will speak to Barder. Probably little in it.' He stood up to shake the other's hand.

'Are you kicking me out? I'm the Pearl Harbour early warning guy, and you show me the door?'

'I have my citizens to protect, and you have the BBC to please. We mustn't disappoint either.' Thomson was putting on his coat while standing up from his chair, nearly failing in both. 'Ah, I almost forgot. A young chap you might want to see—son of an old friend of yours. Cybulski. You will remember Bogdan Cybulski, from Kutno, 1981?'

The journalist was a blank. 'Can't be. I am good with names. Kutno, of course. I was there in December that year. Some turncoat taped the Solidarity meeting and handed it to the SB. Brought the whole house down, that did. Martial Law was the best moment in my entire career. Bloody marvellous. I would remember a Bogdan Cybulski if I met one.'

Spiro concealed his surprise. People kept lying to him about old man Cybulski. 'No matter. It's not important. And the Yazov thing—I am sure it is nothing, but if you do see your ministry friend again do try to bend him a little, won't you? And if the gossip is good . . .'

'Sure. And next time will be on the record.'

Tom asked Gosia to help him with this history essay. He would make what use he could of notes he had made with Carter on the events of 1968. He did attempt to read some Polish sources, but he was confounded by the library loan system in which he had to know the name of the book he sought, write it down on a chit for the librarian who would then disappear through a door behind her desk, then (maybe) reappear with the desired item fifteen minutes later. There was always Topolski. Topolski, whose book Wilk had given him on his first day, wrote almost nothing on the matter, shuffling it away in an aside. Tom made Gosia translate from English, 'Dissatisfaction had, by the way, been expressed much earlier, especially during student revolts in March 1968, but the vicious circle was broken only by the plenary of December

1970, which removed from power those who had been responsible for the errors in economic and social policies.' By the way. Tom already knew about the campaign against Jews in public life, so he wrote about that. Topolski mentioned casualties but didn't name or number them.

Gosia did her best to help. 'Tomek, I have the Polish words, but I am not sure I understand your English ones.' But for him she would try. She wrote it out by hand in pale-blue ink. Tom saw how hard it was for her, both as a work of translation and as a set of challenging new ideas to assimilate. She screwed up her lips and tucked a curl behind her ear. 'But, Tom, there were really so few Jews left in Poland by then. There were no Jews to be against.'

Tom wondered how much responsibility he had for explaining her own country to Gosia. 'Anti-Semitism can exist without Jews, Gosia. I mean, people need only imagine a plot for them to believe it. There were Jews in Poland, even then, Gosia. The irony is, many of them were high up in the Party. The campaign in 1968 was a nasty attempt, using age-old anti-Jewish prejudices to gain influence within the Party.'

'I can believe that!' she exclaimed. An entire argument and counter-argument played out in Gosia's head and across her face, but she said no more.

'Did you write this, Mr Day? Of course, I know you did not as the handwriting is too feminine. And the Polish, truthfully speaking, is too good. But apart from that, this is your work?'

Tom confirmed to Pepliński that it was. He had just finished reading it out, falteringly, to the class. Pepliński had addressed him in English before turning to the rest of the group in their own language. 'Would someone like to challenge our friend from Belfast on his analysis of our recent history? I am certain Mr Day would welcome any questions and do his best to answer them.'

One student complimented him on his style; one other dared say that she had not read about those events, so did not feel she could comment. Still another said nothing at all but sat with his long legs stretching lazily in front of him, clicking his pen.

'Wonderful! Thank you, everyone,' said Pepliński with obvious sarcasm. 'Mr Day, have you any final wise words?'

As Pepliński had spoken to him in Polish, Tom endeavoured to reply in kind. He was stung by his professor's remark, implying that he was less qualified to discuss history which was not his own. 'I study Polish history in Belfast,' he stuttered, 'because it is important. Your history is not only yours.' Tom remembered at that moment what Spiro had told him about the Poles' devotion to an idea of their past. 'We all tell our stories,' Tom went on, sure that he was failing to explain himself even this simply. 'It is good to hear another person tell our story. They may have another perspective because they look from another side. Sorry . . . that's all.' Tom gave up.

As the students left the classroom, they smiled encouragingly at their foreign friend. Tom stayed back, sure that Pepliński would want words with him. 'Sorry, Professor. By now, I had hoped to be able to speak much better Polish. I shouldn't pronounce controversial ideas if I cannot put the words together to defend them.'

'Your Polish is fine, Mr Day. And as for controversy, I heard none. In fact, I rather feel you missed your opportunity. Admittedly they are a diminishing number, but my little band of students here might learn something from you if you were more willing. You have read the books they have not been allowed to. You could have told them about the imaginary anti-Zionist campaign, for example how police raided the university in Cracow and were faced by a united resistance of academics and students. Your own historians have written these books. If you have not read the books, then shame on you and on Carter for not obliging you to.'

'The shame would be all mine,' admitted Tom. 'I try, but I still don't know enough.' He thought of the reading he had not done for his professor in Belfast, the music that Spiro wanted him to appreciate, and the poetry that Aleks wanted him to. 'I cut too many corners, let too many people down.'

Pepliński was not about to let him off the hook. 'Tom, you will amount to nothing if you see an opportunity and walk away from it. Sit down.'

Tom obeyed. He thought of Gosia. He had brought her into the room with her translation of his essay, and now it seemed to him that Pepliński had referred to her too. She had other men chasing her and giving her a good time, yet she had shown patience with him. But for how long? Pepliński was reaching to a high shelf and fetching down a photograph. A young Pepliński, perhaps with his girlfriend and another man. Tom, the older man seemed about to tell him, should seize his opportunity with Gosia. 'What was her name?' Tom asked, pointing at the photograph.

'I thought perhaps you would recognise her.'

Tom looked again, imagining there was no way he could know the face of the woman in the picture. Even in black and white, her eyes appeared ice-blue and her hair—pulled back in a small ponytail—was blonde. He shook his head.

'Back then, in '68, she was a chemistry student, Janina Błońska. We were close politically. That was enough then, but when I think of those times and recall this photograph, I do wonder why we were not also close romantically.'

'It's pani Shaw. My Polish teacher in Belfast.'

'Correct. I conclude from your surprise that she never told you about me?'

'No. She knew, of course, that I was coming here. She must not have realised that you were a teacher here.'

'You have not looked at the other man then. It's Martin. To you, Professor Carter. He spent much of the early part of 1968 here—a break, I imagine, from his Moscow studies. We became firm friends. He was in love with Janina, for sure. Janina and I were active in the student protests after the authorities banned the theatrical production of the Mickiewicz work, *Forefather's Eve*. Many of us were beaten or arrested. Academics, those who sympathised, were dismissed.'

'Yes, I know that. Magda and Bogdan Cybulski were both forced to leave Warsaw. They are parents of my—'

Pepliński interrupted. 'We knew Magdalena Cybulska from afar. She was a post-grad—fearless, although she would claim that it was others who took the real risks. When the government tried to claim that the protests were orchestrated by the Jews and Moczar launched his campaign of anti-Semitism, Warsaw became increasingly dangerous for the likes of Janina.'

'Because?'

'Because her mother was Jewish. As with many others like her, she had survived the war only by her parents placing her with a Catholic family. Her mother and father both died in the gas chambers, and Janina grew up forgetting all about them. With her looks, she easily passed for

Polish. Her new family were good to her, but she somehow always knew they were not her parents. She called them uncle, auntie. One day she simply asked, and they told her. It was not a secret to her friends. She was certainly not ashamed to be Jewish. But by 1968, it had become another reason why she needed to stand up to the Party. Under pressure from Moczar, the rector was forced to identify all Jews registered at the Warsaw University and rapidly thereafter they began to be expelled. By then, Martin Carter was back in Northern Ireland, and he convinced Janina to join him there. The government was happy to allow Jews to emigrate.'

Tom tried to make sense of what he had just learned. Shaw, Carter, and Pepliński all knew each other twenty years before. The coincidence of that was less surprising when he reminded himself of how he came to be sitting here. That they should also have known Magda Cybulska and that her son should have been the one waiting in Wilk's anteroom to escort him to Dom Studenta: that *did* seem to be a coincidence fit for a paranoiac. 'Professor, why am I here?'

'That, Tom, is an excellent question. But the answer is rather mundane. You are here because you are my student. You are also Janina's and Martin's student. We all became teachers and understood from that moment on that our best contribution to the freedom of Poland—to the freedom of thought—would be through our students. Martin found you and with Janina's help, prepared you to come here where you could become my student. There is no mystery. We have each taught very many students although it is true that you are the only one we have shared.'

'Aleks is my friend. Why is that? How did that happen?'

'How do friendships happen? I am not a philosopher. I have no answer for that. But I understand that Aleksander Cybulski is a fine young man, as are you, so it is no surprise to me that you are attracted to each other.'

'Professor Carter once invited me to look for parallels between events. In fact, I had just presented an essay on 1956. He told me that Poles often did make comparisons between one event in their history and another. We are now a generation on from 1968. It's twenty years. Are you set for another anti-government protest, another crackdown?'

Pepliński slipped the photograph back between the books of his top shelf. 'Yes, Tom. For sure we are.'

⌐‿⌐

Tom was again standing on the station platform with Gosia, watching the train for Gdańsk pull in. This time they would both get on. Teenage soldiers heading home on leave; square-shouldered grandmothers returning from the markets in the south and east; skinny men whose jeans and jackets bore a residue of petrol. They and their luggage competed for space on the platform. Gosia would, she said, clamber into a carriage first, find a compartment with spare seats and signal from there to Tom, who would heave their bags to her through the compartment window. They did this and others did it too so that, the length of the train, canvas shopping bags and military-issue rucksacks, and string-bound parcels were passed from fingertips to grasping hands as if they were boarding a train in India rather than Europe. Tom pushed past smokers in the narrow corridor to find his seat opposite Gosia.

He had already told her about Pepliński, Błońska and Carter, and about Magda Cybulska too. 'It is fate that you are here,' she had said, and she had concluded that they were meant to be together. 'You even don't know how much that I had hoped that this would happen to me.' They talked also about his other teachers—Paszyńska, Bańda—but not about hers. 'My touristic direction is not interesting,' she had declared.

Pani Bańda had shown her class the Kieślowski film, *Blind Chance*. Despite having been made some years before, it was only now being made available to watch. Gosia did not know it at all. 'The film is also about fate, Gosia,' Tom explained. 'Randomly, depending on whether or not he catches his train, the main character Witek will join the communists, or be an activist, or become a doctor. He will be happily in love, or he will never again meet the girl he loves.'

'And is it a happy ending for Witek?'

'No. He dies. Well, I suppose you could say that the film has three endings, all determined by whether or not he catches his train. But the final scene shows him, as a doctor, taking a flight to Libya. He seems happy, successful. You think, that's it. But then the plane explodes. There is no sound, just the image of the plane blowing up, and then a black screen.'

'Why did Bańda make you watch this film, Tomek? I don't like this film and I did not even watch it.'

Tom did not know exactly. He assumed it was part of her endeavour to educate them all in Polish culture as well as language.

'But this seems very negative about my country, Tomek. It says people do not choose ideology, that it is only chance. We are only ... I do not know the word, ofiara.'

'A victim.' This word had come up in the class discussion of the film. Detlef had spoken it.

'Victim, yes! I cannot believe this, Tomek. Humans are not only victims. They can be happy or unhappy, but their character is also important.' Every *h* came hard from the back of her throat.

'You mean lucky, not happy, I think.' Tom had noticed how, in Polish, these words were the same, as if a person's happiness were the same thing as their luck.

Gosia looked crossly at him. 'I don't want that you laugh at me. It is not right, this pessimism from a teacher. Look how our country is built up since the war, how beautiful is Warsaw now, how beautiful is Gdańsk—you will see. This is what makes the right direction of our cultural and social forces.'

'You sound like Wilk!' Tom laughed, but Gosia did not. 'OK. You are much more beautiful than Wilk.'

She was still cross, but Tom thought he detected the beginning of a smile.

Out of the train station in Gdańsk, Tom followed his girlfriend to the tram stop and onto the Number 2 and like her, punched a ticket. He stood so she could sit. The tram jangled and groaned as it climbed north out of the city centre and passed a Second World War tank, cemented on a plinth. It then rattled through another commercial district towards what was plainly a communist-built housing development with wave upon wave of ten-storey blocks all breaking (Gosia told him he could not see) towards the coast. Tom's knees wobbled like he was surfing. The tram took a sharp right turn for another half-mile before coming to its final, juddering halt.

'Welcome in Jelitkowo!' Gosia announced. 'We have the best beach in the whole Tri-city.' Tom thought she might be about to rehearse the promotional material from her training at tourism college, but she spared him. 'My father's house is in the woods.'

The house, from the outside, looked much older than the others around it. Gdańsk, before the war, had been the Freie Stadt Danzig, before that, a German port, and long ago part of the Hanseatic League. Already some of the architecture they had passed since the station, including the station itself, was certainly the work of builders not labouring under socialist-realism. The Kamiński house, not ancient, was pre-war. Germans would have lived there once, Germans who may have left behind their furniture, their cutlery, their food even; Germans who would have been supplanted, within days perhaps, by Poles who had trudged from the east, Poles such as the Kamińskis from Lwów.

Doctor Kamiński was standing at the entrance, tall, bald, at the top of a flight of six steps. His clothes—a black three-piece suit and white shirt—reminded Tom of an undertaker. He greeted his guest formally, in an English which—though limited—was almost Victorian and may have been rehearsed. 'You are welcome, Mr Day, in our home. Please.' He did not speak to his daughter but gave her a glancing kiss on one cheek. She, in turn, muttered something to her father intended for Tom not to hear.

If the house was older and possibly crumbling on the outside, inside it was modern and bright and brilliantly clean like Tom imagined the doctor's surgery might appear. Doctor Kamiński's wife had died when his daughter was a teenager. Gosia had said, on the one occasion the subject came up, that she could barely speak about her to her father. Kamiński scrubbed this house himself. Tom looked around wordlessly but nodded his head to show admiration.

'My father has worked his entire life very hard,' Gosia said proudly as if to answer Tom's questions about where the wealth must have come to pay for this kitchen, this furniture. 'He works still when his patients say they don't like the new doctors. They say they must pay *łapówka* to the hospital, to get even a good service. Łapówka?' She looked to her father to help translate.

'Bribe,' Tom confirmed. 'People have to bribe their doctors?'

Kamiński nodded vigorously then shared a story with his daughter that was obviously already familiar to them both. Tom caught none of it and wondered if there were a special family argot spoken only between the two of them. Gosia translated. 'Women who are pregnant, who must go to the hospital when their baby is ready, have some notes in their hand.' She showed her fist, clenched. 'They must decide who they should give the bribe so that their baby is born well.' She and her father were both laughing, Tom could not understand why. 'Sometimes life in Poland is satire.'

In the early evening, Gosia decided that the three of them would walk along the Jelitkowo beach. The path through the wood was grass and sand. Kamiński walked unsure of his balance as though he rarely came this way. Gosia raced ahead to what looked to Tom like an alpine cabin, a pinewood shack with gaudy painted flowers and pop music playing incongruously from external speakers. She came back with three trays of fries, each the size of her palm, each coated in ketchup. Tom was not hungry, but it seemed important to enjoy this for Gosia was re-enacting some favourite memory. Indeed, even Kamiński looked less funereal as he guided fries into his mouth. Father and daughter spoke in their private language, and Tom dropped behind as it was clear to him that they were talking about the woman they had both lost. He found a bin already overflowing with rubbish and placed his laden chip tray on top. Although he had taken his eyes off them only for a moment, when he looked up, he could not see them. He quickened his pace in the direction of the beach. There were a few children playing there, keeping up a ball in a sort of circular volleyball. A dog was burrowing furiously, digging thirstily for water; a young couple, each aware of their own beauty, each parading the other as they walked hand-in-hand; no sign on the beach of a young woman with an older gentleman. Gosia and her father had simply vanished.

Tom wondered what he should do next. Naturally he could return to the house and wait for them there, but he also found himself retrieving the route back to the train station, already devising his escape should his abandonment be real. It made him feel stupid to think that he could be lost here. He might just take his own walk, pretend that he was here for his own pleasure. If he still had his chips, he could be eating them here, or if the dog were his, he could be exercising it. He might go for a run, of course (he had a sudden genuine urge to do that), but he was wearing his coat and so would only look like a man running away from someone. His disorientation was momentary but left his heart racing. He looked out to sea, his eye caught by a small boy recovering a ball. The ball had already been claimed by the current, but the boy, his hair the colour of the sand, was determined to get it back. When the only option was to wade in, he did, up to his waist, and came back with the ball aloft. Tom watched him wander alone without celebrating southwards along the edge of the beach. His eye drawn that way, Tom saw some figures within the tree line walking darkly away. There were two or perhaps three— passing between the trees, it was difficult to count them. Tom decided it might be the father and daughter, so he walked purposefully in that direction, still on the beach so stumbling occasionally in softer sand, keeping them within his sight. They were crossed by others coming in the opposite direction so that, more than once, he thought he had lost them. As he gained on them, he began to consider the problem of how to reach them from the beach, now more than a metre below the level of the path. Closer now and he was sure it was them; it was them. He could see them clearly though they were talking crossly now and not like the father-daughter of just a few moments ago. Tom could hear them more distinctly than he could before as if the less familiar they were with each other, the more understandable they were to him. Gosia was accusing her father and mocking him for any defence he tried to make, sounding not like a daughter.

'She was dying.'

'I had my duty. . .'

'You went away. . .'

'Libya!'

'A beautiful home.'

'I had no choice.'

Tom caught partial phrases as they dropped from the pathway above him. The fragments did not reassemble into a whole. He would have to ask Gosia about it all later, but he was now directly below them and needed to attract their attention.

'Hallo!' he called to them.

Gosia stopped short, angry to have been interrupted. She looked around but could not see him.

'Hallo!' he called again. 'Gosia, I'm here.'

She peered down and when she saw him it was as if she were remembering him. 'Tomek! You are there. Why are you there?' Without waiting for an answer, she ran ahead to where another path let onto the beach, and she waited for him there. She had forgotten her father. Tom looked but the boy with the ball had disappeared.

Later they had supper and Doctor Kamiński retreated sullenly to his office.

'Gosia, why are you so angry with your father?' Tom was recalling the argument on the beach.

'Oh, Tom, I think you cannot understand.' She grasped his hand and rubbed hard at his fingers, each in turn as if doing so could help her choose what to say. 'My father tries to be my mother. He knows that I miss her and he feels guilty.'

'Why should he feel guilty?'

'That is easy to understand, Tomek. My father is a doctor but he could not save his wife. He worked too hard to heal others but was not there to heal her.'

'I am sure it was complicated, Gosia.'

She nodded ruefully as if that word would have to do. 'Tom, in Poland is always complicated. In Martial Law, in that night there were hundreds on streets in Gdańsk, injured people, many injured.' Gosia allowed a tear to run to the end of her chin. 'My father had to go there. I think he did not want to, but it is a doctor's promise, so he went out. Leaving my mother ill, with only me. We have no family in Gdańsk—my father and mother came both from Lwów—and in those times we were not sure of our friends. So I was frightened. He knows this, so he feels guilty also about this. So in this way, he tries to be now like my mother.'

'He seems like a good man, Gosia. And he has provided a beautiful home for you. I don't see many people living this way. Obviously, as a doctor ...'

Gosia interrupted him without actually speaking: it was an instinctive move of the head, a shift in her breathing. The impulse forced a decision to speak. 'Doctors are not paid in Poland as in your country, Thomas. I told you people will pay bribes. You do not need to bribe a person who is already paid well.'

'But surely your father could not earn all of this through receiving bribes?' Tom indicated the marble tiling on the floor, which matched the work surfaces in the kitchen.

'I don't know what is the correct word now. I admit it. Bribe? What exactly this word means in your language, I don't know. My father is a hard worker, for sure, and he is an intelligent man. He does not get *too much* money for this, but we have more than other doctors' families. In those flats we passed today on the tram, those blocks that last eight hundred metres, in those live doctors and professors and dentists and writers and electrics and water engineers—I don't know the words in the dictionary for them all, but they all live in those flats. It is the socialist way. We have no homeless people in Poland. That's good, no?'

'Yes.'

'Of course. What am I saying? Yes, it is good that everyone has a home, and they are equal. But we are not equal because we live in this house. You must be asking this, how can this be? I tell you, Thomas, in one word. Libya!'

Tom's mind flicked involuntarily to Azil with his figs and bananas and Semtex.

'Just as your Witek in the film, Thomas. It is reality. Some people, lucky people, could go one year, two years, to work in Libya. They earned a huge fortune and could bring the money, *hard* money, back to this country. It is all. Can you see?'

'I see that your father did what he could to provide for his family. Are you complaining about that?'

Gosia thought before she spoke. 'Yes, I do complain although I know it is not fair. My mother was healthy when he left us for two years. Then he returned and she was sick. We have not been a proper family for many years. It's true, I complain, and it makes him sad. He thinks he should not have gone to Libya—he should not! Others cannot.'

To Tom, it was as if Gosia were conflating what was fair for her family with what was fair for the country. Was it a failing of her English or of her personal morality? He wanted to tell her to be grateful to the man who clearly loved her, but he understood that no good would come of him insisting on that. 'What do you think he should have done?'

'I wish he had stayed with us, not gone to Libya. We could have been happy living without this furniture. Then he would not have had to go out on the first nights of Martial Law, but stay with Mother and me.' Gosia saw the look of scepticism on Tom's face. 'I know you cannot understand this. You think he had to care for the injured. I can't explain to you everything. He did not want to go. He *had* to while his wife lay dying in a rich man's house.'

Tom was surprised, even appalled, by the line. It was like she had used it before, perfected it after many retellings even in English. And to what end? It did not succeed in drawing his sympathy if that were its purpose. He wanted the subject to change so he would not have to think of her conceitedness.

Gosia also wanted to talk about something different. But for Tom overhearing her at the beach, she would not have made her father's politics a matter for conversation. She doubted her ability to fashion the language, to say nearly the truth but not it all. Tom would be not nearly so sympathetic to her father if he knew the injured he had attended to on those nights were the militia and riot police. After Libya, the Party would never be done demanding the repayment of its favours. As she was discovering now for herself.

'Papa does not like me being in Warsaw. He thinks it is not safe for me there. He takes it as a sort of punishment of him.'

'Punishment for what, Gosia?'

'It is too hard to explain.'

'Is this connected to what you were talking about on the beach?'

Gosia froze.

'Is it connected to your mother?'

Gosia broke into a smile, ill-fitting Tom thought with mention of her dead mother. 'Yes, it is about that,' she said.

'He doesn't mind you being with me?'

Gosia started to answer then checked herself. 'He likes that I have friends. He does not know, I think, that you are my boy, but he likes you because you are sympathetic. He says it is his fault that I am still in Warsaw, that I am there only because of him. It is true, a little.'

'But, Gosia, it is good that you are in Warsaw. You would not know me otherwise.'

'I want to show you Michał,' she announced suddenly, her voice tinkling. Michał was always useful when she wanted to clear her mind of anything important.

'Show me to him, or him to me?' Tom lacked the urge either way, but he could see her determination to put the other conversation behind them. 'Does he live far away?'

Michał lived with his parents in a flat in one of the enormously long blocks they had passed in the tram earlier in the day. Gosia had made Tom wait while she changed her top and reapplied her make-up. Tom wore the same clothes he had all day. He had expected them to walk or perhaps ride the tram, so he was surprised when a taxi pulled up outside the house. Gosia seemed to know the driver or at least she spoke to him in a way that implied she did.

'The elevator stinks,' she complained as they took the lift up to the eighth floor. Tom wondered whether this was an Americanism that Michał had taught her. He met them at the door. He was over six foot tall, in his mid-twenties at least and not at all as Tom had imagined. As he was encouraged to remove his coat and shoes, he noticed that Michał was barefoot and that his toes were long and heavy. A television was blaring in another room, but Michał led them directly to his bedroom. Gosia sat with him on his bed, leaving Tom the chair by himself. This was next to a sideboard with photographs of Michał as a young boy in the scouts, a pennant also with some scout motif and a pair of Russian-Polish dictionaries. It was the room of a tidy teenager.

Tom was happy not to follow their conversation. He wanted Gosia to be able to relax, and he wanted too to have an evening where a discussion did not have to depend on his ability to understand it. The other two joked easily together, recalling mutual friends and incidents they had survived. Gosia's hand rested comfortably on Michał's knee, his arm reached around her shoulders. They listened to music that Gosia chose. Michał did not seem curious to know about this other boy in his room—obviously Gosia had already given some explanation. The sky darkened on the other side of the net curtains, and there was a chill entering via the open window. When Tom spoke, it was rude because it was sudden and in English.

'I am tired,' he said. Gosia pouted in childish disappointment. 'I can walk back alone if you would prefer that.'

Gosia made a comment he did not understand but which made Michał laugh. She did not move immediately, but finally she did push herself away from the Pole.

'Michał thinks you are not polite,' she told him as they walked back. 'Is that what you think?'

'Thomas, don't be absurd!' She dropped the hand she had been holding. 'You were jealous. It was obvious. Michał thought it was funny.'

'I am not jealous, Gosia, although it is clear that's what you want.'

'Why I want you are jealous? Why *do* I want you *to be* jealous? Ah, your crazy language!'

'I don't know, Gosia. Perhaps you want me to fall more deeply for you than I have. You think, perhaps if you show me your good-looking friend, I will be forced to act. To act? I don't even know what I am saying now.'

'You think Michał is good-looking? Maybe he is. He is only my friend.'

'That's not his opinion, Gosia. He thinks he is your boyfriend.'

'Yes, that is true. I am awful to him. I say terrible things, but he tells me he loves me. Not tonight because you were there, but he does tell me that. It is sweet. It is sweet to hear those words from a man, Tomek.'

She wanted him to say it. Regardless of the role she was performing for Staniewicz, she did want Tom to say it. Tom, at that moment, did not feel it or want to say it. He did not even feel that she loved him, just that it would please her to hear it.

'It's OK,' she offered with a smile. 'I know what is in your heart.'

Tom doubted that she did, but if it were a lie, he was happy just then to accept it.

Back at the house, the doctor had prepared Tom's bed in a spare room. Gosia gently blocked his way into her room. 'We could be quiet,' he said.

'My father does not care,' she said. 'He knows I am a woman. But you are right about Michał. I must be honest with him before I can be with you to the end, completely. You are right.'

'I don't want to be right! You can let me in tonight and tell him tomorrow.'

Gosia treated that as a joke and closed the door on him.

Paszyńska had set Tom an essay on the Polish *economic miracle* of the 1970s. 'No doubt, Mr Day, you will find reasons to dismiss our government's achievements,' she had said. Tom wondered whether this was exactly what his lecturer was hoping for. She had suggested a number of authors—all Polish and all on the approved list. But when Tom bravely presented his chit to the SGPiS librarian, he was told that none of them was there. In fact, she had used a more comprehensive phrase than that. They did not *exist*.

The same thing happened to Aleks the following day when he requested books on the trade relationships within Comecon. They also did not exist, apart from the textbook he had already and which his lecturers dutifully taught from. 'They're taking our books away, Tommy boy,' he said. Indeed, over the following few days, several other students made the same observation. When their teachers became aware of their new reality, they on the whole refrained from setting any wider reading. Aleks kept a log of all the texts he learned had been stripped from the shelves: anything to do with 1968 or any of the other post-war flashpoints, treatises on Poland's economic ties with the Soviet Union, texts on the state of infrastructure in the Communist bloc. 'We are an economics college. If they take these books away from us, what is there for us to read?' Aleks protested. The librarians, used to being the dominant partner in their exchanges with students, shrugged and closed the hatch.

Pepliński's lessons were cancelled again. A polite notice on his door, written on his behalf, explained that he was ill. Norbert claimed to have seen him in the college coffee bar. 'He looked like shit. For a change.' Norbert himself had received notification that he must make an appointment to see the dean of students. As a fourth year student, he was obliged to attend the military studies course. If he missed more than three lessons, he could not pass the course, and the military instructor's mark was a condition of graduation. Had he missed many, Tom asked. 'All of them. Fuck it.' Aleks set to work scrounging appropriate clothes for his friend to wear at the meeting with the dean, which would take place at the start of the final semester.

Aleks tapped a new secret source of paper and set the printer to run on all-night production with a supervisory rota comprising himself, Tom, and Norbert. For his shift Tom had had to send Gosia home. On Aleks' insistence, Gosia was not to know about the newspaper. 'It is more than a matter of trust, Tommy,' he had explained to his offended friend. 'If the powielacz is discovered, the names of everyone connected with it are bound to come out. You are protected because you're foreign.

Norbert no longer cares and I . . . well, I am a hero.' Aleks wrote about the disappearing books. He also printed news of the repression of NZS members in Lublin, and the sudden appearance—first in Wrocław then in Poznań, Bydgoszcz and Toruń—of mysterious graffiti, depicting dwarves in many forms and sizes. They were calling this the Orange Alternative. Reading the white spaces—the so-called *białe plamy*—in the official press, Aleks detected more mentions of comments coming from the Kremlin in relation to social unrest in Polish cities. Already in Warsaw students had noticed a heavier militia presence, including on university and college property. Agata and Wioletta told them that police were harassing clubbers outside *Hades;* this also found its way into their newspaper. Aleks advertised NZS events, a public meeting in support of academic freedom, a petition for formal recognition of the union's independence, a one-night performance at Warsaw University of Adam Mickiewicz's verse play *Forefather's Eve,* the first such production anywhere in the country since the play was banned exactly twenty years before.

Gosia called in to Dom Studenta most evenings. She was by now quite friendly also with Wioletta and Agata, so Tom sometimes found her in their room. Once she was there also with Kinga. He had to stop himself again from using any of the unpasteurised language Norbert had taught him to describe beautiful girls. Someone asked Wioletta to play her guitar; Piotr sang some songs from his scouting days, and Gosia joined in when she realised she knew the words. Another girl took the guitar and strummed more aggressively, playing in songs which were more plaintive. Kinga, it transpired, had a voice to match her face. Tom enjoyed listening despite not understanding very much. Agata told him they were metaphors. 'It's not good to say what's in your heart,' she told him. Tom and Gosia kissed, but he could not seem to find time alone with her. She left before ten o'clock. There were many days like this in March.

Jakub drove his baby Fiat up from Kutno, not to see Aleks, but because he had business with Piotr. Piotr had just days before returned from Frankfurt, driving another cream-coloured Mercedes, the boot of which was stuffed with goods more easily purchased in Germany. He had a case of Nudossi hazelnut spread, two trays of Rondo coffee, and six pairs (various sizes, all black) of Zeha sports shoes. 'Like Adidas,'

Piotr claimed to Tom, who decided to buy a pair to replace his own worn-out trainers. In the boot were also hidden three cameras, all of the Praktica make. Piotr was hopeful of selling these at the Russian market at the stadium. Jakub was most interested, however, in the cheap Rotkaeppchen wine which Piotr had smuggled back. He bought one crate for the wedding party, which had now been put off until the summer and another crate which he intended to sell on to make money to pay for the wedding. Piotr, flush with cash, offered to buy some more of Tom's pounds at seven times the bank rate.

'I take some of your new złoty after the match,' Piotr wagered. Poland was playing Northern Ireland in a friendly in Belfast, and it was showing in the TV room in the student hostel. Piotr explained that, due to Tom, there was more than usual interest in the game, and Piotr intended to take some bets. Piotr was pessimistic about his own team's chances. 'Polska is too old,' he moaned. 'Lato, gone. Boniek, he's finished.'

The football had begun by the time Piotr and Tom found their way to the floor at the front of the TV room. Within seconds the Northern Irish was a goal up. Tom stood up to cheer, and the others in the room swore at him and threw at him anything they had to hand. There were nearly as many in the room as there were watching the match in the stadium. Tom's favourite, Whiteside, was having a good game as was the youngster O'Neill. They seemed in control of the game until, about half an hour in, Boniek played the ball forward to Dziekanowski who hit it low and hard into the bottom left corner of the Irish goal. The room lifted in a united cheer apart from Tom who stayed where he was on the floor and received more abuse. After the half-time break, both sides used all of their substitutes, but the score remained the same. Bingham and Lazarek shook hands, each manager satisfied with not losing. Piotr was even happier, having to pay out to no one who had predicted their side's victory. The game was over, the news came on, the sound was muted, and most people in the room left to return to their rooms. So it was only then that Tom noticed that Kinga was sitting there still astounding him with her beauty.

'Hallo, Irlandczyku!' she beckoned, and he came to her. Beside her, though Tom barely saw him, was another student, older than the others—blond, wearing denim, and tall even when sitting down. 'Here is Dariusz.'

The men shook hands. 'We've met before,' said Tom, uttering the words before the memory was fully formed. '*Hades* in September, I think. You were absolutely drunk.'

'Yes, I would have been,' said the other. 'Sorry I don't remember.'

'He was with Gosia!' Kinga shouted in his ear, delighted as a sheepdog to have all her animals gathered.

Just then, Tom realised exactly who the other man was. He was Dariusz Michalski, the leader of the NZS in the Red Fortress. 'You know my friend, Aleks. You have a bed in our room. We call you *Nikt*.' Looking at the man now, Tom was baffled he had not noticed him in the room before. He seemed fabricated for the purpose of being looked at. Nobody was the wrong name for him.

'Yes, Cybulski. Sorry . . .' He craned his neck to see past Tom to the television set, where the news was still on. Two men, each in different uniforms, were shaking hands in front of an enormous desk. The desk appeared weighed down by some sort of bronze bird, so highly polished it reflected the flashes from the cameras from the rank of photographers.

'Something important happening?' Tom asked.

'Too early to say,' replied Darek. 'That is Polish Interior Minister Czesław Kiszczak. And the man whose hand he is so vigorously shaking is Soviet Defence Minister Dmitry Yazov.'

'Polish and Soviet officials get together all of the time, I am sure. But why would an interior minister be meeting a defence minister?'

'That, Tomasz, is the right question. Why indeed? And why have they chosen to let the people know about this one?'

'That's not Poland,' Kinga interjected. 'That's the Russian bird on the table. See, has two heads.'

'There are protests on the streets already,' Tom offered his analysis, remembering what Spiro had said. 'The government looks weak because of the price rises. They have arrested people, but that hasn't stopped the unrest and the strange graffiti. This is the Russians applying pressure by summoning the security people to the Kremlin.'

'It's more, Tomasz. It's a threat.' Michalski placed his hand on Kinga's knee, kissed her full on her lips, and stood up to leave. 'See you around, Tomasz.' Then he was gone. A minute passed before either Kinga or Tom could decide what to do.

'Kinga,' Tom asked, 'did you ever speak to Dariusz about me?'

'No, Tomek. Why I do that?'

'No reason. But he knew my name, that's all. Perhaps Aleks told him.'

'You have right, it must to be Aleks.' Kinga was satisfied with that until another thought occurred to her. 'Or Gosia?'

To Kinga and to Tom the thought both unnerved them and made sense.

———⌣———

Tom wore his white shirt and decided also to borrow a tie from Piotr. Aleks met his mother at the station and took a taxi from there. Pani Bańda, too excited by the prospect of again seeing the star actor Holoubek on stage to eat a full meal with her family, had a sandwich instead. Professor Pepliński looked through some old photographs with his wife before deciding finally that yes, he would go. Thomson, acting on a tip-off from Staniewicz, turned up with a cameraman and established a position outside the Warsaw University Theatre. He understood that the words, *Dziady Cz. III*, written on the posters outside the theatre—and normally translated to English as *Forefather's Eve Part III*—had not been allowed in public since the last time the play was performed in the National Theatre twenty years before. Now, like then, was a tense moment in which to stage a play with an explicit anti-Russian sentiment—Thomson formed the words in his head that he later planned to say to camera.

Inside the theatre was already dark, the stage and backdrop painted all black. Magda took her seat between her son and her son's friend. Pepliński sat at the back, hardly inside the auditorium at all, with a view of all below him—his students, students of other teachers, others like him who had seen the same play when last it was staged. Bańda, a cultured woman, sat at the front as she always liked to, four rows in front of her amusing Irish student. The NZS organisers had sold many more tickets than there were seats, but no one minded as young people occupied the steps in the aisles between and at the sides of the paid-for seating.

There is no curtain. A single spotlight silences the audience, illuminating the ghostly features of Gustaw and his guardian angel, a coarse blanket on the floor the only marker that this is a Russian cell and Gustaw is its prisoner. He sleeps, he awakens. His angel and company of spirits speak to him, he shall be free!

> 'I shall be free—yes, and full well I know
> The sort of grace the Muscovite will show,
> Striking the fetters from my feet and hands
> To rivet on my spirit heavier bands!'

He sleeps, he awakens. He rises and on one side with a piece of coal, he writes

D. O. M.

GUSTAVUS

OBIIT M. D. CCC. XXIII. CALENDIS NOVEMBRIS.

Then on the other side with the same coal, he writes

HIC NATUS EST

CONRADUS

M. D. CCC. XXIII. CALENDIS NOVEMBRIS.

Gustaw-now-Konrad leans against the window (a lighting effect only). He sleeps. A spirit—really a young student from a village outside Warsaw—speaks as if directly to the audience.

> 'O man, didst thou but know how great thy power!
> One thought of thine, like hidden lightning flashing,
> Through gathered clouds can send the thunder crashing
> In wasteful storm or pour down fruitful shower.'

They, even those who don't know that this speech ends the prologue, cheer in a collective release. Wilt thou plunge down to hell or rise divine?

The cheering subsides when the lighting picks out prison guards standing at the back wall of the stage, drinking in threes like present-day militia. By theatrical convention, they do not see the group of student prisoners out of their cells, singing, arguing and drinking by candlelight.

138

They gather in Konrad's cell as it is the largest. Despite the tsarist *ukaz*, which has seen hundreds of arrests in Wilno, schools shut and students denied either the right to complete their studies or to be publically employed, Zegota naively believes the Russians can be paid off, that they will not be sent to Siberia without charge. 'But we are innocent.' Others are more worldly-wise. Tomasz knows that Senator Novosiltsov, to re-establish his favour with the tsar, will find a Polish plot among the Literary Society at Wilno University. One last unhappy course remains for us: to choose some few men for the sacrifice, who'll take upon themselves the blame for all. I was the leader of your comradeship so it's my place to suffer for my friends. Choose out some brothers who will go with me.

The younger members of the audience cautiously applaud, not sure of the rules, but soon their applause gathers the support of others, the older people, those who knew better, and the whole audience is in an uproar of consent. His fellow prisoners mock Tomasz for liking the discomforts of his cell too well. He prefers significant martyrdom to meaningless freedom. One of their number was in the city today. He saw the *kibitkas* carrying scores of youngsters off to Siberia. One youth caught his eye, too weak to carry even his own chains yet bravely smiling and waving to the crowd. 'Poland has not perished yet!' Someone in the audience strikes up a verse of the national anthem, and the actors on the stage and the people in the audience are now players in the one production. The young man (the actor playing Konrad) must command their attention again. He is singing blasphemously 'like Satan' losing his mind, pledging revenge upon the Muscovite.

'Then vengeance, vengeance on the foe, God upon our side or no!'

A bell rings (or is it the siren of the militia?) and the guards are at the gate, there to restore order in the theatre. The scene is ended. The audience stand to applaud and some leave the auditorium for the interval.

Tom stands with Magda and Aleks at one side of the foyer. He sees pani Bańda at the bar chatting to old friends. Pepliński is near the door, apparently contemplating an early departure. Through the glass in the door, Tom can see another man wearing a pale-grey winter coat. The man looks familiar to him, but he cannot remember from where.

'Professor Pepliński says he knew you back in 1968,' Tom began. 'Or he knew of you.'

Magda seemed surprised, perhaps flattered. 'No. But he would have known Zygmunt Schaff. Schaff was a great philologist. I was his post-grad student. Pepliński may have taken classes with him. I know that many would turn up for his lectures, even those not officially enrolled in his courses. He was Jewish, of course, a survivor of the Holocaust and a critic of totalitarianism. Students would analyse his lectures for their implied condemnation of the government. He employed me—informally, I was not paid. It was more of an internship—to type up his lectures and to distribute them wherever I could. They were never anonymous. His name was always at the top and the bottom of the pages. It was his way of defying the censorship. When *Dziady* was banned in January '68, students and intellectuals protested against the censor. There were police beatings on university campuses in Warsaw and all across Poland. By March, elements within the Party had reacted to the protests by launching their own campaign of anti-Semitism.'

'Moczar.' Tom recalled his talk with Pepliński.

'Yes. Jews were removed from their teaching posts. Their books were removed from the libraries. For Schaff, it was like the Nazis had returned. He was old, he had no fight left, so he accepted the invitation to go into exile.'

'Like my Polish teacher in Belfast, Janina Błońska.'

'There were many, perhaps thousands, Tom. Schaff went to Israel where it was impossible for us to remain in contact. I suppose he is no longer alive.'

'But you, Mom, kept his work going.' Aleks had been standing quietly, proudly, to one side. 'You kept typing his work.'

'I had his key. His office was filled with his old notes, everything he had ever committed to paper, it seemed. I selected some things—I could not do it all—and typed them, as before, with his name. I dropped copies in student bars, cafés near the university, academic common rooms. No one knew it was me—or perhaps a few did because eventually I was arrested. I was a strange thing for them. Bogdan had already been removed from his lectureship and was in the factory in Kutno. Little Kuba was with me, alone in Warsaw, and I was pregnant with Aleks. I could have gone to the West—it was suggested. Instead, I could work as a cleaner in the hospital in Kutno. Good enough for a Jew-loving intellectual is what they thought, and I agreed with them. It was an easy choice.' She found her son's hand behind her, knowing where it would be and gave it a gentle squeeze.

'So,' she continued, 'when Aleks told me that they were restaging *Dziady* here twenty years on, I did have to be here.'

'Me too,' agreed Tom. He wanted to be able to tell Janina Shaw and Martin Carter that he stood where they had. 'But I think there will be trouble tonight after the show. I have just realised who that man is outside.' He pointed to the journalist, who could now be seen with his cameraman. 'It's Sebastian Thomson. He is the man that Bogdan translated for in Kutno. If he is here, it is because he expects something will happen.'

'OK,' Magda said simply. It was like a resignation. It also permitted Aleks to leave. 'Let's go in, Tomek.'

Aleks' seat remained empty for the second part of the production. As before, Konrad is in his cell in the centre of the stage in a state of delirium. This is his Great Improvisation. The young actor, willed on by the audience, is giving the performance of his life. The actor- Konrad compares his own acts of creation—his verse—with those of God. Is God truly so great? This is the God who allows Poland to suffer—like his Son on the Cross—dismembered by foreign invaders. The audience is hushed, aware that this is their great poem, that the boy on the stage, not the Father, is their hope. The monologue is over. Angels and demons battle for the young man's soul. Eva and Marcellina pray for him. Then Gustaw Holoubek is seen at the front of the stage. He is two metres from pani Bańda. He was Konrad when she last saw him, old then for the role of a student but perfect in his integrity. Now he is Father Peter, having his own vision of the person who will restore Poland's freedom. The Son of a foreign mother, in his blood old heroes/ And his name will be forty and four.

The audience, schooled in their nation's literature, know this to mean Adam—Adam Mickiewicz, the great national poet himself. They have been waiting for Holoubek to deliver this line, they have the sound of it already in their own heads, and they applaud with relief that the verse drama has arrived at this point. It is nearly over. Konrad has recovered, knowing that his crucified country will be resurrected. It ends. Bańda stands, and Magda stands and the whole audience stands, those in the seats and those on the steps. Peter and Konrad, Tomasz and Zegota, the devils and angels, the students and their prison guards all stand and take their bow. Some feel that Gustaw Holoubek, in his priest garb, ought to address them as himself, but the lights have dimmed on the stage and come up instead on the auditorium like for an instant the crowd is the hero. People look around them, searching for familiar faces or for a sign of what to do next. Pepliński, being nearest the door, is consequently the first to leave, so the crowd follow after him. He leads them, by chance, on to the street in front of the university theatre, and he has a decision to make. Possibly the followers make it for him. He turns right towards the Mickiewicz monument. There is a small gathering there already, made up of people who could not get into the theatre and others who saw a crowd and joined it. The ZOMO riot police are there too, waiting for the switch moment when they can call a theatrical audience an illegal gathering. Sebastian Thomson arrives in a rush, trailed by his cameraman. Aleks too is there with his camera, moving to remain on the fringe of the crowd. Tom, not yet arrived, feels the need to protect Magda although she is the experienced one. Ahead of them a student has scaled the monument with an NZS banner. Tom recognises Dariusz Michalski. Perhaps that is the moment. Or it happens when a girl starts up a chant that others repeat. The group already at the monument is met by the crowd led by Pepliński. He is standing taller now, more sure of his place. The ZOMO are nervous: they have their orders, but they first need a moment. The student on the monument, the girl chanting, the old man directing the mob. A stone is thrown; it is not clear from which side. But the police, like organised beetles, charge with their shields before their helmets and their batons raised, looking for soft heads to crush. Immediately there are screams, cries of shock and panic. They are like appeals to witnesses, but all the streets—the boulevard which is Krakowskie Przedmieście, the square in front of the Royal Castle, the roads leading down to the river and up to the parade ground—are at once deserted, the only people in the city the ones in uniform and those in the crowd. Out of the chaos a ring of students surrounds the base of the monument to protect either the poet in bronze or the protesters hanging off him. Some older citizens seek sanctuary on the pavement, off the cobble, but they have left some of their comrades behind. They can see them, caught up among the flying fists and striking police sticks, picked out by the white spotlights atop the ZOMO vans. A young man has loosened a cobble from near a storm drain, has weighed it in his hand, and has hurled it at the line of police. He is quickly joined by others, who hack at the ground with their heels and chuck the stones over the heads of their friends. Tom now feels Magda fragile beside him, so he crouches over her. His ear stings and he ducks reflexively. There is a crack like a can on a kitchen top, followed by a rushing sound like a kettle about to whistle. Tom knows what this is. Still ducking, he checks that it is Magda's hand that he has in his, and he pulls her to where his instinct tells him there is safety. The teargas, indiscriminate, disperses many of those who are still on their feet and strips the monument of those still clinging to it. The ZOMO themselves (in protective masks) drag away the bodies on the ground. They open the backs of their vans to those they have selected for arrest, some like war casualties still draped in the banners they had brought. Thomson is reporting urgently down the lens to viewers of the BBC. Magda is applying her handkerchief to the gash above Tom's ear; it is so bloody, she already needs another. She looks out for her youngest son and sees him, the width of the boulevard away, near to the ZOMO vans, protected apparently by the camera flashing in front of his face. He has pictures of girls, their faces stilled in a rictus of fear, and pictures of bewildered well-dressed veterans. And he has one photograph, safe inside his Praktica camera, of Professor Pepliński in handcuffs and under arrest.

EWA 1999

EWA HAD A HEADACHE. HER REPORT ON DARIUSZ Michalski's *lustracja* declaration sat on her screen, dwelling mainly on his UK tax returns and how he came by his millions. She hardly saw this as news at all, and she was beginning to think that Aleks Cybulski, her boss at the paper, had put her on to the story as a way of sidelining her. On the other hand, the inside pages of rival newspapers had their own stories on Michalski, and they all seemed to agree on one thing: there were only two viable candidates to replace the sitting president in the palace at Belvedere. One was the tabloid press baron and former Communist Party propaganda chief Jacek Mazur, the other was Dariusz Michalski. So if she was going to make something more of it—if she was going to prove her worth to Cybulski—she had until that evening to do it. Because that evening the candidate Michalski was holding a New Years' Eve party which she was expected to attend. And she had a headache.

She pulled open the file from the Public Interest Spokesperson. There were the anodyne entries covering the candidate's biography—his birth in 1963 in Ostrów Mazowiecka to Urszula and Adam, both described as agricultural workers, his school education, during which he won the regional Olympiad for English. His politicisation at SGPiS is unexplained; he was suspended on two occasions by Vice-Rector Marcin Wilk before the final strike in May 1988, each time because of his unorthodox way of challenging the rules. In 1987 officials in the Interior Ministry (specifically Stanisław Staniewicz) took the decision

144

to gather closer intelligence on him. They recruited the tourism student from Gdańsk, Małgorzata Kamińska, as an informant. There are several short entries on the file in her name and two longer—evidently embellished—reports from her course director Dudek. (Staniewicz has scribbled in the margins of these latter reports to the effect that he holds little store by them.) Kamińska describes her befriending and attempted entrapment of Thomas Day, who was at that time on a study placement there from his university in Belfast. In her reports from September to Christmas 1987, she writes that Day 'knows nothing', or has 'no contact yet' with the target; his closest friendship is with Aleksander Cybulski from Kutno. On him, she comments 'He does not trust me' and 'He leaves the room when I come in'. There is a notable change in her mood from about February 1988. Thomas Day is becoming more closely attached to her, and he is engaging more directly with political agitation. He is treated for a minor injury after he becomes embroiled in the riot following the student production of *Forefather's Eve* in March. Dariusz Michalski then moves into the dormitory of Day and Cybulski. (Someone, perhaps Staniewicz, doodles here 'as expected'.) Kamińska subsequently has frequent engagement with the target and his girlfriend Kinga Andrzejewska, and her reporting becomes more detailed. Michalski is revered by his fellow students; he joins in anti-Party songs in the hostel (named here as Dom Studenta, in the vicinity of SGPiS); there are prolonged periods of unannounced absence. He boasts about missing compulsory classes. He attempts to represent his roommate Norbert N in his appeal against dismissal from the university for failing to attend military studies classes. Most of this is reported to her by Thomas Day. In the lead up to the May strike, Kamińska is present as Michalski, Cybulski, and other student agitators prepare for the occupation. 'DM is the unquestioned leader. He gives everyone a role (AC is chief propagandist). He speaks about 'Warsaw' and 'Gdańsk' referring to the contacts he has with the wider NZS leadership. His mood is almost always optimistic.' Reading between the lines, it is obvious that Staniewicz is pressuring her to sleep with Thomas Day as a way of ensuring her continued access. She is not happy about it, saying she didn't agree to be an informant so she could be a prostitute. That must have taken guts. Anyway, the upshot is for the week of the occupation, Kamińska is shut out—she files no reports for that period.

She makes one brief, final entry: 'Liaised, as instructed, with Michalski at Europejski Hotel. Duties discharged.' There is only one further note on the file made by Staniewicz of the Interior to the effect of Michalski accepting voluntary exile in West Germany. Ewa knew that, within months of these events, the Polish government had entered into the round-table talks that would rapidly see them democratically ousted from office.

As far as she could tell, the only unusual aspect to Michalski's file was that he appeared to have been monitored indirectly via the pillow talk of the Irishman, Day. Ewa made a list of the threads she wanted to follow up:

Małgorzata Kamińska—did she return to Gdańsk? Did she continue to inform on others?

Thomas Day—what is known about him after May?

Kinga Andrzejewska—is she available for a quote on the candidate?

Staniewicz—dead?

Marcin Wilk—dead?

She herself would call the women; there was no time to interview them in person. She would give Janusz—the intern—the dead-end job of tracking down Staniewicz and Wilk. She put her pen through Thomas Day: no likely further interest there.

'Hello. Is that Mr Kamiński? This is Ewa Kowalska from *Wyborcza*.'

'Dr Kamiński. The press again!'

'Yes, I am sorry, Dr Kamiński.' Ewa noted that she was clearly not the first to speak to them. 'I am trying to get in touch with Małgorzata Kamińska—your daughter, I presume? There is much interest now in Dariusz Michalski naturally, so we just wanted to hear what your daughter remembers about him. They were friends, I think?'

'I don't believe they were friends, no. I don't recall her ever mentioning him. There was one young man she brought to my home here, the Irishman, but that's all as far as I remember. I am sorry I cannot help you more.'

'No, Dr Kamiński, that's very kind. I wonder, can I speak to your daughter?'

There was a long silence at the other end of the line. Kamiński seemed to be struggling for breath. 'The other newspaperman knows already. You people should check these things before bothering old people like me. Gosia is dead. It's just me and my grandson now. The Irishman never came again.'

The emotion that Ewa detected from him was anger rather than grief. Perhaps, as a doctor, he could detach himself even when the loss was his own. He described, quite clinically, the circumstances of her death.

'I am dreadfully sorry, Dr Kamiński. I wasn't told that your daughter had died, or that she had a son.'

'Miss Kowalska, I must insist that you do not write about this in your newspaper. It would be too upsetting for her son.'

'You have my word.' She was certain the Mazur press would salivate over this story once they got hold of it. 'Your grandson must miss his mother terribly.'

'It happened so long ago, Miss Kowalska. He never knew his mother. It has only ever been Marek and me. It is enough for him that I now have to explain to him that his mother was a spy.'

Ewa put the phone down. She left her desk and went to the toilet. She looked long and hard at the face in the mirror. Her features, untouched that day by make-up, appeared harsh to her. The LCD lighting gave her a mortuary pallor, her lips too thin for a woman of her age. She opened her bag for her lipstick and blusher and applied her new face.

Janusz was waiting for her at her desk. 'Bad news, Ewka.'

'Don't call me that. What bad news?'

'Your man, Marcin Wilk.'

'What about him?'

'Not dead, I am afraid. So I hear. You are going to have to trace him yourself.'

'Can't you do it?'

'Not if you want me to dig up Staniewicz. Now, he *is* dead. But I am told there are certain files I can access if I turn up at the right place.'

'Okay, you do that.' Ewa was just a little jealous that her junior colleague might be following the more interesting lead. 'But don't fuck it up.'

'Will do my best not to, Ewka.'

'And when you get back, I will get Cybulski to fire you.'

Kinga Andrzejewska was living in Düsseldorf, Germany, the CEO of a medium-sized technology company. She was delighted to talk to *Wyborcza* about ex-patriot Poles making their way in the new Europe.

'I employ more than forty people here,' she explained. 'Germans, Turks, a few Poles. Günter, my partner, is the chief engineer. I run the business side of things.' Then because she thought that perhaps the journalist calling her from Warsaw might want her to say it, 'It would be better if Poland were a member of the European Union. I could employ more Poles here, and more easily export back to my own country some of the technology we make here.'

Ewa had several channels she could now pursue. She chose to proceed cautiously. 'Your degree from SGPiS must have helped you when you set up your business, Miss Andrzejewska?'

There was a loud chuckle down the line from Düsseldorf. 'Degree! I never got one of those. Politics got in the way of my education, Miss Kowalska, from the beginning right through to the end. When I started my economics programme at SGPiS, we were taught according to standard Marxist orthodoxy. You could tell the teachers' hearts were not in it, but they had no real choice. Then when communism collapsed in Poland in summer 1989, the whole underlying ideology of our course collapsed with it. There was no value in continuing with it. Shortly thereafter, a West German consultancy firm moved into Warsaw and snapped up bright young students like me. Within months I was working in Cologne, in a united Germany. I have never gone back.'

'That is an inspirational story, Miss Andrzejewska.' Ewa remembered the pretext of her call. 'Might you set up a business in your own country, should we ever join the EU?'

'Well, that all depends on there being the right political climate there.'

Ewa decided to press. 'Indeed, Miss Andrzejewska. Can I ask, do you still have the right to vote here? You will be aware, I imagine, that there is one candidate in particular—Dariusz Michalski—who wants to push ahead with EU accession talks.'

Germany laughed again. 'I was beginning to wonder, Miss Kowalska, when you would get around to asking me about Darek. What do you want to know? I am afraid I will disappoint you if it is scandal you are after.'

Kinga gave her account, which tallied with everyone else's so far. Michalski was intelligent, handsome, much-admired. 'I know that he came in for some criticism for ending the occupation strike when he did—saying he had bottled it. For me, it was the reverse. It took considerable courage on his part to call it off, to stop the violence before more people got hurt. That is leadership, Miss Kowalska, don't you agree? And it was prescient too. Within a few short months, Solidarity was talking to the Party, and the whole regime disintegrated. I loved him—we all loved him. Apart, obviously, from Gosia.'

'Małgorzata Kamińska?'

'She was spying on him all along, so the papers say. I am afraid, she rather took me in. I don't believe the boys ever trusted her—besides Tom—but I quite liked her at first before I knew what she was up to. I suppose that is all in his file.'

'Yes. And I spoke to her father this morning.' Ewa dropped her professional guard for just a moment. 'I must say, I feel rather sorry for him, alone with his grandson.'

'Dr Kamiński worked for the Party. He administered to the ZOMO and militia during Martial Law. I don't think he needs your sympathy.' There was a pause on the line. 'You say he has a grandson?'

'Yes, after his daughter died, it was just the two of them. The boy must have been very small.'

'I . . . That's . . . But . . .' Kinga made several attempts to begin her sentence.

'You did not know?'

'That's not what I understood at all. Gosia called me—it must have been July or August, just a few months after the strike after Tom had been sent back to Ireland and Darek had disappeared—and she told me she was leaving. She had a chance to leave Poland. She had a friend in Norway. She sounded happy. I was angry with her because it seemed so sudden, and she had seemed so in love with Tom. She told me she did love him, but after all that had happened in Warsaw, she could not bear to stay. She begged me to be happy for her, so I said I was. In a way, I was. That was the very last I heard from her. Tom wrote to me—he could get nothing from Gosia—so I told him that. I thought it was the truth. And all along, he had a son he knew nothing about! It is a tragedy, Miss Kowalska.'

'I told the Doctor I would not write about it. *Wyborcza* is not interested in publishing this kind of thing although I have no doubt the Mazur press would love to get their hands on it.'

'They mustn't know! You must bury this as deeply as you can! That poor boy.'

'That won't be easy, Kinga,' Ewa warned, deliberately switching to use her interviewee's forename. This was the reason she had not chosen Janusz to make the call. 'Michalski has placed himself—and therefore his past—at the centre of public attention. The *lustracja* law obliges all public figures to make a full disclosure.'

'I am not a fool, Miss Kowalska. I know what the law says. But this is not Darek's past. Besides being spied upon by her, he had no connections at all with Gosia. If the public must know about her and her son, then surely it will be Thomas they will want to hear from, not Darek.' In the pause that followed, Ewa could hear Kinga open a bag. 'Do you intend to contact Thomas? I don't seem to have an address or number for him any longer. It has been more than eleven years, after all. But you are aware, I suppose, that he works for the BBC? The *World Service*—well-known, I understand, although I never listen.'

When she hung up on Andrzejewska, Ewa put a request into the paper's digital team to make an online search for a Thomas Day at the BBC in London. There was no sign yet of Janusz's return with information on Staniewicz. She wanted a coffee but she did not fancy making it for herself. Cybulski had not been seen emerging from his office since she had called in on him that morning. The newsroom was busy chasing down stories on Yeltsin's resignation in Moscow and Putin's elevation. At best, she had a tabloid tale of the candidate, the Mata Hari and the fatherless boy. It was not a story she had the stomach for. At least if the Staniewicz line did throw up anything of interest, it was unlikely to be salacious. What of Marcin Wilk, the vice-rector whose office Michalski and others had occupied—what more could he know that the file did not?

Wilk was not so easy to track down despite his unusual surname. SGPiS had a last-known address which they were unwilling to release to her. They found unconvincing her plea that she was trying to trace her favourite teachers. The best promise she could extract from the secretariat was that someone would call a number, tell whoever answered that Ewa was wishing to contact them, then leave it up to them to call the paper. Ewa hung up, sure she was at a dead end. Within minutes her phone rang. It was a woman—Wilk's daughter. The old vice-rector was in hospital as he had been on and off for about four years, his lung condition compounded by mounting forgetfulness. The daughter did not mind if the journalist paid him a visit ('He is impossible to upset.') and so gave details of his ward.

Ewa was surprised to find the hospital looking like one of those modern palaces she saw on American television, and certainly she did not imagine she would find Wilk in a private room. But there he was sitting up in bed with an attractive nurse feeding some runny pudding to him.

'Ah, Miss Kowalska!' He nearly spat. 'I have been expecting you.' He ran his hand over the back of his head to flatten his hair. The nurse left him with an instruction not to be too long without his respirator.

Ewa pulled a chair around from the foot of the bed to be closer to him. She felt strange at the immediate intimacy this suggested. She had not sat like this since she had nursed her own father. 'Mr Wilk . . . may I call you that?'

'I would prefer professor, but I forget that myself sometimes so I will forgive you if you occasionally slip into informality. I will, however, call you Ewa.'

Ewa nodded that she was fine with that. 'Professor Wilk, I know you grow tired and that you will need your oxygen again soon, so I will get straight to it. Perhaps your daughter mentioned that I was writing about the historic strike that affected SGPiS in May 1988?'

'She did.' Wilk noticed a drop of pudding on his lower lip. He licked it off with such relish, Ewa had to look away. 'Although she did not describe it as historic, as you just did. There were many such strikes that spring and summer. There was nothing especially unique about ours.'

'Except that it was nearly unprecedented at SGPiS—the Red Fortress.'

'That label was an exaggeration, at least by the mid-1980s. By then, there were simply fewer Party children willing to associate with the regime. I was not at all surprised when the strike began.'

'Because you were informed?' Ewa was careful to make this a question, but Wilk did not readily reply. 'Were you receiving intelligence on the underground activities of your students?'

'Let me see.' Wilk rolled his eyes ceiling-ward as if to recover his memories from there. Then his eyes seemed to forget what they were doing there and closed in an instant slumber. Ewa was exasperated, just as she had been when her father slipped into stupidity. She nudged him forcefully until his eyes unblinked. 'Yes!'

'Yes? Yes, what?'

'In answer to your question, Ewa, I did receive some intelligence.' He chuckled, apparently at the word. 'That Cybulski—your boss, I realise now—was printing propaganda was no secret although we never found his press until much later. Useless piece of shit he is. But you are not really interested in what I think of him, are you?'

'No. But he is not a piece of shit, Professor Wilk.' She waited until she detected a nod of apology from him. 'What do you remember about Dariusz Michalski?'

'That man never thanked me, you know? Twice I suspended him when I could have thrown him out on his ear, and twice I let him pick up his studies where he had left off. Not a card or a bottle of vodka, nothing at all. I used to get such a lot of gifts, Ewa, you would not believe. My wife reckoned it was the only thing that made being married to me worthwhile.' Wilk settled back into his pillows as if he had concluded proceedings. Then just as unpredictably, he sat forward again. 'I rather liked him. I did, somewhat, the more independent ones. He was clever, amusing, quite humble. Out of his depth, obviously, with the strike business. You see, he was seriously out of step with his own side.'

'How do you mean? The students remained loyal to him till the end, I have heard.'

'The students, yes—what would they know? They just did as Michalski instructed. He told them to demonstrate: they demonstrated. They went on strike when he wanted them to and walked out when he called it off. He absolutely had a hold over them, just as you can see now with some people he wants to vote for him. I might vote for him myself!' Wilk laughed so hard at his own irony, he needed to fit his oxygen mask to regain his breath.

Ewa took a moment to entertain and then dismiss the thought. Surely the ex-Communist Mazur could rely on the vote of the former Party man? There was something else interesting in what Wilk had just said. 'Why do you say he was out of step?'

'The student strike was an embarrassment more to Solidarity than it was to the government.' Wilk stated it as an incontestable fact. He said some more in the same vein, about the pressure he was certain Michalski was under to end the protest, about the predictability of the SB storming the building, about how—in the end—Michalski had done the right thing to prevent further violence.

'Cybulski's reports from that time do not give the impression that the SB attack on the student occupation was predicted.' Ewa flicked furiously through her notepad for a line she half-remembered. She found it. '"The mood among the students was upbeat. They were sure that, with Michalski negotiating with the rector, an announcement at least on official registration of the NZS was imminent." That, to me, does not sound like they were expecting defeat.'

'Those are the words of your boss, Miss Kowalska. That does not make them the truth.' Wilk shut his eyes again, painfully suppressing a spasm in his lungs. Ewa had more questions, but it was clear that Wilk would be giving no more answers. The nurse returned and wordlessly held the door open for Ewa to leave.

'You all had better hope that Mazur does not get in!' Wilk called after her with almost his last breath. 'The first thing he will do is blow the doors off the archives, the secret files—the watchers, the ones they watched. Oh, the prospect of all of that could almost make me vote for him myself.'

Ewa walked rather than take the metro two stops back to the office. It was cold. To her ear, there was something even in the name of the city that betokened bitterness. It did not matter that it was her city. She never got used to the driving wind and obstinate snow. Concentrating on the weather, she found it hard to analyse what she had learned. But it seemed clear to her that everyone from his university nemesis to his former girlfriend still admired Dariusz Michalski. There was a sidebar story of a tragically orphaned boy in Gdańsk and a mother-spy, who somehow failed to flee to Norway when her lover left for London and her target took exile in West Germany.

There was a note from Janusz on her desk when she got there, telling her to find him in the office mess. She never went in there; the coffee was so awful. No one ever went in there. 'Ewka!' he called to her as if she might not see him sitting there alone.

She walked to him reluctantly, not wishing to reward his impertinence. 'Why do you call me that? I don't like it when you call me that.'

'That's what Cybulski calls you,' Janusz reasoned.

'That's different,' Ewa replied, unable to mount an argument without her keyboard and screen. 'Don't do it.'

The intern shrugged like he really didn't care. 'Do you want to hear what I learned?'

'Yes, of course. You have been at the Ministry of the Interior.' Ewa hadn't meant to sound like she was reminding herself.

'First off, Staniewicz was something of a major-league bastard. He ran a string of informants who, like Małgorzata Kamińska, had a parent who owed him something—usually some favour that had come their way due to his pull with the Party. Kamińska's dad spent time earning serious money in Libya, for example. Did you get that?'

Ewa admitted she had not. She watched as Janusz literally draw a tally mark in his pad.

'I stopped writing down their names after I reached forty, figured I was wasting my time, as they had no connection to Michalski. But Staniewicz was keeping a close eye on dissidents in every corner, not just students like our man.'

Ewa was not surprised. It would have shocked her, however, if even a small proportion of the intelligence amounted to anything. She accepted the common assumption of socialism as experienced in her country: it would have been fine if they had been any good at it. As for spying on their own people, the points would have to be given for effort rather than execution.

'Tell me that's not all you got.'

'Just warming up, Ewka.' The intern shifted his position to dodge the expected blow from his superior. It didn't come. 'The reports from Kamińska were mainly student gossip. Once she had inveigled herself into the group, I think she actually developed a minor obsession with him.'

'You mean with the Irishman, Day? I heard she was in love with him.'

'Yes, sure, that. But I didn't mean him. I think she became obsessed with Darek Michalski. You see it in the way she keeps mentioning what he's wearing, or when he cuts his hair, or how he sings a particular song. That's not normal detail for a spy to report on.'

'Do you have much experience of reading espionage files, Janusz? No. She was not a teenager, even then. I believe she knew exactly what she was doing, and she was no smitten schoolgirl.'

'You would like me to move on.' If Janusz was grumpy, he recovered quickly. 'By May 1988, at the time of the rising student protests around the country and then the occupation strike at SGPiS, information supplied by Kamińska was supplemented by observational notes from professional watchers. Michalski was running the NZS at his university, but he was also meeting student leaders from colleges all around Warsaw. He had clandestine meetings and phone calls with activists close to the top of Solidarity. There are no taps, unfortunately, but Staniewicz gets the impression that they—not Michalski—are calling the shots. Staniewicz wonders why only seven take part in the occupation of Wilk's office, why two of them were not even enrolled at SGPiS. He even doubts that Michalski was fully in control by the time he cancelled the occupation. But there are no intelligence reports covering that—just his scribble in the margin of a routine briefing.'

'So Staniewicz thinks that Michalski was less of a big shot than is usually made out?' Ewa pondered this new interpretation while staring into the eyes of her junior. She was focused on an object rather than him because that helped her to concentrate, but it unnerved him nonetheless. When she realised this, she looked away. 'Is that not exactly what we would expect? What self-respecting Solidarity official is going to allow himself or herself to be bossed by a boy? The fact they are meeting him at all boosts, rather than diminishes, his claims to have played a part in the end to communism here. What else?'

'Z.' Janusz allowed Ewa the chance to underplay his investigative journalism one more time before going on. 'Ring any bells?'

'Cut the crap, Janusz. Who or what is Z?'

'Z or Z, is Michalski's man in the SB. He is the one Michalski talks to throughout the negotiations, the man Michalski bargains with for union recognition and the other stuff they wanted. On day three of the occupation, the SB reconnect the phone in Wilk's office just so they can have an hourly chat with our guy. They arrange for extra water, fruit, coffee, bread—everything the students will need to keep going. At one point Staniewicz reprimands Z for helping to prolong the strike. It's Z's job to talk Michalski back off the ledge. Z describes Michalski as bright, sane, under pressure . . .' Janusz was consulting his notes. 'Yes, and willing to compromise.'

'What could he have meant by that?'

'There's no telling. The next night the whole drama was over.'

'Well done, Janusz.' Ewa tried to find a tone he would imagine was genuinely encouraging. 'Michalski kept a channel open with the SB. That could look embarrassing to him now. Of course, at the time, it was probably just good sense, you don't organise an occupation without giving your opponent the opportunity to give in to you. But it is interesting that, that has not come up before—it was not in any of Aleks Cybulski's bulletins back then. That can only mean that Michalski kept it from him or told Cybulski to keep quiet about it.' Ewa imagined the editorial conference she might need to have with the deputy political editor of her paper. 'You can write that up, Janusz. If we ever do a piece on this, you will get an additional reporting credit. I will see to it.' Ewa expected the intern to leap out of his seat with gratitude, but he remained where he was. 'You are still here. Was there more at the ministry?'

Janusz looked past Ewa's shoulder. He had chosen to meet her in the office diner because it was always guaranteed to be empty of people. He knew that what he had found in the bowels of the ministry was potentially explosive.

'I think, above all else, Staniewicz was worried that the student strike might succeed beyond even its own expectations.' Janusz sensed Ewa was about to interrupt. 'Just wait, let me go on. He was convinced that the SGPiS authorities would cave in and follow the University of Warsaw to officially recognise the independent students' union. No big deal, you would think. Staniewicz didn't agree. There is a telegram in Russian—one of many—that he sent to the deputy in the Defence Ministry in Moscow, in which he says, "Tell your boss, the Polish Party has no stomach for the fight", or words to that effect. Good question,

Ewa: why is someone from our Interior corresponding with someone from their Defence? No idea, but he is, and with some passion and frequency. And who is this deputy's boss? Good question again. The Defence Minister at the time is one Dmitry Yazov. Remember him? No, you don't pay attention to Russia, as you made clear this morning. Dmitry Yazov is one of those whose attempted coup against Gorbachev in August 1991 brought that whole show crashing down around their ears. It seems Yazov was operating behind Gorbachev's back for some while before that. How Staniewicz knows that or just suspects that—I don't know. Maybe I missed it, maybe it's not there. But he works it out and decides to get in league with Yazov or at least someone close to Yazov but at his own level. And at first it is just warnings about how rubbish the Poles are at keeping order in their own house, but it evolves—it's like he is working this guy over—it becomes something much bigger. He starts feeding lines to this guy, stuff he wants Yazov to say publicly and to Kiszczak, our Interior Minister. And Yazov obliges. He starts laying into Kiszczak, telling him by telegram he's got to arrest student dissidents and Catholic intellectuals across the country. Yazov warns Kiszczak that the Poles cannot rely forever on the Kremlin turning a blind eye to the crumbling legitimacy of the Party, that if the population don't like necessary reforms, they will have to be imposed with force. For Kiszczak, this is like déjà vu, a rerun of 1981 when he chose to implement Martial Law to get the Polish army to invade their own country rather than risk a Warsaw Pact scenario. Through Yazov's deputy, Staniewicz is told that Red Army units in Warsaw are on exercises, that they have gunboats nudging towards the Bay of Gdańsk. These apparently are standard Soviet manoeuvres when they want to turn the heat up. Staniewicz is delighted at first, sure that it will be enough to stiffen his colleagues' sinews. Who orders this threat from the Reds? Another good one, Ewa. No one. No one does. It's a hoax. The Soviet military is not about to invade Polish sovereign territory—or whatever they would have called our pathetic independence then— because only Gorbachev can sign off on that, and that's not his way. He cannot order an *actual* incursion, but Yazov can at least give the impression he has. It seems our friends Yazov and Staniewicz share a devotion to Marxism-Leninism-Stalinism so long as it keeps the status quo.'

157

Ewa insisted on speaking. 'I have no idea, Janusz, how you came by documents that have eluded everyone else. Let's leave that for later. But I need to be clear, you are saying that diehards in the Kremlin and unreconstructed Commies here colluded in the phantom invasion of Poland in 1988. That they did this even though it would certainly undermine the efforts of our government to accommodate the opposition and would likely also hole Gorbachev under his own waterline. That's what you are saying?'

'Yes.'

'And this stuff is just, like, lying around?'

'Not just lying around. I had to look for it. But it can be found. If I found it . . . I doubt I am the first. It's in Staniewicz's indictment file. Within a week of the strike, they had carted him off to prison. This is the sort of stuff no one wants to hear about these days. Under Yeltsin, the line was we are all friends now, no need to rake over the messy stuff from the past.'

'Messy stuff like Katyń, you mean?'

'That'll do for an example. Keep the past locked up, except who knows where we might be now with Putin set to take the keys to the Kremlin?'

Ewa was certainly ready to believe Janusz on this final point. Two dead grandparents were a testament to an enduring absence of justice. 'Okay, Janusz. So now you are either going to be arrested or win an award. Yazov was conspiring with Staniewicz and maybe others here to impose a hard line against the wishes of our own government and Gorbachev. How does this connect with Dariusz Michalski, if it even does?'

'Z. Remember him? Staniewicz appoints Z of the SB to keep Michalski warm, to keep him supplied, and to make sure lines of communication remain open.'

'You said that already.'

'Staniewicz is not convinced his colleagues will buckle under the pressure from Yazov. They will soon realise that the soldiers are still in their bases and the Baltic fleet has still not been sighted off Gdańsk. And Kiszczak may have grown his own set. So he instructs Z instead to tell Michalski that the Reds are coming. He tells him that if the students keep up with their little games, the government will fall before they can make any concessions. The Kremlin will install some Moscow men in their place, like Czechoslovakia in 1968, and all deals will be off. He doesn't quite tell Michalski there are Red Army soldiers at that moment on Krakowskie Przedmieście, but he does lay out for him our raison d'état—the euphemism of the day, the ever-present Polish reality of its geopolitical position on the western edge of the Soviet empire. Staniewicz is banking on Michalski having limited alternative sources of information hidden inside Wilk's office.'

'Cybulski is there with him—it's in his reports from the time,' Ewa interrupted. 'They have a television in there, where they get snatches of news about other protests. He says that these helped keep the mood in the room upbeat—they were not alone.'

'Z knows about the TV. Staniewicz does too.'

'They plant false stories there? Soviet military movements?'

'It's not said.' Janusz flicked uselessly through his notepad. 'I'd say yes, but I don't know for sure.'

'That's a lot of pressure for a young man. Do you have any evidence in your notes that Michalski listened to him?'

'None. None that I found. But Michalski did call it all off.'

'After he was assaulted by the SB. Only then. That doesn't sound like he was persuaded by their arguments and lies.'

'You're right. That's what happened. He was beaten up.' Janusz closed his notebook.

'Is that it?'

He nodded slowly.

'It's quite enough, Janusz. Not bad for an intern.' Ewa's eyes fixed on her colleague's pad. She knew what she must do. She picked it up and slowly put it into her pocket. 'I hope you don't mind. But you are not a journalist, not yet. You are not protected. Later you might be forced to reveal more than you should. I won't have to. I can say I must protect my sources, and Cybulski will stand by me.'

'Your sources? But they are not yours, Ewa.'

'Well, as of now, *you* are my source, Janusz. It's the only way we can write this. We might just be ending the career of our country's greatest hope before it properly gets started. We can't afford to get this wrong. Do you understand?'

Janusz did. Then he remembered, 'Staniewicz is dead.'

'Yes,' sighed Ewa. 'And thank God for that.'

The two were careful not to re-enter the newsroom at the same time. Janusz made himself useful to those writing a profile of Putin. Cybulski had emerged from his office, having decided that Yeltsin's departure would be their lead political story whatever the foreign news guys opted for. Ewa sat undisturbed by her desk, where she found a note from the digital guys. It contained the telephone number and address in London of the BBC announcer, Thomas Day.

Janusz wondered how he would tell his boss the one final thing he had discovered.

WARSAW, MAY 1988

THE CUT ABOVE TOM'S EAR HAD HEALED, BUT HE STILL HAD not returned to his classes, apart from his Polish lessons with pani Bańda. She did not discuss the play *Forefather's Eve* with him despite knowing they had both been there and witnessed the arrest of Professor Pepliński. Neither did she bring poetry or art or film into the lessons. Instead she drilled Tom, Nelson, and the others in the use of the imperfective and perfective forms of the past tense. The Slavs in the room had little trouble. The imperfective aspect governed the ongoing, habitual, never-ending. The perfective was for those situations which were done with, over, forever in the past. 'Grammar reveals the soul,' Bańda said, and Tom could well believe her.

Azil, the Libyan, had theatre tickets. Hana would not go without Jana, so he asked Nelson to accompany him instead. 'You come, Tom. It's an American show. I have two more tickets. Bring your girlfriend.'

Gosia was thrilled. 'This show comes to Poland every two year, I think. Rarely I know people can go. Michał will be jealous. Azil is a resourceful boy if he has fixed the tickets. Can he arrange still two more? It would be fine for Kinga and Darek also. Ask please!'

Up With People! was coming to the Hala Kongresowa at the Palace of Culture. Rather than borrow a tie again from Piotr, Gosia made Tom buy one to wear with his white shirt; she wore a short black dress, in jersey fabric. Kinga and Darek appeared, looking like Miss World and her model escort. Even in the foyer of the Congress Hall, with its red walls and red carpet, people turned to admire the couple as if their presence there boosted the esteem of the event. Inside the enormous amphitheatre, Nelson and Azil sat to Tom's left; to his right sat Gosia, Darek, and Kinga. Tom noticed how, even during the performance, both Gosia from one side and Kinga from the other would lean into Darek, say something amusing into his ear, then fall back into their seat laughing. Tom wished that he too could be sitting nearer to Darek to share a joke about the antics on stage. The performers were children or adults in charge of children wearing clothes in primary colours. Their message—sponsored it turned out by Nivea cosmetics—was of love and peace, reinforced by paper doves and cut-out hearts. Jesus was present everywhere where there was hope although he failed to make an appearance that evening. The crowd was mainly in agreement. Azil was less certain and became more morose with every song. When the audience was implored to get to their feet, he refused, and Tom sat with him in happy solidarity. Gosia and Kinga whooped and cheered like the evangelised, Darek caught helplessly between them. A young man, with curly hair to his shoulders, came confidently to the front of the stage and sang to them of global unity via a mic taped to his forehead, and indeed the globe itself descended on ropes behind him. The properties manager had done a poor job with the makeshift-prop world, for the strong stage lighting clearly picked out beneath its painted surface the white-on-red lettering PZPR of the Polish United Workers' Party. For many in the audience, this delighted them all the more.

There was toothpaste and face cream on sale after the show and tapes of the performance. Azil and Nelson left the two couples, who decided to eat cake in the Café Kulturalna. Gosia was still singing the last song. Darek rolled a cigarette and drank coffee. Kinga asked Tom if he had enjoyed the show.

'I think Chopin would have been better.'

'Good man!' said Darek, his voice raised and alarming other members of the audience still leaving. 'I won't ask you to name your favourite piece. It will be his 'Ballade Number 1 in G Minor'. Or it should be. Kinga, let's take these two to Chopin's *dworek*—Tom, you haven't been to his birthplace? Or let's all go to a Sunday concert at Łazienki. I know Tom goes there, don't you?'

'Yes, I do.'

'I knew it!' He crunched Tom's shoulder. 'And we must educate you further, Tom. I cannot believe we have had you all these months already. So much wasted time.' Darek seemed determined to make up for it all now.

Tom's mind turned back to the performance that evening. 'I admit I don't understand what just took place in there.' He pointed back up the sweeping stairs towards the hall. 'I doubt we could be in a more communist place, the palace imposed on Warsaw by Stalin, in the hall where the Communist Party itself holds its congresses. The auditorium was packed with the old and young of the Party, unless I am wrong.'

Darek was nodding assent.

'You, Darek, must have been taking some sort of risk just being here,' Tom went on because no one interrupted him. 'Other student leaders and intellectuals like Pepliński have been lifted off the streets. There are militia everywhere, especially around the university. Even the napkin holder there has a red star on it!'

'It does. Ha, you are right!' Darek was overjoyed at Tom's apparently novel observation. 'But where, if not here, would be the last place to look for me?' Kinga chose this moment to go to the toilet. 'Tom, you must not worry about me, or even your friend the professor. If the SB wants to arrest me, they won't have to look too hard. And if they do, we are not Romania here or even East Germany. I will surface again with all my limbs still. Gosia, am I right?'

Gosia had not expected to be asked and responded as if she had not quite been listening. 'I did like the show. Polish culture can be so monoton.'

'Monotonous.' Tom translated. He could see her point but chose not to concede it. 'There may be a darkness about your theatre or poster art, for example. But you get the culture your times deserve.'

'Again, good man! Gosia, you have a fine one here. Our artists paint in greys, but below it, you can see pink and yellow and bright purple.'

'The hidden messages, the satire, you mean?'

'It's a difficult art form to translate for you, Tom. But I see you have the temperament. So did you detect satire with the *Up With People* people?'

He did not, just a saccharine intensity. 'I think they are too dull to be satirical.'

163

'You mean to say, stupid or lacking in colour? Both, I bet. English, what a fantastic language to be ambiguous in.'

Gosia was struggling to keep up. Darek did not notice or did not care.

'Tomek, tell me this, why did the government invite this celebration of kitsch into the home of communism?'

'The first answer I would give, the Party is not intelligent.' Tom sought a way of explaining this further. 'It's like with their arrests of activists. They generate fear by an apparently calculated arbitrariness—they pick up some, but not other more obvious targets. But it's not calculated. It's arbitrary only because they mainly don't know what they are doing. So with this show. The public censor let it through because he didn't have the wit not to. The second reason imagines that the Party does have some intelligence. The Party thinks that an American show, whatever its message, will convince some to think that the government is not so dictatorial after all. Look, we have Nivea!'

'We do have Nivea,' Gosia interrupted as if that were the subject. Then more seriously, she said, 'Is not so bad in Poland as in other places. Sure, we are not as . . .' she could not find the word she should use. 'Like in Yugoslavia. Still, I am patriotic.'

'A true patriot does not look at their country and say, "Sure we aren't that free, but we aren't that bad either." They say, "We should not be this unfree".' Darek physically turned away from Gosia. 'Tom, I like your analysis, but it is not complete. Whereas I agree that the Party are donkeys, it is worth taking them seriously because even donkeys have big teeth.' He was delighted at his own turn of phrase and laughed loudly. Again, people milling in the foyer turned and stared. 'What do these people think they witnessed tonight? Are they even aware that this is a team of hippy evangelists but without the crucifixes and without the sex? No, hippy is wrong here because these children really love their parents. Their virtues are American, and they travel the world painting it the same colour. They are Christo-capitalists. That's it!'

'Darek, Christo-capitalists in an atheist, Communist state?'

'This is where I sometimes believe our government can be capable of satire. They are taking the piss. It is like they are saying you cannot have capitalism because imperialism is its highest form, but you can watch some capitalists on a stage pretending to love world peace. International solidarity, just not solidarity in one country!'

A woman, perhaps the manager of the café, flicked the light switch off to indicate she wanted her customers to leave. Then—because she feared she might have been too subtle for the foreign language speakers—she let fly with her own, expletive-strewn analysis of these young people. The café—not in fact a room but just a differently floored part of the foyer—was now in comparative darkness, so the three stood outside its shadow to wait for Kinga.

Tom noticed how rarely Darek spent time in his room, how even more rarely he slept there. Aleks would often speak of him. Darek had to meet people in other parts of the city. Sometimes he would stay over in other dorms or sleep on sofas in other people's flats. Gosia confirmed that students at her college had also heard of Dariusz Michalski. 'I think he is known, yes. It may be because he is good-looking. Our students are not so very political. Here is so radical!'

'Not really,' Tom countered. 'Most people at SGPiS pay little attention to the NZS or its demands. Aleks is always complaining about their apathy. That's why he . . .' Tom stopped himself from revealing the part Aleks played in promoting the independent union though he could see no reason to hide it from his girlfriend. 'It is why he talks about it all of the time. That's why you think we are so radical here. It's just Aleks talking.'

'Non-stop!'

Gosia was to spend another weekend in Gdańsk, and Tom found himself missing her already. 'Michał is sick,' she explained. 'Sometimes I think he needs me more than you. He believes he is still my boyfriend.'

'You must tell him he isn't.'

'Are you jealous, Tommy?' Gosia simpered.

'I am jealous that he seems to be the one keeping you out of my bed, yes.' Not for the first time, Tom wanted her to see that the situation was ridiculous.

'Tommy, I know you want to sleep with me. And you will, I promise. But I must be ready.' Suddenly her tone changed. 'I am not a whore, you think I am? I will not sleep with you just because someone say I should.'

'Who says you should sleep with me, Gosia? I don't hear them.'

Gosia shut herself up until she was sure she could speak correctly. 'No one says it, Tommy. But the society wants me to. There is a pressure even a man cannot understand it.' She became sullen, and when she did, Tom sensed she became secretive. There was something in her composition she did not yet want him to see.

'Michał.' Tom decided to be conciliatory. 'You said that he has problems with his stomach?'

'Is a big problem in Poland, I think. So many problems, it is the diet. People die in hospital.'

Tom ventured into an area he had not been before. 'Was that how your mother died, Gosia?'

'No!' She laughed. 'My mother's trouble was psychological. It is why my father could not help her.'

'You are very strong, talking about it. You don't seem sad.'

Gosia looked at him as if marvelling he could be so simple-minded. 'That's not so deep a thing to say, Tommy. I notice you use longer words with Aleks or Darek, not so superficial. It's because you talk to me, or you don't know how to. It's funny, but I not laughing. I don't want a superficial boy.'

A moment earlier she was promising to sleep with him. Now she was spurning him for a man with a poor stomach. 'What kind of psychological trouble, Gosia? How is that something you die of?' She turned her face to the bedroom wall. 'You don't have to answer. But you should know I am not superficial.'

Wioletta and Agata were having a party in their room. 'Is it someone's birthday or name-day?' Tom wanted to know.

'No,' Wioletta replied, 'I was just practising my guitar, and then there were these people.' Darek was one of those who had turned up, but he was laid out on a bed, making up for lost sleep. Aleks was beside him as if waiting to catch his words as he awoke. There were a lot of other people, including Norbert and several friends of his whom Tom had met but did not know. Tom was happy to contribute a half-litre of decent vodka. Agata cut bread. Aleks brought in a jar of pickled cucumbers that he said had originated on his father's allotment. Piotr had two whole slabs of East German chocolate, a gift, he said, 'From our fraternal comrades.' Tom could follow a large proportion of the Polish chat by now. Gosia wanted Wioletta to play some of her favourite scouting songs, but this time she refused. 'I don't like those songs any longer.' Norbert led the first toast and the second. He then called for a different type of song, but nobody present knew how to play it, so Piotr took the guitar and plucked out some of his Led Zeppelin. Several started chatting in small groups at that because only a few knew any of the words. Agata offered to make tea with her heating element, but the boys preferred to drink vodka. Darek woke up and started talking privately to Aleks. Aleks did not take notes, but their conversation was very businesslike. Aleks nodded instead of speaking back as if he were agreeing to a set of instructions. He then left. Tom could guess where to. Darek—with a gentle insult to Piotr—called to be given the guitar, and with that Norbert stopped talking to his friends and Wioletta shushed Agata and Piotr sat back on a bed and studied his Led Zeppelin score.

Tom had not heard Darek play, neither did he even know he could. Darek bent his face towards the soundhole and along the neck of the guitar as he played, contriving to look soulful rather than amateurish as he did. His voice was surprising, for it came out as Leonard Cohen. There was a chorus and those who knew it joined in quietly out of respect to Darek or the message of the song or both. Tom did not ask Gosia for a translation because she seemed lost in her own thoughts, but fortunately Norbert was on hand.

'It means our country is shit,' he said. He was drinking between rounds.

'What did the dean say to you about graduation and military studies?' Tom remembered that Norbert should have had his meeting by now.

Norbert nodded in Darek's direction. 'Ask man with guitar,' he said.

Tom inferred this was bad news. 'Are you being thrown out?' He added a hand gesture to make sure Norbert understood.

'No, throw out!' Norbert affirmed. 'Dariusz bastard make dean give me a chance. Chance the final. But I must go to army class with the others. All of them. Is shit.'

Tom did not attempt to convince Norbert that this was good news when he was so clearly taking it badly. Darek had overheard their conversation and changed his song, now a humorous one, aiming it at the unlucky Norbert. Even Tom picked up the words of the chorus, which he sang with the same enthusiasm as the others. He knew well the words for *fucking idiot*. Norbert had taught him.

It was a quiet day in the glass-painting shop in the Old Town. The old man had had time to rearrange the frames, hanging all the coloured initials in alphabetical order, making a gallery of white eagles—some with, most without, their Sandomierz Crowns, and stacking for discreet viewing his collection of pre- and post-Partition maps of Poland, inter-war Poland, People's Republic of Poland. He had sold one panorama depicting the city walls in the seventeenth century. For his own home, he had finished his etching of the Hebrew word *Chai*, completing the letters ח and י. He had had plenty of time to keep an eye on the Square.

He saw the British man coming, watching as he first bought a pink cordial drink from a vendor's cart and lingered by the landscapes of a street artist just outside his shop. The man came in. Szulman knew from before that he spoke good Polish.

'Hello, Szulman,' the Briton said. 'It's a pleasure to see you again.'

'And you too, sir. It has been a while. Are you looking for something for the embassy or for your own flat?'

'Neither today, Szulman. I want you to help my young friend here.' Szulman was surprised to discover a younger man appear from behind his customer. 'He is from Ireland, but he understands us well enough.'

Szulman came round his counter to shake the Irishman's hand. The old man was nervous. He was not meant to get this close to people he was watching. 'I don't understand. How can I help him?'

'He is looking for someone. And I believe you know where they live.'

Spiro and Tom followed the glass painter's directions to the Żoliborz district of the city to a three-storey apartment building in a cobbled side street with only two cars parked on the broken pavement. The intercom dash on the ground floor confirmed that the top storey flat was occupied by Mr and Mrs Błoński. The female voice which emitted from the intercom grille was tiny and uncertain. Spiro spoke back to it, explaining that they were friends of Janina. Buzzed through, they climbed the bright, well-swept stairs to the top, where they were met by the voice, now embodied in a tall woman with once-blonde hair piled neatly atop her head. She let them in without further introductions. Inside, she insisted they not take off their shoes but took their coats and hung them away in a cupboard. She went to the kitchen to make tea, leaving them in a sitting room that seemed to be suffering from too much furniture. A reproduction of the *Mona Lisa* hung on a wall near the balcony.

'I thought you might come to see me,' she said to Tom as she rejoined them. She spoke in Polish, simplified for Tom to understand. 'Janina told me she had a student here in Warsaw. She didn't tell you where I lived?'

'No, unfortunately,' Tom replied.

'That's typical of my daughter!' Mrs Błońska laughed generously. 'Did she tell you about me at all?'

'Again, no,' Tom confirmed. Then because he wanted to imply no criticism of her, he added, 'I did not ask her about her life. It was my fault.'

'The young are not curious these days. I am not surprised you did not ask. I am surprised by your excellent Polish. Janina said you were not very good, forgive me for saying.'

It was Spiro's turn to laugh. 'He can say many things now that I am sure your daughter would never have taught him.'

Spiro explained who he was, and he brushed aside his host's embarrassment when she apologised for not having better cake to offer a representative of the Queen of England.

'Mrs Błońska, did you know that Professor Pepliński had been arrested?' Tom asked the question, Spiro keeping his grammar in line. 'Pepliński is my teacher here and was a friend of your daughter.' Tom pulled out the photograph that Aleks had taken of the moment of Pepliński's arrest.

'Artur? Yes, I remember. Poor man,' she said, stroking the injured face in the picture. 'I think he was in love with Janina, or so it seemed. But then, everyone was. She was so beautiful. Blonde, like me.'

'She does look like you,' Tom agreed, realising he was also paying the older woman a compliment. 'But she was not actually your daughter, was she? Pepliński told me.'

'No.' Błońska brought her hands together on her lap. 'Our similarity was a coincidence, but it helped to save her life, perhaps mine also. Her father—not her father, but my late husband—grew to honestly believe she was really ours, that God had intervened to give us a child we could not have ourselves. We were a happy family. It hurt us terribly when Janina left.'

'She called you auntie and uncle?'

'Yes. From the very beginning. It was the war. I had to explain to my neighbours where I suddenly had this baby from, so I said she was my niece, that my sister had died in a bombing raid in Warsaw, leaving this poor infant behind. It happened a lot, it was not so hard to believe and, well . . . like you said, we were alike.'

'How did Janina come to be with you?' Spiro put his teacup down to ask the question, somehow signalling greater respect that way. 'She was Jewish, we know.'

'You also are Jewish, Mr Spiro, are you not? Also a survivor. I am certain your story is as enthralling as our Janina's.' Błońska did not wait for Spiro to tell his story but left, went into her bedroom, and returned with a battered shoebox. She rifled through a few photographs resting near the top, picked one out, and tapped it on the side of the box to remove some of its dust. 'Their wedding day,' she explained. 'Janina's mother and father. Aren't they so funny-looking, when you think how beautiful their daughter would become? They are so *dark*. When you think of Janina and how fair she was, she was like a real Pole.'

'She was, and they were,' Spiro corrected her. 'I mean, Mrs Błońska, the Jews lived here alongside Poles for centuries. This was their home.'

'Of course, Mr Spiro. I am not one of *those* Poles. There are anti-Semites in every country, sorry to say, not only this one. And as with other countries in the war, there were Poles who, like us, risked a lot to assist the Jews. I would like our Jews back again, but sadly I doubt they will ever. Not even Janina will come back.'

Tom was still looking at the picture; he could see no resemblance there to his teacher. 'Why you, Mrs Błońska? Why did the baby come to you?'

'We lived in neighbouring blocks on Kościelna Street since before the war. We should all have left much sooner, but the human spirit is a liar, Mr Day. It convinces you that things will get better or—if they are worse—you will withstand it all. So we stayed. The baby was born, then the ghetto was established. I saw them—all of them, the Jews I mean—pack up the things they were allowed to keep and start to make their way to the ghetto. I stood on the street and watched them. I think perhaps I was crying. I was only a young woman but already married and already despairing at my inability to become pregnant. I did so want a child. I think they saw me first, saw me crying. They cannot have planned it—I don't know, perhaps they did because they had this photograph together with a small bundle of their daughter's things—they simply approached me and implored me to take their baby. They looked so . . .' Mrs Błońska broke off to clear her throat, raising a hand to her mouth. 'They were dying already, I think. The baby, Janina, was healthy and fat from being on the breast. Her mother must have had very little more to give.'

'You say they implored you,' Spiro interrupted gently. 'What did they say to you?'

'That, Mr Spiro, is the only question Janina asked after we confirmed to her we were not her natural parents. She of course wanted to know the last words we heard her parents speak. I am ashamed to admit, I do not know.'

'You forgot. That is understandable.'

'I did not forget, Mr Spiro. I think I never knew. I think they said very little in fact, and if they had, it would likely have been drowned out by the screaming and the bullying by the Nazis. I remember their faces—their faces begged me. And then Janina and her bundle were in my arms. They never even looked back. I think they were already broken, Mr Spiro, you know how it is. That, however, is not what I had to tell Janina. For her, I painted a scene of desperate sorrow and agony. It is not what happened, but it was nevertheless more close to the truth. You understand me.'

It was not a question, but Spiro nodded. 'Thank you,' he said. He would have said something in Hebrew, but he realised it would have been lost on her. Mrs Błońska had acted bravely but on behalf of one little girl only.

'Between us, nothing at all changed after we told her. She loved us just as before. She was always independent of us as if she knew she would soon move away. But she always treated us with great affection. She knew it would break my husband's heart if she left the country, but under Moczar there was no choice.'

Tom reminded himself who Moczar was. 'This was the member of the government, the man leading the anti-Semitic campaign in 1968.

Under his command, the rector of Warsaw University revealed the list of students who were Jews?'

'That's right.' Mrs Błońska ignored the numerous errors in the Irishman's grammar and pronunciation.

'But, Mrs Błońska, why was Janina registered there as a Jew? All her life with you she had lived as a Catholic, I presume?'

'She had. My husband in particular was quite religious. They would attend Mass and the other holidays together. She would have listed herself as Catholic on her original enrolment, but when she realised she was Jewish, she insisted on amending her record, even though already by then life for the Jews in Poland was uncomfortable.'

'So why did she do it?'

'Because it was the truth.' This was Spiro. 'All of her life, from the very beginning, the same lie had been told in order to protect her. She had survived because she was placed apart from the Jews. She could survive again if again she stood apart from them. But this time, when the choice was her own, she chose to stand with them. I am right, I think, Mrs Błońska?'

Błońska had been studying Spiro, listening intently to him. 'Do you think so, Mr Spiro? For you, the truth must be such a contorted thing. We never thought of it that way, but it would be so nice to believe those were her reasons. To us, she simply said that they knew she was Jewish, she wasn't ashamed, she would take what was coming. Over the years, when we have spoken, we have never really spoken about those times. "Life moves on" was some sort of motto for her. And she has had a good life in Belfast although of course we worry for her there.' She turned her attention on Tom, just then appreciating that he somehow carried a piece of her daughter. 'Mr Day, can you imagine that my Janina was unable to come to Poland when my husband died—they would not issue her with a visa. Only twice were we allowed to travel to see her, on each occasion alone. They knew we would not emigrate if one of us was forced to stay home in Poland. You have seen more of her than we have . . .' Błońska clearly wanted to ask a question, but one would not form.

'She is a very good teacher, Mrs Błońska. Better than I am a student.' Tom searched for other phrases that might comfort but realised he had already said enough.

Mrs Błońska was happy with what she had heard. 'Adults can be so reckless with their young, don't you find? We push them out in the world when we know how dangerous it is. What's it for, do you think?'

They had done what they had hoped to do by paying the visit, but something more occurred to Tom. He spoke further, now not supported by Spiro. 'Artur. Mrs Błońska, Artur Pepliński is in prison. Do you remember I told you?'

'Yes, of course. This is awful.' She was looking again at the photograph that Tom had brought. 'What did he do?'

'He did only what the students did back in '68, students such as Janina. He watched a play. He spoke the truth. He is a good person, Mrs Błońska, and he should not be in prison. Please, tell pani Shaw . . . I mean, please tell your daughter that Artur Pepliński needs her help.'

Błońska held the moment—and the picture—like together they were something sacred. 'May I keep this?'

Twenty minutes later, Spiro and Tom were again on the street. 'What was all that about, Tom? Janina Shaw will already know that Pepliński was arrested. Carter will have told her, assuming you told Carter. What can she do to help?

'She can press the Polish embassies in Dublin and London. She can alert the Polish diaspora to the growing political oppression. She will know what to do.'

'And why will she act now if she has not already acted?'

Tom smiled. 'Because her mother will tell her that her student from Belfast paid her a visit, that he speaks much better Polish than anyone could have imagined, and that helping Artur Pepliński is the one truthful thing to do.'

Sebastian Thomson hired a car from his hotel (Victoria) to drive the couple of hours to Kutno. Bogdan Cybulski had left a message for him at the reception but refused to speak to the journalist over his phone. Thomson drove with his road map open on the passenger seat; he paid attention to the unpredictable ruts in the road rather than the silver birch lining the carriageways.

Magda opened the door to the journalist, hushing him immediately while accepting a chaste kiss on each cheek. Bogdan appeared at the door and ushered Thomson back down the stairs to the hire car, giving him directions to take them both to the Cybulski allotment.

'Why so nervous, my friend?'

'They are arresting people all across the country, Sebastian, in Kutno also. Talking to a BBC reporter is more than enough cause. We can't be too careful.'

'You have always evaded it in the past, Bogdan. I thought you were unarrestable?'

'That's not a word, Sebastian. And it's not a fact. Plenty of Cybulskis have spent time in prison. I don't want it to be my turn or my younger son's.'

It had cost Bogdan a lot to contact his old friend again. Thomson was the only man in the world who knew he was the source of the Kutno Tapes. Not even Jakub, whose recorder he had taken from his room, had any idea. That no one seriously suspected Bogdan of the leak was proof that the BBC man was as good as his word. They were sitting together, knee to knee, in Cybulski's tiny makeshift shed. The Englishman, in his suit, was out of place and unhappy. 'This is ridiculous, Bogdan. I don't have the time to be dragged out here to the middle of literally nowhere. What you had to tell me you could have done over the phone. State Security in Poland is not at the level of the Stasi or Securitate, let alone the KGB. Your phone doesn't have a tap on it, a fault, for sure, but not a tap. You are paranoid.'

Bogdan pulled out a piece of paper from his jacket pocket and began reading from it. 'Lisek, Kozłowska, Wiśniewska, and Wójcik, all arrested in the past three weeks, only the two women since released. They had all spoken to me on the phone in the days preceding their arrest. Zając returned from my flat last weekend to find his own had been searched. Just communicating with each other was enough for them to be charged with conspiracy. I am followed in my car. Jakub's fiancée refuses to come to our home. She is so spooked. Hopefully the gorillas won't have recognised your car. Otherwise we might find them hiding out in the barn over there.'

Thomson looked to where the Pole had pointed. Something white lifted from its roof and rose into the air: a stork. 'Okay, Bogdan. Let's say you are right. What do you want from me?'

'That's not the first question one expects to hear from a journalist. It is usually they who want the help. I have something to give you, and a promise I want you to make in return.'

'That's only a bargain if the two items are of equal value,' Thomson reasoned. 'Tell me the promise you want me to make, and I will consider its worth.'

'Do you remember my son, Aleksander?' The reporter nodded. The boy had been about twelve years old when he had last seen him, just before the Martial Law. 'He is a student at SGPiS in Warsaw. All he would talk about after he met you was how he too would become a journalist. He has an illegal printing press hidden somewhere, which he uses to publish anti-government propaganda and news about the Independent Students' Association.'

'That sounds risky.'

'It is. I want you to help him any way you can that does not put him in more danger. You have sources in the Interior? Mislead them about the students, point them in the wrong directions. You can do that?'

Sebastian Thomson scratched the back of his head. 'I don't know, Bogdan. That sounds like inserting myself into the story to change the course of it. I'm a BBC man. At the very least I have to maintain a veneer of impartiality.'

'Sebastian, there is no story you have ever told about Poland that you did not alter just by telling it. All information that you receive—from our side or the Party's—is given with a purpose, to present the most positive possible case. You know this. All I ask is that you look out for my boy, knowing that he has looked up to you all these years. And I do not ask you this favour for free.'

'Yes, I was wondering about that. Say I can drop a few breadcrumbs leading away from Aleks, what information will make that worth my while?'

Reflexively, Bogdan scanned the horizon and the other shacks in the vicinity. 'Zając,' he said finally. 'My friend with the ransacked flat I told you about. What he came to my place to tell me could change everything here. He said that there is a power struggle going on at the top of the Party, of the government. He said all of these arrests were the work of those in the Interior and Defence ministries determined to give Solidarity no quarter. He said there was a pattern, noises coming out of the Kremlin followed by actions on the streets of Warsaw, Gdańsk, and elsewhere.'

'That's nothing, Bogdan. That's barely a story. The Kremlin is always putting the screw on their socialist brothers.' Thomson knew already from Staniewicz in the Interior that the Russians were worried.

'But Zając has heard that that is only half of the story.' Bogdan struggled to keep his voice above the whisper it had been at until now. 'Others at the top of the government—possibly including the president himself—are following a different track. They have sent out . . . I don't know the word, in insects, it is antennae . . . feelers? Yes, they have sent out feelers to the opposition to explore the possibility of talks leading to a more democratic organisation of society. There are no terms yet, or Zając at least does not know them, but there has been nothing like this since August 1980.

'That's it, Sebastian. That's your information.'

Thomson had been scribbling notes in shorthand. Again his free hand moved to the back of his head. 'Bogdan, who is this Zając guy? None of my sources in Warsaw have this or anything like this.'

'His brother drives one of the ministerial limousines. I believe him. It doesn't matter whether you do or not because you won't be able to report it until you have sources to corroborate. But now you have this you can ask some questions. That's the way it works, right?'

'Correct. Bogdan, if you are right—if there is a power struggle going on—you had better hope the right side wins.' He paused to allow his thoughts to catch up with his shorthand. 'If the hardliners come out on top, you, your son, all those you associate with are in danger. On the other hand, if the moderates—those who are seeking to negotiate—if they are to come to the fore, then the likes of Aleks stirring up trouble at the university is only going to make it harder for them. Have you considered that, Bogdan? Students causing havoc on the streets of the capital is only going to play into the hands of the SB hard nuts. Don't you think you should warn your son?'

'Of course I have thought of that. But what should I tell him, to give up the struggle when it is the struggle that has persuaded at least some of the communists to come to the table? I could not tell him that, and he would not listen to me if I tried. No. This is why you are here, my friend. This is why you must watch out for him.'

'Bogdan, you do know that it is not up to you to save the country from another Martial Law?'

Cybulski looked out upon the enormity of the landscape. The line of trees, broken allotment shacks, ancient farmyard buildings, none of them could leaven the essential flatness or disrupt the majesty of the expanse. 'This, Sebastian, is our great prize and our curse.' Cybulski noted that the other man seemed barely to be listening. 'This landscape has inspired our poets and our painters. Look at it! It is like gazing upon the universe. It can make the heart sing.' Cybulski paused. He would make the Englishman see. 'You have nothing like it on your land. You must go to the literal ends of your earth, to your coast and look out upon the sea, before you perceive anything like this. But it turns out you are the lucky ones.'

Thomson nodded. He knew where the Pole was going with this.

'Our land is flat. Armies march across our land as if it were their own. Every Pole knows it. It is in our reflexes.' Bogdan shifted his position on his stool as if he were shifting subjects. 'I am an old man, Sebastian. Responsibility, secrecy, these are the things which age a person. I was wrong in 1981. I thought, if they had the tapes, they would hear the voices on it—those in the Galeria who argued against a general strike—and realise we were genuine partners. We were convinced, most of us, that all-out action then would precipitate a Warsaw Pact invasion. That would have been ruinous for the country and for Solidarity. That had to be avoided. But I hadn't reckoned on Jacek Mazur. He got the tapes and presented them as a conspiracy, treason. It wasn't invasion we then suffered but the next worst thing, Martial Law. Sebastian, you know that Kuba was arrested then, and you know that he suffered and suffers still. And you know it was my fault.' Bogdan raised his hand sharply to silence the other man. 'It is no good to tell me that others are more to blame. Only I am his father. That is my responsibility. And it has made me an old man.'

'Then, Bogdan, there are very many old men in this country.'

Thomson weighed up the bargain. He had indeed been given a remarkable lead; such talks, if they were planned and did take place, could spell the end of single-party rule in Poland. After that, who knew? What was required of him was only to distract attention from an unknown student protester in a university known only for its compliance. 'I will do what you ask, Bogdan. Your son will be fine, I promise.'

The two men stood up to shake hands, but instead they embraced in the way they had watched countless communist leaders embrace. It amused them both. 'Sebastian, the irony is that, should we succeed in freeing our country, that will be the end of me: the files will be strewn all over the streets of Poland.'

'We must be careful what we wish for,' Thomson agreed as they walked back to the hire car. 'By the way, your son is already better known than you might imagine. An acquaintance of mine at the British embassy suggested I might want to meet him. He knew Aleks was your son. Of course, I had to deny all knowledge of you. One has to protect one's sources.'

Back in Warsaw, nearing the Victoria Hotel where the modern city met the old, Thomson drove straight into a crowd of protesters. He kicked himself for spending so long outside the capital when he had been telling his news producers for days that the opposition would soon take their action onto the streets. He had been tailed, he was certain, the whole way back from Kutno. He dumped his car on Królewska Street about a hundred yards short of the hotel, ran to the lobby, and made a call to his cameraman upstairs. No answer. Of course, he would be grabbing footage of the crowd. All Thomson could do was to go back outside and do some old-style reporting, speaking to anyone whose English was good enough, gaining some intelligence that he could piece together for a report to camera later that evening.

He learned what he already knew. People—at least these people, two or three thousand of them—were still enraged by the government's pricing policies and what they saw as their failure to supply the shops. I have no toilet paper since March. Only vinegar is in the shops. A loaf of bread is smaller each month. Thomson had heard these complaints before but knew that they were no less real for being familiar. He heard from them that there were similar protests in Cracow, Gdańsk, Lublin, and Szczecin, and that more were planned over the coming three days. Were they afraid of the ZOMO, the riot police? They not here at the moment. Only the gorillas in leather jackets are here, look at them. For now they stay back. The militia maybe attack us. Thomson saw the line of police blocking the march of the protesters into Castle Square and he saw the plain-clothed SB gathered near the taxi rank, by the subway, around the Sigmund Vasa Column. Thomson did not have the Polish to make much sense of the banners, but it was enough to know that these people were workers. They were on strike and they were supporters of Solidarity.

In his basement cell that evening, Aleks invited Tom to listen in to the BBC *World Service*, which had a report from their man in Warsaw, Sebastian Thomson. 'That's the guy my father translated for back in '81,' Aleks reminded him. 'If he is here again, it must be because he expects something big to go down.' Aleks prepared some rapid copy and set the printing press running. 'Tonight is an important night,' he announced. 'We'll let Warsaw know we are ready.'

The posters bore the simple black-on-white legend of the NZS and demanded an increase in the student stipend to compensate for the huge rise in prices for basic goods. Together, with a bucket of paste made from a mix of water and flour, the two friends walked the lengths of Independence Avenue and Marchlewski Street, the parade grounds before the Palace of Culture and the Grand Theatre and plastered their posters on lamp posts and trees, government buildings, and apartment blocks. They returned to Dom Studenta, unseen, in time for just three hours of sleep.

They heard the complaints coming from the canteen before they had even reached it. The breakfast being served was a single bread roll for each student, on a plate with a square of butter and a cup of warm sweetened milk. When the noise in the canteen became too great, the ladies behind the serving hatches merely pulled down the grilles. Reports soon reached the students from others who had sought out alternative sources of breakfast, that the shops were already closed, *Sold Out*. Rumours spread that the university authorities were deliberately starving them, aware of the protest planned for that morning outside the Military Academy.

'My stomach is empty,' Norbert groaned. 'But my feet are still good.'

Norbert had again been told he could not graduate for failing to turn up for lessons in military drill. After Michalski had won him a reprieve, it was Norbert's intention to play the game until the end of the term, but when other students started being suspended also, he sided with them and stayed in bed. From under his shirt he pulled a rolled-up poster with NZS in large lettering and a demand to re-instate all students ejected for skipping compulsory classes.

'I am impressed,' said Aleks, shaking his friend's hand. 'Such a lot of paper!'

Students were already gathering at the steps to SGPiS when Aleks, Tom, Norbert, and others from Dom Studenta arrived. Gosia had decided not to join them—she had classes she could not afford to miss. Kinga was there already. Darek was standing on an upended beer crate, someone handed him a megaphone, and he started up a call-and-response chant. Another dozen students joined them. Aleks whispered to Tom that he did not recognise these last few and speculated that they were there to cause trouble. He took out his camera and photographed them as he did others in the crowd. Darek led the group down the steps and along Independence Avenue as far as the Military Academy, which was the focus of the protest. Students from other colleges were already there so that in total there were perhaps three hundred. A small group—some in a comic rendering of a soldier's uniform—were enacting a kind of street theatre. A soldier would shoot a student, the student would die, the student's mother would thank the soldier, the student would stand up again alive, the mother would shoot him herself, the soldier would thank the mother. This manifestation would recur with minor details added each time until all the students were dead and only the soldier and mother were left standing. They then shot each other. The ZOMO—the real riot police—stood by watching all of this, pretending not to watch it, for it was surely a crime and a crime to witness one and not act on it. And they had been instructed, if at all possible, not to make any arrests today. Not that the protesting students knew this. They continued their games and their songs. They satirised Party slogans ('Army today, tomorrow . . . and on Thursday?'), none of which Tom understood. He wanted to be helpful to Aleks, but he noticed that his friend was busy with his camera, openly taking pictures of the protesters and surreptitiously snapping the ZOMO too. Without the menace of the riot police, it looked as if the protest might dissipate prematurely until Darek again grabbed hold of the megaphone and sat on the ground. The whole crowd followed his lead and sat. They started singing 'Give

Peace a Chance'. This for a reason which eluded Tom but which Darek anticipated riled the ZOMO to the point where a few began to break ranks and had to be restrained by their own. This was the song that could go on forever. That was the point of it. Darek chose the point to call it to an end, silencing his followers with a long *shhhh* into the megaphone. And they were completely silent. The traffic on the Avenue had already been blocked; if there had been workers on the metro that day, they were not there now. The city conducted a silence in sympathy. Only the uneasy shuffling of police boots on gravel, a nervous click of someone's gun against their belt buckle. The quiet held. Tom wondered for how long it could possibly hold. Would the pigeon flying to rest on the top of the Academy building upset the quiet? Would the distant honk of a frustrated driver's horn? It seemed the stray noises only served as counterpoint to the silence, enhancing it. The ZOMO could have disturbed the performance, but it appeared they too were bound by the spell until, that is, Darek elected to stand up. It was a ridiculous fantasy, he knew, but Tom at that moment recalled Konrad from *Forefather's Eve*, the stricken prisoner who belatedly recognised the messiah in himself. Darek was standing still. And everyone else stood still with him—even accidentally, the riot police, whose only instructions had been to do nothing. Perhaps that was what gave Darek the inspiration for his next move, for without warning, he struck up a comic march, stepping in circles until everyone had caught up with him, and he could march them back up Independence Avenue that day miraculously unmolested.

The party that night was in Tom's room. Agata and Wioletta had bought cake in the only shop in Warsaw still selling it. Piotr had dipped into his foreign currency reserves to pay a visit to the Pewex store and brought back gifts of expensive *Żubrówka* and *Wyborowa* vodka and a bottle of *Napoleon* brandy. Aleks arrived late, having spent the evening sourcing photographic paper and fluid to develop his pictures. Gosia returned to Dom Studenta that night especially for the celebrations. Overall, Tom counted more girls in his room than was normal, and it was obvious that Darek was the attraction. He had scored a triumph, leading an NZS protest that was not broken apart by either the university or state authorities. Wioletta asked Tom if today's demonstration was not exactly like one in his own country and did that

181

not prove that, already in Poland, it was possible to live in truth. Tom accepted a vodka shot and agreed that it was; it did.

Darek, even with Kinga sitting impressively on his knee, was paying attention to the conversation. 'My friends,' he began (in English at first, for Tom's benefit). 'We are deluding ourselves if we think that Václav Havel would approve of us today. For him, *living in truth* is not about the protesting but about the everyday living as if the regime were not there.' Having silenced his audience for the second time that day, this time into sullenness, he continued in Polish, berating them for their complacency. 'We do not live in truth if we only have bread and butter for our breakfast. It is still commonplace for SB to enter colleges of learning and arrest academics and students who speak their mind. Pepliński and others are still in prison. Norbert, here, will still not graduate in the summer because he refuses to play at soldiers. We do not live in truth if we consider our act of protest a victory when our object of protest remains lost.'

No one could disagree with him. Fortunately, the music on Agata's cassette player kept playing.

'I'm hungry,' groaned Norbert, grabbing a piece of Agata's cheesecake. Enough people laughed at that to allow the party to get going again. A round of drinks waited to be drunk. Tom and Gosia retreated to a corner of Tom's bed. Darek kissed Kinga as he apologised for having to leave early and was followed from the room by Aleks with his camera slung over his shoulder.

The party drifted into Wioletta and Agata's room, leaving Tom and Gosia alone. It was rare for them to find any privacy; such were the arrangements in Dom Studenta. They kissed and fumbled in each other's clothing as they had many times before. And as before, a point was reached and Gosia emitted a squeak which was the signal to stop. 'Don't you think that tonight would be a good time?' asked Tom with more patience than he felt. He was still riding the euphoria from that day's demonstration but sensed there could not be many more days like these. 'Let's live in truth, Gosia!' He laughed but pressed on. 'I mean it. You trust me, don't you? And I trust you. That should be enough.'

Gosia stroked the Irishman's face. 'I am happy that you trust me even if you don't say that you love me.' She extricated herself from him and sat up in the bed. Where once her words had flowed, they now sounded placed. 'Here is not a good place, Tom. If we make love, I don't want it in this place.' Gosia, as she had before, drew down a veil. At such times, it seemed to Tom that there were secrets or things that she wanted to tell him that were too painful to utter. Somehow, the thought of making love to him made her sad.

'Why do I make you unhappy, Gosia?'

'You? Oh, Tommy, Tomek, Tom! You are so little to blame. This is my situation.' She touched her head and her heart then placed her fingers on his lips so he could say no more.

Elsewhere in the city, John Spiro was preparing for his visit to the Ministry of the Interior. Prompted by the journalist Thomson, Spiro had spent days listening to TASS news agency broadcasts and reading *Isvestia* and *Pravda*. His Russian was certainly still good enough to read the predictable text despite the florid formulas that sought to mask their true meanings. Glasnost had reached far enough into the Russian press for it to quote a young politician on the founding of her new Democratic Union party. Spiro read her views about the strengthening of the rule of law and the spreading of liberal ideas, pondering their implications for Poland. TASS carried reports of a meeting between Gorbachev and the Patriarch of the Russian Orthodox Church, in which they agreed state support for celebrations marking the millennium of Christianity in Russia. *Only under Gorbachev,* Spiro thought to himself. *But for how much longer?* A small item in *Pravda* referred to troop exercises in Lithuania SSR and a cordial meeting between Defence Minister Dmitry Yazov and his Polish opposite number. These meetings took place all the time, Spiro knew, and no Soviet troop exercise was too trivial to report. The glory of the Red Army was always topical.

However absorbed he was by the Kremlinology, it was not the main item in his in tray. Her majesty's embassies in Washington, Tel Aviv, and London had been assailed by letters and demands for personal appointments to protest the arrest of Polish intellectuals. It appeared that Janina Błońska had gone to work. The Polish ambassador to London had already been called in to the Foreign Office, but now the Warsaw boys had to make their own representation.

'Spiro, this is one for you. Pop along to the Interior. Kiszczak won't see us unless it's me, so you might have to make do with the sinister one, what's his name?'

'Stanisław Staniewicz, sir.'

'That's the one. Show him that list of names. Tell him the Poles abroad are not happy, even suggest we have intelligence that Gorby might call off his planned visit in September. Do we have intelligence like that, John?'

'Not really, no, sir.'

'No. Well, it can't harm to suggest otherwise. Take my driver, why don't you? Maybe you will get to see the man one notch up from—'

'Staniewicz. Yes, sir, quite possibly. Thank you, sir.'

Spiro had no illusions about the power of the ambassadorial Rolls; he was even made to wait outside while Staniewicz finished his evening calls. Finally, he was admitted.

'Good evening, Mr Spiro. Sorry about that, but when Moscow calls . . . You know how it is.'

'Not really, no.'

'Not even the Americans? Don't they just occasionally push you in directions you would rather not go?' Staniewicz offered the diplomat a cigarette.

'Sometimes, but they have to try harder than a phone call.' He took the cigarette and lit it with the under-minister's desk lighter. 'We take our heat from our own Foreign Office.'

'How many political prisoners are they asking us to release? We have quite a few, you know.'

'Ideally, we would like them all out. But failing that, we would settle for quality over quantity.'

'That's funny. I thought you would say the opposite.' Staniewicz took a long drag on his cigarette then looked at it with scorn. 'Quality—I wish! This country is shit enough without these bloody intellectuals and students fucking it up even more.'

'Do you know, Stanisław, I think you have got it all wrong. This would be a fine country without your security service goons. How does it add to the wealth of the nation to lock up an ageing historian?'

Staniewicz flipped open a file already sitting on his desk. He registered Spiro's surprise. 'Yes, I knew you were coming. So which one is the historian?'

'Artur Pepliński from SGPiS. Arrested in March for standing in the street.'

The apparatchik was running his finger down the list of names but stopped before he reached P. He remembered now. 'Pepliński is no innocent, Mr Spiro, whatever your Irish friend may have told you. I had to sit on a stage at his university last November while your young man delivered a speech written for him by his professor which could have landed them both in prison. We suspended him, warned him, but he came back and continued to run his classes erratically.' He pulled from the file a cutting from a foreign newspaper. On it Spiro recognised the photograph taken of Pepliński's arrest in March. The elderly Mrs Błońska had done her job.

'Erratically?'

'Yes, he made errors, historical errors. That's not something we can let our state employees do, Mr Spiro.'

'So you have spies in his classroom! How low will you lot stoop, using children as agents of the state?'

Staniewicz allowed the cloud of smoke between them to clear. 'You British make such an art of hypocrisy, sometimes you do not recognise it yourselves.' He lifted a strand of stray tobacco from the corner of his mouth. He picked up the Pepliński file. 'Then, Mr Spiro— and I now refer to the street you mentioned that we pulled him off— he led an illegal demonstration following an irregular production of the Mickiewicz play. That's provocative behaviour from any citizen, unacceptable from a teacher.'

'That sounds like you have been watching him for some time. That's unusual even for you, isn't it?'

'We have not been watching him, Spiro. It's just that he seems to spend a lot of time with people we do watch.'

Spiro knew he was meant to interpret the politician's words as a warning. He had already referred to Tom and indicated he was aware of Tom's relationship to the embassy. He decided to counterpunch. 'I see that Yazov has been busying himself with your affairs recently. That can't be comfortable.'

Staniewicz narrowed his eyes, the better to look through his interlocutor, before relaxing. 'You have been reading the Soviet press. Very wise. Yes, well, I don't think you have much to worry about there.'

Spiro noticed that Staniewicz had lit another of the cigarettes he disliked, so he offered him one of his own.

'Thank you. One day—perhaps sooner than we all think—you and I can both smoke your superior Western cigarettes. Holding on to our socialist dreams may take more of a fight than either we or our patrons are prepared to put up. You must have noticed that our enthusiasm for making arrests is already dwindling.'

An instant passed before Spiro realised the communist was not being ironic about his dreams; this really would be a loss that no amount of American tobacco could compensate him for.

'Street demonstrations are now a daily occurrence. My boss—I mean my boss here, Kiszczak—has lately decided to go easy on them. That for now appears to be the way the wind is blowing. You might as well know that it is not a wind that I favour or that favours me. Our best hope is that the radicals push too hard, too quickly. Under those circumstances I might . . . those with real influence might be able to interest the Russians again in saving our backsides.'

'You would rather see another Martial Law? Really, Staniewicz, with Gorbachev in the Kremlin, you astonish me. You would never pull that one off again.' Spiro then recalled what Thomson had told him before. For some, Gorbachev in the Kremlin was a provisional arrangement. 'Stanisław, whatever you have planned, I must insist that you give my embassy ample warning. We have citizens we would need to clear out. But what you are talking about would be a catastrophe.'

'As ever, John, in Poland the ball is never entirely in our own court.' He stood up to shake the other man's hand. 'I will see to it that your friend Pepliński and the other academics—the quality as you put it—are returned to their families shortly. I will be doing myself a favour with Kiszczak. It does one no harm to look out for oneself at these times. We may, in any case, require their cells for others.' This amused him greatly.

Spiro tossed his packet of cigarettes on the table for the Pole. 'Have these, Stanisław. Perhaps you will acquire a taste for them.'

Spiro left the ministry, sending the ambassador's Rolls away empty. He had to get a message to Tom.

———⁓———

Breakfast did not improve. Norbert was not reinstated. Under Michalski's guiding hand, the key to the linen cupboard was found and pots of red and black hoarding paint were liberated from a construction workers' lockup on Independence Avenue. Aleks was awarded a bonanza of paper for his press and enough ink so that even pani Elźbieta would struggle to explain it away. Tom was detailed to help craft messages in English that could be smuggled out to the foreign press. He intended to use his knife to call Spiro, but there was a long line of others at the phone each time he tried. Norbert appointed himself at the head of the team bent on recruiting more members. Kinga was to investigate the strength of support among academics. Agata and Wioletta volunteered to find and then horde quantities of non-perishable food. ('Imagine a siege,' Darek told them. 'Cater that.') They dragooned Piotr into the effort. Michalski himself, in coordination with other NZS leaders in other colleges, compiled a set of demands that would be replicated across the country. And with black paint and red, these demands were scrawled on stolen bedsheets and hung from windows in lecture theatres and in student houses and across the central foyer of SGPiS. They demanded legal registration for their independent union, reform of the higher education law to include self-government for universities and high schools over employment of staff, publication, and their programmes, and for the NZS to be allowed to organise academic and cultural events and for students to have more choice over courses and an end to compulsory military studies. Finally, they demanded that ZOMO and SB officials be banished from school and college grounds.

Their protest was coordinated with a national one-day strike. There were greater numbers demonstrating outside Warsaw University, and students at the Technical College were reliably belligerent. Even some lectures in the College of Tourism were boycotted. But the actions at SGPiS were the most eye-catching. Sons and daughters of the Party were not expected to down their books, bar entry to their classes, or picket their library. It was not supposed to happen that traffic on the side street of Stefan Batory would be turned back due to their numbers. That was where Dariusz Michalski positioned himself and where Aleks Cybulski took his photographs and where a BBC cameraman shot pictures through the railings of the adjacent park.

At first it looked as though their protest would pass off peacefully, watched closely but not molested by the police. Students converged on Stefan Batory, blowing their whistles and beating their makeshift drums. A baby Fiat was commandeered as a stage, and from it Michalski and other NZS organisers gave their speeches and made their demands. Each was met with a cheer as the students increased in number and confidence. An enterprising rock band showed up with portable amps, and for half an hour, they entertained the crowd by noisily repeating the only three songs they had written. They induced their audience to say what they thought about the director of the university, the prime minister of the country, and the secret police clustering on the fringes. A speaker from national Solidarity (nobody recognised her or could later recall her name) angered many in the crowd when she suggested they go back to class, apply their pressure gently, and trust in the adult leadership of the opposition. 'We need to work with *this* government,' she implored. 'Not the one that might come after it.' Some took her advice as permission to leave the demonstration. Sensing a premature end to the protest, Michalski grabbed her mic, climbed back on to the Fiat, and started an impromptu chant of 'We are here. We are staying.' There were many present there who had protested earlier in the week outside the Military Academy; they remembered Michalski from that event and to their colleagues Aleks overheard them say, 'Michalski, he's the one!' and 'They should put that one in charge of the opposition.' The crowd thickened again. Another band, hearing about the free gig their rivals had performed, showed up with yet more amplification equipment, and someone found a way of plugging it into the street's electricity cabinet. By the afternoon, Jakub Cybulski had appeared from Kutno and with Piotr was selling bottles of beer from the back of a beat-up Mercedes. Girls and boys were walking about with peace symbols painted on their faces.

All the while, no traffic had been able to pass up Stefan Batory. Men, returning from work expecting their midday meal, found there was no way through and hooted their car horns. It seemed at first to contribute to the gaiety of the day, but soon these drivers realised that

188

by combining the sounding of their horns, they could drown out the band and the speakers on the roof of the Fiat. Presently, the wives of these men came out to support them. Up to that point, they had either been too entertained or too intimidated by the demonstration to want to stop it. Now they were emboldened and they started issuing their own individual demands. ZOMO arrived, preceded by a rumour that they had left behind devastation in the Old Town where the Warsaw University protest had been going on. The shields of the riot police, or of more than one of them, were smeared in engine grease, but to someone in the crowd, this looked like blood. The student mass, so recently jubilant, was now confronted by local residents in their cars and on their pavements, and it seemed the ZOMO were on the people's side. The people were the gathering of senior citizens trying to enter the park, the construction workers blocked in their truck on the way to the metro dig site, the woman on the pavement with a protective arm inadequately stretched around a baby's pram. These were the people the ZOMO would defend with their bloody shields and flailing batons. The mic rolled in a quarter arc on the bonnet of the Fiat until one of the earlier speakers—a boy whose badly pitted skin made him look much younger than the rest—grabbed it and without mounting the platform, shouted into the boiling street, 'A student is dead! They killed an innocent student!'

It may have been this that sparked the riot, or it may have been the decision at the same time by the ZOMO to charge at the students with their batons raised. Young people crashed into each other in their attempts to avoid a beating. The woman with the pram reversed it into an entryway and gained some safety. The guitarist ripped his leads from the electricity cabinet and lifted what equipment he could. The BBC cameraman filmed his star reporter while police charged, and students counter-charged behind him. An empty beer bottle got past a shield and struck a ZOMO on the face. Cars parked up on the street and now abandoned obstructed those students who tried to escape so that many were frightened by their own mass. Aleks photographed a girl with a head injury, a V of blood mocking her peace-loving face paint. A group of boys (Norbert may have been among them—they masked themselves by pulling their T-shirts over their faces) rushed the line of riot police, striking at them with poles they had ripped from their protest banners.

189

One ZOMO collapsed to the ground and was, for a few seconds, set upon by the students until they were in turn repelled. Shots were fired. 'They are killing us!' someone screamed. The BBC cameraman could not tell whence the firing had come—if it had been firing at all—and the pictures he would transmit jerked from the line of police to the line of protesters back to the police. The panic was general. More than one was crushed against the line of cars, trying to escape. 'ZOMO, murderers!' The local residents, unwilling to sacrifice their street, ducked into their cars and retreated into their doorways. A student fell against a kerb clutching the side of her head, a victim of a fist misdirected from her own side. The ZOMO remembered their training and recycled their front line. They advanced stride by coordinated stride like a malicious chorus line. The protesters retreated into an ever-condensing space. In the squeeze one stumbled into the pram, knocking it over and sending its cargo of watermelons spilling into the street. They rolled like the heads of children.

Within minutes all but a core of students had been utterly dispersed. Michalski found that the mic no longer worked so raised his voice as best he could and called on the few remaining to retreat with him to the rectorate in the main building of SGPiS. 'Pull back. Get off the street. Find safety.' He pulled Aleks' ear to his mouth and shouted quick instructions. They had a contingency in the event of this level of violence. Aleks shouldered his camera and from Agata took her bag of *kiełbasa,* bread, and cheese. He looked around for Norbert but couldn't find him. Kuba pulled at him from behind, thrust a piece of paper into his hand, and shouted something into his face that no one but Aleks himself could have heard over the din on the street. He pushed his brother angrily away and seeing Tom, he grabbed his arm and dragged him out of Stefan Batory, back up Independence Avenue towards SGPiS.

The university building was weirdly silent, the students scattered, their protest banners already pulled down. The porter and her family paid no attention to Tom and Aleks as they staggered into the atrium and headed towards a flight of stairs. Tom was feeling a sharp pain in his foot from something heavy that had landed or stamped on it in the commotion. Only inside the building did he notice the injury, and only now in the contrasting silence did he register a ringing in his ears from the clamour outside. He experienced it like deafness; for balance, he held tight onto the banister rail and followed his friend upstairs. They reached the door marked 010, the outer office of the vice-rector. The secretaries had already fled, and Marcin Wilk was remonstrating with two young men Tom did not know. The two men had such a menacing presence it made Wilk look vulnerable in his own space. He tried raising his voice against them but was quickly overcome by a fit of coughing that robbed his legs of all strength. He fell into a secretary's chair. The two young men, having conquered Wilk, then debated how best to dispose of him; neither was willing to vacate the territory they had just gained. To Aleks, they nodded that he should proceed into Wilk's office to make it ready for the others. That left Tom. They ordered him to deal with Wilk while they joined Aleks in the main office.

Tom was still unsteady on his feet. He hooked his arm around the university official to lift him up. Through the older man's back, Tom could feel the effort of his lungs as he continued to wheeze and cough. To Tom it was like cradling a sick animal; there was something repellent about touching a thing so pathetic. He would have to overcome his own pain, and his imbalance, to get the man downstairs and to the porter's office, where Tom thought it would be safe to dump him.

'Thank you,' muttered Wilk. 'Let me just rest here for a moment. I hope you have enjoyed your stay with us.' The vice-rector could manage little above a whisper.

Tom was lost for the correct words. It was as if the vice-rector were hosting him at a polite reception. 'I did not imagine it would come to this,' he said. He had enjoyed himself, but now it seemed Wilk was calling it to an end. 'I still have a couple of months.'

'I don't think so. Well, you may have. But I certainly will not.' The coughing once more took control of the frail man's body.

Tom was baffled by the ambiguity of what Wilk had said, and it embarrassed him. Was he talking about his leadership of the university, the position of the Party in the country, or his own life? At that moment, it was not hard to believe he meant all three. Did the man want sympathy from Tom? 'I'm sure you can recover,' Tom said, aware only then that his words were as ambiguous.

Wilk spluttered, amused. 'Ah, you have learned much with us!' Tom had lowered him back into one of the secretary's chairs. 'You should go back in,' he said when his breathing had eased. 'They still need you in there. I had hoped you would be a good influence on them. Perhaps you still can be?' He finished on this unanswerable question.

They were interrupted by one of the two strangers. 'Back in here,' he barked. Tom hoisted the ill man again to his feet and helped him past a sprawling cheese plant into his own office.

Darek, Kinga, and Agata were already there. 'We came by other way!' was Kinga's response to Tom's quizzical look. With Aleks and the two strangers, that made seven in total, plus Wilk. Michalski immediately started issuing instructions as he realised that these early decisions were crucial to the entire enterprise. He ordered that the enormous conference table be pushed onto its side and placed as a bulwark against the door to the outer office. It took three of them to manoeuvre Wilk's iron-framed desk the short distance to the corner to cover the second door. This, Tom then realised, was how Darek and the girls had gained entry. Tom remembered what Wilk had told him about that door the first time he had been there on his first day in Poland. He had spoken of how it *rained* in the corridor beyond his private toilet on the other side, that they did not have the money for the renovation required to fix the leaks at that end of the building. The corridor, and the stairs from it, had been shut down. Tom had told Aleks about it. That Darek had chosen it as his way in was proof that he had planned to occupy the office all along.

Darek spoke differently to the two unknown men like they were veterans to be treated with another level of respect. Still, he considered himself to be in charge; he uttered something that Tom could not decode, and the two began searching the room. One—Bartek—checked the phone that was still on the desk; he pronounced it working and free of bugs. The other—Cesary—ran professional fingers across the tops of picture frames and around the central hanging light fitting. He too was happy the room was clean. Tom recalled the vice-rector's nervous reaction when he speculated that, on the other side of the door to the derelict wing, there may be secret recording equipment. He realised now that it was no joke. Their initial duties executed, Bartek and Cesary took up sentry positions at each of the doors. Anyone thereafter wanting to use the toilet had to ask Cesary first.

Tom sat with Wilk on the long sofa, wondering what his role would be there. Kinga and Agata were busy at the drinks cabinet, assembling in that place all of their provisions. For Michalski they announced the inventory: three types of sausage, a substantial hunk of cheese, five loaves of bread, and several tins of meat paste. In the cupboards they had found a store of tea, water, and vodka. There was even a kettle. Dividing by the eight persons present, Kinga estimated it could last them three days. 'Two at the most,' Michalski decided, and he glanced first at Wilk and then at the phone. 'We will have to call for more food.'

Aleks pressed buttons on the giant television set and was surprised when it flickered into life. A man in thick-rimmed glasses was reading the early evening news. The prime minister had that day been visiting a farming collective in the Suwałki region and could announce a sharp rise in production to meet the needs of Polish kitchens. A housewife was interviewed to say how delighted she was. A report from the Soviet Union showed the mothballing of a class of ICBMs, following the landmark agreement with the Americans in December. It showed Gorbachev with a white coat and hard hat as if he were personally decommissioning the weapons, Minister Yazov looking less than comfortable behind him. There followed a brief segment on the social disturbances in some of the major cities that afternoon, which made no mention of violent clashes or of the death of a student at the hands of the riot police.

Aleks switched off the set. 'Do they even know that students are on strike and we are here?' he asked the room.

'Of course. We had no choice but to get off the street—it wasn't safe. The secretaries will have reported us to the porter downstairs. The authorities may choose to keep it hushed up. It would be your job, my friend, to make sure they cannot.' Darek picked up the phone. 'It works. You can use it.'

'I have a number,' Aleks said simply, as if in wonder, to himself. He produced the paper that his brother had forced into his hand towards the end of the battle on Stefan Batory. As if making a calculation, he turned away from the phone. 'Later,' he said. 'It's too soon. There will be no one there to take the call.'

Michalski seemed satisfied with that. 'Whatever you say, Aleks. I know you will do the right thing.'

Agata was at the window. From there she had a view down Independence Avenue to Stefan Batory Street. 'There is no more shooting. I am right, there was shooting? It's all quiet out there like they have imposed the police hour.'

Tom did not understand the phrase. Like everyone else, Agata had been speaking Polish and for the most part, Tom had understood what was going on. Now, with Wilk, he found himself seated beside a translator. The 'police hour' was the curfew.

'They have closed off the avenue. They want no one to approach the university, it seems. And they have switched on every street light, for a change,' Agata continued. 'That will be so no one can hide if they are out when they shouldn't be.' She strained her eyes right to see towards the city centre. 'Wait,' she said, 'there are people near the Palace of Culture.'

'In uniform?' Kinga asked. Agata, her hand drifting resignedly down the net curtain, simply nodded her reply.

'Which uniform—Polish or Soviet?' Wilk had now recovered his voice. He was very amused at his own question. 'You had better hope it's the former!'

Tom watched Michalski's face redden then slowly regain its pallor. 'Tom,' he said, 'please keep our guest quiet.'

'What should he do, gag me? Why not? I am already your hostage.'

'You are our patient, Mr Wilk, not our hostage,' Michalski reminded him with as much civility as he could muster. 'When we found you, you were gasping for breath until Thomas settled you and gave you a seat.'

'I am *Professor* Wilk. Is it normal practice in health care to use your gorillas to barricade the patient in, Mr Michalski?' Having unsettled his temper, Wilk again lost control of his breathing and so tactically withdrew from the struggle.

'For now, at least, *Mr* Wilk, you are in the safest place for you. As Agata has just told us, there is a curfew, and you will not wish to be caught outside.'

Wilk's coughing continued unabated for several more minutes. Darkness crept across the Warsaw sky. Tom left the sofa for Wilk to stretch out; he unhooked the woollen tapestry from the wall and laid it across the patient. That was indeed how Tom now thought of him. There was nothing else which would do as a blanket. In the gathering gloom, Kinga made tea, which all but Bartek and Cesary accepted. No one moved to switch the light on. After a while, everyone settled into their positions, settled into their thoughts. Tom sat on the floor with his back leaning against Wilk's sofa. He was pondering still Wilk's question from earlier, about having enjoyed himself in Poland. The question, or perhaps the phrasing of it, seemed asinine now. It begged no insight at all into the experience. He thought of the last words he had spoken with Gosia only the night before. He had made her promise, and they now had a plan. But after this, what would happen to their plan? Wilk was surely right. They were all out of time. It was inconceivable that any of them—certainly not Tom—could go back to their studies when finally they emerged. At the very least, Wilk would expel them all, and Tom would be forced to return to Belfast. What sense could he make of this for Carter? He had found pani Shaw's mother, and he had tried to intervene on Pepliński's behalf, but in short, he had ended up in a student prank that could only bring disgrace upon him. A prank, moreover, which involved taking hostage the vice-rector of his university, who might very well be dying on the sofa behind him.

There was now near silence in the blackened office. Wilk breathed effortfully in his sleep. An occasional siren reached them from the street. A whispered conversation between Aleks and Darek crept through the dark. Tom heard Aleks pick up the phone and dial the number he had been holding in his pocket. The line purred briefly before a voice broke in on the other end. Aleks spoke urgently, quietly and in English. Tom strained to listen but could make out very little. Aleks was talking to someone he did not know, reporting their position in Wilk's office. Besides Wilk's, he heard his own name and Michalski's. There was then a substantial pause during which Aleks appeared to be listening to the other speaker. He set down the receiver without speaking again.

None, with the possible exception of Wilk, slept well. In the morning he found a bowl of fruit which had somehow escaped the attention of quartermasters Kinga and Agata. He happily shared it around with glasses of tea. It sufficed as breakfast. His sunny mood was matched by Darek, who had discovered scissors and glue inside the vice-rector's desk. With Kinga's help, he unhooked the curtains and the nets from the window and laid them flat on the floor where the conference table had recently stood. Kinga applied the scissors to the curtains and cut out, as large as she dared, the letters N, Z, and S. They were easily glued to the nets. Aleks photographed them as they worked. Their task was then to drape their new-fangled banner out of the window. Bartek and Cesary were useful for that, pinning it securely to the window latch so that it did not drift down to Independence Avenue. Aleks said he was sure this would gain the attention they needed. He had seen a BBC camera on Stefan Batory during the riot the day before; they would broadcast those pictures and report also on their occupation.

'Will it be on the television?' Tom asked.

Aleks consulted the clock on the wall. 'Broadcasting has not begun for the day yet. We can wait.'

Waiting was not that easy. Construction work on the metro was suspended. Bartek and Cesary, whose patience before had seemed an element of their training, were now grouchy. Fortunately for everyone, they took their bad tempers out on each other, channelling their aggression into violent arm-wrestling contests. Tom had an urge to run. A fit man was not fit when his job was to remain in one place. His foot, though injured, would not hold him back if he had clean air in his lungs and green grass to run on. He limped to the window to find the park he could run in in his mind.

'You should rest your foot, Tomek,' said Kinga softly.

Tom looked at her. With his back to the window, there appeared a halo around her. 'I don't know what happened. Something hit my foot. It must have been on Stefan Batory.'

'A ZOMO van ran over it, Tomek! Your bones will be broken. Rest it, please. I didn't bring first aid.' Kinga looked to Darek for a better idea. He shook his head.

'Do you have any paper?' Agata was snapping at the hostage. 'How, in an office this size, can there be no paper? Tell me, where is it?' She was shaking Wilk, who pursed his lips as if by doing so he could restrain his coughing. It also meant that he could respond to her plea with his eyes only. She should search the built-in unit behind him. She ravaged the cupboard like a hungry person, found the paper she wanted and also a bundle of pens. She sat on the floor with these, a loose parquet tile beside her clacking like a torture. Kinga sat beside her, stroking her hair, calming her. 'I am going to write you a song, Darek,' announced Agata matter-of-factly.

Aleks had also noted the tension growing in himself, brought on in his case by a personal oversight. He had neglected to bring into the main office one of the secretary's typewriters. They had since barricaded the door and his opportunity had apparently passed.

'Not necessarily, Cybulski,' said Michalski with a levelness he always used with Aleks. 'Bartek, Cesary, what are the chances?'

Neither of the heavies could understand why any of the occupation party should need a typewriter. On the other hand, they were happy to engage again in physical force against an inanimate object, and they foresaw no danger at the present moment. As far as anyone could tell, their protest continued to proceed unnoticed. With less effort than it had taken to lodge it there in the first place, they shoved the conference table to one side, far enough for Aleks to open the door, duck under a cheese plant, and return quickly with pani Elżbieta's monstrous green typewriter. Delighted with his booty, Aleks bore it to the vice-rector's desk at the other end of the room, inserted a fresh sheet of paper, returned the carriage, and started to type. The clacking was a happy sound, punctuated at regular intervals by a joyous ding.

'What are you writing?' asked Tom from his station by the sofa.

'This!' replied Aleks as if he need give no further explanation. He typed frantically, catching up on all of the previous day—the peaceful demonstration on Stefan Batory, the arrival of the ZOMO and the descent into violence, the reports of a student's death, and the strategic retreat to the SGPiS building. It was their stronghold, their fortress, and he played with those words for a headline. He summonsed Darek over to coach a quotation from him.

Michalski had been rolling a supply of cigarettes. 'Say this: "The events of May 1988 can now be written into the history of our nation. Rational argument was met by intransigence beyond reason. A tiny but determined band of ordinary students, armed only with the intellects their education brought them and the values handed down to them by parents and forefathers, confronted the stony face of Polish socialism. The Battle of Stefan Batory will be remembered by those who witnessed it and sung about by those who only heard about it."'

'Exactly!' yelped Agata from the floor.

Darek continued. '"The strike of students goes on. They will continue to boycott their lectures. But the battle is now a siege. From our current vantage, we cannot tell how this history will unwind. But we are sure that there is no freedom without solidarity. There is no truth without liberty, no dignity without independence." How about that?'

With a few more keystrokes, Aleks had caught up. 'Great. I will add some words of condolence about our fallen brother or sister.' He looked up from the keyboard. 'Does anyone know the sex of the student who was killed in Warsaw?'

'Someone said it was a girl. That spotty boy with the microphone—I am sure he said the victim was a girl.' Kinga approached Aleks at his typewriter to help him with the details.

Speaking as if he were typing, Aleks said, 'As we await further news of the stricken student, we know already that the blame for the violence of Stefan Batory lies squarely with the riot police. Consider those words, "riot police". Before they arrived, there had been no riot, and nothing but a celebration of music and word for them to police.' He paused to type his draft.

'Leave your pleas for the court, Cybulski.' Wilk was positively enjoying his captivity. 'The only way any of you come out of this is under arrest.'

'For what crime?' asked Tom, still moved by the speech Darek had orated to paper.

'Only a decadent could ask such a question,' Wilk spat. 'For public assembly designed to disturb the social balance, for false imprisonment of a venerated Party member, for wilful damage to state property.' He gestured to the curtains billowing in the spring breeze like the day's laundry. 'For, most possibly, bringing down upon our state the full force of a Warsaw Pact intervention. You are children! You have no idea about the forces you are playing with.' He stopped there. This time the force of his words was not undermined by a subsequent spasm of coughing. They hung in the air as surely as did the curtain out the window.

'Once again, our guest has been rude,' Michalski said. 'This is unfortunate, as I know you to require medication and I know you keep it in your flat rather than your office. Soon, your wife—who, as the spouse of a venerated but wayward Party man, is accustomed to your staying away overnight without explanation—will finally insist that the militia come for you, and the militia will look for you here. Then, if not before, our action will become widely known. We will, of course, request for you the drugs that keep you alive, while at the same time making our own simple, well-rehearsed demands. This might take hours, or it might take days but, Mr Wilk, whether it is the former or the latter, it is no time for us to wait who have been waiting already so long.' The typewriter clicked, as if it were recording the student leader by its own volition. It was Darek's turn to laugh. 'You see, Mr Wilk. We are not quite the children you took us for.'

Kinga judged it time to put on the television. The news was just beginning. The first item was the continuing industrial action across Poland. Miners in Katowice were on strike, pictures of their blackened faces appearing like archive footage. The Lenin Shipyard in Gdańsk had been called out. Lech Wałęsa was given a rare minute of airtime to explain their protest. Worshippers outside the Arka Pana church in Nowa Huta had been gathering in a protest that was at once political and religious. Universities across the country had been shut. The newsreader, adjusting his glasses, did his best to apportion blame for these disturbances to the appropriate forces in society. There was no reference to their own action, but the students in the room were jubilant. Darek and Aleks hugged, Agata and Kinga held hands and danced the way infants do, the loose tile clapped. Even Bartek and Cesary permitted each other a handshake. Tom, still sitting where he had been all along, noticed the television picture fade and die. The power must have been cut. Darek was the next to spot it; he went directly to the phone. It too was dead.

'No line, Mr Michalski?' teased Wilk. 'They have decided to ignore you all. That is unfortunate for the both of us. You will have no means by which to bargain for your ridiculous political demands, and I . . . I will not get my drugs. I wonder which of us ought to be the more disappointed.'

Their mood of celebration had been easily quelled. Already cut off from their friends, already separated from the actions taking place around Poland, the shorting of their electricity divorced them still further from both.

Their second afternoon passed more slowly than their first. Kinga divided the food so that there would be some left for the evening and the next morning, though not much. Wilk refused to eat. Kinga chided him. 'Who ever heard of a wolf who wouldn't eat?'

'I won't be your prisoner, so I won't eat your prison food.' Nevertheless, they set his ration to one side: they would not be accused of starving him more than themselves. Tom kept his water glass full, and Wilk did drink from that.

By the early evening, the police had again opened Independence Avenue to traffic and those who passed by on foot. University classes were still suspended due to the continuing strike: had they not been, their occupation of the vice-rector's office would surely have been discovered earlier. It was this isolation, the back the universe had turned to them, which unsettled Darek the most. He blamed himself for not anticipating that the authorities would ignore them, and he saw the effect inaction had on his friends. He smoked all day until there was no tobacco left in his pouch.

He stood at the window, their improvised banner hanging ignored below him. 'Agata,' he called over his shoulder. 'How is that song of yours coming along?'

Agata waved the paper over her head. 'I have added to it a verse about The Wolf losing his appetite.'

'Perfect! Do you have a tune? Well, teach us it, and we will sing it at the tops of our voices from this window, and we will see if we cannot stop the traffic again and make those people down there look up.'

Bartek and Cesary declined to leave their posts and Wilk would not be co-opted, but all the others gathered around the window, and to the tune of a rocked-up 'Stairway to Heaven', they brought their protest back on to the street. They earned immediate cheers from a small group just below them. They heard the words of the song, saw the NZS on the banner, and called up their support. A few may have realised the singing was coming from the rectorate. They tried the door to the building and found it shut, as it had been since the disturbances the day before. This sparked something of a street-level celebration. Darek called on them to assemble their friends. By dusk, there was a group of about fifty there. They moved on when the ZOMO arrived, but not before they—and the banner flying storeys above their heads—were caught by a BBC camera. Aleks' phone call had not gone to waste.

Aleks was determined to maintain whatever records he could of their occupation. He had taken photographs from the window as the ZOMO arrived to remove their supporters; he photographed the people in the room, all except Bartek and Cesary, who saw themselves as professionals for whom anonymity was a requirement. Aleks spent the long evening in subdued conversation with his leader, with Aleks as amanuensis. If they had worries about their tactics, they kept those worries between themselves. One of their concerns must have been the dwindling supply of food. Even though Wilk was still not eating, they might have breakfast in the morning but no more.

The room was in its second night of darkness. Wilk was asleep, troubled by hunger and shortness of breath. The girls lay in each other's arms. It was Tom who noticed the television flicker back to life. The screen filled with the head and shoulders of a woman before a totally black backdrop. She was reciting a poem in a trained, actorly way: 'Po końcu świata/ po śmierci/ znalazłem się w środku życia.'

Tom knew the poem: it was the one Aleks had translated for him at Christmas. He spoke the next verse over the actor. 'This is a table, I said. This is a table. On the table there is bread, a knife. The knife serves to cut bread. People live on bread. One must love a man. I learned by night, by day what must one love. I replied: man. I found myself in the midst of life.'

Tom hobbled across the room to where Darek and Aleks had been talking, sitting on either end of the desk. He stood before them and spoke English to them. 'I do not know what you two have planned. I don't know how we come out of this well. But I do know that now is not the time to give up. The power is back on, which means that phone is probably working too. Why have they given us our electricity back? I think it's because they want to communicate with us. My guess is that if we are patient enough, they will call us first. Do that: wait. Make them have to listen to us. Your demands are reasonable: people live on bread, but one must love a man. This is about your rights, your dignity.'

Aleks spoke next. 'What have I made of you?' He embraced his Irish friend. 'But, Tom, the old man is suffering. We can't have a second death on our hands. Wilk does need his drugs, and god knows he needs to eat. He has calculated that we will quit rather than let him decline further. We might be occupying his office, but he is determined to sit us out.'

Darek touched Aleks' elbow. 'True, Aleks. Tomek, do you have an answer to that? I think you do.'

Tom nodded slowly. 'The people outside do not know that Wilk is refusing food. They don't know how poorly he is. They don't know how much time they have got. We play with that ignorance. Correct?'

Darek agreed. 'And what else?'

Tom pondered for longer. 'They don't know for sure that Wilk is not on our side? They have their own suspicions of him.'

'Especially after that speech he allowed you to make last November,' Aleks said.

'Excellent!' Darek concluded. 'And so, we wait for them to call us.' The decision was made.

The phone rang in the morning before any of them had woken. Darek picked up the receiver and spoke quietly into it. After about ten minutes, he set the phone down again.

'They are sending up food . . . and drugs for the old man.'

'And our demands? Will they recognise the union?' Kinga had appeared at Darek's elbow.

'He—the one I spoke to—said they were being considered. He implied that people at the very top were aware that we were here.' He hooked his arm around Kinga's waist. 'But in the meantime, we will have proper food to eat!'

There was jubilation in the room, before Darek silenced them all. 'One more thing he—the person I spoke to—said. He said no one died. He said no student was killed, or even that live rounds were fired.'

Agata and Kinga held tight to each other. 'That's good,' Kinga said. 'But, Dariusz, what does it mean?'

Wilk spoke before the student leader could. 'It means you have an agent provocateur.' He continued with a wheezy chuckle: 'You have someone in your midst, planted there to stir trouble.'

The likely truth of the man's words struck them all at once. Darek was the first to recover. 'It changes nothing,' he insisted. 'We are still here. We can prolong our protest here longer than we could on Stefan Batory. And now we have food arriving!'

Meat, cheese, cake, bread, and water were brought into the SGPiS building and left at the door joining Wilk's and his secretaries' offices. When Bartek was certain it was safe, he, with Cesary, pulled the heavy table away from the door, reached around, and dragged the food bags in. Having decided that this was not his captors' food, Wilk agreed to eat;

he gobbled some of the pills which were also found in one of the bags. He was quickly revived.

Agata was at the window. 'Our friends have returned,' she reported. 'I think I can see Piotr down there.'

A small demonstration of about a hundred students had again gathered across the road from the university. This time, they had banners of their own, repeating the demands of the NZS for formal recognition and for legal guarantees that the SB and ZOMO could not harass students on university grounds. There were signs for 'Academic Freedom' and others aligning the concerns of the NZS with those of Solidarity.

'What good can any of them do?' asked Wilk, rising from his sofa. 'The louder you protest, the harder it will be for the authorities to accede to your demands, the more likely this will end with Russians and Czechs on our streets. You do understand that, don't you? In a People's Democracy, it is the Party which must interpret the will of the people. It is an enduring truth.'

'And yet, even you must concede that it isn't so,' Darek countered. 'Outside stand the sons and daughters of the Party you so revere—they are with us. You cannot ignore that for long, even if seven students barricaded into an office can be ignored. History is not with you, Mr Wilk.'

The noise outside only grew in intensity as the morning moved into afternoon. Students, who realised they had boycotted another day of lectures, joined the protest. One of the bands from the Battle of Stefan Batory reappeared. Having added another song to their repertoire, they plugged in electric guitars to leads passed through ground-floor windows. Agata recognised the tune. 'That's my song!' she cried. 'They have learned our song.' And she found herself actually crying. The others joined her at the window, and from there, they took up the chorus of their protest anthem. The crowd outside responded when they saw their heroes above them. One joker called out that he wanted Wilk to appear at the window too, and a chant went out of 'Wilk! Wilk! Wilk!'

'They love you, Mr Wilk,' said Darek, not bothering to conceal the mockery from his voice. 'You aren't their hostage, you are their hero! Your standing in the Party apparatus will be assured after this.'

Darek and the others had turned their attention inwards towards the vice-rector. As they did, the cries outside took on a different quality, turning to screams. Darek darted back to the window to witness the riot police appear out of nowhere to rush the protesters, striking them with their batons. Two police struggled to get hold of a banner, and for a moment at least, it looked as though they were brandishing it in triumph above their own heads. None fought back, but a few students were dragged by their hair and their clothing into the back of a police van. The van was driven at speed up Independence Avenue and out of sight. In only seconds, the street had been cleared, and the sound of a single man's footsteps ricocheted off the featureless walls as he hurried to get out of sight.

The Wolf was smiling. 'They will come for you here next.'

Aleks waited until the early evening to put on the television for the news. The images were grainy as if shot from extreme distance, and the sound recording had been lost from the reel; but the eight in the room could clearly see the water cannon and the CS gas being used by ZOMO in Nowa Huta to disperse worshippers and rioters outside the Arka Pana church. They were as silent as the footage; even Wilk seemed disturbed. The newsreader in the studio cautiously picked through the script written for him, talking of the need for the leading forces in society to reassert control and quoting the archbishop's call for calm. There followed a piece about tractor production at Ursus, another about the pope investing new cardinals in Rome. The world had been shaken, but it would right itself again. The final item—placed as if it had no connection to the previous—was a thirty-second interview with Kiszczak, the Minister for the Interior, thanking the state security and police for their vigilance and remarking on their eternal comradeship with the Soviet Union, who were naturally following events in Poland closely.

Tom confessed to not understanding much of the report. Wilk translated for him, concluding with his own interpretation. 'General Kiszczak is under a pressure,' he said. 'This is not his talking. It is not maybe our government talking. This is the Kremlin, but not even the entire of the Kremlin, I don't think. Your friend, Mr Michalski, must also understand this. I have told him that workers' protests cannot succeed in a proletarian state—it is an error of logic. Our government must be rational, and if it cannot, then the Soviets will.'

'This is a threat of Soviet invasion, or of martial law?' Tom was incredulous. 'Because students have organised a sit-in of your office?'

'No, Tom,' Aleks corrected him. 'Not for that reason alone. You have watched the pictures from Nowa Huta. Ask yourself: why has the censor allowed us to see that? They want us to see the security reaction, and for that, they have to show us the protests. The report did not mention other disturbances in Gdańsk and so on—and here—but the viewers will know of them and know what's coming next. We watched it from our own window this afternoon.'

'What we saw today was nothing,' Kinga interjected. 'That, on the street, was a party compared to what could be. That is why we must stay, why our fight is the right one. I can no longer live in a country where people are afraid to speak their mind.' She was standing squarely in the centre of the office, as if that were the stage from which to defend their position. 'I vote we stay.'

Everyone looked to Darek. Until that moment, the question of whether they should give up their occupation had not been put—it had not been in doubt.

'Are you operating a democracy in here, Michalski?' Wilk challenged him. 'I had thought every decision was yours alone. Now it appears that people have a say. Is it time for another of your speeches?'

Michalski had seemed ready to speak. Instead he moved further to the side, closer to the desk which had somehow over the few days become his own. He sat on what had been Wilk's chair and swivelled it towards the wall, the phone on its cradle near his hand. 'I agree with Kinga,' was all he said.

Independence Avenue was again blocked to traffic; the metro remained unbuilt. Their banner made from curtain fluttered again unseen from their window, but elsewhere in the city, writers were composing manifestos, SB were arresting dissident activists, Solidarity officials were considering their next moves, and government ministers were waiting by their phones. Michalski was also on the telephone, speaking in a hushed voice, pressing for their demands to be met.

'Someone is sitting on the road,' Agata reported from the window. She looked up at the sky, which was not yet dark. 'They are lighting a candle.' There was a weariness in the room so that no one else stood with Agata. 'No, they are not alone. Wait a minute.' She counted. 'There is a line of people coming from . . . it looks like Dom Studenta—they are all holding candles and they are gathering on the road.' Agata looked northwards along the avenue as far as she could. 'I can't see any militia, not yet.' She looked back towards the student gathering. 'There aren't any banners. I don't think they are even talking. It's like they are holding a vigil.' Agata now spoke to the room: 'They are *praying* for us.'

At that, Darek did rouse himself to stand by Agata, and together, they looked down upon the meeting. 'They are not only students,' he said. 'There are people coming out of the flats opposite too. There are families. They all know we are here, and why we are here.' The gathering became a mass of people, all clutching lit candles and holding silence. Many sat on the road, while others stood around them.

For the first time, Wilk was drawn to the window. He looked shaken. 'This will not end well. Dariusz, look!' He pointed to the southern edge of the group. Three men, all in plain clothes, had appeared without candles. 'SB,' Wilk added simply. 'The SB will disrupt a political gathering, even if it looks like a religious one. Look, now there are others.' He pointed, this time to four men emerging from Stefan Batory Street.

They came as silently as the silent protesters had. One by one, the SB picked boys and girls from the ground and walked them to dark vans, which, as could now be seen, had been waiting there all along. There were no screams, but the scene was as violent as any they had witnessed before. The operation was painstaking, meticulous, cruel in its completeness. When there were just a handful remaining, they too were hauled to their feet and marched away. The night had fallen in the meantime, and the lights had come on to bathe the empty street in a sulphur glow. Candles left to burn in the street guttered out. Darek wiped a tear with his sleeve.

They bedded down for their third night in the office. On Darek's insistence, Wilk vacated the sofa, and Bartek and Cesary each took their turn to sleep there. Everyone was exhausted, so only Tom was awake when Darek lifted the phone after just one ring. Tom understood that through the day, Michalski had been discussing matters with others in the NZS, or even Solidarity. He had relayed to them information about other protests that had not been reported on the news. Through those contacts, he had secured them more food, which, as before, had been delivered via pani Elżbieta's outer office. Tom understood, as apparently had the others, that he was not to interrogate Michalski about his calls—certainly not in front of Wilk—and recognised how, after each call, Michalski seemed somewhat more burdened. Tom turned in his armchair to try to get back to sleep.

But Wilk was awake. 'Who, Mr Michalski, are you talking to when you are talking on the phone?' Wilk asked the question, knowing there would be no answer.

A helicopter was buzzing the sky, sometimes closer to their building, sometimes further away. It was the sound of nights in Belfast; not for the first time, Tom felt very far from home. Or this might be the noise of Russian aircraft, Warsaw Pact soldiers marching across his dream.

One of the men on the sofa—it turned out to have been Cesary—crept to the desk and, as quietly as he could so as not to disturb the rest, shifted it enough for him to slip through the door to the toilet. None liked to spend any longer there than was necessary, not only because of their security, but because of how unpleasantly wet and dilapidated that wing of the building was. Tiles lay smashed on the floor where they had fallen from the wall, the banister rail leading down the stairs at the end of the corridor had partly collapsed. Tom heard Cesary whistling to himself for comfort.

It ended shortly after that. The squad of SB, all clad in black fatigues and beetle-eye helmets, barged into the office through the door that Cesary had left ajar. They made the maximum noise so as to confuse the sleepers, who could offer no resistance. Bartek was apprehended by two police. The conference table was cast aside, and Wilk was spirited out through that door. Michalski was already gone, pulled by three or four SB out the door they had come in and rushed down the derelict corridor and stairs, shouting over his shoulder to Aleks to grab his camera. Cesary was missing; Tom, Aleks, and the girls remained guarded in the office. Moments later, they could hear Darek screaming. After the intimacy of their three days together, his cries seemed to come from an impossible distance. He might already be dead. Aleks, the chronicler, could wait no longer in the room: he rushed past his guard to the corridor, to find his friend.

Darek was at the foot of the stairs, his SB assailants standing around him, their work apparently done. There was blood on the floor, and Aleks' photographs captured this, the bruising on Michalski's face, his broken nose and missing tooth. Aleks clicked his camera, when his instinct was to help his friend.

'It's over, Aleks,' cried Darek through his smashed mouth. 'Someone will die. It has to stop now. Tell everyone the strike is over.'

The SB grabbed him roughly under his arms and dragged him along the wet corridor, his feet trailing in the slime.

A security policeman wrestled Tom down the main stairs of the SGPiS building, past the still-closed porter's office and into a waiting car. It was two o'clock in the morning. Tom took a deep breath of the chilly air before ducking into the back seat. It drove off at speed, giving him no opportunity to orient himself. They stopped at a nondescript building. Tom was never sure whether it was a police or university property. He was locked in a room with a bed and told to sleep. He dreamt that it had never happened, that he had spent the early summer days with Gosia, that they had made love. They were in Gdańsk, staying at her father's seaside house in Jelitkowo. Her mother was there too, well and beautiful like her daughter. Before he was awake, it dawned on Tom that this was all a dream, that he would never walk again on the Jelitkowo beach. He woke up crying.

He was arraigned before a panel of university deans. Others—not as lucky as he—were at that same moment in front of a judge's bench. He had violated the trust placed in him when they had first agreed to his stay. The violation, as it pertained to Marcin Wilk, was criminal: the vice-rector was now seriously ill in hospital, not expected to recover. They had no hesitation in expelling him from his course, and as this terminated the conditions of his visa, he would be obliged to leave the country forthwith. He was invited to speak in his own defence.

'I am sorry about Professor Wilk,' he said. He was sorry about a great many more things, but none of the men in front of him would care about any of that. He was met outside the chamber by John Spiro.

'Let's get you back to your dorm,' Spiro said, as kindly as he could.

'How long do I have?'

'Just two days, Tom. We will get you a flight to London, but until then, you had better lie low.'

'What about the others, what's happening with them?'

'News is patchy on that. For some reason, they don't feel obliged to tell all to British embassy officials. The two girls have been sent home and told they won't graduate. Same for Cybulski, although they have oddly allowed him to keep his camera. Expect to see his pictures appear in Sebastian Thomson's reports. Michalski is still detained. Judging, however, by the official response so far, I think they will treat him leniently. The deputy minister in the Interior Department, Staniewicz, went so far as to praise Michalski's decision to end the strike. With you on a flight home, the government seem about to draw a line under the whole affair. They would prefer it if you said nothing.'

'What you're saying, Spiro, is that as I am being deported, you would rather I didn't make any more fuss. Your job now is to keep this out of the *Sun*, the *Times*, and the *Belfast Telegraph*. Well, my apologies if I have messed up your day.'

In Dom Studenta, people came and went much as they always had. The porter, as always, ignored Tom as he entered with Spiro. Tom's room was already vacant: the posters removed from the walls, the sheets from the beds. Unusually, the curtains were pulled back and the windows open, which let in an air and a light that seemed alien to the room. 'I didn't realise we were allowed to open those,' said Tom.

'You packed quickly,' Spiro joked, pointing at the bag and rucksack at the end of Tom's bed.

'It wasn't me,' said Tom, not in the mood for humour. 'Someone else went through my things, folded them, sniffed them, whatever. They may have nicked stuff too, for all I know.'

Spiro wrinkled his nose at the smell of dust and bleach. 'Maybe the same person who did the cleaning. You should look through, make sure it's all there.' The diplomat reached for a pen and something to note down a record of goods stolen. Day was, after all, still a British citizen abroad.

'Don't bother,' Tom stayed him. 'It's not the worst thing to have happened to me.'

'No,' Spiro admitted. At first he had been angry with his young charge for getting caught up in the strike and occupation of Wilk's office;

it had certainly caused for him a number of difficult conversations with his ambassador. But he was proud too, and not really surprised. And he understood Tom's bewilderment and loss. They had spoken on the way about the fact that Tom would never be allowed back in the country. 'Tom, I know that you are not ready to hear this yet, but we may not have much time later. When you get to London, you will be met at the airport by someone from the Foreign Office. They will want to debrief you.'

'What does that entail?'

'Hard to say exactly. They will certainly ask you about your involvement with Michalski. They will be interested too in your relationship with Wilk.'

'And you? Will they ask me about you?'

'No, Tom. They know about me already. After the debrief, they will put you on a plane back to Belfast. Of course, you don't have to go back there. The FCO person might find something else for you to do, say in London.'

'Why would I stay in London?'

'You don't need to decide now, just give it some thought.'

Tom sat on the end of his bed. He remembered a time when he was glad of this bed, when he was exhausted and did not know where he would be sleeping in this strange city. Then Aleks had found him a room.

'Is there something else I can do for you, Tom?'

'Two days, you said. Where should I stay?'

Spiro had already booked Tom into the Europejski Hotel on the edge of the Old Town. Two days' isolation there before flying to London was the diplomat's version of tidying up.

'Gosia. John, I haven't seen Gosia since before the strike.'

'Are you sure, Tom? I speak here as a friend, not just your embassy representative: are you sure you want to be messed over by the girl at this late stage? After everything I have already told you? When this is done, there will be no coming back—you are aware of that, aren't you? You won't see her, and you won't be hearing from her. Love, under the circumstances, is a non-starter. Oh, shit!'

Tom allowed himself a smile at the other man's discomfort. 'Good man, Spiro. It's the least you can do.'

All personal effects had been removed from College Director Dudek's office, the pattern sewn for him by his daughter, the framed photograph he kept of his unloved wife. His desk had been wiped clean, his sofa had been pushed further against a wall, and his secretary had been reassigned. The strike that had even reached the College of Tourism had swept Dudek from his job. Stanisław Staniewicz, seated behind the desk, had survived the immediate turmoil but calculated that he too would soon be out of a job. Kiszczak would remove him and almost certainly have him arrested for his connivance with Yazov. And that ruthless bastard Mazur would come along to brush it all away. That was still to come; first he had some mess of his own to clean up. He checked his watch.

Kamińska appeared at the door. Staniewicz gestured for her to come in and close the door behind her.

'How are you, Gosia?' he asked, surprising himself that he actually cared.

'Tired of Warsaw. I want to go home. Since I failed you, can't you just let me go home?'

'Failed me? That's an interesting perspective.' Staniewicz allowed himself a sardonic laugh. 'You think you have been working for me only, not for any greater good?'

'Oh, stop it! There is no greater good here, none that either you or I still believe in. Please let's not waste any more time pretending otherwise. You sent me to watch Tom, because I am pretty and you were sure he would fall for me. You did not count on me falling in love with him first.'

'Gosia, it is true we expect too much of our citizens sometimes. Your emotions should not have entered into it. I handled you poorly. You had no training. You ought to have learned that your role is to manipulate your subject's emotions without letting in your own.'

'You are a heartless bastard, Staniewicz. It was also forbidden for my father to put me and my mother before the system. That was your doing too. You have not changed at all. The system will no doubt go on, empty as it is, for as long as we live, adjusting where it has to but essentially surviving. You will probably survive too. Just don't tell me that you or it stand for anything noble.'

'I will settle for that if it means survival, Miss Kamińska. So I wonder, in what sense do you think you have failed?'

Gosia dropped her hands, heavy and powerless, to her sides. Emotion caught at her throat, which she waited to pass. She had still not found the words when she started to speak. 'This . . . It would have been so much . . . People have suffered who did not have to.'

'People you love?' Staniewicz wondered how the doctor, Gosia's father, would have uttered the words.

'People I did not know, but whom now I know.' Her sentence sounded formal even to her. She could not speak otherwise to this man. 'It would have been better for them if I had managed to stop them.'

'Again, you surprise me, Gosia. You did very important work for us. The information you supplied was most useful. It is a pity that only you and I will ever know it.'

Gosia looked dully around the office. She had had it confirmed that she had passed her course and would be allowed to graduate, despite the lessons she had missed. She thought maybe she could establish a small tourism business in Jelitkowo with her father, perhaps convert their home into a seasonal boarding house and register it with Orbis, the state travel enterprise. She might even get to travel herself.

'Why did you want to see me?' she asked, dragging herself back into the nearly empty office.

Staniewicz sighed heavily and lifted a package from the desk drawer. 'Because I have one more job for you. Dariusz Michalski, like dissidents before him, has been offered a one-way ticket out of Poland, exile in the West, where he can do us no more harm. We have him in a secure hotel for now. Apparently, the boy is already homesick—did you know he comes from Ostrów Mazowiecka? So he is having second thoughts. This package is his ticket, visa to the West, and enough hard currency to last him six months. I have been told it is my job to give it to him and to make him accept it. My boss would rather his hands were not on it, and I feel the same way, which is why I am asking you to take it to him. Gosia, if you think you failed me before, it is absolutely crucial that you do not fail me now: you must do everything you can to make him take it—everything. Do you understand?'

Gosia thought of her college room. Her bedroom lay unmade. She felt a thrill unconnected to Tom. In her room was a wardrobe with a black jersey dress she knew she looked good in. Above her sink was a bottle of perfume, as yet unopened. There was a silver bracelet with her name she would give him, as a gift before she left.

'I must tell him I was spying on him?'

'He will work that out.'

'Then I can go home?'

'I promise.'

'Where is he? You say he is in a hotel.'

'Not far from here. The Europejski.'

—◡—

'Please tell me this security is not all for me?' Tom was ushered into the hotel foyer by Spiro. Two militia vans were parked outside, and inside the reception area itself a soldier was stationed at each exit and doorway.

'*I* am your security. Wait for me there.' Spiro left his charge in the middle of the foyer while he made enquiries at the desk. He looked and sounded angry as he returned to Tom with the key and pressed the button in the lift for the fourth floor. He didn't speak until the Irishman was fast in his room.

'It's Michalski,' he blurted, as if to that point he had been holding his breath. 'The fucking incompetence of these people! They *knew* I was taking you here, but did that stop them from holding Michalski here too? Did it fuck!' He dropped Tom's bag on the bed. 'I mean, who thinks that's a good idea?'

'Can I see him?'

'Exactly! That's exactly what you will want to do, and the same with him once he finds out his deported mate has got the en suite upstairs. Shit in hell. Do you know, Tom, you are the lucky one to be getting out of here? Believe me.'

'Have you had a tough day, John? Do you want to sit down? I am sure I could order a glass of water for you.' Tom was enjoying the other man's loss of cool.

'And you can shut up.' Spiro sighed deeply and shook the crap out of his head. 'Right, you sit there and don't go away. Don't move, if you can afford it. Give your foot a rest. Clearly, I have stuff to do now which I had not planned on doing.'

'John?'

'Yes!'

'Can you bring up lunch for me? I haven't eaten since . . . since last week.'

The absurdity of the situation made both men laugh. Tom promised not to leave his room if Spiro promised not to lock him in. Spiro would return later with news, and in the meantime, he would send up food.

The hotel room was enormous, larger than his dorm for four in Dom Studenta. It was dominated by the bed. The bed was clothed in a golden quilt, edged with bronze satin. Beneath the quilt, the sheets were so crisp they were brittle; it was all Tom could do to resist climbing between them. He was tantalised by that thought and by the promise he would keep later with Gosia.

He kicked off his shoes and stepped to the window. Past the nylon curtains, he strained to look right. There, he knew, was the vast Piłsudski Square. In it would be the Tomb of the Unknown Soldier and, beyond that, the Saxon Gardens. Tom curled his toes on the carpet, his feet reminding him that they had not run in over a week. A soldier was posted below, outside some sort of military establishment. Tom fancied the soldier had glanced up, making eye contact with him, and Tom stared back, daring the soldier to look away. The soldier and he were about the same age, about the same build. Tom craved to know more about him—where he was from, what he dreamed—and whether from the pain in his broken foot or hunger, he felt his heart pounding. He moved away from the window when there was a gentle knock at his door. His lunch had arrived.

Later, he watched television for the news. The reporter spoke too quickly and monotonously for Tom to know what she was saying, but the pictures were of Wałęsa and other leaders from Solidarity meeting in Warsaw, apparently to discuss their response to the latest strikes of workers and students. There was no mention of the occupation in SGPiS, or of his own deportation. The two international channels—CNN and BBC—were similarly silent on the strike. He wondered whether, elsewhere in the same hotel, Darek would have been watching the same programme. Indeed, Tom found himself comparing what he knew of his own situation with what he imagined of Michalski's. Spiro had said that Darek might be treated leniently, that after all, the authorities had welcomed his decision to call off the strike. Did that treatment stretch to being accommodated in one of the capital's best hotels while, for Aleks at least, conscription in the army seemed a likely outcome? But then Tom remembered the police and security personnel in the hotel reception: Darek was certainly more prisoner than guest. He wondered if his friend also had a double bed and whether that bed was covered in a golden blanket and whether his bathroom had—as Tom's had—musky-smelling soaps and creamy shampoos.

Tom turned the taps on his bath. He let the yellow water run through the hole before inserting the plug and tipping in a bottle of lotion. He wanted the tub to fill; it wouldn't matter if the water spilled over as he climbed in, he wanted to feel the luxury of too much hot water on his body. First, he unbelted his jeans and let them fall to the floor. His fingers trembled as he unbuttoned his shirt, excited either by the steam rising in the bathroom or by what he knew was coming later. He slipped off his socks and his pants and dipped his toe in the too-hot water. He plunged his whole body in, slipping to the end of the bath, sending a wave of water and foam crashing over the end. The heat made him gasp. He knew that if he survived the first few moments, his body would adjust. Soon he was able to stretch out again. He rested his head on the rim of the tub and watched as tiny bubbles made the hairs on his legs stand on end. Even with the bathroom door open, the mirror steamed over. The heavy, wet air was hard to breathe; he focused on slowing his heart rate. Finally, everything—his heart, the steam, the plane of the water—was becalmed, and he lay there for long minutes with his eyes closed. Unbidden and unhurried, his mind replayed the events of the previous week, and as it did, new questions surfaced—questions about what happened and about what would happen next.

His eyes opened. The heat had gone out of the bath. The water droplets on the mirror lost their own cohesion and streamed down the mirror in tears. Tom climbed out of the bath and grabbed a towel.

He dropped his rucksack on the bed, and it bounced like a body. He had to choose what to wear; it felt like a strange choice to make. He spilled the guts of his bag over the quilt, and it reminded him of the occasion many months before and many miles away when he had packed for his year in Poland. His East German trainers were there, and his white shorts and T-shirt. The Polish soldier's boots that Janusz had given him, not worn since the last of the snow, took up the space once filled by toilet rolls. He went back to the bathroom and found a tiny bottle of some generic scent. He splashed it all on his face and chest. Gosia would comment on it, say it did not smell of him, complain a little, but find it amusing. He waited for the perfume to evaporate before he buttoned on his white shirt. He felt ridiculous and juvenile because his towel was still wrapped around his waist. He dried his bottom half off, found a pair of pants, and pulled on a pair of jeans, wishing they were fresher than they were. He didn't bother with socks. His hair was black and sticking to his neck, when there was a knock at the door. It was Spiro.

'Wow, you look—and smell—a whole lot better. Here, take this. I hope you have your passport handy?'

Tom took in his hand his flight ticket for the following day. He felt a sudden swelling of injustice. 'Why can't I stay, Spiro? Why can't they give me another chance?'

'Because, Tom, you took the vice-rector of the university hostage. Quite apart from the small matter of behaving like a democrat in a communist country, they cannot very well overlook the false imprisonment of one of their own. Frankly, they could have jailed you.'

Tom nodded; he didn't really have the fight in him to continue making his defence. 'Did you find Gosia? When is she coming?'

'I did. You have an hour to wait, if you can contain yourself that long.' Spiro winked. 'She had no clue what they had done with you, or even whether or not you were still in the country.'

'I take it she was pleased?'

'Yes. Of course, she was pleased. I'd say she was a bit nonplussed that you were staying here.' Spiro reflected back on the conversation he had had with her. 'Naturally, she was suspicious of me, having never met me. Perhaps at first, she thought I was laying some sort of trap. Everyone is a bit jumpy at the moment, understandably. But certainly, she is pleased that you are still here.'

'Did you tell her I am leaving tomorrow?'

'Look, Tom, I didn't want to. But she didn't believe me when I said I didn't know.'

'You cracked? All that interrogation resistance training you did with the diplomatic corps really paid off, didn't it?'

'She was good, man. I was powerless.' Spiro held his hand up so as to quickly change the subject. 'Look, I don't want it to cramp your style any, but I will be waiting down in the foyer for when you are both done. You are still under my protection, you understand. I will have to escort her off the premises, so to speak.'

'You really need to take another look at your job description, Spiro. Okay, an hour?' Tom considered asking the older man for advice as to how he should spend the intervening time, but dismissed the idea. He could brush his teeth or read a book or turn on the TV or watch the soldier outside.

He did all those things. The time crept by slowly and well past the hour he had been told to wait. The sentry below had not changed; he would occasionally execute a four-step march to his left, perform a turn as smooth as a swimmer, and march back to his assigned spot. Whether he was exercising his own initiative or acting on drilled instruction Tom was not sure, but the man's performance was flawless, if pointless.

She was exactly an hour late: her precision rebuffed Tom, who thought that perhaps he was the one at fault. They did not argue. They undressed each other completely. Tom noticed that there was a thread hanging loose from her jersey dress. She was near to tears from the moment she arrived, and Tom was sorry that he could not handle her more gently—and sorry too that he could not occupy the exact emotional place where she was. He knew they should talk, but talk was too likely a distraction from what he had in mind. He breathed her in instead: her perfume was new, or suffused with another scent, not one he recognised from her. Her body—or his body with her—was novel too, forming unfamiliar shapes against his. It came to his and glanced away. She seemed fatigued, already spent, unable to give more than she was, so allowing him inexpertly to take the lead.

Finally, Gosia rolled away from him. She pulled on her knickers and walked to the bathroom, shutting the door softly behind her. Still naked, Tom sat up at the head of the bed with the sheet to his waist and waited. He did not know what for. He did not know her business in the bathroom, but he could hear the water running in the bath. Now he was ready to speak, she was not there. He felt suddenly, unassailably tired. He may have dozed. When he was next aware of her, she was sitting, fully clothed, beside him on the bed. The bathroom light was still on, a glow in a distant corner of the room.

She ran her thumb along his hairline, like a mother might a sick child. 'That was nice, Tomek.'

'Do you have to go? Why do you have to go?'

'I do. I don't expect you to understand. It is better if I go.'

'Again? But I have hardly seen you. You were not there when the strike began. I wanted you with me in that office.'

Gosia turned away cross, trying to disguise the fact. 'That was not my interest.' She paused, as if to battle several conflicting ways of expression. 'It was better I was not there, believe me.'

'I missed you, Gosia.'

'Don't talk to me about it, please. I did not ask you to strike, and now you must leave Poland. And Darek must also go. This is not my fault.'

'Darek? What do you know about Darek? Have you seen him?'

Gosia recoiled from the vigour of his questioning. 'Please, not an interrogation! Soon it will not be a secret any longer. Darek . . .' Emotion sounding like self-restraint caught her words. 'Your friend will go to Germany to have a new life. People are talking about this—that's how I know.'

'Gosia, I don't want to argue. We have so much to talk about. We need to plan for. . .'

'Yes, Tomek. There is much we can talk about, but nothing to plan for.'

'What does that mean?'

'Why are you so young?' She was exasperated at his refusal to accept the fundamental truths of their situation. 'It is our *reality*, Tomek. It does not matter now if you love me. You must leave. My time with you is over. I cannot be with you now. They will not allow me to travel to see you because they know I would never return here. It would be better if you did not love me—my role here would be easier.'

'Your role, Gosia? You are not making sense.'

Gosia swatted away what remained of his incomprehension; she could explain to him no more clearly. She stood up. 'I am going now. I should have brought you something of me to take home, something sentimental. You would like that. I am sorry I have nothing. You can try to remember your Polish girl, if you like. Goodbye, Thomas.' She bent down to kiss him, but he was as cold as stone.

She was gone. He had not managed to say goodbye; he had not acted at all. He swung his feet to the floor, kicking his pants. He put them on to go to the window, hoping to catch a final sight of her. He could hear dance music coming from somewhere else in the hotel and feel it throbbing through his feet. It was reminiscent of the music from *Hades*. Below on the street two women (prostitutes, Tom assumed) were giggling as they walked past the soldier on duty. The nylon of the curtain felt cheap against his fingers, and the smut of the window came off on his fist as he cleared a circle to see better. The chill of the glass gave him goosebumps; with his clean hand, he smoothed them away from his chest and stomach. His fingers came to rest inside the band of his pants. He saw her before he was aware that it was her: she was not alone, but with Spiro, in a greater hurry than he. They got as far as the parade square together before he split to the left, she walking straight in the direction of the Saxon Gardens.

He felt again the air through the window on his skin, so he stepped back until he saw his whole reflection in its frame. He climbed back into the bed, curling up beside the hollow left there moments before by Gosia. And he danced with her to the music still playing.

LONDON AND WARSAW, 31 DECEMBER 1999

F OR ANYONE WATCHING, HE WAS QUITE EASY TO SPOT: NOT many people were leaving Bush House in Aldwych at that time of the morning, not many of them were jogging, and even fewer would have chosen to wear white shorts and T-shirt in December. Tall and thick-limbed against the white Portland stone, but for his black hair, he looked not unlike one of the classical statues that stood above the portico. His movements, however, were lithe and rapid. At 2 am he had absolute freedom of the streets of London: he was often observed taking a different route home on different nights, and on this occasion, he set off straight up Kingsway. In his head, he mapped Russell Square, the new British Library, and a near-derelict St Pancras station. From there, he knew a backstreets route to Islington and Canonbury to get to his flat on Canonbury Mews.

Tom always took the bus to work. Tradition (and his bosses at Bush House) dictated that he dress smartly, even for what they called blind work. Tom might have one of the more recognisable voices on the World Service, but few would have spotted him in the street as he walked in his suit to Essex Road, or on the 341 bus to Aldwych. Even the commissionaire in the reception, whose profession was to recognise people, only pretended to know Thomas Day. The building, after all, was full of actors. Anonymity today, if not normally, was welcome. Until today, Tom thought he knew all he needed to know. Today he had a bomb to carry around in his head.

Tinsel still infected his workspace. Other carrels in the newsroom were vacant, their usual occupants taking time off to be with their families. For this reason, Tom was given the job of listening to one of that evening's lead features and writing the introduction which he would later record to tape. Sebastian Thomson had sent in a gruelling report from Grozny: the city had been under attack from Russian bombers since September, ordered by new prime minister Putin. The targets had been Chechen rebels, but the cries of women and children in their bombed-out homes dominated the sound file. Tom listened to the tape four times; he called up other reports from the archive, dating back to when Chechnya proclaimed its independence from Russia upon the collapse of the Soviet Union, then on the earlier phases of the Chechen War. He listened a fifth time to Thomson's report, again to the cries of the women and children, imagining by now that he could recognise individual voices. That of one child, a boy, stood out for him: this child was not crying but talking defiantly, saying something that Tom did not understand but it called to him nevertheless. Thomson's voiceover obliterated the boy. Day wrote a draft of his intro piece then set it aside to take dinner in the canteen.

He had a row with a lady in a paper hat. The potato was not fully baked, and the beans were cold. It was not the lady's fault (Tom understood that much), but she was the face of the catering operation at that moment, she was the frontline, so she had to accept the full force of his criticism and make whatever recompense she could within her ambit. He said this loudly to her while other colleagues waited behind, hoping he would quickly shut up and go back to being gentle Tom. They were glad in the end to let him sit alone with his pudding and warm custard. The dinner lady pressed on through her tears.

When he got back to his desk, he decided his first Grozny draft was inadequate. He started again. It did not matter that he couldn't understand them; he wanted to hear the voices of the children without Thomson's overlay. If he'd had the technology—and the authority—he would have re-edited the tape; he felt the audience could have coped with less from the star journalist. As he had neither the means nor the permission to alter the report, he focused again on his introduction to it.

For three months, shells from Russian planes have been dropping on the homes and hospitals, the orphanages and playgrounds of the Chechen capital of Grozny. Our East European editor, Sebastian Thomson, has been there and filed this report for the World Service.

Fine, that was a start—there was room for a further sentence to be inserted but he was happy with the tone. Tone was a contested concept at the BBC, one which certain editors would rather do away with entirely. To *say* anything, it was important first to disguise it so it appeared to say nothing. So long as Thomson's report mentioned the playgrounds and the orphanages (and it did), it was all right for Day to do so. All he was doing was foregrounding; he would dig into the audio one more time, to find something else to bring to the fore.

His editor passed his script. 'Do it again, Day,' she called in from the other side of the recording booth. 'How are you saying "Grozny"?'

Tom never had to retake. Whether he was reading his own words or someone else's, all he had to do was *read words*, and he had been doing that all his remembered life. He read it again into the mic.

'Jesus, Day! Have you been drinking? Just say it straight.' The editor pulled her cans up to her ears while Tom tried for a third time, desperately pushing from his mind the matter that had begun to invade it.

He finished his third take and pushed his chair back on its wheels. 'That'll have to do you,' he called over his shoulder, leaving the soundproof room. The editor, still not happy, pretended she was. The sound recordist thought he could digitally remove the wobble from the announcer's voice.

Tom had two hours before he took the live handover from Radio 4 at one in the morning. He badly needed to sort his head. For all that his job required no skills not possessed by most of the adult population, he somehow managed to do it better than most, and it had given him a good life. He could ill afford to lose it. It paid him just well enough to afford the inflated mortgage on his mews flat, and there was the occasional perk. The staff Christmas party had been one; despite himself, Tom allowed a small smile at the recent memory of that. He got invited, from time to time, to charity gigs sponsored by the sort of internationals living in London who actually listened to the World Service. That was always good cover. There was the event in Northolt. The sun had shone all day, high in the sky, lowering into the evening, glinting through the dusty windows. He got to meet survivors and families from the Polish RAF squadrons who flew their Hurricanes and Spitfires out of there in the war. Back in the day, they had danced on the dance floor of the Orchard clubhouse, served by maître d's in slick hair and black tails, or lounged on the green, waiting for the klaxon to call them. 'In thankful memory of the gallant Polish airmen', the plaque said. The clubhouse now must have looked different from how it had been then. Sometime in the '70s, the walls had been panelled with wood which now, after decades without varnish, was faded and brittle. They smelled burnt in the sun. Tom sat on late into the evening with the charity's principal donor, an expat. He was tall and handsome and blond, as exotic as the original Polish pilots must have appeared. What was it John Spiro had once said to him? 'If they are telling you a good story, ask yourself what story they aren't telling you.' The Pole was frank, unencumbered by his past. Sometimes things were not as they once seemed, he said. Life is about the chance things, but also about the decisions one makes when the chances are presented.

Tom survived the one o'clock link without incident. By then, the first item of news was the belief that Yeltsin would choose the last day of the millennium to announce Vladimir Putin as his successor. Yeltsin was spent. Putin, out of the nowhere of his KGB past, had placed himself as the unavoidable choice. Beating up on the Chechens had done Putin no harm, Tom considered. He refrained from adding any evaluative inflection to his voice and passed on to the other stories, such as the viral spread of the computer bug which was predicted to bring down flights and wipe out Wall Street. He survived his six minutes. He waited for his red light to go on, clicked his pen shut, and leaned back in his chair exhausted.

'Bet you won't be running home tonight, Day,' came the blokeish voice of his producer.

It was true, his body ached. But his mind ached too, and for that, Tom knew no better cure than to jog through a deserted London at two in the morning. 'No other way,' Tom replied, acting the poor voice-man. He knew he had to speak to his producer before he clocked off for the night; his behaviour earlier in the evening would not have gone unnoticed. An explanation would ensue, saying nothing very much, and Tom would be advised to take some time to himself.

'No point embarrassing yourself, Tommy,' the producer said in the locker room, himself embarrassed.

'Cheers, Geoff,' Tom replied, pulling his T-shirt over his head. 'It is just something I need to deal with. Normal service will be resumed shortly.'

'Yes, of course. You do that.'

Tom straightened his shorts and made sure of the laces on his trainers. He was waiting for Geoff the producer to leave so he could start his warm-up. 'So, that will be that, then?'

It was two in the morning by the time he had got rid of Geoff and secured his things in his locker. He saluted the commissionaire at the reception as always, and he was already sprinting before he was out of the door of Bush House. He thrilled to run up the central reservation of Kingsway without fear of traffic. He dodged left only because he preferred to run through the square gardens of Bloomsbury, which shared their night-time with squirrels and the homeless. There were lights on still in some of the Georgian townhouses. If Tom had his way, they would not all be dazzling hotels, but still run by landladies for the benefit of waifs and revolutionaries. It was a life he might once have imagined for himself. His room would have been draughty; he would have warmed up soup on a single-ring stove while typing translated poems, wearing fingerless gloves; his landlady would have indulged his passion for listening late-night to Chopin recordings and overlooked late payment of his rent; a pet of some sort would have lived the inverse life, driven by the primes of food, not thought, spinning on a wheel in a cage. Black cabs blaring on the Euston Road woke him, and he stepped back on to the pavement. The new British Library from the outside looked more like a red-brick fortress than a place he could read or sleep in. Not for the first time, he was wolf-whistled by the male prostitutes outside Kings Cross, as he kicked off north-east towards and through the gardens of the Barnsbury Estate.

The lights inside the all-night corner shop were almost blinding. The pint of milk Tom placed on the counter looked blue, and the half loaf of sliced bread in its silvery wrapper might have been designed for a space station. He paid for the items before remembering that both were likely to go to waste.

'No cigarettes for you tonight, sir?'

'No, Mr Sharma. I still haven't taken up smoking.'

'The exercise will kill you first!' It was the shop owner's favourite joke with this client.

Canonbury Mews was in fact a crescent, defended from the main road by a shield of London planes. The bell at the front door still bore the name of the previous occupant, or maybe of someone who had never lived there. The stairs up were permanently grimy; the door at the top would not have deterred for long anyone attempting to gain unbidden access. Such a person would have first encountered a hallway of coats, shoes, and discarded clothing, all clearly belonging to one male. The living room was tidier if only because it contained very little of anything: a television, a black leather sofa, a stuffed cardboard box. Other than that, there was a tiny kitchen, a bedroom, a bathroom. The glass shelf below the bathroom mirror contained all the bottles of all the products the occupant had tried but failed to use up. A well-sprung double bed filled the bedroom, and on it was a suitcase, open and not quite packed. Heavy woollen socks sat beside the case, a sweater reached into it with one arm. In the living room, a letter—separated from its envelope—rested on a cushion on the sofa. It was handwritten. The window had no curtains, meaning that when the light was on and the sky was dark, it was easier for someone to see in than it was to see out. The light at that moment was not on. If someone had been standing at the window, they could have looked left down the crescent of Georgian houses and watched a jogger in white shorts and T-shirt come pounding their way. They would have watched him struggle, as if slowed by the drag of age or by a simple reluctance to complete the final strides.

Ewa Kowalska placed her call to London. Although they were faintly interested that someone from the *Wyborcza* newspaper in Warsaw wanted to speak with him, no one was of any use: he wasn't at work, they didn't know where he was, and they would not give out his private number. Ewa was not bothered. With Janusz's help she had already gathered enough research on Dariusz Michalski to justify demanding an interview with him. She had an invite to his New Year's Eve party that night and she would use the occasion to make her approach.

Day was not the only one she could not track down. Aleks Cybulski, her deputy editor, had last been seen early that afternoon. (Or *heard*, in fact. An almighty banging could be felt through the building as Cybulski tackled the defective heating in his office with a hefty spanner.) Ewa badly wanted to speak to him about her story, to get his advice and his sanction to confront Michalski. The two men had once been close, and she would rather avoid breaking her career in the same moment she made it. She had thumbed through the intern's notebook and her own to make a combined summary, hoping in that way to locate exactly where her story was. Michalski's lustration file had already revealed that he had been spied upon by the student from Gdańsk, Małgorzata Kamińska, who had been instructed to befriend the Irishman, Thomas Day. The file also included details of the fortune the candidate had made in the West and his UK tax returns, including his donations to London-based charities. Michalski had accepted exile in West Germany once the strike came to an end. Documents uncovered by Janusz indicated that an SB man codenamed Z had maintained communication with Michalski during the occupation, including passing on bogus news of a Soviet military build-up and the threat to Poland's territorial integrity. This plan was hatched between Staniewicz in Warsaw and Yazov in the Kremlin, despairing at the determination of the Warsaw government to tackle the wave of strikes across the country. Michalski had called off the strike after he was assaulted by the SB during the raid on Wilk's office. Wilk suspected that the student leader had lost control of the situation by then. His girlfriend, Kinga Andrzejewska, held the contrary view: every decision he made was a mark of his leadership. From her, Ewa had learned that both the death of the spy and the birth of her son had been unknown to them all.

Ewa had promised Kamińska's father that she would not print that story. As Kinga had said, it had no bearing on Michalski or his fitness to lead his country. There surely *was* a story about high-level collusion behind the backs of both Polish and Soviet governments, but again, how could she tie this to the candidate? The connection, if there was one at all, was Z. Ewa wrote out the questions she would try to ask Michalski at the party that night. Over her screen, she could perceive the blurred movements of others around the newsroom and their muffled discussions. The Yeltsin resignation was the only subject in the office—that and their feverish efforts to dig up more about his successor Vladimir Putin. Janusz, the intern, was sitting alone at his screen, apparently reading reports from the Russian news agencies. Ewa watched him, momentarily distracted from her own task. Quite a day for him, she thought. And no one to tell. A cream-coloured card poked out from beneath her keyboard. It was the invitation to Michalski's party. For the first time, she noticed it was to her 'plus guest'. She felt a flutter of adrenalin or panic or dismay at being forced into a decision. Her headache returned.

'Janusz,' she called to the intern, who arrived in an instant. 'You are going to a party tonight. Look smart and don't embarrass me. And fetch me a coffee.'

'Yes, Ewka.'

Aleks had some time to kill before he had to leave to pick up his guest. His senior writers had taken charge of his section today: the main story was Putin; the other columns of the political pages would largely be filled up with the stories they had written over the previous three or four days. No one liked to be too busy on New Year's Eve, apart from Aleks. He was only calm when the office was hectic. Having time to kill, as he seemed to have now, left him ill at ease. He heard things and sensed things in quiet moments, things he would have more happily ignored. The water moved in the heating pipe in the way it was designed to, but today he perceived an airlock. Behind his desk, on his hands and knees, he smashed his spanner resoundingly against the offending pipe, until he could no longer hear the hiss or drip. He swore a couple of times so that his colleagues could hear that too.

He would have to find out how much Ewa had learned. By now, she was bound to have called the old doctor in Gdańsk, and she would have discovered—as he had himself—that Gosia had died and, before that, had given birth to a son. Neither the boy nor his grandfather knew who the father was until Aleks told them. He had gone to Gdańsk to do it. It was the only way.

The man clearly had money, or at least used to have. Was it Kinga Andrzejewska who told him that Gosia's father had earned his fortune in Libya, and was a Party quack? Aleks could not remember now. All he really remembered of her was that he had never trusted her and that he'd had to swear Tom to secrecy about their printing press. Still, it was a surprise even to him that she had turned out to be an informant. Dr

Kamiński's house stood three storeys tall on its own plot of land in a wooded area by the beach. He found himself wanting to like the old man. In the end, he liked the boy better.

It was Marek who answered the door. The boy was still only ten, but he was tall and blond and could have passed for older. 'You are the journalist,' he had announced, thereby reversing the introductions. 'You are the one who hates my mother.'

Aleks was let in and given tea. He sat on an armchair, with the boy and his grandfather on the sofa opposite. A scatter of magazines lay between them, their pages creased from being stood on. Around, the furniture and other items in the room gave the impression of never having been moved. 'I don't hate your mother, Marek. I never did. I did once spend a lot of time in her company, although we did not get to know each other well.'

'You were an activist.' The boy again. He was twisting something silver on his wrist, a bracelet.

'Yes, I was.'

'My mother was your enemy, then.'

'In some ways, one would have to say you are right. But I did not know that then, none of us did.'

'Of course you didn't. She would not have been much of a spy if you had all known all along.'

'I guess not.' It occurred to Aleks that for the boy who never knew his mother, now to be able to call her a spy was some sort of recompense for the dubious glamour of it. He needed her to have been good at spying. 'She certainly fooled me.'

'And that politician.' This time, it was Dr Kamiński who spoke. 'If he had just stayed in Great Britain, where he was making all that money, and not come back to be a politician, we would not have to deal with this. It's only because of the *lustracja* that Marek has to know his mother was an informant.'

'You knew? You knew then? We are not on the record here, Dr Kamiński.'

Kamiński glanced at his grandson, as if to check with him how much truth he could bear. Or perhaps he was assessing his own fortitude. 'I didn't know, but I should have. She told me that she had been called to a meeting with Stanisław Staniewicz, that he had brought up our past association.'

Cybulski watched for any reaction from the boy, but he sat stoically; he was not of a mind to start blaming his grandfather for his mother's entanglements. 'Staniewicz had been your benefactor. He was the one who arranged your work visa in North Africa, let you bring your hard-currency earnings back into the country. For you, he had been a useful man to know.'

'He liked owning people, Mr Cybulski. He had made his way up the Party ladder, first in Gdańsk, before moving to the capital, but he never lost sight of those who owed him—even those lowly ones like me. He took Gosia's cooperation as payment in the end.'

'So, you don't believe your daughter was motivated by ideology?'

The question seemed to surprise the doctor. 'You remember those times, Mr Cybulski. When was anyone ever motivated by ideology? We have ideology now, to be sure, a wholesale privatisation of ideology. A friend is a business client you can exploit; an education is just an exaggerated line on a CV. Nobody reads anything anymore unless it's a get-rich-quick manual, or that scandal sheet, *Oni*. I can see you agree with me, Mr Cybulski. Well, you would: you write newspaper stories which you suspect no one reads. I read your paper, Mr Cybulski, but I might be the last one.'

Cybulski found it odd to be lectured on capitalism by an old communist who had made his money through his connections. Perhaps it took a cynic to see the world clearly. 'Dr Kamiński, did Gosia ever talk about Dariusz Michalski?'

'Honestly, I had never heard of the man until last week when he said he wanted to be president, and then *Oni* and the other papers published his lustration. She did talk about some of them in general, but not so they would stand out. She had a great friend here, Michał, whom I always thought she would settle down with. Michał was distraught when she died, and he was always very good with Marek. Do you remember that, Marek?'

The boy shook his head.

'No. Well, Michał met someone else, they got married, and that was the end of that.'

Aleks nodded along encouragingly through this, content that the old man really did not know anything about Darek. Should other journalists track him down, which undoubtedly they would, it was far better if Kamiński genuinely had nothing to tell them.

'Of course, there was the Irishman.' The man uttered this as if he were not sure it was an authentic memory. 'Gosia brought him here once. Quite well-mannered, if I recall, tried to speak to me in Polish. Forgotten the name.'

'Thomas. Tom. Tomek.'

'Was that it?'

'Yes. We shared a room. He was her boyfriend.'

'Really? It did not look that way to me. But then, my daughter could be so dismissive of boys.'

During this last exchange, Aleks kept his eyes on Marek, who held his stare back while twisting still his silver bracelet. The fact that it also suited his purpose did not minimise the fact that for Aleks, there really was no choice now.

'Marek, the Irishman your grandfather has been talking about—he is your father.'

The boy simply stared back. But for the merest flicker of his eyelids and creasing of his temple, Aleks might have concluded he had not heard at all.

Aleks decided to continue talking. 'Actually, it was him that your mother was spying on. Staniewicz reckoned it was more likely that Tom would lead her to Dariusz. She met Tom in a student nightclub. Indeed, I think we were all there that night. She started hanging around our room after that. They became very close, or at least they seemed to. Tom was in love with her, I am sure of that. He never suspected that she was using him to inform on Darek Michalski. I doubt he even knows it now.'

'Is he your friend?' Marek spoke at last.

'Tomek was my very great friend.' The force of his own words rocked him: he was suddenly aware of the extent of his own loss. 'Whatever your grandfather says about the country today—and I do agree with him—Poland was not an easy place for most people to live in back then. Very basic items, such as paper and toilet roll, were luxuries to us. Tom never once complained, never once added to our shame when we felt embarrassed. He shared what he had with us, as we did with him. He once bought a winter coat for a student in his own class. It was an expensive coat, and I told him off for spending too much on it. But what a thing to do! Through all the dangers we encountered that year, he suffered them too. He was injured once by the riot police because he was shielding my mother with his body.' Aleks was caught by the tears welling in his eyes. The boy had to know this about his father. 'I loved him, I suppose. That's true. Not in the way he loved your mother, but yes, what else can I call it? I shared my greatest secrets with him, and he proved worthy of my trust.'

'Where does he live?' Marek had surely been listening, but he was spare with his questions. It was his way of maintaining control.

'Yes, I have an address for him in London. But I have not communicated with him in a long time. It's unforgivable, after what I just told you.'

'It is, Mr Cybulski. I would never neglect a true friend.'

'I will contact him for you, if you like.'

Marek was already decided. 'No, I shall do it. I will invite him here. But I need the address from you.'

'Of course.'

Aleks had promised the doctor not to write about him or the boy and urged him not to talk to other journalists. He gave Marek the address he wanted. Nature would hopefully take care of the rest.

The radiator was dripping. He recognised that the source of his anxiety was neither the heating system nor the unwanted gift of free time. Ewa had been busy on the story he had given her. By now, she would have concluded as he had that Thomas Day was the father of the spy's child. As a piece of human interest, it posed no additional threat to the candidate. For the boy's sake and the old man's, Aleks would have preferred there be no mention of Gosia's life after the strike, but if there had to be, then the focus might as well fall on Day. Tom would understand that, he hoped, or he would have to be made to. No, that was not why Aleks was anxious. It was what the doctor had said about Stanisław Staniewicz. Aleks knew nothing about the former minister's role in the affair, other than he had ordered the spying operation. Whether he had taken a closer interest than that, Aleks could not tell, but if anyone could find out, it was Ewa Kowalska.

Aleks took a taxi to Okęcie airport, having first stopped at Central Station to buy a ticket. The plans to rename the airport after Chopin would never catch on, he was sure. Varsovians had had enough of that already. When the monument to the old Soviet secret police chief, Feliks Dzierżyński, was toppled in his very own square in 1989, Aleks had been

231

there and cheered with the rest. Calling it again by its old name, Bank Square, was hardly something to celebrate. Marchlewski had lost his avenue to John Paul II—that, despite the time it took to say it out loud, was a more popular change.

He sat in the back so as not to irritate the driver. Snow ploughs had cleared the roads, scattering grey snow in their wake. Like giant windbreaks, the road was lined with supersized billboards. He could have teeth like the model in the picture if he booked an appointment at this exclusive clinic. Life insurance was his to have at a price his beautiful family would want him to pay. Jacek Mazur—his ears small like a child's—beamed out from behind one of his papers, flanked on either side by improbably gorgeous women. *Oni czytają*, this one said: They are reading. Other ingenious slogans in the same vein included 'They are listening' and 'They are watching.' The meaning of 'they' was shiftable in the Mazur universe: sometimes it was his loyal readership, or, when he hinted at conspiracy, 'they' could be the mysterious complex of liberal politicians, academics, and foreigners who continually sniped at the current president. Cybulski himself had been in the Mazur crosshairs, as had his editor. Now it was the turn of Dariusz Michalski.

The driver caught Aleks' eye in his rear-view mirror. 'I'll vote for him.'

Aleks looked away. He did not want this conversation.

'You Warsaw types won't like it. You are a Warsaw type, I can tell. You don't like Mazur because you don't get him.'

Cybulski did not appreciate being taken for a metropolitan. He was provoked enough to look again in the driver's mirror.

'Mazur is like us,' the cabbie continued, pointing at his own chest. 'He knows we like looking at girls during the week, and then we go to Mass and pray on Sundays!' His mirth drove him into the middle lane. 'That's a proper Pole. There will be no backsliding into communism with him—he knows all their secrets. That's what I like about the man: there is no pretence. He was what he was, and now he can turn that to everyone's advantage. He will clear out the judges—just you wait—all those guys appointed by the Party in the old days, still clinging to their jobs. Out with them. And there are still people at state radio and television who never left after communism ended. Mazur knows who they are. We won't be sorry to see them go. So what if the Europeans don't like it? Everyone knows we are Slavs really. What do you call that new guy in Moscow—Putin? Mazur will be just fine with him. Ha! I can see it on your face, how much you don't like it.'

It was true. Cybulski normally avoided catching taxis in the capital for this very reason. He knew there were large numbers of people who believed as the taxi driver did. The election was still ten months away, and the polls showed Mazur was unlikely to achieve the 50 per cent he would need in the first round to be elected. However, his post-Communist, Right-wing hard-man stance appealed to many, and in Putin, he might find himself with an ally in Moscow. Michalski, from the point of view of most voters, was a blank slate. They might distrust what they did not know, or they could project onto him their aspirations. Having lived abroad since before the revolution in 1989, he could take neither the blame nor the credit for what had happened since. For now, Michalski was the most serious challenger and stood a realistic chance of gaining the Belvedere Palace. Mazur stood in his way.

Darek had said little so far—maybe he would set out his platform at his party that night. He might well call on Cybulski to help shape his message, just as he had done eleven years before. Perhaps that was the source of the journalist's anxiety. Would he still be up to the job?

Aleks paid off the driver and entered the arrivals lounge for international flights. He found a coffee shop and sat at one of the tables. The waitress seemed to know what he needed and placed a sturdy cup and saucer in front of him. 'Kawa po amerykańsku,' she said, leaving him alone with his drink. He still had time to kill.

Tom had barely slept. Once he had showered and packed, it was already four in the morning. He lay in bed for four hours before giving up and making his call. No answer, so he left a voicemail. 'John, it's me. There has been a complication. I have to go back in.' Then he left for the airport.

His flight was busy with Poles heading home for the New Year. Their voices seemed strange to his ear; he knew their language once. He had Marek's letter in his coat pocket. The boy had written it in schoolbook English and gone back to correct his own mistakes, marking insertions with elegant downward-pointing arrows. The letter did not elaborate upon what its author viewed as the essential facts. It stated simply that he, Marek, was Gosia's son, born in February 1989. His mother had given birth to him and then died sometime shortly thereafter. (Marek did not seem clear on exactly when.) He lived alone with his grandfather in Jelitkowo, Gdańsk. Thomas was his father. He knew this from Mr Aleks Cybulski, who had also given Marek his address in London. Finally, he invited Thomas to visit him. Tom read the invitation as a command.

The man he saw looked too old and had lost most of his hair, but he was Aleksander Cybulski. He stood apart from the line of chauffeurs and others waiting for their clients or loved ones. Neither man had rehearsed what to say first, so instead, they embraced each other and allowed the tightness of their bodies to speak for them. It seemed they had a lot to say, for neither wanted to let go of the other.

'So the millennium bug didn't bring your plane down?'

'It seems no.'

'Are you are still running in those ridiculous shorts?'

Tom nodded happily. 'Are you are still printing a newspaper no one knows about?'

'Not far off,' Aleks agreed. 'Good. So nothing has changed.' Both men would have gladly assented to that.

The taxi dropped them at Central Station so Tom could place his bag in left luggage. 'I am looking for what has changed since I was last here,' said Tom, gazing around at the station and the Palace of Culture looming beside it. 'That certainly was not there.' He was pointing at a green-glassed skyscraper. The word 'Marriott' was scribed across its top.

'Are you sure? No, you are right. They built it in 1989—you left the year before that.'

Left. At the time, the word had been intended as final. Tom would never be welcome back.

'I thought that was it, Aleks. I never thought I would see this place again, or any of you. That was the brutality of it: we were all disbanded, dispersed to our various corners. It was a cruel way to treat us . . . we were only children really.'

'It seems longer ago to me than it actually was, as you can tell.' Aleks ran his fingers over his smooth head. 'So much has changed since then. The irony for us is that our banishment was so short—only a year before the regime collapsed. But you did not come back. Darek didn't either, until now. Norbert actually opted to stay in the army.'

The two men laughed at the memory of their old drill-dodging roommate. Both tried to picture Norbert in uniform and buzz-cut hair. 'I thought we could walk,' Aleks suggested, 'if you don't mind the weather?'

It was cold, but there was an absence of wind for now. In Warsaw, that always made the difference. They ambled towards the Old Town, unhurried by the rushing out of the old millennium, determined to take their time. Tom tried to orient himself while following his friend. The street plan was laid out as before, although a new type of building—steel-framed, glass-clad—was going up everywhere. Perhaps there were more cars on the roads; certainly there was a greater variety. Leaving the traffic behind for the Saxon Gardens was like entering a vast indoors. A recent snowfall damped all external noise and obscured the edges between path and grass. They could have been alone.

'So, Norbert is in the army. What about Piotr? Did he make his fortune?'

'Of course. He turned his smuggling into a legitimate business, and now has two car showrooms in Kutno. He still takes me out when I go home, just to show me how wealthy he is. I lost touch with Agata and Wioletta. Kinga, the last I heard, is in Germany.'

Tom nodded wordlessly, picturing all of these people as they were eleven years before. Kinga had written to him for a while, then stopped. He did not ask about Darek and he did not mention Gosia; inevitably that would be their last conversation. They came out of the Saxon Gardens at the northern edge of Piłsudski Square nearest to the Grand Theatre, before heading east towards Krakowskie Przedmieście.

'Do you know where you are yet?'

'That's the Adam Mickiewicz monument ahead. The Royal Castle is off to the left, and then the Old Square.'

'Well remembered.' Aleks stopped his friend in front of the Mickiewicz statue. 'His fault, in a way, don't you think?' Two children were repeatedly climbing to the top of the stepped plinth and jumping to the ground. They were tiny, made bigger and rounder by their layers of winter clothing. 'Mickiewicz was writing at a time when there was no Poland, only the idea of it. He felt we were a virtuous nation, sacrificed by our eastern and western neighbours. It is little wonder his plays continued to resonate with us. For the Communists, he posed a particular problem: how could they silence the national poet? Did you know, for a time in the '80s, it was nearly impossible to buy his works in the shops? You would go into a bookshop and they would tell you they were sold out because he was a bestseller. That was the word they used in Polish—as if in our communist paradise, market forces were to blame for our shortages of poetry! In reality, they just printed as few copies as they could get away with.'

Tom took his bearings at the edge of the pavement. 'I was here, I think, when the stone hit my head.'

'And you saved my mother.'

'I wonder about that, Aleks. I am not sure she did not save me that day, making sure we were not in the line of fire. If I took the hit, I was glad to. I mean, not just to take it for Magda—I was happy to be hit if that meant I was now included. That's the right word. I was never going to suffer the same way you all were, because at some point, I would be allowed to go home. But for a while, I would be able to join in. No, that's not it. It was not a game.'

'It may have been a game for some, Tom.'

'But not for you, Aleks. Not for your family, or for Darek or Pepliński. To be *included* with you, to be trusted by you—and possibly even make some difference with you: that is what I wanted.'

Aleks put his arm on his friend's shoulder and walked him in the direction of the Old Town. 'You did make a difference, Tom. I am sure. But we were all so young then, and we did not see the picture outside our own frame.' They had reached the main square. Again, Tom mentally compared what he could see with what he could remember. Aleks continued: 'What we saw was other students protesting, and the miners and the shipbuilders. What we only learned later was that Solidarity were having secret talks with the government, beginning the process that would end in their collapse.'

Tom nodded absently. His eyes focused on one corner of the square.

'In some sense, the street riots in Nowa Huta and our strike at SGPiS only made it harder for the negotiations to take place. The government came under a lot of pressure to clamp down hard on us. There were ministers there who remembered Martial Law with fondness.'

Tom was looking vainly for the glass-painting shop, the one run by the old Jewish artisan. Szulman had helped them find Mrs Błońska, the one with the *Mona Lisa* in her living room. And that had helped get Professor Pepliński released. Szulman and his shop were gone now. They still sold cut glass there, but the manufactured variety, the sort that could be bought in any mid-end district in any European city.

Aleks showed his guest into the Gessler restaurant. The wind was now picking up a drift of snow and depositing it around the rim of the marketplace, but the iron crocodile sign hanging outside stubbornly resisted.

'The opposite would also have been true, Aleks.' He was considering what his friend had said about the secret negotiations. 'The government needed a compelling reason to talk to Solidarity. Authoritarian governments only talk to the opposition when they see their authority draining away. That's what we . . . that's what you represented: the leadership of the university and of the mines and shipyards and of the government had no authority left.'

'Fine, I will accept hero status if you insist on conferring it upon me. And if you let me buy you dinner.' Aleks might have anticipated the Irishman would order from the 'peasants' kitchen' options. 'Noodles and cabbage are not as popular as they once were, but feel free to eat what you like.'

'Spiro took me here once,' said Tom later, between spoonfuls of borscht. Aleks' face was one-half lit by a candle mounted on the vaulting.

'Who is Spiro?'

Tom was amazed to recall that the two men who had been so much a part of his year had never met. 'Spiro worked here in the British embassy. He sort of looked after me, although he would be the first to admit that he didn't do a good job of it. In the end, he was the one who put me on the flight out of the country.'

'It's funny you never mentioned him to me.'

'Not really—he asked me not to. He was aware of your underground newspaper. Actually, I think he might even have read it, although he claimed not to. He gave me the impression that he knew about you and your family, even before I met you.'

Aleks stiffened. 'That's a lot not to have told me about, Tom. Was he working for British Intelligence?'

'No. Well, how would I know? I don't believe so, any more than any British diplomat stationed in a communist country would have been. But he was certainly knowledgeable, I will give him that. He knew about the Kutno tapes, for example—that meeting your father was at, with the secret recordings. As I said, he asked me not to tell you about him.'

'Why would he do that?'

'Aleks, I can't say for sure. But he was my embassy man, and I would have needed a good reason not to do what he asked. I liked him—there is that too. He did say something about being able to help us more if you didn't know he was there.'

'Were you spying for him, Tom? I mean, you might as well tell me if you were. Everyone else appears to have been an informant of one type or another.'

'No. Spiro was on our side. I have no doubt about that. That's not spying, if you are all on the same side.' Even if it meant passing on information that was another person's secret.

'You have the same moral certainty you had back then, Tomek. I admire that.' The Pole shifted his head position slightly, enough to leave his face in shadow. 'Where is your Spiro friend now?'

'He followed his ambassador out to Africa. No clue after that.' Tom would not say much more than that. But he was stopped short in any case by what Aleks had just said. Morally certain was not how he would have described himself. His life had so far followed none of the glittering trajectories promised for it. No one in London besides a voicemail knew where he was right now, or cared. In fact, in ten years there had never been another person he would have wanted to tell about what was now on his mind. He had a choice to make now, one which was forced upon him by actions he had taken as a much younger man. That—Aleks was right—was a time when he knew himself better, when he was more morally assured. Decisions, then, were easier to make. Not now. He had thought he could ask Aleks for his advice—he might still—but he was aware now that with Spiro, he had offended his friend.

The waiter placed a bottle of chilled vodka between them. Tom grabbed it, tipped it upside down and smacked its bottom, cracked its lid off, and glugged the sluggish fluid into two glasses. '*Do dna?*'

'To the bottom,' Aleks agreed. Sitting in the candlelight shadow, he inspected the Irishman closely. Aleks was not just a friend now; he was a journalist. Hearing what people were saying, anticipating what people might do, when they might try to conceal both—these were his instincts. He knew why Tom was here, and he knew the dilemma he was grappling with. Aleks was clear that his duty was to behave as a friend. A friend to whom was the only question.

They drank more and talked about their lives in London and Warsaw.

'I listen to you sometimes, Tom, on the World Service. In fact, I was listening last night. That report from Grozny was very powerful.'

'I agree. I wish it were mine. It was your friend's, am I right?'

'Sebastian Thomson. Why do you say he is my friend? My father worked with him, for sure, but I hardly know him.'

'But you worked with him too. After Michalski was attacked by the SB, your photographs—you gave them to Thomson, did you not?'

'It was the best way to get the message out. You forget, I was only working underground then. No one would have seen the images if I was relying on the *powielacz*.'

'Of course, Aleks. It was the right thing to do, as when you called Thomson from Wilk's office. You did call him then, didn't you?'

'What of it?'

'Nothing, Aleks. Nothing at all. It's simply that you did not want the rest of us to know. Michalski—I presume you told him you had the BBC's number?'

'No. I don't remember. I don't think so. He always trusted me to do what it took to get our message out. He never asked me how.' Aleks had not expected in this conversation to be on the defensive. He never suspected that Tom knew—as he must have done all along—that he had called Thomson. What else had Tom been watching for, sitting quietly those days beside the vice-rector?

'Kuba gave me his number.' If there had to be secrets, Aleks did not want this to be one of them. 'In the chaos on Stefan Batory early on the first day, Jakub was there too—you remember, he was hawking beer with Piotr. He had the BBC man's number on a piece of paper, and when the riot police piled in, he stuffed it into my hand. Then we retreated to Wilk's office. And I cocked up. I was the one who was supposed to ensure maximum exposure, but there we were and no one was saying anything about it. I remembered I had Sebastian Thomson's number, so of course I rang it.'

'Why did Kuba have the number of the BBC's Eastern Europe correspondent? It's all right, Aleks, don't answer. I have had time to think about it. He gave it to Kuba himself. How is Bogdan, by the way?'

'He is good, thanks.' Aleks sought even deeper shade, his head touching the low vaulted ceiling.

'Glad to hear that. Thomson was expecting your call. He was there, on Stefan Batory Street. I saw him. When I saw him I thought, wow, this must really be the revolution. Why otherwise would Thomson be there?'

'He was just doing his job, Tom. He's a brilliant reporter.'

'So what happened when you called him? Wait. You told him where we were, and you asked him to get it on film and broadcast it. Maximum exposure, right?'

'Right. That was my job, Tom. What are you getting at? I had a contact, I used it. So what if I didn't tell everyone who was sitting there? Remember, there were those non-SGPiS henchmen there, and Wilk himself. Secrecy was called for.'

'I agree, Aleks. Secrets were absolutely the order of the day.' Tom poured himself another vodka and drank it without a toast. 'Tell me though, Aleks. Why did Thomson not report the story?'

'I beg your pardon? What would I know about that?'

'I watched the television from the comfort of my hotel room, Aleks. After my hearing and after I was ejected from the university, Spiro spirited me off to a hotel posh enough to have international news channels. Sebastian Thomson was there all right, but not a word about the SGPiS strike. I thought he was your friend—or your father's—but not one sentence did he report of your achievement. I was in that room a long time, Aleks, with not much else to do. He totally ignored you.'

'That was his decision. It made no difference in the end. And he took my pictures of Darek, didn't he?'

'Yes, Aleks, he took them, but did he broadcast them? No. Not then. Not until about two weeks ago, when Dariusz Michalski announced his independent run to be president. I must congratulate you, Aleks. They were marvellous photos. Michalski looks a total mess in them. They would have looked great on television. So why, do you think, did he not do that?'

'I have no idea, Tom.' Aleks angrily shot back a vodka.

'That's OK, because I have my own theory. You see, Aleks, nothing remotely as important as this has ever happened in my life, so I have thought about it a lot. So here goes: we were not the story.'

'What are you talking about, Tom? You were there, you saw what happened.'

'All of it, Aleks. Well, nearly all of it. My point is, there were events taking place outside the office that we were not aware of. I say "we". I was not aware what was happening. But Thomson was. Two days after our strike was called off, he was the first journalist anywhere—here, anywhere—to break the story of the government-Solidarity talks. How, Aleks, how did he get that story? I don't know the answer to that, but I know enough about the BBC to know that he had more than one source. The occupation ends, the strike is called off, and soon after that, Thomson gets his confirmation and he can run his story. So, here is my guess: when you called him from Wilk's office, Sebastian Thomson already knew about the secret negotiations. OK, so now I am thinking, if he knew that then, what would he tell you? When did you first learn that the party was nearly up? I mean, you said it yourself: a strike by the students of SGPiS was embarrassing to Solidarity and a red rag to the hardliners in the Party. Did Thomson suggest you find a way of ending the strike early, Aleks?'

Aleks had been shaking his head through most of this last speech. 'You have it all wrong, Tom. Yes, I knew about the talks, but only at the same time as everyone else—in fact, almost certainly later, as I was in detention for several days. Thomson told me nothing, except that my father had made him promise to look after me. That's why he slipped Kuba his number, when he saw him on Stefan Batory. After that, he wanted details of what was happening in the office. He didn't use them, but I read nothing into that.'

They had reached the bottom of the bottle.

'Honestly, Tom. He told me nothing.'

'I believe you, Aleks. I have always believed you.' Tom stopped while Aleks called for the bill. 'That's the truth, by the way.' He tried to smile away the tension of the previous hour. 'Actually, he did tell you something.'

'What do you mean?'

'His promise to your father, to look out for you. The best thing he could do for you was to not report our story. Are you with me? If no one knew what we were doing, the SB would not have to deal with us.'

'And the talks could proceed.' Aleks was relieved finally to be in agreement with his friend. 'There is just one thing wrong with your theory, Tom. The SB did come.'

Tom laughed. 'They did. But that was our fault. There was nothing that Thomson could do about Agata writing that song, or about us singing it at the tops of our voices from the window. The SB came for us only after crowds of supporters started gathering on Independence Avenue. We brought it on ourselves!'

Aleks paid the bill and helped the Irishman on with his coat. Soon they were again standing in the Old Town Square. 'Are you all right, Tom? Not too drunk?'

'Oh, I am quite drunk, and I had maybe only four hours sleep last night. But it's New Year's Eve and I am back in the land of my expulsion. What's next?'

The walk back to Piłsudski Square did not take them long. The white columns of the Grand Theatre were like extensions of the snow, backlit by the orange glow of the interior. Aleks had acquired concert tickets from the paper's music critic. The critic did not like Chopin, especially when played by a Russian ('I know already what I would write about it'), so passed the offer to Cybulski, who remembered Tom's fondness for the composer.

'Don't take offence, Aleks, if I fall asleep,' warned Tom, as he settled into the plush red velvet of his dress circle seat.

'You won't have time. It's a short recital tonight.' Aleks pointed to the programme: Étude Op. 10, No. 12 in C minor. Ballade No. 1 in G minor, Op. 23.

To mild applause that rippled from the front row of the dress circle to high in the gods, the young Russian came on in a bright red dress and took her seat by the grand piano. She made eye contact only with the keys. The lights in the auditorium and on the stage dimmed to a spot. From the outset, the pianist's fingering was furious and risky, tempting discord. The notes descended in long, pessimistic sweeps. Aleks concentrated his eyes and ears on her left hand, sight fractionally ahead of sound, semiquavers following semiquavers in hypnotic repetition.

Russians had not always been welcome in Warsaw, as the Revolutionary
Étude attested. Chopin, here, had composed a piece fitting the legendary
darkness of their soul. Aleks wondered whether he should not reassess
his own nation's character. Or his own. Earlier, Tom had asked about his
family. It should not have surprised him that Tom had been thinking
again about the secrets he had kept, and those that had been kept from
him. It was natural under the circumstances. But his affection for
Magda, Bogdan, and Jakub was uncomplicated. Kuba (surely, Aleks
could tell him this?) had not prospered under capitalism. The flat he had
hoped one day to rent with his wife had become even more unattainable.
He got into trouble with the police and with alcohol, and finally, his
wife left. She took their daughter with her. Magda had to again become
mother to her son, as he regressed to adolescence. For now, Magda still
worked at the hospital, but her cleaning job had been contracted to a
private company who frequently reminded her that younger women
were cheaper. It did not matter that they didn't clean so well or know so
well the needs of the nurses in the wards. Aleks suspected his mother
had started writing again, and he hoped one day she would be ready to
talk to him about it. Bogdan no longer worked in the arms plant, because
there was no longer an arms plant in Kutno. First the state sold it to
an overseas firm, then the firm closed it and sold the land back to the
regional government at a substantial profit. In some ways, for Bogdan
this had been a blessing, for he could not have put up for much longer
with the way his colleagues ostracised him. There had been whispers
for years, why had Cybulski never been arrested, even taken in for
questioning, when his sons had, his wife had? In the main, the whispers
were jokes at his expense, for them all to laugh at, there also being
respect for Bogdan: he was an academic, but he never placed himself
above others and he never shirked a shift in the factory. Daniel Zając had
decided to stand as an MP in Kutno for Solidarity Electoral Action in
the 1997 election. Zając had been a friend for years, would spend hours
at the Cybulskis'; he had once returned to his own home and found it
turned over by the SB. Bogdan had always said their flat was bugged or
watched or both. In the election, he was happy to campaign with his old
comrade. Zając's secret police file was opened as part of his lustration
declaration, and in it were SB reports naming Bogdan Cybulski as an
informant. No one believed it. Those who knew Bogdan knew the

rumours too, and they dismissed them. But others were ready to believe Jacek Mazur, or the lurid lustration stories he loved to display across the pages of *Oni*. 'They spied.' They even knew the stories contained falsities, because the files were filled with the lies the secret service put there for their own insurance. Zając publicly recalled the occasion when his flat had been ransacked, and for some, Bogdan's association with that was enough to condemn him.

The gallery reacted as one. They took to their feet like one multi-footed body; they cheered and demanded more. Beside him, Tom was also standing, also cheering. The pianist in red had scaled the challenges of the étude and was stoically accepting her applause. Behind her back— Aleks was looking—she was flexing her fingers, readying them for the next piece. Bogdan spent his days, even these harshest of winter days, in his shack on the allotment. He fixed a spade with a new handle.

Tom assumed his friend was critical of the performance: everyone else was standing in ovation. For Tom, the rendition of the Revolutionary Étude was thrilling. His heart pounded, his palms perspired. True, he had barely slept and he had drunk as much vodka as he had eaten food, so his vital signs may have been symptoms of a diminution of body function, or indeed of his emotional state. He and the pianist took their seats simultaneously. In the resumed darkness, he recalled from the programme that she would next play Ballade No. 1 in G minor, Op. 23. She made a confident, if modest, opening of single notes, petering to near silence then sliding into the signature theme. Tom was happy to be in familiar sonic territory. The first theme was supplanted by a second. He was not a reader of music or knowledgeable of it by ear. Often he could enjoy it only superficially, intellectually. When he had gone to the Sunday Chopin recitals at Łazienki, it was always alone—there was just that one time with Spiro, when they first met. There was no one to teach him. He was ignorant of many things and naïve about many more. He had fallen in love with Gosia—and yes, he still believed he had—as a consequence of her love for him. He had felt it from her before he had felt it for her. She had been hesitant about making love to him, and he had inferred it was because she saw it as a precious thing—with him, it would be a precious thing. In time, he had loved her for that too. After their time together at the hotel, he ought to have realised she was telling him it was over—she had not hidden that from him. But he had continued to write to her from home, and for a while, she wrote to him, until without warning, her letters stopped. Kinga explained. There had always been a boy in Norway; Gosia had even told Tom about him, but now it seemed he was a lover, not a pen pal and she would leave Poland to live with him there. It was Kinga, not Gosia, who broke to him that news. For ten years, that was what he had known. That was quite long enough for him to learn to hate her, despise her, then eventually dismiss her. Sometimes, when he was with another woman, Gosia would enter his head. It was her touch, her smell, eventually only her name. He did not miss her, and he did not wish that things had been different, but there had been occasions (the pianist was now repeating the signature theme for the final time) when he had pictured himself with Gosia and a child. Where or when this was, was never clear, and over time, he relegated this dream to an adolescent fantasy. He had learned not to want it; he was not jealous of the Norwegian. Then the boy wrote a letter, calling him Daddy. The word was self-conscious maybe, a deliberate avoidance of more formal terms, but it was touching nevertheless. Tom *was* touched by it. Daddy—he had done literally nothing to deserve the honour. He had not taught the boy to appreciate music or been an influence for good upon him, or even until just days ago been aware of his existence. Until days ago, he was not aware that the boy's mother was dead, neither that nor how she had died. The boy himself had had to tell him. The coda was a reprise. A chord struck clamorously, like some definite punctuation, brought Tom again to an awareness of those around him, an awareness of Aleks' shoulder touching his own. The magical pianist quick-fingered down the length of her keyboard, eked out the ending, and was done.

The audience stood again to applaud. The Russian pianist bowed, no longer screwing her fingers, happy with her work done. She would soon leave the stage, change out of her concert dress, and accept a lift from the theatre director to Central Station, from where her train to Moscow would depart before midnight. Her expenses did not extend to a hotel in Warsaw.

There had been a new fall of snow. But that it was white, it could have been an extension of the luscious carpet of the theatre. Aleks marched unsteadily across Piłsudski Square, while Tom followed two steps behind.

'Where are we going now?' Despite the vastness of the open space, Tom's voice was intimate.

Aleks pointed a little way off. 'Just there.'

Tom was sure he knew the building, but he could not imagine why Aleks would choose to take him there. They rounded into a street leading out of the square. A lone soldier stood guard, shivering outside a military administration building.

'We are going to see Darek!' In Aleks' mind, he was presenting this as a gift to his friend. 'Dariusz Michalski is hosting a party tonight for friends, opinion formers, his political advisors. Now that his lustration has been published, he can properly launch his campaign for the election next year. It's a huge moment for him. He has asked me to be there, I think because he may want me to join his team. He is being attacked weekly by Jacek Mazur, and I might be able to help with that.'

'Aleks, where are we going?'

'Just here: the Europejski Hotel. It is still one of the city's finest.'

Tom froze in the snow. Was this some sort of joke? Did his friend not know that this was where he had last seen Gosia? Tom had watched her leave across the parade square from his window on the fourth floor, alone and vulnerable. He did not know it then, but within the year, she would be dead. 'Aleks, why here, for God's sake?'

Aleks was not aware of the associations for the Irishman, and two strides ahead of him as he was, he failed to detect his distress now. 'This place has some symbolic significance for Darek. He may explain it later.'

They entered the hotel foyer. Tom had reconstructed this place countless times in his head. He knew its configuration: the reception to the left, the lifts ahead and to the right. This time there was no militia, but the man standing alone in the corner with a mobile phone strapped to his waist almost certainly was security in private plainclothes form. As before, there was dance music thrumming from below, and it was in this direction that Aleks led his unwilling guest. There were stairs down. The two men checked their coats into the cloakroom, sharing the tab. Aleks remembered that his invitation was inside his coat pocket, so he had to ask for it back. He was nervously excited.

Michalski's team had booked the hotel's main function room, which would normally be the disco venue for the city's older, wealthier dancers. Hiring it out on New Year's Eve had cost the candidate a lot of money, but no other venue would do. The room was pretty full by the time Aleks and Tom got there. News was that Michalski had arrived but had not yet spoken. Aleks knew many of the other guests, a few of whom he respected. Mainly he forgot to introduce Tom to them. Tom found the bar and happily retreated there. He sought the prop of the bar rather than the drink he could buy there. Another younger man stood there too. He was tall, wore his hair slightly long, and like Tom, was not as showily dressed as most others there.

'*Cześć*,' he greeted Tom, in a non-committal fashion.

'*Cześć*,' Tom replied.

'Oh, you are not Polish?'

'Is it really so obvious?'

The other man laughed. 'It's a terrible language when it's impossible even to say hi! I am Janusz, by the way.'

'Tom.' They shook hands. Janusz recognised the name as being the same as the man in the Michalski file, but he did not connect that information with the man in front of him. 'Why are you here on New Year's Eve? Isn't this crowd a little old for you? Or are you a fan of Michalski?'

'Michalski is all right, I suppose. Better than Mazur. He has a chance in the election. But people don't know him, and if they did know him, they might not like him.'

'Why do you say that?'

'I'm not saying anything.' The intern was not about to betray a day's work to this stranger. 'It's the same with all politicians. It's what they don't tell you—that's what you need to listen out for.'

'Perhaps you are older than you look, Janusz?'

The young reporter laughed. 'No. I am all for democracy. I am just sceptical about those who want to be elected. This would not be my first choice of party to be at tonight.'

'You have not said why you are.'

'Work. My boss is here.' Janusz took in the room with a quick glance. 'Actually, all my bosses are here. The one who thinks she is my boss gave me no choice.' The young man sighed. Ewa was talking to a group of men at the other side of the room. Their suits and their hair were all cut the same way, and Janusz knew them to be Politics graduates over-impressed with their own lowly positions in Warsaw think tanks.

Tom followed the younger man's gaze across the room. 'Your boss looks very pretty.'

'Yes,' Janusz agreed and smiled. 'But she will bust your balls. She does mine every day, today in particular.'

Tom looked more closely at the woman. 'It seems she is still at work.' She was pressing a hand-held recorder in one bored man's direction. 'She is a journalist, right?'

'Along with a high proportion of the rest. We are *Wyborcza*.'

'Ah. That means that I came to the party with one of your other bosses.'

'So Cybulski was with you? Ewa was looking for him all afternoon. What did you say your name was again?'

Tom told him.

'Ewa . . . that's her.' He pointed again at the journalist working the room. 'Ewa tried to call you today in London.' Janusz stopped himself from saying more.

'You have been doing your research, I suppose. I was the spy's boyfriend. Why would you not want to talk to me?'

'Don't worry. You are not the real story here.' Janusz took a drink from his bottle. He had been trying, and failing, all day to catch Ewa's attention. Since she had confiscated his notepad, she had been avoiding him. The problem was, the notepad did not contain everything he had found out about Dariusz Michalski.

'Will I be allowed to keep my secrets, do you think?'

'You, Mr Day, are a private citizen. Dariusz Michalski wants to be president of our country. People need to know the man they are voting for.'

'Do you know him?'

Janusz paused before he replied. 'Actually, no. I know *about* him, I know things that others do not about the student strike and how it all ended. But no, I don't know him. Not like you do.'

'Even I would not claim to know him that well, Janusz, and I was with him throughout the occupation and for long periods before.' Tom looked closely at the younger man. 'I see you are troubled by what you have learned.'

'Do I look troubled?' Janusz stood up straight and pulled down his shirt. 'There was one thing I found this afternoon that I have not managed to tell her—Ewa—yet. The thing is, maybe it does not matter.

Maybe it is the sort of thing that a guy is allowed to say about himself, a simple exaggeration that others repeat so that suddenly he seems a bigger shot than he really is. No big deal in itself. But I didn't tell her this afternoon, when I should have. And now the thing—the no big deal—begins to look like a big deal. And if I tell her, she is bound to have to do something about it because she is a journalist.'

'You are a journalist.'

'No, not yet. As she reminded me this afternoon, I'm an intern only. So I am thinking, perhaps different rules apply to interns.'

'Are you asking me, Janusz?' Tom laughed. 'Well, speaking as one private citizen to another, I would say . . .' Tom laughed again and could not finish. 'Frankly, Janusz, and I say this because I like you: I might well be the very last person who should be advising you on that.'

Ewa Kowalska tolerated parties only in so far as they allowed her either to source a story or to get drunk for free. She was enjoying herself at this one. So far, she had spoken to eight different members of Michalski's staff, all of whom were fans who knew nothing about him. Two were ex-expats, Poles who had followed him from London with legends of his acumen and philanthropy. Their role was simply to create and then repeat statistics for journalists: the size of Michalski's wealth relative to the average Pole, the proportion of his wealth that he gifted to deserving charities, the extent that he would bankroll his independent election campaign. In case this made him appear aloof, they evened the accounting with tales from his Ostrów Mazowiecka youth: how he was from unimpeachable working-class stock, how his mother still swept the floors of the local primary school, how his business empire also supported small rural farmers. Ewa already had all this, but she could now pepper her report with 'sources close to the campaign' and 'Michalski insiders'.

'What would it take to persuade your man to give me an interview?'

'It's too early in the race to start issuing that kind of access, Ewa. You know how these things work.' Ewa did not, but then neither did the speaker. Everyone connected to the candidate—including the candidate himself—was an amateur. 'Dariusz will make a speech a little later. He may take a few questions—we would rather he didn't, but he just loves reporters.'

'Then he is sure to love what I have to tell him,' Ewa pressed. She could not reveal to this gatekeeper what her line of questions would be, so she had to impress him in other ways. 'I want to talk to him about his old student days. I have been in touch with some of his acquaintances from then.'

The man was still not biting. He really was a numbskull, Ewa decided. 'That's one of the most popular passages in his standard speech. If you listen out, he is sure to mention those days tonight.'

'Excellent.' Ewa concluded she had better get drunk and salvage her New Year's Eve that way.

Dariusz Michalski had arrived at the Europejski Hotel but had not yet joined his guests. He was, Aleks was told, hidden away in a private room on the second floor with his closest confidants. Aleks had decided earlier in the day that it was imperative that he speak one to one to his old colleague. He wanted to warn him that Kowalska had been looking behind the curtains of his lustration declaration and that, with the intern's help, she had come very close to some uncomfortable truths. Aleks was perturbed that his protégé had not brought her findings to him directly; he had to find out what she was up to by promising Janusz the intern a permanent position. Now Michalski would need to be told that she knew about Z and the pressure the SB put on him with their lies about a threat of Soviet invasion. Michalski should probably also be told that Wilk was still alive and rambling happily about the shambles of the occupation.

The Michalski entourage occupied two adjoining rooms; Aleks was admitted to the room the candidate was not in. He could see Michalski through the open door, being helped into a tie by a young assistant. His old friend seemed to have spotted him at one point: his eyes widened, his smile returned, but his attention was reverted to his mundane preparations. Aleks was assured that the candidate was humbled he had accepted his invitation and was excited about meeting him later, but now he had to prepare for his speech; for this, only his closest advisors were allowed in. The door was shut between the two rooms.

The disco had started by the time Aleks returned to the main function room in the basement of the hotel. He could see Tom standing with Janusz at the bar, deep in conversation. Aleks surmised that by now, the intern would have told the Irishman everything he and Ewa had uncovered. So, Tom would know that during the occupation, Darek was being told that the Kremlin was threatening a Prague-style intervention.

What could Tom make of that information? Would he add it to his suspicions about what Sebastian Thomson was telling Aleks over the phone? Aleks understood one thing clearly: Dariusz Michalski's only chance of being elected president was if people believed in his honesty and good intentions. For that, they needed to trust that his money was legitimately earned and generously given away. And they needed to believe that throughout his student activism, he never collaborated with the secret police. His decision to end the occupation strike was made to prevent further violence, and not because he was pressed to by the SB. And while he was being spied upon, he personally passed on no information. Ewa, Janusz, Tom—perhaps several others—now knew more than had been officially revealed in the *lustracja*. The candidate, as yet, was unaware of this. Aleks knew—as he always did—that his job now was to protect Darek.

'I see you two have met.' Cybulski joined the other two men at the bar. 'I presume I need make no introductions?'

'None necessary . . . sir,' said Janusz, remembering his manners in time. 'Mr Day was just telling me about his year in Warsaw.'

'Not quite a year, was it, Tom?' Cybulski prompted. 'None of us got to complete what we started, did we?'

Tom was drinking a beer and he bought another for Aleks. He said nothing.

'I guess you were all dismissed from the university, not just Michalski.' Janusz, while engrossed in the conversation, was tapping his feet to the disco music and searching for faces on the dance floor. 'But you all turned out all right in the end, didn't you? Kinga Andrzejewska has a profitable business in Düsseldorf. Michalski is a millionaire. Mr Day, you are a famous presenter for the BBC—that's not bad, given you were deported from here in disgrace. How did you manage to do so well for yourself?'

'Not famous.' Tom set his glass on the bar and ignored the question. 'Aleks, you also made a success of your career. Deputy political editor at *Wyborcza*—you bounced back well.'

'My intern here will tell you that "deputy political editor" is a made-up title. Even my office is not a real office. I have a desk by a leaking pipe, which I am obliged to repair myself. All day, our newsroom has been working on a story—the end of Yeltsin, the rise of Putin—with no direction whatsoever from me. Janusz here, with Ewa Kowalska, has been trying to prove that Dariusz Michalski lied on his lustration. As you will have already heard, what they have found may be interesting but it amounts to nothing. Janusz has considered taking their more salacious findings—those relating to Małgorzata Kamińska—to our enemy, Mazur, at *Oni*. I have had to promise him a better job with us. I am hoping he will not notice that I don't have the authority to do that and, in any case, will conclude for himself that this wonderful country of ours needs newspapers and politicians that the people can trust, that the paper he is at is better than the rest, and that Dariusz Michalski is too.'

'Why do you believe that?' It was Tom who asked the question, but it could have been Janusz. 'What makes you so sure that Darek is better than all the rest?'

The intern had put his beer down and stopped dancing. The music still blared, but for the moment, the three men could not hear it.

'There is no simple answer to that, Tom. I know that there was a time in my life—a time you played your own part in—when I believed in him and he did not let us down. We were all young and naïve then, but we had passion and courage and he had more of both than everyone else. There are many people who fought hard and long for the end of communism, but who have suffered as a consequence of their struggle—we have not all succeeded as Darek or Kinga have. I believe that he understands that. He has always understood that, I think. No journalism I have written since was as important as the reporting I did then, when I risked my own freedom to tell everyone I could why it mattered so much. It still matters; the stakes are still high.'

'You still need to be Michalski's mouthpiece.' Tom continued so there could be no offence. 'He should take you on—you were always brilliant at it. I wonder how good he will sound without you.'

As Tom spoke, his words were stranded above the level of the receding music, to be overwhelmed again now by the excited murmur of the crowd. The candidate had finally arrived at his own party. He was taller and still more handsome than any man in the room. The dancers parted to allow a path for him to a raised platform and microphone. A few bars of 'Stairway to Heaven' from Led Zeppelin played as he smiled into his mic. Ewa joined her boss and her intern at the bar, failing to recognise the third man.

Michalski began by thanking his assistants who had made the last-minute arrangements. He spoke self-deprecatingly about where he came from and about his success so far. He caught Cybulski's eye and was pleased to see him and other friends in the crowd. He noticed Tom too, and his brow creased with an effort of recognition.

'People ask me—I think it's a fair question—how can I expect the voters to trust me if they know so little about me? I can open my files to them and let them see my tax returns, but still they don't know me. Can they put their faith in a man who, in the eleven years when Poland built its democracy, chose to live abroad?' A few of the less sober revellers, still standing on the dance floor, gave their own reply to the questions. 'Well, I can see I have convinced at least a few of you already!' The audience liked that and applauded to encourage him to go on.

'They want to know where I come from. They don't mean where in Poland, but where in my heart . . . where in my head. Aleksander Cybulski knows where I come from.' He pointed out his friend. 'And if I am not mistaken, that is my old fellow revolutionary Thomas Day—he knows where I come from.' He paused to allow the audience to clap for some of their own number. 'A great man once said to me that life is about the chance things, but also about the decisions one makes when the chances are presented. These men, and other men and women, were there at the beginning with me. They called me *Nikt* then: no one calls me "No one" now!' Michalski allowed a cheer to interrupt him but raised a hand to signal his modesty. 'They understood, as I did, that there is no liberty for some until there is liberty for all. It is not enough for some of the brave to live as if they are free—their task is to work and not to tire until all can live free. This is not the work of one person or one group. This was not only *my* work. Many joined in the effort: worshippers in churches, workers in factories, students in classrooms, parents in their homes, artists in their imaginations. It was the work of many. It was not inevitable that we would succeed.' Some in the audience, those who could remember, nodded in confirmation towards those who could not. 'We had our enemies. The enemy we did see was no more, no less dangerous than the enemy we did not see. Yes, we could be invaded by the Soviets and just as easily invaded by our own government, for that, friends, is what Martial Law is. We suffered that . . . your families suffered that as mine did. We were told we must never go back to that, we must never tempt another invasion, but the people who told us that were our enemies too. They preached caution to us, begged us to compromise, invited us to be content with our "as if" freedom. There *was* a price to pay, but for them, the price was always too high. The price a person is willing to pay for liberty is the mark of the man, the mark of the woman. It is the balance of violence. When the SB stormed into that vice-rector's office, armed and armoured as if for war, when without warning they attacked us and beat us, when I looked into their eyes and saw no accommodation, no comprehension even, then I knew at that moment that the balance had been reached. Our strike could achieve no more than it had already.'

Ewa Kowalska moved away from the bar to stand closer to the front edge of the audience. She had questions that it seemed Michalski might not want to answer. She knew the lie he had just told.

'I was arrested, we were all detained. In the history of Poland's liberation struggle, there have been thousands of arrests and detentions—we were the next few. The least was that we were denied graduation. In my case, I was denied my family, my home, my country. My choice was no choice at all: accept exile or be incarcerated indefinitely. We did not know in 1988 what we were to learn in 1989. I could not have dreamed that as I was sent first to West Berlin and then to London, Poland would in the meantime become free again. I dreamed instead that I might somehow carry on the fight from abroad, as generations had done before. It was a dream I first had here, in this very hotel. Here, in the luxury of the Europejski Hotel, is where the bizarre captains of communism decided to hold me while they arranged my transit out of the country. They brought meals to my room but no human comfort. I could not say goodbye to my friends, or even to my family. They isolated me from all news so that it was really a prison, a prison with a double bed and en suite bathroom.'

No human comfort—Tom knew the lie. Until then, Tom had managed to forget where he was. He now recalled his own detention in the hotel, his own double bed and bathroom. What was his own price? He looked at the man and he listened to the distortions he made with the truth. Was that also a kind of violence, and if so, what was an acceptable balance? Michalski had settled on a version of events that suited the narrative he needed to tell, may even have tallied superficially with how he remembered them. No goodbyes, no human comfort? Tom knew the truth of that now as if he had been a witness to it.

'And now, friends, let me conclude with the news I have only just heard myself. It is early days yet, but Polish Television will announce a poll tonight which puts me ahead of Jacek Mazur. We have much work still to do to prevent that man from becoming president of Poland, but with your faith, friends, we are headed for the Belvedere!'

The speech was over. Tom pushed through bodies to leave the function room just as a journalist—it was the colleague of the intern—was asking a question of the candidate about his lustration.

'Candidate Michalski, I have a question for you. What were your connections with the disgraced interior secretary Stanisław Staniewicz during your strike and occupation?'

If Tom had been bothered about the candidate's answer, he could not have heard it; the roar in the room was too loud and he was already too far away.

'What can you tell us about your SB contact, named Z?' Kowalska persisted. By now, she was being jostled by a number of Michalski's think tank fans. 'How will the public respond to a candidate who repeats the lies told in his *lustracja*?'

Tom needed his coat, but Aleks—still inside—had the token for the cloakroom. Tom knew he could not enter that space again, yet every practicality told him he could not leave. The smallness of his problem maddened him; it mattered not at all to another living soul and yet it immobilised him. When he saw the intern fleeing the room (what was his name? Janusz!), Tom grabbed him at both shoulders.

Janusz shrugged him off, lifting his fists for a fight before he recognised his assailant. 'Jesus, are you all right?'

'Yes, perfectly. I just need some air. Get Cybulski for me, will you?'

'He's a bit busy at the minute, trying to control Ewa. In there is not a good place for me to be. Cybulski will sack me before he has even given me a job.'

'Get him!'

Thirty minutes later, Aleks had left the party, and the two men were standing in their coats outside the Europejski Hotel.

'What have you done with your colleague?' Tom tried to show concern.

'Ewa asked her questions, and Darek laughed them off. For now, while only she knows what she knows, he can do that. The questions will only get tougher.' Both men knew what the questions would be about.

'My coming here was a mistake,' said Tom, shuddering.

'But you had to come, Tommy. The boy himself wrote to you.'

'I don't mean the boy. I mean *here*.' Tom gestured back towards the hotel. 'You didn't know, did you? Darek was not the only one kept here before he was forced to leave the country.'

'You too?' Aleks marvelled at the idiocy of it. 'And you are going to tell me that this is where you last met Gosia.' He let the ensuing silence answer. 'Shit!'

Despite the bitter cold, they walked slowly across Piłsudski Square in the direction of the Tomb of the Unknown Soldier. The parade ground was busy with people heading towards parties, hurrying to get there before midnight.

'It really shouldn't matter,' said Tom to the night. 'How long have I hated her? Ten years! A lot of hatred can build up in that time, Aleks. And really, I *did* hate her. All I knew was what Kinga told me, that Gosia had skipped off to Norway. There was a Norwegian—I knew that. I actually saw her off at the train station once as she rushed home to meet him. I should have seen it coming. She even prepared me for it, that last time we met in my hotel room: she told me we could never see each other again. Back then, she was merely stating what we all assumed was the truth. I was expelled from the country and would never get a visa to return; she would never be allowed to see me in the West. It was plain.'

A party was going on, on the western edge of the Saxon Gardens. A cabin was dispensing free cups of beer to anyone who wanted them. Aleks and Tom stood for a while on the fringe of the party drinking the freezing lager. Tom found that he was looking for faded handbills, pasted to trees and walls.

'You hated her too, I think.' Tom touched his cup to Aleks' to prove no ill feeling.

'Her son asked me the same question.' Aleks found that he wanted to sit down or, failing that, to keep walking. Standing still made him unsteady. 'I didn't hate Gosia. I resented her. I wanted you to spend less time with her and more time with me.'

'You were jealous.'

'Not only that. I believed, in a way, that the time you were with her was somehow bad for you. I thought you were better off in my company. I know that sounds arrogant now.'

'No, now it sounds sensible. How did you know she was bad for me even then?'

Aleks waved his hands in the air, as if by accident he might connect with something solid. 'I was not alone in thinking that I had a special power for sniffing out the untrustworthy. And I was not alone in mainly being wrong about it.'

'What did she say about me, Aleks? You have read her reports, I know you have. What's in there?'

'Come on, let's get going. We will freeze here.' Aleks walked his friend out of the park and on to Marszałkowska Street, which thousands of people had commandeered to count in the new millennium. Trams careened up and down both sides of the street, ringing their bells in alarm more than merriment.

'Yes, Tom. I read the file. But the one on Michalski, not you. You were never her target, it was always Darek.' Aleks saw that this wounded his friend. He wondered at the conflicts he was suffering. 'Initially anyway, you were just her job. Do you remember the first time you met?'

'In *Hades*, of course.'

'Darek was there too, wasn't he? Getting close to you was a better bet of getting close to him. Darek moved in and out of our lives that year— he was at the end of one suspension and spending time building his contacts in the NZS. Her idea . . . her handler's idea was to present you and her as a package for when Darek turned up again. You would appeal to him because you were foreign; she would appeal to him because she was your girlfriend.'

'How well did that work?'

'Not very. For most of the time, she had very little to report. She knew nothing at all about our printing press, for example.'

'You asked me not to tell her. I kept it a secret from her.'

'You did. I probably never thanked you for that.'

'Don't mention it.' They were now standing more or less in front of the Palace of Culture. A sound stage had been erected, but no bands were playing at that moment, just recorded music. An enormous countdown clock filled the sky behind it. Aleks found more beers for them to share.

'The file does not reveal if she loved you, Tom. You know that, right? The file was never going to say that, one way or another. You are the only person who can judge that. At some point, after taking you on as an assignment, did she grow to love you?'

'What does it matter now?' Tom stared up at the absurdity that was the Palace of Culture, his eyes counting off the layers. He wondered what point it had now, what point had a castle on the hill when the king had departed. He drank from his beer because he no longer wanted to hold it.

'It matters, Tom, because of your son.' Aleks reached a hand to his friend's shoulder because at that moment, it seemed he needed to be steadied. 'I cannot work out why she never told you about him, never told you she was pregnant. Unless it was itself an act of love—she assumed you could never know your son, so she relieved you of the responsibility by not telling you. But it was a monstrous way to treat the boy. He never knew, not even a clue. His grandfather was no wiser.'

'Until you told them.' Tom recalled the clipped, formal words of Marek's letter.

'Yes. And I gave the boy your address because he wanted to write to you himself. He is quite some guy, as you will see.'

'Why did you go there, Aleks? What took you to Gdańsk after all these years?' The band had now appeared on stage, and they were already blasting out electric music. The clock behind them showed the minutes draining out of the century. 'Did you know she was dead?'

'No,' shouted Aleks over the music.

'It was for Darek?'

Aleks just nodded. It was impossible to explain over the noise that he had made the trip to the Kamińskis because he had wanted to ensure there would be no trouble for Darek there. He was glad of the noise, for how would he explain to Tom that Gosia's death was a bonus? Beside him, Tom was shouting something, but in the din, Aleks could make none of it out. Whatever the situation, Tom would need to take the train, and Aleks could report quietly that the spy's son had found his father. The crowd were counting down from ten. Gosia would never again cause him or Michalski trouble. Seven, six, five. The doctor was surprised to hear that the Irishman was the father. Three, two. The boy had appeared, strong and blond at the front door. A spray of fireworks cracked the night. Neon zeroes filled the sky.

The two friends joined the celebration. They embraced each other long enough to see out their younger selves, the men they had once been, the lives that had somehow continued unchanged until that moment, long enough to glimpse the people they would need to become. For Aleks, there was the hope too that the embrace would transfer to Tom the determination even now to take the train to Gdańsk.

The band started playing and everyone was dancing, Tom and Aleks too. Tom felt like he had never slept and would never find sleep again. Finally it struck him that he was back in Poland and that fact alone made him happy. For the moment, it did not matter what had gone before, and he could postpone thinking about what must happen next. He just danced.

They danced until the drink ran out. 'I know place!' cried Aleks, rejoicing again in his honoured role of the resourceful one. He ran to a tram stop, Tom close behind, and leapt on the first tram heading southwards down Marszałkowska. After just a few stops, Aleks declared it a bad tram, climbed off it, and clambered on another, with Tom barely able to keep up.

'This is better,' Aleks decided. He blocked Tom when he tried to punch a ticket. 'Tonight we not pay. Poland is free!'

They had travelled some distance and Tom was unsure of his bearings, and it was fine because Aleks was with him. The tram reached its terminus, but there was a free night bus to be had and that took them further. Through the smeary window, Tom tracked the man-high pipes that ran overground down the central reservation. He was thirsty. He recalled this avenue, Armia Ludowa: once he had run along it to get to the park for his secret meeting with the man from the embassy. He had listened to Chopin for the first time and learned how to make a phone call with a knife, that no one could trace and no one could listen in on. As if disabled by a multitude of choices, the bus stopped at the Plac Na Rozdrożu intersection.

'It's the parting of the ways,' declared Aleks. Tom followed his guide to a bar—wooden, even alpine—that looked like it had been dropped in the middle of the roundabout.

There were few other revellers there, most having left for other parties or simply gone home. Both Aleks and Tom were aware that they still had hours to pass and a pub was as good a place as any. Drinking was similar to celebrating; drinking let them talk, and it would also allow them later to forget. Tom had already noticed that Aleks' English was deteriorating.

They sat with beers between them. 'Why did I end up in your room, Aleks? Why, the day I arrived in Warsaw, did you take me to your dorm in Dom Studenta?'

Aleks looked over his friend's shoulder, puzzled. 'I don't remember that. We must watch the time.'

'Of course you remember! It was the first time we met. I was with Wilk, you were in his secretaries' office. You were supposed to take me to the international students' house, but you made me come with you instead. Why did you do that?'

'I don't remember. We had extra bed.'

'You had *two* extra beds. One became mine, and the other would later be Darek's—you knew that already. You took me to Dom Studenta because you wanted me to meet Michalski. Why?'

'Tommy . . . You like Dariusz, yes? So what's the problem?' Aleks knocked his glass against Tom's to show there was no problem. 'You were friends, right? And now, with our help, he will become president.'

Tom could see that that was the simplest explanation. Aleks had taken him in because he liked the look of him and thought they would become friends, and together be friends with Michalski. 'Did Wilk want you to take me to your room? Aleks, were you asked to keep an eye on me in Warsaw?'

Aleks laughed. 'Never would I not work for the Wolf! You are getting paranoid.'

'But you told me even then that his secretary—what was her name, pani Elżbieta—had arranged my dinner pass for Dom Studenta, even though I was registered in a different house. Why would she do that?'

'Ah, pani Elżbieta! Beautiful, don't you agree?'

Tom was resigned; he no longer cared. Maybe Wilk had asked Aleks to watch over Tom for the year. If he had, then the vice-rector had obviously put his trust in the wrong man. Perhaps Aleks had some half-formed plan to bring Tom and Darek together, that the three might act in combination. If so, he was obeying his instincts for fixing things. It did not matter now; Tom was glad that he had—glad even despite the mess they were in.

Aleks sat on the wooden bench, with his head rested on the table between them. He was asleep. Tom nudged his friend's elbow, but he did not stir. Tom felt alone. Dariusz might still be at the party, or he might have left to consider with his advisors how to respond to new questions from journalists. Carter, Pepliński, Spiro—he was a grown-up now, and these men were not around to help him. Aleks—resourceful, romantic Aleks—was his only friend here, and he needed to sleep. Tom was alone.

'Dariusz is in trouble, Aleks.' There was a noise from the sleeping pile, but nothing more. The few other drinkers in the bar were engrossed in their own troubled dramas. Most were sitting alone, deserted by the parties they came with or still waiting for their friends who did not come. 'I think he cannot be elected president. He lied. He lied tonight and he must have lied on his lustration declaration, and I think your colleagues know it.' Tom turned his glass in its own wet circle. His head was beginning to hurt. He wished his friend were awake now to hear the facts, but their time was running out.

'It was a set-up. The SB storming into Wilk's office, grabbing Darek, and dragging him out by the other stairs to beat him up—it was all staged. That end of the building was abandoned, the assault happened before anyone could get there, then you turned up with your camera. Perhaps you knew, perhaps you didn't—it doesn't matter. Darek assumed that your photographs would circulate and he would have cover for ending the strike.' The lump in front of him did not stir. 'The "balance of violence", remember that? He said it again tonight. When the violence became too great, it was time to make a tactical retreat. Everyone accepted it at the time—the government, Solidarity. Why? Because they had arranged it.'

Tom sensed that the sleeping mass opposite him was holding its breath. 'Darek was taking calls while in Wilk's office—we all saw that and assumed he was negotiating food for us and drugs for Wilk. He was, but he was also talking to someone at the SB. This is what your colleagues at the paper have found out today. I don't have a name. They may have a name. This guy was telling Darek about the government talks with the opposition, that the strike put those talks at risk and that the Russians were getting feisty. Darek was given a way out: agree to the raid on the occupation, get a little roughed up, then call it all off on the spot. Whatever followed would follow, but there would be exile for him.'

Aleks did not move but swore loudly in Polish.

'I am sorry, Aleks, it is true. I know because Michalski told me himself.'

Slowly, like it was dependent on an ancient mechanism, Aleks raised his head. '*Kiedy?*'

'When? In London, maybe three years ago. He was sponsoring a charity—Polish RAF veterans—and I was invited. It was a beautiful day, I remember. They unveiled a plaque in Northolt. They were playing cricket outside, or some such, I can't remember now but it was very English. We drank cider. He was totally exotic. I mean, Darek always stood out, but here he was alien and even so he was in his element. We chatted for a long time. He was completely frank about it. When we met at the start of the day, he had no intention of running for office, and the latest *lustracja* law had not been passed. He felt comfortable talking to me; I think he even felt he owed me an explanation. That's when I learned that Gosia had been spying on me. He knew. He . . .'

Tom blocked himself from having that thought. He needed to tell Aleks about the SB. 'Actually, he laughed as he told me. "We nearly fucked it up," he said. "They were only meant to beat me gently! But they shoved me and I slipped on the stairs and nearly broke my neck." That's how he smashed his eye and lost his tooth. He slipped. "But I made sure Cybulski got the picture."'

Aleks spat, '*Kłamstwo!*'

'It's not a lie. He did not feel ashamed back then, in London. If anything, he felt vindicated by how events turned out. And he was right. Actually, when he told me, I wasn't surprised. I felt I had known all along. Ask yourself honestly, Aleks: didn't you know already that Darek had coordinated the end of the strike with the SB?'

Aleks had woken up in a bar he didn't recognise with a stranger speaking a foreign language. He couldn't find the arguments to defend himself, and some deeply buried survival instinct urged him to flee. He stumbled out of the back of the bench he found himself on, clambered to his feet, and made for the brightest light, which he took to be the exit. Outside, he gasped a mouthful of wintry air and tried to clear his head. The stranger was at his elbow. The road he was on headed off in every direction, a parting of the ways. An occasional car shot past or screeched around the roundabout. There were too many options, and the choice he made next might not be an escape. Something told him that time was passing, more quickly than he could keep pace with it. A two-carriage tram juddered to a stop directly in front of him. He didn't see its number, but he climbed aboard anyway just before its doors clanged shut. He was startled by the brightness inside, all the lights on when there were no other passengers. The tram lurched in a wide arc; Aleks clung to the upright bar so as to not fall over. The other man was there still. Aleks knew the man, but he was also certain that right then he needed to be rid of him. Aleks told him to go away. The tram rode through several stops, hurtled down a straight avenue. On his left, Warsaw's embassies and palaces flicked past him, their security lights trained on themselves, casting blocks of shadow. At his back was the vast blackness of a royal park. Trees have no lights of their own, he mused; they are glorious in the light, but they darken quickly in the gloom. A park is a light vacuum, a tomb. The tram stopped, Aleks got off, the man followed. Aleks tried to run, but unaccountably, one foot would not properly follow the other. There were shops here in the daytime, and fashionable restaurants. Aleks did not know these places, though he knew where he was. They had shut their eyes and shut their mouths, like all should do at night— don't come here, don't look in our windows. Angry suddenly, Aleks tried telling the other man to leave him alone. *You have no business here. All you can do is harm. It's best that you leave. You have no time.* There was a monument, some hero on a horse with steps and a low iron railing. The sight of bushes nearby reminded Aleks that he needed to pee. When, all night, had he used the toilet? He had not noticed how desperate he was until that moment, and all of a sudden, he was frantic. He fumbled with freezing hands to release himself. The other man stood beside him and he too steamed into the bush. *Can't you see that it is important that you leave? Have you not already done us enough harm?*

'Aleks, gdzie jesteśmy?'

The same question again and again. What made the man think that Aleks had any clue where they were? A night bus was parked across the road, its lights on and door open. Aleks staggered across the road without looking while his shadow still had his dick out. The driver was snoozing. Aleks shoved him awake. *Are you working? Is this service still running? See, I have some cash.* The driver was slow to react, giving the other man plenty of time to catch up. Whether the bus was in service or not, the driver turned the key, shut the door, and set off. Maybe the driver was simply looking for a quieter spot to sleep off his own New Year's Eve drinking. Devotional charms hung from his rear-view mirror, and he had sellotaped a photograph of a child to his dashboard. A cushion—crocheted in a peasant design—propped up his seat. He had made his cabin his home. An empty bottle rolled beneath his seat. Aleks sat at the end of the bus. He could still not get the foreigner to see sense. All he kept repeating was 'Aleks, *gdzie jesteśmy,*' Where are we? *I don't know where we are, Tom! I thought I did. I don't even know where this bus is going—those windows are black where I thought we would see lights. I thought that at last, we might be able to make good on our promises—those promises we made when we fought the communists, the promises they made to us when the communists went away. I thought we could have a country where good people like my father would not have to live under another suspicion, where my mother might have a job deserving of her courage and her intelligence. I thought Dariusz Michalski could get us there, or get us close. Whatever you say about the SB, I still believe in him. He is still the finest man I ever followed. But others will not see it that way. His opponents—even those who were themselves communists—will call him a collaborator. Those who profited most under the old regime profit still under this, and those hypocrites will not hesitate to take Darek down. Stop asking me where we are! Why can't you understand what I am saying? What do you want from me? Leave here!*

The bus trundled to a halt at a road closure sign. The driver turned off the lights and opened the door for his two passengers to disembark. Aleks knew that however hard he might try, he could not lose his follower. He looked up, saw the Palace of Culture in the distance, and walked towards that.

For the past hour, Aleks had spoken to Tom only in Polish, as if he did not recognise the Irishman at all. Tom was lost, and all he could do was track his drunken friend in the hope he would eventually sober up. The city had changed. It was not so long since he was last there, but a revolution had occurred in the meantime. He did not think it was an illusion that there appeared to be more of it, stretched beyond its previous boundaries outwards and upwards. Landmarks he anticipated seeing on his left were instead on his right, suggesting he was heading north when he thought they were going south. A few streets had changed their names, and a few statues had lost their pedestals. His own inebriation did not help. Was it drunkenness or mental disarray that explained Aleks' behaviour? Either way, he was Tom's only hope. It would have been better for everyone had the facts about the conclusion to the strike not come out, but there was no prospect now of concealing them. The *Wyborcza* journalist and her intern already knew too much, and what they did not know they would uncover soon. The Michalski campaign would not survive the barrage of questions. Who was his SB contact? Whose idea was it to stage the end of the siege? How much had he been paid to accept life as an exile? The truth would be demanded, as if that were the highest virtue. They would insist upon a truth stripped of all complexity, blind to its own time. Their truth would not need to be kind, understanding, or even true.

Tom was now walking behind the other. He had no hat, and he had left his gloves somewhere. Against the icy wind, his coat was not up to the task. Above, there were three or four moons, or jagged reflected crescents of moon, playing among the glassy high-rises of Warsaw new town. A few stray fireworks, having forgotten to explode earlier, now let loose their payload with a joyless crump. But the colours were jolly, they held out hope.

The pair approached the Palace of Culture from one of its four compass points—which one was not clear to Tom. The edifice soared upwards in decreasing oblongs, set in its square base, looking pretty much the same from this aspect as from any other. The surrounding roads and buildings also formed four mostly equal sides; if there were any outstanding features, they were obscured for now by the palace itself. As a landmark, therefore, it was duplicitous, pointing to itself rather than indicating the way to anywhere else. *Gdzie jesteśmy*?

'Aleks, you must listen to me. You must stop and listen.' Tom made his friend sit on a step at the base of the palace. The stage stood where it had hours before, when the clock had counted a thousand years out. Empty tins of Polish beer rolled together, rolled apart, rolled together again. Pages from *Oni*, the tabloid newspaper, blew about in red and white.

'The boy is not my son. Aleks, Marek does not belong to me.' Tom had saved up the words for his friend, but aloud, they stunned even him.

'I feel now as if Gosia never lied to me. She did not tell me about Marek because he was not mine.' Tom pulled the collar of his coat

265

around his chin. He looked ahead rather than at Aleks, but he felt sure he was listening. 'Perhaps if she had not died when she did . . .' The thought was as enormous as the building he sat below.

'Tom. Tomek. You know how she died? I know how she died. Ewa knows. You?'

'Yes.'

'How do you know?'

'The boy told me.'

'Of course.'

The ground before them was vast, intended for parades and mass demonstrations. It was perfect too for the lone protest, ideal for one individual to stand solitarily, stating their singular grandeur while grandness surrounded them. The right setting for an apocalypse, massive or minor. A pigeon flew in and flew out again, as ignorant as it had arrived.

Aleks interrupted his friend's thoughts. 'How do you know, Tom? How can you be sure Marek is not your son?'

'Some truths are simple, Aleks, my friend. We never made love.' He waited for a reaction, but there was only stillness. Tom himself was suddenly loquacious, finding together the words and the person to tell them to. 'That's right. Not in the Student House, not in Gdańsk, not even in the place it was meant to all happen: Hotel Europejski. I *wanted* to, absolutely! Every bit of me was ready, but she always put it off. I think I know why now. She said something once about how "they" expected us to have sex, but that she was not a prostitute. At the time, I thought she meant that there were social expectations, as we were boyfriend and girlfriend. But it was not that. Her spy handlers wanted her to get closer to me, to make sure I fell for her. *They* wanted her to make love to me— and I wanted it too—but she would not do that for them. Even if she did love me, she would not do it for them. Even at the very end. Even when the game was up and I was in the hotel and Spiro brought her to me. Even though I wanted so badly to be with her, and we both knew we would never see each other again—even then. Even though I loved her.'

'Tomek,' Aleks spoke at last. 'I was sure the boy was yours. It's the only reason I gave him your address. You were the only answer that made sense.'

'The only answer? To what?' Tom was tired. He did not want to argue again.

'The question of who is the boy's father.'

'That was not your only question, Aleks. I know you. I know where your love and loyalty lie. There was and is always another question: how can you protect Michalski?'

Aleks, his face reddened by the cold, reddened further. But he was tired too. 'The woman who spied on Dariusz Michalski had a secret child nine months after he was sent into punitive exile. There are journalists less curious than my Ewka—there are journalists there . . .' Aleks pointed furiously at a page from *Oni*, drifting disconnected from any others. '*They*! They would find the boy and tell everyone he was Michalski's. They would not need it to be true. They would delight in the ending of his political career, whatever the cost to the boy or his grandfather. So yes, knowing that you had to be the father was . . . it was helpful. I admit that. I know what that says about me. But, Tommy, I also thought it was true.'

'Naturally you did. I don't doubt you believed that.' Tom breathed deep, head still hurting from alcohol, still aching from the stuff he knew that others did not. 'You know who the father is, Aleks.'

In that instant, Aleks did know.

'He told us himself earlier tonight, didn't he?' said Tom. 'Darek was there at the hotel, two floors down, on the night Gosia came to see me.' There was the merest tremble in his voice, a residue of loathing or jealousy. 'She kept me waiting over an hour. She went to him, then she came to me. And so, of course, we did not make love. She had already made love to him.'

Aleks was shaking his head; not enough of this made sense to him yet, but he had already accepted it as true. What would have motivated either Gosia or Darek to do what they did? Then the problem simply resolved into its simplest form.

Tom spoke the words. 'She had watched him for months, and well, like the rest of us, she fell in love with him in her way. Darek—suddenly, violently, he had been defeated and his punishment was to be banished from everybody he knew and loved. Gosia arrived in his room—perhaps it was her last mission—and . . . I doubt he gave it a second thought.'

'You don't blame him?'

'I blame her! But I have stopped hating her.' Having arrived at this point, it seemed enough to Tom: this could be his final declaration.

'Tom, what do you want from me?' It was a question he had asked before. Even now, Tom understood that Aleks would be searching for a way to salvage his hero's campaign. Michalski could issue a clarification to his lustration, depict a young man grappling alone with forces much greater than himself. The country might accept that. It would not accept a president who had abandoned his son, even unknowingly.

'Aleks, where are we?' Tom was now standing facing the palace, laughing at it. 'And how do I get to the Central Station from here?'

'I have your ticket, here.' He tapped his coat pocket and checked his watch. 'Your bag is at the station. You have seven minutes, if you still want to make the train.'

Both men were now standing, each with the feeling that they may not see each other again. As if to deny that, they gave each other only a small handshake. Tom went to speak but was interrupted. 'No, there is no time. You should run.'

Warsaw Central Station was not far from where they had been behind the Palace of Culture. Tom opened the buttons of his coat to allow himself to run more freely. He was at the station within moments. At five o'clock in the morning, even the impressive lighting inside could not expel the pervading darkness, and there was little comfort for the homeless from the cold. Skipping past the few other passengers, Tom retrieved his case from left luggage, still clutching the ticket Aleks had given him.

'It leaves in three minutes,' he said.

Three minutes could be forever to Tom. He had a memory of leaving the great hall, and he traced the steps of that, running down the gaping stairs and on to the landing from which all platforms could be accessed. Platform 2 was his. Tom knew the way like he had rehearsed it, but slowed his run as if he barely wanted to get there. The escalator down to the platform juddered, having also not made up its mind. The train wasn't there. The clock on the platform scored the time inexorably, though its hands recoiled with every advance. Warsaw was not where the train began, and it would go much further beyond Gdańsk.

The ticket told him his carriage, and painted marks on the floor told him where to wait. A food vendor was opening her kiosk, making noise that reverberated around the underground cavern. Her keys jangled in the padlock, the metal retracting grille shuffled upwards like an audience clapping; she whistled. There was joy and foreboding in every sound. The train slid in and, without a fuss, aligned itself with the edge of the platform. Tom checked his ticket again for the right train, the right carriage, the right seat. Unwatched, he grabbed the handle of his suitcase, hauled his tired body up the steep iron steps, and edged sideways down the corridor to his compartment. He sat upright, with his head cushioned. When the time on the platform clock matched the time on his ticket, the train jerked forward. His head nodded. The train pulled silently and indifferently away from the city.

T H E   E N D

Lightning Source UK Ltd.
Milton Keynes UK
UKHW040624150223
416722UK00033B/866/J